Ernest Bracebridge

School Days

by

William H. G. Kingston

Double9
BOOKS

Ernest Bracebridge
School Days
by William H. G. Kingston

Copyright © 2024

All Rights reserved.

ISBN: 978-93-67146-00-2

Published by

DOUBLE 9 BOOKS
2/13-B, Ansari Road
Daryaganj, New Delhi – 110002
info@double9books.com
www.double9books.com
Tel. 011-40042856

ABOUT THE AUTHOR

W.H.G. Kingston (1814–1880) was an English author known for his adventure novels, particularly those set at sea. He gained popularity for his vivid storytelling and ability to engage young readers, often incorporating themes of bravery, duty, and the spirit of adventure.

Kingston's works frequently focused on naval life and the experiences of sailors, reflecting his interest in maritime history and the British Navy. He wrote numerous novels, including "From Powder Monkey to Admiral" and "The Three Midshipmen," which depict the challenges and triumphs of young protagonists in a nautical setting. His writing is characterized by rich descriptions and strong moral lessons, emphasizing virtues like hard work, loyalty, and respect. Kingston's contributions to children's literature helped shape the genre of adventure fiction, and his stories remain appreciated for their excitement and positive values. His legacy continues to influence maritime literature and inspire readers with tales of courage and exploration.

CONTENTS

Chapter One
The School, the Master, and his Boys

It was a half-holiday. One of our fellows who had lately taken his degree and passed as Senior Wrangler had asked it for us. He had just come down for a few hours to see the Doctor and the old place. How we cheered him! How proudly the Doctor looked at him! What a great man we thought him! He was a great man! for he had won a great victory,—not only over his fellow-men, not only over his books, by compelling them to give up the knowledge they contained,—but over his love of pleasure; over a tendency to indolence; over his temper and passions; and now Henry Martin was able to commence the earnest struggle of life with the consciousness, which of itself gives strength, that he had obtained the most important of all victories—that over self.

There he stood, surrounded by some of the bigger boys who had been at school with him; a pleasant smile on his countenance as he looked about him on the old familiar scenes. Then he shook hands with the fellows standing near him, and we all cheered again louder than ever. He thanked us, and said that he hoped he should often meet many of us in the world, and that he should always look back with pleasure to the days he had spent in that place. At last he once more waved his hand and went back into the house.

The instant dinner was over, out we all rushed into the playground. Those were happy times when, directly after it, we could stand on our heads, play high-cock-o'lorum, or hang by our heels from the cross-bars of our gymnastic poles without the slightest inconvenience.

Our school was a good one; I ought to speak well of it. I have, indeed, a very small opinion of a boy who does not think highly and speak highly of his own school, and feel thoroughly identified with it, provided it is a good one. Our school, at all events, was first-rate, and so was our master. We were proud of him, and believed firmly that there were very few men in England, or in the world, for that matter, who were equal to him. He won the affections of all of us, and as it seemed, with wonderful ease. How he did it we did not trouble ourselves to consider. I have since, however, often thought over the subject, and have had no difficulty in guessing the cause of his influence. He was a ripe scholar, and thoroughly understood what he professed to teach: then he was always just, and although he was strict, and could be very severe on occasions, he was one of the kindest-hearted men I ever met. We all thought so; and boys are not bad judges of their elders. He was a tall, fine man, with a florid complexion. His eyes were large and clear, and full of intelligence and expression. And then his voice!—how rich and mellow it sounded when he exerted it. His smile, too, was particularly pleasing; and, old as he was, at least as we thought him, he entered heartily into many of our games and amusements; and it was a fine thing to see him stand up with a bat in his hand, and send the ball flying over the hedge into the other field. He had been a great cricketer at College, and had generally been one of the eleven when any University match was played, so we heard; and that made him encourage all sorts of sports and pastimes. He pulled a capital oar; and we heard that he had been very great at football, though he had long since given up playing: indeed, I doubt if there was any game which he had not played well, and could not still play better than most people, had he chosen. Such was Doctor Carr—the Doctor, as we called him—of Grafton Hall.

Grafton Hall was a fine old place, situated on a healthy spot, and surrounded by good-sized grounds: indeed, no place could be more admirably fitted for a first-rate gentleman's school.

The house was a large Elizabethan building, with a number of good-sized airy rooms, and passages, and staircases. The hall served, for what it was originally intended, as a dining-hall.

The Doctor had built a wing, in which was situated our school-room, and a lofty, well-ventilated room it was. We had several lecture-rooms besides; and then the large old courtyard served as a capital playground in wet weather, as well as a racket-court; and in one corner of it we had our gymnasium, which was one of the many capital things belonging to the school.

A fine wide glade in the park, which had been thoroughly drained, served us as a magnificent cricket-ground; and there was, not far from it, a good-sized pond, through which ran a stream of clear water, where we bathed in the summer. It was kept clean and free from weeds, and even in the deepest parts we could, on a sunny day, see the bright pebbles shining at the bottom.

I need not now give a further description of the dear old place. We were most of us as fond of it as if it had been our father's property. I do not mean to say that it was a perfect paradise. I do not fancy such a place exists in the world; and if it did, I must own that schoolboys are not, as a rule, much like angels. Still the Doctor did *his* best to make it a happy place, and an abode fit for boys of refined minds and gentlemanly habits and ideas. It was generally our own faults if anything went wrong.

When a new boy arrived, the Doctor took him into the school-room, and lecture-rooms, and dining-hall, and through the sleeping-rooms, and playground, and gardens; indeed, all round the place.

"Now, my lad," he used to say, "you will remark that everything is well arranged, and clean, and neat. I trust to your honour to refrain from injuring anything in any way, and to do your best to keep the place in the good order in which you see it."

On no occasion had he ever to speak again on the subject; for we all took a pride in the handsome, gentlemanly appearance of the house and grounds, and effectually prevented any mischievously inclined boy from injuring them. All the other arrangements of the establishment were equally good with those I have described.

The Doctor's wife was a first-rate person; so kind, and gentle, and considerate. We were all very fond of her; and so we were of the good matron, Mrs Smith, who kept all the people under her in such excellent order.

The ushers, too, were all very good in their way, for the Doctor seldom made a mistake in selecting them. They were good scholars and gentlemen, and generally entered with zest into most of our sports and games. But it is time that I should return to that memorable half-holiday.

The Doctor had not long before erected a gymnasium, which was at this time all the rage among us. We never grew tired of practising on it. The moment we came out of the dining-hall the greater number of us assembled round it.

Some swarmed up the poles; others the ropes which hung from the bars above; several performed various exercises on the parallel bars; while four seized the ropes which hung from a long perpendicular pole, and were soon seen, with giant strides, rotating round it, till they scarcely touched the ground with their feet.

Numbers were likewise hanging on to the horizontal bar; sitting on it, swinging by it, circling it, kicking it, hanging to it by the legs or the feet, performing, indeed, more movements than I can well describe.

There were also several wooden horses, or rather logs of wood on legs, on which the boys were mounting and dismounting, vaulting on to them, leaping along them or over them, kneeling on them, jumping off them, and, indeed, going through a variety of movements which might give them confidence on horseback.

Several swings were in full action. Very few boys were sitting on them; most of them were standing upright; some were holding on with two hands, others only with one; some standing on one foot, and holding on by one rope; others leaning with perfect composure against one rope; but all were moving rapidly in one way or another; indeed, the effect to a person unaccustomed to the scene must have been very curious.

One of the most active fellows we had at that time was Richard Blackall. He was not quite the cock of the school, though, for his size, he was very strong; but at all gymnastic feats he beat nearly everybody. His chief rival was Miles Lemon, who could perform most of the exercises he could, and did some of them better. Lemon was not so strong as Blackall, but he had a more correct eye, and a calmer temper; both very important qualifications, especially in most athletic exercises. He was, in consequence, a better cricketer, and a still better fencer. Even at the broadsword exercise, although at first it might appear that Blackall was far superior to Miles, the latter had more than once given proof that it was hard work for any one to gain a victory over him.

Blackall's great fault was a strong inclination to bully. He was a tyrant, and utterly indifferent to the feelings of others. If he wanted a thing done, he did not consider what trouble and annoyance it might give others, but, confiding in his strength, he made all the smaller boys do what he wanted. If they refused, he thrashed them till they promised to obey him. He was a great talker, and a never-ceasing boaster of what he had done, and of what he could do and would do. As he certainly could do many of the things he talked about, it was believed that he could do everything. Some believed in him, but others did not. Such a person was, however, sure to have a number of followers and ardent admirers, who quoted him on all occasions,—stuck by him through thick or thin, right or wrong, and looked upon him as one of the finest fellows in existence.

Among the most constant of his followers was Robert Dawson—Bobby Dawson he was always called. He was not a badly inclined little fellow, but he had no confidence in himself, and, consequently, wanted to lean on somebody else. Unfortunately he chose Blackall as his supporter.

Among the smaller boys who aspired to be considered something above the common was Tommy Bouldon. He was a determined, independent little fellow. He was very active, and could perform more feats of activity than any other boy of his size. He was a fair cricketer, and was sometimes chosen by some of the bigger fellows to play in their matches. This made Tommy rather cocky at times; but he was a good-natured chap, and managed to live on good terms with everybody.

Tommy, like Blackall, was rather apt to boast of what he had done, or he purposed doing; but in one respect he was different;—he never exaggerated in his descriptions of his past exploits, and seldom failed to perform whatever he undertook to do.

The boys I have described were among the many who were exercising away with all their might and main on the gymnastic poles.

Blackall was going up a ladder hand over hand, without using his feet, while Lemon was swarming up a pole. When they reached the top, giddy as was the height, they crossed each other and descended, one by the pole and the other by the rope, head foremost; then, without stopping, each climbed on some horizontal bars.

Lemon first hung by his hands to the bar he had seized, and then he drew himself up until his chest touched the bar; then, lowering himself, he passed one of his feet through his hands, and hitched his knee over the bar; then he swung backwards, and came up sitting on the bar with one leg; it was easy enough to draw the other leg after him. Throwing himself off, he caught the bar again by his hands, and curled his body over it.

"That's all very fine," exclaimed Blackall, who had been sitting on a bar observing him; "but, old fellow, can you do this?"

Blackall, as he spoke, threw himself off the bar, grasping it with both hands; then he passed the left knee through the right arm, so as to let the knee rest in the elbow; then he passed the right knee over the instep of the left foot, and letting go his left hand, he grasped his right foot with it. Thus he hung, suspended by his right hand, and coiled up like a ball. After hanging thus for a couple of minutes, he caught the bar by his other hand, and, uncoiling himself, brought his feet between his arms and allowed them to drop till they nearly touched the ground. Then he turned back the same way. Once more lifting himself up, he threw his legs over the bar, and dropping straight down, hung by his bent knees, with his head towards the ground. A little fellow passing at the moment, he called him, and lifted him off the ground; a feat which called forth the loud applause of all his admirers. This excited him to further efforts, and he was induced to continue still longer when he found that Lemon did not seem inclined to vie with him.

While the exercises I have described were going forward, the Doctor made his appearance at the door of the yard, accompanied by a boy who looked curiously round at what was taking place. After waiting a minute or so, the Doctor led him on through the grounds.

"I wonder who that chap is!" observed Tommy Bouldon. "He looks a regular-built sawney."

"Oh, don't you know? He's the new fellow," answered Bobby Dawson. "I heard something about him from Sandon, who lives in the same county, ten or a dozen miles from his father's house. The families visit,—that is to say, the elders go and stay at each other's houses,—but Sandon has never met this fellow himself, so he could only tell me what he had heard. One thing he knows for certain, that he has never been at school before, so he must be a regular muff, don't you see. His father is a sort of philosopher—brings up his children unlike anybody else; makes them learn all about insects and flowers, and birds and beasts, and astronomy, and teaches them to do all sorts of things besides, but nothing that is of any use in the world that I know of. Now I'll wager young Hopeful has never played football or cricket in his life, and couldn't if he was to try. Those sort of fellows, in my opinion, are only fit to keep tame rabbits and silkworms."

Master Bobby did not exactly define to what sort of character he alluded; and it is possible he might have been mistaken as to his opinion of the new boy.

"Well, I agree with you," observed Tommy Bouldon, drawing himself up to his full height of three feet seven inches, and looking very consequential. "I hate those home-bred, missy, milk-and-water chaps. It is a pity they should ever come to school at all. They are more fit to be turned into nursery-maids, and to look after their little brothers and sisters."

This sally of wit drew forth a shout of laughter from Bobby Dawson, who forthwith settled in his mind that he would precious soon take the shine out of the new boy.

"But, I say, what is the fellow's name?" asked Tommy.

"Oh, didn't I tell you?" answered Bobby. "It's Bracebridge; his Christian name is—let me see, I heard it, I know it's one of your fancy romantic mamma's pet-boy names—just what young ladies put in little children's story-books. Oh, I have it now—Ernest—Ernest Bracebridge."

"I don't see that that is so very much out of the way either," observed Bouldon; "I've known two or three Ernests who were not bad sorts of fellows. There was Ernest Hyde, who was a capital cricketer, and Ernest Eastgate, who was one of the best runners I ever met; still from what you tell me, I fully expect that this Ernest Bracebridge will turn out no great shakes."

While the lads were speaking, the subject of their remarks returned to the playground. An unprejudiced person would certainly not have designated him as a muff. He was an active, well-built boy, of between twelve and thirteen years old. He had light-brown hair, curling slightly, with a fair complexion and a good colour. His mouth showed a good deal of firmness, and he had clear honest eyes, with no little amount of humour in them. He was dressed in a dark-blue jacket, white trousers, and a cloth cap. Dawson and Bouldon eyed him narrowly. What they thought of him, after a nearer scrutiny, they did not say. He stood at a little distance from the gymnasium, watching with very evident interest the exercises of the boys. He had, it seemed, when he first came in with the Doctor, been attracted with what he had seen, and had come back again as soon as he was at liberty. He drew nearer and nearer as he gained more and more confidence, till he got close up to where Dawson and Bouldon were swinging lazily on some cross-bars. Blackall was at that moment playing off some of his most difficult feats, such as I have already described.

"I say, young fellow, can you do anything like that?" said Tommy, addressing Ernest, and pointing at Blackall. "Dawson here swears there isn't another fellow in England who can come up to him."

"I beg your pardon, did you speak to me?" asked Ernest, looking at Tommy as if he considered the question had not been put in the most civil way.

"Yes, of course, young one, I did. There's no one behind you, is there?" answered Tommy. "What's more, too, I expect an answer."

"Perhaps I might, with a little practice," answered the new boy carelessly. "I'm rather fond of athletic exercises."

"I'll be content to see you get up that pole, young 'un," observed Tommy, putting his tongue in his cheek. "Take care you don't burn your fingers as you come down."

"I'll try, if I may," replied the new boy quietly.

He advanced towards the pole, but another boy got hold of it—rather a bungler he seemed; so Ernest left him to puff and blow by himself in his vain efforts at getting up, and went on to one of the swinging ropes. He seized it well above his head, and pressing his knees and feet against it, steadily drew himself up, to the surprise of Bouldon and Dawson and several other lookers-on, till he reached the lofty cross-bar. Was he coming down again? No. He sprang up and ran along the beam with fearless steps till he came to the part into which the top of the pole was fixed. Most of the boys thought that he would come down by the ladder; but, stooping down, he swung himself on to the pole and slid down head first to the ground. There he stood, looking as cool and unconcerned as if he had not moved from the spot. The feat he had performed, though not difficult, was one which neither Dawson nor Bouldon had yet attempted. It raised him wonderfully in the opinion of those young gentlemen.

"Very well, young one," exclaimed Tommy in a patronising tone. "I did not think you'd have done it half as well. However, I suppose it's *the* trick you have practised. You couldn't do, now, what that big fellow there, Blackall, is about?"

"Oh, yes," said Ernest quietly. "I can kick the bar, or swing on it, or circle it, or do the grasshopper, or hang by my legs, or make a true lover's knot, or pass through my arms, or hang by my feet. You fancy that I am boasting, but the fact is this, my father won't let us do anything imperfectly. If we do it at all, he says, we must do it well."

"Oh, I dare say that's all right, young one," observed Tommy, turning away with Dawson. "I see how it is. He has been coached well up in gymnastics, but when he comes to play cricket or football it will be a very different affair. A fellow may learn one thing or so at home very well, but he soon breaks down when he comes to practice work."

A few only of the boys had remarked Ernest's performances. Most of them were too much engaged in their own exercises to think of him. He felt rather solitary when left to himself, and wished that Dawson and Bouldon would have stopped to talk to him, not that he particularly admired their manners. He was well prepared, however, to meet all sorts of characters. School and its inner life had been described to him by his father with faithful accuracy.

Although at the time few, if any, private schools were to be found superior to Grafton Hall, Ernest did not expect to find it as happy a place as his own home, much less a paradise. A number of little boys were playing a game of ring-taw in a corner of the yard. Ernest walked up to them. No one took any notice of him, but went on with their game. "Knuckle down," was the cry. A sturdy little fellow, with a well-bronzed hand, was peppering away, knocking marble after marble out of the ring with his taw, and bid fair to win all that remained. Ernest had long ago given up marbles himself, but he did not pretend to forget how to play with them. He thought that if he offered to join them it might serve as an introduction.

"If you will let me, I shall like to play with you," he said quietly, catching the eye of the sturdy player.

"With all my heart," was the answer.

"Thank you. But I must buy a taw and some marbles," said Ernest. "I did not think of bringing any."

"Oh, I will lend you some," answered the boy. "Here, this taw is a prime one; it will win you half the marbles in the ring if you play well."

Ernest thanked his new friend, and took the taw and a dozen marbles with a smile. He was amused at finding himself about to play marbles with some boys most of whom were so much younger than himself. His new friend had cleared the ring, and a fresh game was about to begin. He put down eight of his marbles, and, as there were several players, a large number were collected. The first player had shot out four or five marbles, when his taw remaining in the ring, he had to put them all back and go out. Ernest was kneeling down to take his turn, when Blackall, tired of his gymnastic exercises, came sauntering by.

"What are you about there, you fellows? I'll join you," he exclaimed. "How many down? Eight. Oh, very well."

Without more ado he was stooping down to shooting from the offing, when Ernest observed that he had taken his turn.

"Who are you, I should like to know, you little upstart?" cried Blackall, eyeing the new-comer with great disdain. "Get out of my way, or I will kick you over."

"Indeed I shall not," exclaimed Ernest, who had never been spoken to in that style before, but whose whole spirit rose instantly in rebellion against anything like tyranny or injustice. Without speaking further, he stooped down and shot his taw with considerable effect along the edges of the ring of marbles. It knocked out several, and stopped a little way outside.

"Didn't you hear me?" exclaimed Blackall furiously. "Get out of my way, I say."

Ernest did not move, but took his taw and again fired, with the same effect as before. Blackall's fury was now at its highest pitch. He rushed at Ernest, and lifting him with his foot sent him spinning along the ground. Ernest was not hurt, so he got up and said, "I wonder you can treat a stranger so. However, the time will come when you will not dare to do it."

"Shame! shame!" shouted several of the little fellows, snatching up their marbles and running away, for they were accustomed to be treated in that way by Blackall.

Ernest was left with his first acquaintance standing by his side, while the bully walked on, observing—

"Very well; you'll catch it another time, let me promise you."

"That's right!" exclaimed Ernest's companion. "I'm glad you treated him so. It's the only way. If I was bigger I would, but he thrashes me so unmercifully whenever I stick up against him that I've got rather sick of opposing him."

"Help me," said Ernest, "and we'll see what can be done."

The other boy put out his hand, and pressing that of the new-comer, said, "I will." The compact was then and there sealed, not to be broken; and the boys felt that they understood each other.

"What is your name?" said Ernest. "It is curious that I should not know it, and yet I feel as if I was a friend of yours."

"My name is John Buttar," answered the boy. "I have heard yours. You are to be in our room, for the matron told me a new boy was coming to-day, though I little thought what sort of a fellow he was to be. But come along, I'll show you round the bounds. We may not go outside for the next three weeks, for some of the big fellows got into a row, and we have been kept in ever since."

So Johnny Butter, as he was called, ran on. He let Ernest into the politics of the school, and gave him a great deal of valuable information.

Ernest listened attentively, and asked several questions on important points, all of which Buttar answered in a satisfactory way.

"This is a very jolly place altogether, you see," he remarked; "what is wrong is generally owing to our own faults, or rather to that of the big fellows. For instance, the Doctor knows nothing of the bullying which goes forward; if he knew what sort of a fellow Blackall is he would very soon send him to the right-about, I suspect. We might tell of him, of course, but that would never do, so he goes on and gets worse and worse. The only way is to set up against him as you did to-day. If everybody did that we should soon put him down."

Ernest was very much interested in all he saw. Notwithstanding the example he had just had, he thought that it might be a very good sort of place. Buttar introduced him to several boys, who, he said, were very nice fellows; so that before many hours had passed Ernest found himself with a considerable number of acquaintances, and even Dawson and Bouldon condescended to speak rationally to him.

A number of boys having collected, a game of Prisoners' Base was proposed. Ernest did not know the rules of the game, but he quickly learnt them, and soon got as much excited as any one. His new friend John Buttar was captain on one side, while Tommy Bouldon was leader of the opposite party. Each chose ten followers. A hedge formed their base, two plots being marked out close to it, one of which was occupied by each party. Two circles were formed, about a hundred yards off, for prisons.

"Chevy, chevy, chevy!" shouted Buttar, rushing out.

Bouldon gave chase after him. They were looked upon as cocks of their set, and the chase was exciting. Bouldon was very nearly catching Buttar, when Ernest darted out to his rescue. Now, Tommy, you must put your best leg foremost or you will be caught to a certainty. What twisting and turning, what dodging there was. Now Bouldon had almost caught up Buttar, but the latter, stooping down, was off again under his very hands, and turning suddenly, was off once more behind his back.

"'Ware the new boy; 'ware young Bracebridge," was the shout from Bouldon's side.

Tommy was in hot chase after Buttar, and there seemed every probability of his catching him. On hearing the cry, he looked over his shoulder and saw Ernest close to him. He had now to think of his own safety. From what he had observed of the new boy, he saw, that though he was a new boy, and had never been at school before, he was not to be despised. He had therefore to imitate Buttar's tactics, and to dodge away from his pursuer.

Ernest had evidently been accustomed chiefly to run straight forward; he was very fleet of foot, but had not practised the art of twisting and turning. Another boy of Bouldon's side now ran out in pursuit of Ernest, who, having executed his purpose of rescuing Buttar, returned in triumph to his base, while one of his side ran out, and, touching the boy who had gone out against him, carried him off to the prison.

Several others were taken; Bouldon at length was caught, so was Buttar, but he was quickly rescued by Ernest, whose side was at length victorious, having committed every one of the others to prison.

Ernest, who had contributed very largely to this success, pronounced it a capital game. He gained also a good deal of credit by the way he had played it, especially when it was known that it was for the first time, and that he had never been at school before. The way in which his companions treated him put him in very good spirits, and he became sufficiently satisfied with himself and with everything around him. He felt that he could do a number of things, but he was diffident from not knowing of what value they might be considered by other boys. He had heard that some savages despised the purest pearls, while they set a high value on bits of glittering glass, and so he thought that some of his accomplishments might be very little thought of by other boys. However, by the time the tea-bell rang, he had fully established himself in the good opinions of most of the younger boys; even two or three of the elder ones pronounced him to be a plucky little chap.

The evening was spent in a fine large hall which had been fitted up for playing. Before each breaking-up a platform was raised at one end, and speeches were delivered from it, and more than once it had been fitted up as a theatre, and the boys had got up, with some effect, some well-selected plays. There were some tables and desks at one end, and rows of shelves on which were placed boxes and baskets, and cages with birds and tame mice, and indeed all sorts of small pets. A few of the quieter boys went in that direction, but the greater number began to play a variety of noisy games.

"I say, who's for a game of high-cock-o'lorum?" exclaimed Bouldon.

"I, I, I," answered several voices.

"Come along, Bracebridge, try your hand at it."

Ernest declined at first, for he did not much admire having a number of fellows jumping over his head and sitting on his shoulders, but Tommy pressed him so hard that at last he consented to try. His side was to leap.

"Go on, go on!" shouted Buttar.

Ernest had for some time practised vaulting; he ran, measuring his distance, and sprang over the heads of all the boys right up to the wall.

"Bravo!" cried Buttar, delighted, "you'll do, I see; there's no fear of you now."

Ernest felt much pleased by the praise bestowed on him by his new friend, and turning round he waved to the other boys to come on. The last boy failed, and his side had to go under. He proved as staunch, however, with two heavy boys on his shoulders, as any of the most practised players, and his side were much oftener riders than horses.

"I say, though, you don't mean to say, Bracebridge, that you have never been to school before?" said Buttar, as they were summoned away to their bedrooms. "I should have thought, from the way you do things, that you were an old boy."

Ernest assured him that he had never been in any school whatever, and that he had associated very little with any boys, except his own brothers.

"I'll tell you how it is," he continued; "my father says we should do everything on principle. He has made us practise all sorts of athletic exercises, and shown us how we can make the best use of our muscles and bones. The balls of the foot and toes are given us, for instance, as pads from which we may spring, and on which we may alight, but clumsy fellows will attempt to leap from their heels or jump down on them; however, I'll tell you what I know about the matter another time. He has us taught to row and swim, and climb and ride. He says that they are essential accomplishments for people who have to knock about the world, as all of us will have to do. He has always told us that we must labour before we can be fed; it is the lot of humanity. If we by any chance neglected to do what he ordered, we had to go without our dinner or breakfast, as the case might be; so you see we have learned to depend a good deal upon ourselves, and to feel that if we do not try our best to get on, no one else will help us."

"Oh, yes! I understand now why you are so different to most new boys," answered Buttar. "Well, your father is a sensible man, there's no doubt of it. I got on pretty well when I first came, much from the same reason. My mother never let us have our own way, always gave us plenty to do, and taught us to take care of ourselves without our nurses continually running after us. Now I have seen big fellows come here, who cried if they were hit, were always eating cakes and sweet things, and sung out when they went to bed for the maid-servant to put on their night-caps; these sort of fellows are seldom worth much, either in school or out of it. They fudge their lessons and shirk their work at play; regular do-nothing Molly Milksops, I call them."

And the two boys laughed heartily at the picture Buttar had so well drawn.

Off each room was a washing-place, well supplied with running water, and a bath for those boys who could not bathe in the pond. Ernest's bed was pointed out to him. Approaching it, he knelt down, and while most of the boys were washing, said his prayers. Only one boy in a shrill voice cried out in the middle of them, Amen. When Ernest rose up he looked round to try and discover who had used the expression. All were silent, and pretended to be busily employed in getting into bed; two or three were chuckling as if something witty had been said.

"I will not ask who said, Amen," remarked Ernest in a serious voice. "But remember, school-fellows, you are mocking, not a poor worm like me, but God Almighty, our Maker." Saying this, he placed his head on his pillow.

"A very odd fellow," observed two or three of the boys; "I wonder how he will turn out."

Chapter Two
Ernest's First Days at School

The next morning, when he got up, Ernest was told, after prayers, to take his seat on a vacant bench at the bottom of the school, till the Doctor had time to examine him. He felt rather nervous about his examination, for he had been led to suppose it a very awful affair. At last the Doctor called him up and asked him what books he had read. Ernest ran through a long list; Sir Walter Scott's novels, and Locke on the Human Understanding, were among them. The Doctor smiled as he enumerated them.

"I fear that they will not stand you in good stead here, my man; the books I mean are Greek and Latin books. What have you read of them?"

"None, sir, right through. I know a great number of words, and can put them together, and papa and I sometimes talk Latin and Greek together, just as easily as we do French and German and Italian."

"I have no doubt that you will do in the end," observed Doctor Carr. "I make a rule, however, to put boys who have not read certain books in the class in which those books are about to be read, and let them work their way up. I reserve the power of removing a boy up as rapidly as I think fit, so that if you are diligent I have no doubt that you will rapidly rise in the school."

Ernest thanked the Doctor, and in the forenoon went up with his new class. He felt rather ashamed at finding himself among so many little boys, and still more at the bungling, hesitating way in which they said their lessons. They were just beginning Caesar. He found that he could quickly turn it into English, but he took his dictionary that he might ascertain the exact meaning of each word. The Doctor called up his class that day, though he generally heard only the upper classes. Ernest began at the bottom, but before the lesson was over he had won his way to the top of the class.

"Very good indeed, Bracebridge," said the Doctor with an approving smile; "you may read as much Caesar as you like every day. I will beg Mr Johnson to hear you, and when you have got through it you shall be moved into the next class."

Many of the boys thought this a very odd sort of reward, and were much surprised to hear Ernest thank the Doctor for his kindness. They would have considered it a greater reward to be excused altogether from their lessons. Much more surprised were they to find Ernest working away day after day at his Caesar, and translating as much as Mr Johnson had time to listen to. He read on so clearly and fluently that most of the boys declared that he must have known all about it before. A few felt jealous of him, and tried to interrupt him; but he went steadily working on, pretending to take no notice of these petty annoyances launched at him. In the course of a fortnight he was out of the class and placed in the next above it. This he got through in less than a month, and now he found himself in the same with Buttar, Dawson, and Bouldon. They welcomed him very cordially, though they could not exactly understand how he managed so quickly to get among them. The two latter, however, were especially indignant when they discovered his style of doing his work.

"It's against all school morality," exclaimed Tommy, with a burst of virtuous anger. "How should we be ever able to get through half our lessons if we were to follow your plan? You must give it up, old fellow; it won't do."

"I am sorry that I cannot, to please you," answered Ernest. "You see, I want to read through all these books, that I may get to higher ones which are more interesting; and then I want to get to College as soon as possible, that I may begin life. Our days in this world are too short to allow us to waste them. If I get through school twice as fast as any of you, I shall have gained so many years to my life. That is worth working for—is it not?"

"My notion is, that we should do as few lessons and amuse ourselves as much as we can," answered Tom Bouldon. "When we are grown up there will be time enough to think of employing time; I do not see any use in looking forward to the future, which is so far off."

"What are we sent into this world for, do you think?" asked Ernest.

"I'm sure I don't know," answered Bouldon.

"To spend the money which is left us, or to go into professions to make our fortunes," observed Dawson.

"I should think rather to prepare for the future," remarked Ernest. "So my father has always told me, and I am very sure that he is right. We are just sent into this world to prepare for another, and that preparation is to be made by doing our duty to the best of our power in that station of life in which we are placed. It is our duty when we are boys to prepare for being men, by training our minds and bodies, and by laying in as large a share of knowledge as we can obtain."

"Oh, that's what the saints say!" exclaimed Dawson, with a laugh. "We shall very soon christen you the saint, Bracebridge, if you talk in that way."

"I don't mind what you may call me," said Ernest, quietly; "I only repeat what a sensible man has told me; I am very certain that he has only said what he knows to be the truth."

Neither Dawson nor Bouldon would be convinced that Ernest was talking sense, but Buttar, who was listening, drank in every word he said. He had at first felt an inclination to patronise the new boy, but he now tacitly acknowledged him as his superior in most respects, except perhaps a small amount of the details of school knowledge.

Ernest, however, had been too carefully trained by his father to presume on this superiority. He, of course, could not help feeling that he did many things better than most of his companions, but then he was perfectly conscious that if they had possessed the advantages his father had given him, they would probably have done as well.

With the ushers he was a favourite, especially with his own master, who was under the impression that the rapid progress he made was owing to his instruction; while Doctor Carr soon perceived that he was likely to prove a credit to the school. Ernest, however, was not perfect, and he had trials which were probably in the end good for him. Some of the elder boys were jealous of the progress he made, and called him a conceited little puppy. Blackall, who was only in the third class, and had from the first taken a dislike to him, did not like to see him catching him up, as he called it. With mere brute force Ernest could not contend, so that he got many a cuff and kick from the ill-disposed among the elder boys, which he was obliged to take quietly, though he might have felt the inclination to resent the treatment he received.

At length he began to prefer the hours spent in school, because he was there certain of being free from the annoyances in the playground. The bigger boys did not condescend to play with hoops, but Ernest was very fond of all games played with them. Buttar and he were generally on one side, opposed to Dawson and Bouldon.

"Who's for prisoners' base?" exclaimed Buttar coming out from school into the playground with his hoop in his hand.

Plenty of boys were ready to join, and soon there was a tremendous clattering away with hoop-sticks and hoops, while Ernest was seen with a light thin hoop, dodging in noiselessly among them. His hoop-stick was as light as his hoop, which he never beat. He merely pressed the stick against it, and in an instant, by placing the stick on the top, could either stop or turn, while he kept it under the most perfect command. The sides were soon arranged. Out he darted with his swift hoop towards the enemy's prison, which he circled round; and though Tom Bouldon was on the watch to catch him, he kept dodging about till another of his own side ran out, in the hope of knocking down Bouldon's hoop. Bouldon was in honour bound to follow Ernest till he touched his hoop, or drove him back to his base. Ernest drove on his hoop to a considerable distance, with Tommy after him. Jones, one of Ernest's side, pursued Tommy, Dawson pursued Jones, and Dawson, in his turn, was followed by Buttar, and so on, till every one playing was out with the double work of having to try and make a prisoner, and, at the same time, to escape from the boy pursuing him. To a spectator not knowing the game, it might have appeared as if all was confusion: but those playing knew exactly what they were about, and felt that all their energies and science were required to enable them to play well. Ernest's great aim was to lead Bouldon into such a position that Jones might catch him. This he at last succeeded in doing, and Tommy and his hoop were sent into prison, and as no one was at the base, there he had every chance of remaining some time. Meantime, Ernest rushed to the base, to be ready to capture any one who might get back on the opposite side and endeavour to rescue Bouldon. He was joined speedily by Jones, who had only to look out so as to escape from Dawson. Dawson might have caught him, but, being himself pursued, he had to take care of his own safety. When Dawson saw that Jones had escaped him, he could with honour return to his camp; but his pursuer was nimble of foot, and had a light hoop, and just before he reached his base, he, or rather his hoop, was touched, and he had to take up his place in the prison. Thus the game continued with great animation, victory appearing now to lean to one side, now to the other; but on each occasion when their side got the worst of it, Ernest and Buttar made such well-directed efforts that they speedily restored the day. Now, all but three on their side were captured. Out sprung Ernest with his hoop, flying like the wind; and while his opponents were looking on at the rapidity of his movements, Buttar, who had thrown himself on the ground, as if exhausted, leaped up, and dashing along, had recovered a prisoner before any one could overtake him. Ernest in like manner regained another, and wheeling round as soon as he had entered the base, he was off again, and had sent an opponent to prison, and rescued another friend, without for a moment stopping. Sometimes he would tell Buttar exactly what he was going to do, and so well were his plans laid, that he seldom failed to accomplish his design. This gave him confidence in himself, and gained him the perfect confidence of his companions. At length Ernest and Buttar succeeded in putting every one of their opponents in prison, and loud shouts from their side proclaimed that they had won the well-contested victory. The game was over; the light hoops were laid aside, and Dawson proposed that they should play at English and French. Their chargers, as they called their heavy hoops, were brought out from the play-room, and the two parties, joined by a good many more, drew up on opposite sides of the field. Even some of the bigger fellows condescended to join in the game. It was generally supposed to depend more on strength than skill. The strongest hoops were used, and if a hoop was once down, the owner was obliged to retire from the field. Just as they were about to begin, Blackall passed by. Dawson instantly called to him—

"I say, Blackall—there's a good fellow—do come and be our captain. Here's my biggest hoop—it's a stunner! Under your guidance it is sure to gain us the victory."

"Well, I don't mind helping you," answered Blackall, carelessly, eyeing, however, Ernest and Buttar, for both of whom he had an especial dislike.

"That won't do," observed Buttar, who was one of the captains of his party. "Stay, I'll get Lemon to join us. He won't mind taking a hoop-stick to help us; and he, and you, and I, together with a few other good fellows and true, will be able to hold our own against Dawson and Tommy, even though they have Bully Blackall with them."

Buttar soon found Miles Lemon, who, though he was reading an interesting book, jumped up with the most good-natured alacrity, and undertook to act as the leader of their party.

"Oh, you fellows were afraid to take care of yourselves!" exclaimed Blackall, when he saw Lemon and Buttar approaching. "Well, we will see what we can do."

There were full thirty boys on each side—nearly half the school. None of the bigger boys, of course, condescended to play with hoops. Blackall and Lemon, indeed, made it understood that they only joined as leaders, and on no account for their own amusement, while there were a good many small boys who were considered too weak to take part in so rough a sport. The armies were drawn up in double line, one at each end of the gravel playground. At a signal given, they rushed forward to the deadly strife, some striking away at their heavy hoops with all their might, and using clubs rather than hoop-sticks. Ernest offered a great contrast to those heavy chargers. He entered the battle with his light hoop and hoop-stick, and when the signal was given, rushed forward in the van to commence the strife. On came Blackall, highly indignant to see a new boy taking the lead in so prominent a way. He struck his hoop with a force sufficient to overthrow not only Ernest's hoop, but Ernest himself; but the young champion knew well what he was about. Instead of waiting for the blow, by a dexterous turn he brought the edge of his light hoop against the side of Blackall's, which went reeling away among the following crowd, and was instantly upset. Ernest was in time to treat another hoop of the second line in the same fashion, and then he sprang on with a shout of victory to the end of the ground. Several times the two parties changed sides, and each time five or six hoops went down, sometimes more. It was a regular tournament, such as was fought by the knights of old, only hoops were used instead of horses, and hoop-sticks in lieu of lances; but the spirit which animated the breasts of the combatants was the same, and probably it was enjoyed as keenly. Blackall stood on one side, eyeing with revengeful feelings the success which attended Ernest wherever he moved. Backwards and forwards he went; and although constantly charged and marked out for destruction by the biggest fellows on the opposite side, always avoiding them, and seldom failing to strike down one or more hoops in every course. Blackall could not understand how it was. He was not aware what a well-practised eye, good nerves, and a firm will could accomplish. Ernest's father had instilled into him the principle, that whatever is worth doing at all, is worth doing as well as it can be done. So, when he took a hoop in his hand, he considered how he could use it to the best advantage; and from the first, he never played with it without endeavouring to perfect himself in some method of turning it here or there, of stopping it suddenly, or of twirling it round.

A second time that day did Ernest's party come off victorious. Some said that it was owing to Lemon having joined them: but Lemon himself confessed that he had not done half as much execution as had young Bracebridge. From that day Lemon noticed Ernest in a very marked way, and when he spoke to him treated him as an equal in age. Some of his first companions declared that, to a certainty, Bracebridge would be very much cocked up by the attention shown him; but they were mistaken, for he pursued the even tenor of his way without showing that he by any means thought himself superior to his companions.

The Easter holidays arrived. Those who lived near enough to the school went home; but as the boys were generally collected from widely separated parts of England, Scotland, and Ireland, the greater number remained. They had greater liberty than at any other time, and were allowed to make long excursions with one of the masters, or with some of the bigger boys who, from their good principles and steadiness, were considered fit to be entrusted with them. Lemon was high enough in the school to have that honour, and so Ernest and Buttar always endeavoured to belong to his party. Lemon was very glad to have them, as he found them more companionable than many of the bigger fellows, and he had no difficulty in keeping them in order. Tom Bouldon was also frequently of their party. He had tried others, but after some experience he found their society by far the most satisfactory.

Blackall, although a bully, stood pretty well with the masters. He had cleverness sufficient to get through his lessons with credit, and he had sense enough to keep himself out of mischief generally. Doctor Carr now and then had uncomfortable feelings about him. He was not altogether satisfied with his plausible answers; nor did he like the expression of his countenance, that almost sure indicator of the mind within. Still the Doctor hoped that he might be mistaken, and did not forbid Blackall, who was appointed to the office by one of the masters, to take out a party of youngsters. Far better would it have been for the boys had they been kept shut up within the walls of the school-room on the finest days of the year than have been allowed to go out with such an associate. Blackall wanted to be considered a man, and he thought the sure way to become so was to imitate the vices and bad habits of men. Too well do I remember the poison he poured into the ears of his attentive and astonished hearers. About five miles off there was a village with a few small shops in it. One of them contained books and stationery, and cigars and snuff. It was much patronised by Blackall, not for the former, but for the latter articles. He thought it very manly not only to have his cigar-case, but his snuff-box. Lemon never failed to ridicule him to the other boys for his affectation of manliness. He did this to prevent them from following so pernicious an example.

"See that fellow, now, making a chimney of his mouth and a dust-hole of his nose," observed Lemon, when one day he and his party passed him, with several of his companions, lying on the grass on a hill side, three or four miles from the school. Blackall had a huge cigar in his mouth, and a small boy sat near him, looking pale as death, and evidently suffering dreadfully.

"What's the matter, Eden?" asked Lemon, kindly, as he passed him.

"Oh—oh! it's that horrid tobacco! I thought I should like it; but I'm going to die—I know that I am. Oh dear! oh dear!" answered the little fellow.

"I hope that you are not going to die," said Lemon; "but you will not get well sitting there in the hot sun. Jump up, and come with us. Bracebridge and Buttar and I will help you along. There's a stream of clear cold water near here; a draught of that will do you much good. Think how pleasant it will be trickling down your throat, and putting out the fire which I know you feel burning within you."

The picture that Lemon thus wisely drew was so attractive, that the little fellow got slowly up, and tried to walk along with him.

"Where are you going to take Eden to?" shouted Blackall, when he saw what was occurring.

"Out of mischief," answered Lemon. "We are going to the seaside, and— some fresh air will do him good."

"He is under my charge, and you have no business to take him away from me," said Blackall.

Lemon had become much interested in poor little Eden, who was a promising boy, and who he saw would be ruined if left much in Blackall's society. He therefore, like a true-hearted, conscientious person, resolved by all means to save him. He did not say, like some people, after a few slight efforts, "I have done my duty. I warned him of the consequences, and I am not called on to do any more." When he wanted to draw a boy out of danger, he made him his friend; he worked and worked away; he talked to him; he showed him the inevitable result of his folly; he used arguments of all sorts; he worked on all the better feelings the boy might possess; and what was of still more avail, he did not trust to his own strength for success—he prayed earnestly at the Throne of Grace—at that Throne where such prayers are always gladly heard—that his efforts might avail: and others wondered, more than Lemon himself, how it was when Lemon took a fellow in hand that he always turned out so well. For this important object he struggled hard to obtain popularity in the school, and succeeded; for no boy of his age and size was so popular among all the right-thinking and well-disposed boys as he was. On this occasion he resolved not to leave Eden in Blackall's power.

"If he wishes to come, I shall certainly allow him," said Lemon.

"He was committed to my charge by Mr Ogilby, and you have no business to take him away," cried Blackall, still leaning lazily on his arm, and continuing to smoke.

"To make him sick and wretched; to teach him to smoke and to drink beer and spirits, and to listen to your foul conversation—you reprobate!" answered Lemon calmly, as he stopped and faced Blackall.

"By God! I'll thrash you for that as soundly as you ever were in your life," exclaimed Blackall, taking his cigar out of his mouth, and rising to his feet.

Earnest's heart rose to his mouth; Buttar clenched his fists tightly. Putting Eden behind them, they sprang to Lemon's side, and looked defiantly at the approaching bully. None of the other boys of either party stirred. Blackall did not like the aspect of affairs. He knew that though, from his greater strength and weight, he could thrash Lemon, he could not hope at any time to gain an easy victory; and from what he had observed of Ernest, he suspected that if he did strike, he would strike very hard and sharp. Buttar also, when once he was attempting to thrash him, had given him such a hit in the eye that the mark had remained for a fortnight at least, to the no small satisfaction of those whom he had been accustomed to bully. He therefore stopped just before he got up to Lemon.

"Come," he said, "I don't want to quarrel. Let Eden remain, and I'll cry *pax*."

"Certainly not, Blackall, you've let Eden do what is forbidden; you are setting him a bad example. I shall therefore be glad to take him away from you. He wishes to accompany me, and I shall let him do so," was the answer.

"Oh, you're a puritanical saint, Lemon,—all the school knows that," said Blackall with a sneer with which he hoped to cover his own retreat. He had been telling the fellows around him that he felt very seedy, and as he looked at the firm front of his three antagonists he had no fancy to commence a desperate fight with them.

"I wish to deserve the good opinion of my schoolfellows, and I do not believe that they will agree with you," said Lemon. "If hating vice and despising the low practices in which you indulge will make me a saint, I am ready to acknowledge the impeachment, and I can only say that I hope the poor little fellows may see the hideousness of sin, and loathe it as much as they do the vile tobacco-leaves you give them to suck, and the spirits and beer which you teach them to drink. Stop! hear me out. There is nothing immoral in drinking a glass of beer or in smoking, but in our case they are both forbidden by the Doctor, whom we are bound to obey. Both become vices when carried to excess, as you, Blackall, carry them, and would teach your pitiable imitators to carry them; and I warn you and them that such practices can only bring you disgrace and misery at last."

Lemon, without saying another word, turned on his heel, and, accompanied by his two sturdy supporters, was walking away.

"Do you mean to say that I drink?" shouted Blackall, with an oath, as soon as he could recover from the astonishment into which this unusual style of address had thrown him.

Lemon turned round, looked him full in the face, and said, "I do." Then he went on the way he had been going. Blackall did not say another word, but staggered back to the bank on which he had been sitting, and endeavoured to re-light the end of the cigar he had dropped when he got up. He knew that Lemon had spoken the truth. Already he had that day stopped at more than one road-side ale-house and drunk several glasses of beer. "*In vino-veritas*," is a true saying. Blackall when sober might pass for a very brave fellow: his true character came out when he was drunk, and he showed himself an arrant coward, as he had done on this occasion. The boys who remained with him looked very foolish, and some of them felt heartily ashamed of their leader. Some resolved to break from him altogether, but he had thrown his chains too firmly over others to allow them to hope or even to wish to get free from him. Lemon, Ernest, Buttar, and their companions continued their walk, carrying poor little Eden along with them. He confessed to having chewed a piece of the cigar and swallowed it, before he discovered that it was not intended to be eaten. Happily for him, he became violently sick, and then, having washed his face in a brook and taken a draught of cold water, he was able to enjoy the beautiful coast scenery the party ultimately reached.

"Is not this much better than sitting smoking and boozing with that thick-headed fellow, Blackall, and his set?" said Ernest, addressing young Eden.

"Indeed it is," was the answer. "I'm sure if Lemon will let me come with him, I will gladly promise never to go out with Blackall any more."

"Stick to that resolution, my boy," replied Ernest. "I'll undertake that Lemon will let you accompany him; and now let us go down on the beach. These sands look very tempting."

The whole party were soon on the sands, strolling along and picking up the various marine curiosities they found in their way. Most of the party wondered at the odd-shaped things they picked up, but had not the slightest notion of their names, or even whether they were animal or vegetable. Ernest knew very little on the subject, though he had read a book or so about the wonders of the sea-shore; but Lemon was able to give his party nearly all the information they required. One of their number was called John Gregson. He was looked upon by the school generally as rather stupid. He seldom joined in any of their games; and when he did, played them very badly, unless they were such as required more judgment than practice. Now, however, he showed that he possessed some knowledge which the others did not. Ernest had picked up a roundish object with a hole through it, and partly covered with spines, which Tom Bouldon stoutly declared to be a fish's egg.

"It must have been a very large fish, then," observed Ernest. "Those prickles, too, are puzzling. Perhaps they grew after the egg was laid."

The general opinion was that Gregson knew something about all sorts of out-of-the-way matters.

"I say, Gregson, this is a regular-built *egg*; isn't it?" said Bouldon, as soon as he could be found. He was discovered up to his knees in a pool among the rocks, with a hammer and chisel in hand, working perseveringly under water.

"No; you first make a statement totally at variance with the truth, and then ask a question," answered the young naturalist, looking up from his occupation, but apparently not well pleased at being interrupted. "That is the *Echinus esculentus,* or sea-urchin. Just let me finish knocking off this magnificent anemone, and I'll tell you all about it."

"Anemone! Oh, I know—one of those curious coloured sea-weedy things I've seen girls collect at watering-places," observed Bouldon, whose knowledge of natural history was not very extensive. "I'd save you all that trouble; let me cut it off with my knife."

"Not for the world; you'd kill it, to a certainty," exclaimed Gregson. "See, I have knocked off a piece of the rock to which it is sticking, and I may now put it into my jar. Now I could cut off any portion of it, and the part cut off will turn into a new anemone, but if I were to injure the base the animal would quickly die. They belong to the class scientifically called *Anthozoa* or living flowers, because from their external appearance they seem to partake of the vegetable nature. Just look into that part of the pool which I have left undisturbed. See, there are two of them feeding. Look how they stretch out their long tentacles to catch hold of their food. Ah! that one has got hold of a tiny shrimp, and is tucking it into his hungry maw, which is just in the middle of its flower-like body. Is he not a handsome fellow? What beautiful colours he presents! Ah! I thought that I should see something else in the pool that you would think curious. Look down close. There are three or more little globular bodies floating about like balloons. The animal is the berve. It has ciliated bands round it, like the marks on a melon. What a beautiful iridescent light plays over them! They enable it to move over the water, while with its long tentacles it fishes for its food. At night those cilia shine with a phosphorescent light, and have a very beautiful appearance. Stop! oh, don't go away without looking more particularly at this submarine forest. The woods of America in autumn do not present more gorgeous colours. That beautiful pink weed is the *Delesseria sanguinea.* Let us pull up some and take it with us to dry it. It will keep its colour for years and its smell for months. See, those are shrimps cruising in and about those delicate branches, and crabs crawling round their stems, and sandskippers darting about; ah, and there comes a goby! Did any of you ever see a goby? Look at him!—what bright eyes he has got! He is hardly bigger than a shrimp, but he is their deadly enemy. He eats up their eggs and the young shrimps, as well as sandhoppers, and indeed anything living which he can get into his big mouth. In his way he is just as terrific a fellow as the shark. He is very hardy, too, and will live in an aquarium with perfect contentment provided he can get enough to eat."

"Well, I had no notion that so many curious things were to be found in a little pool of water," observed Bouldon. "I've looked into hundreds, but never found anything that I know of."

"Oh, I have not mentioned a quarter of the things to be found even in this pool," answered Gregson. "Ah, look at that soldier-crab now! He has just come out from among the sea-weed with his stolen shell in which he has stowed away his soft tail. I'll tell you all about him—"

"Not now, Greggy, thank you," exclaimed Bouldon, who was getting somewhat tired of the naturalist's accounts. When Gregson once began on his favourite subject he was never inclined to stop. Nor was that surprising, for no subject is more interesting and absorbing to those who once take it up—nothing affords more pure or unmixed delight.

"But I say, Greggy, you promised to tell us about this sea-egg, or whatever it is called," said Buttar. "Come, I want to hear."

"Well, look at this starfish," answered Gregson, drawing a five-fingered jack from his jar. Then, taking the echinus in his hand,—"These two fellows are first cousins, very nearly related, though you may not be inclined to believe the fact. The thing you call an egg was as much a living being, capable of feeding itself and producing young, as this starfish. If I was to bend round the rays of the starfish and fill up the interior, I could produce an animal very like the echinus. Both of them have also a mouth at the lower part, and their internal structure is very similar. It is curious that as the echinus grows he continually sends forth a substance from the interior which simultaneously increases the sides of all the plates which form his shell, and thus he never finds his coat too small for him. The spines which appear so rigid when he is dead, he can move when alive in any direction, and they are an excellent substitute for feet; while he can put forth tentacles from the centre orifice, which serve him as hands. Did you ever see a starfish walk? Well, he can get very rapidly over the ground and up steep rocks. He can bend his body into any shape, and the lower surface is covered with vast numbers of tentacles, with which he can work his onward way; and it is extraordinary what long journeys he is able to accomplish by perseverance."

Gregson wound up his lecture by promising to commence a salt-water aquarium, and most of his companions undertook to make another excursion with him for the purpose of conveying back a sufficient supply of salt-water and living curiosities to stock it. They all agreed that they had mightily enjoyed their day's excursion. Ernest, for the first time since he had come to school, felt rather ashamed of himself that he knew so little about natural history, especially of the sea, and he resolved to take every opportunity of making himself acquainted with the subject. Just before they reached home they passed through the field where they had left Blackall and his party. Most of the boys had gone away; but they saw three or four collected together at the bank where the bully had been sitting. He was there; and his companions were bending over him endeavouring to rouse him up. Several empty porter bottles lay near, which plainly told what was the matter with him—he was helplessly tipsy. Lemon, and Ernest, and Buttar went forward to help to drag him along. He looked a picture of imbecility and brutishness. He knew none of them; and only grinned horribly when they spoke to him. Though they felt he richly deserved punishment, it was a point of honour to endeavour to save a school-fellow from disgrace, so they hauled him along and got him into his room and put to bed without meeting any of the masters or the matron—an undertaking they could not have performed except in the holidays. Nearly all his companions next day looked very wretched and complained of headaches—a pretty strong proof of the ill effects of drinking. Alas, how many youths have been hopelessly ruined by the example and counsels of a wretch like Blackall!—and how many, in consequence of habits such as his, have sunk into an early and unhonoured grave, after continuing for a time a trouble and shame to all belonging to them! Let masters and parents watch carefully against the first steps taken, often through folly and idleness, towards so vile a habit; and most earnestly do I pray that none of my young readers may be tempted to adopt so destructive a practice.

Chapter Three
Our Grand Hare Hunt

"Who's for a jolly good game of hare and hounds?" exclaimed Tom Bouldon, rushing into the play-room, where a number of boys were assembled, soon after breakfast, on a lovely day during the Easter holidays. Nearly everybody replied, "I am, I, I, I."

"That's right; we couldn't have finer weather, and it's sure to last. I've been talking to young Bracebridge, and he has undertaken to do hare," observed Bouldon. "I know what some of you will say: he's a new fellow, and isn't fit for the work; but there isn't such a runner in the school. You see how he enters into all the games, though he has never played them before. I'll bet he'll make as good a hare as we've ever had, if not a better. That's my opinion."

This oration of Tommy's had the desired effect. With but few dissentient voices, Ernest was elected to the honour of acting hare. Tommy hurried out to inform him of the fact. Ernest was not well prepared for the undertaking. He had only entered two or three times before into the sport, but still he sufficiently understood what was required of him, to feel that he should make a very creditable hare. He, however, thought that it would be more satisfactory if he was to consult with Bouldon and Buttar, as to what line of country he should take. They told him that if they knew, it would spoil their fun; so they went and found Lemon, who gladly undertook to give him his advice on the subject.

In the meantime, all hands were busily employed in making scent; that is, tearing into the smallest possible pieces all the bits of paper they could lay hands on. Ernest's consultation with Lemon was soon over. Having put on his across-country boots, a short pair of loose trousers, and taken in his belt a hole or so, grasping a trusty stick in his hand, he set off by himself to have a look over the country.

The whole party of hounds numbered upwards of forty. There were some very good runners among them; and, what was of more consequence, several who knew the country thoroughly; so that Ernest knew that he must put forth all his energies. This, however, was what he took delight in doing.

No people but those who have played at hare and hounds, can fully appreciate the excitement, the interest, and the pleasure of the game; or the proud feeling of the hare, who finds that he is successfully baffling his pursuers when he is distancing them by the rapidity of his pace, or by the artfulness of his dodges; still all the time, whatever twists and turns he may make, knowing that he is bound to leave traces of his scent sufficiently strong to lead on the hounds.

The greater part of the day was consumed in preparations for the hunt. Everybody engaged looked out their easiest shoes, and their thickest worsted socks. Still a huntsman and a whipper-in were to be chosen: Buttar proposed asking Lemon, and Bouldon seconded the motion. But then it was suggested, that Ernest had consulted him as to the course he should pursue. One or two cried out for Blackall. "No, no; let us ask Lemon," said Buttar again; "if he knows too much about the course Bracebridge is to take, he will not go; but if he thinks it is right, he will. We can always trust Lemon's honour, you know."

No one dissented from this opinion. Probably Lemon himself was scarcely aware how popular he really was; and certainly he would have been fully satisfied with the grounds on which his popularity was founded. At last, Lemon was met coming into the playground. Several voices assailed him with "Will you be huntsman?"

"Will you be huntsman, Lemon?"

"I must take time to consider; it is a serious undertaking," he answered, laughing. "I will see what Tommy and Buttar have to say."

They expressed their own opinions, and mentioned all that had been said. "Very well, I can take the part very conscientiously," he added; "I merely advised Bracebridge in a general way, what course to take; and when he knows that I am to be huntsman, he will deviate sufficiently to prevent me from being able to follow him, unless I get hold of the scent."

In the evening, when Ernest came back, he expressed his perfect readiness to have Lemon as huntsman. Bouldon was chosen as whipper-in.

"And I'll try to be one of the fleetest hounds," said Dawson, "since I'm neither hare, nor huntsman, nor whipper-in."

Lemon possessed many qualifications for his office; and, among others, a capital horn, on which he could play very well. We always got up our games of hare and hounds in first-rate style. The huntsman, besides his horn, was furnished with a white flag, fastened to a staff shod with iron; while the whipper-in had a red flag. The hare had as large a bag as he could carry of white paper, torn into very small pieces. Frequently, too, the hounds dressed in blue or red caps and jackets, which gave the field a very animated appearance; far better in one respect than a real hunt with harriers, because we were certain that the hare was enjoying the fun as much as the hunters, and whether he was caught or escaped, would sit down afterwards to a capital dinner or tea with them, and "fight his battles o'er again."

The morning for the hunt arrived. It broke, bright and beautiful! with just enough frost in the air to give it freshness and briskness.

The boys were up soon after daybreak, and had breakfast at once, that they might be ready to start at an early hour, and have the whole day before them. They assembled, just outside the school-grounds, in a small wood, which would conceal the hare from them, when he broke cover, and enable him to get a good start.

The hunt was to be longer than any that had ever been run, and as there was every probability that all the scent would be expended, it was arranged that Buttar should accompany Ernest to carry an additional bag of paper.

The huntsman sounded his horn cheerily, and all the hounds came pouring into the woodland glade, accompanied by the Doctor, who seemed as eager as any one to see the sport.

"Now, Buttar, are you all ready?" said Ernest, as they buckled up their waist-belts, and grasped their leaping-poles. "Too—too—too," went the huntsman's horn.

"Off hare, off hare," cried the Doctor. "Ten minutes law will give you a fine start; you'll make play with it—away, away!" He clapped his hands. Off flew Ernest and Buttar, fleet as greyhounds, and very unlike the timid hares they pretended to represent.

The Doctor held his watch in his hand. The hounds meantime were getting ready to start; one pressing before the other, taking a last look at shoe-strings, tightening in their belts, rubbing their hands, in their eagerness to rush out of the wood and commence the pursuit. They kept looking up at the Doctor's countenance, to endeavour to ascertain by the expression it wore whether time was nearly up. Those who had watches were continually pulling them out for the same object. At last the Doctor was seen to put his into his pocket. Lemon gave a cheerful sound with his horn.

"Away, lads, away!" cried the Doctor, full of animation. The instant the order was issued, the hounds made a magnificent burst out of the wood, in full cry, led on by the huntsman, waving his flag, and followed by Tom Bouldon, as whipper-in; an office he performed most effectually. The Doctor stalked after them, enjoying the sport as much as anybody; and, I have no doubt, longing to enter more fully into it, and to run along with them.

Away went the pack, cheering each other on, across a field in which they had found the scent. At the bottom of it ran a rapid brook, as they all well knew. There were stepping-stones across it. It required a firm foot and a steady eye not to fall in. It was a clever dodge of the hare to gain time, for only one could cross at a time. There was scent on each stone, to show he had crossed. Two or three slipped in, but were speedily picked out again by their companions; and forming rapidly, continued the chase on the other side, up a long green lane, with high hedges on either side. They had to keep their eyes about them to ascertain whether he had gone through the hedge, or kept up the lane. On, on they went! at last a pathway, over a stile, appeared on the right, leading through a thick copse. They dashed into it, but soon found that the pathway had not been kept; and through briar and underwood they had to force a passage; now losing the scent, now catching it again; a wide, dry, sunny field lay before them; along it, and two or three others of a similar character they had to go; and then across another brook, over which, one after the other, they boldly leapt. Once more they were in a green lane, with deep cart ruts in it. Before them was a mud cottage, with thatched roof, and a small, fully cultivated garden, enclosed by rough palings, in front of it.

An old couple looked out, surprised at the noise. "Oh, they be the young gentlemen from Grafton Hall. What can they be after?" they observed to one another.

"I say, good dame, have you seen a couple of hares running along this way?" exclaimed Tom Bouldon, striking his staff into the ground, for the hounds had lost the scent.

"No; but we seed two young gentlemen a scampering along here, and up that there lane. Bees they demented? We didn't like to stop them, though somehow we thought as how we ought."

"Lucky you didn't; they'd have kicked up a great row, let me tell you," answered Tommy, laughing heartily. He had not time to say more. The shout of "Tally ho!" and the merry sound of the huntsman's horn, put all the pack in motion. The lane led up hill, and then widened out on some wild open rounded downs, with here and there a white chalk-pit, showing the character of the soil. Up it they tore—for the scent was strong, and they were eager to make up for the time they had lost.

Every one was well warmed up now, and would have leaped across a chasm or down a precipice, or performed any other desperate achievement which they would not have attempted to do in their cooler moments. They breasted the steep downs in magnificent style. The scent led up some of the most difficult parts. For half a mile or more it led along the very summit of the ridge, but a fresh sweet breeze came playing around them, invigorating their muscles, and making them insensible to fatigue. The scent led over a high mound, along the edge of a chalk cliff. As they reached the summit, two figures were seen on the top of a similar height. All were of opinion that they were Ernest and Buttar. They looked scarcely half a mile off. The figures took off their caps, and waved them: this act dispelled all doubts on the subject. Some began to fear that they should catch the hares too easily, but Lemon assured them that there was no fear of that, and so they soon found. Down the steep they dashed, till he shouted to them to stop, and to turn off to the left. A long line of chalk cliffs intervened between them and the opposite height, and the scent led along their edge. Ernest and Buttar had, in the meantime, disappeared; after a run of a quarter of a mile, once more the scent was lost.

"Lost, lost!" shouted Lemon; and the hounds as they came up, went off in every direction to try and find it. In vain, for a long time, they hunted about, till a white spot was seen at the edge of the cliff, a little farther on. The cliff was here more practicable. They looked over; several pieces of paper appeared scattered on little green patches down the precipice. Fearlessly they began to descend, though to some people it would have been nervous work. The difficulty they found showed that Ernest and his companion had in no way lost ground, but had probably gained on them. Now they all reached a ledge, beyond which the descent seemed utterly impracticable. Still Ernest and Buttar evidently had got down.

"Where the hares have gone, we must follow," cried Lemon, to encourage his party. "Hunt about for a path—where there's a will there's a way! Hurra, now!"

The hounds kept examining the ledge in every direction, and at a distance they must have looked like a swarm of ants, so busy did they appear. Still without success; and some of the more fainthearted declared that they should have to climb up the cliff again, and find some other way down, or give up the chase.

"No, no, nonsense," said the huntsman. "There is a way down, and the way must be found."

I must now go back to describe the progress of the hare and his friend.

I have read of "the hare and many friends," but they were very unlike young Buttar; no one could desire a stouter or a stauncher friend. Before starting they had well laid their plans, and determined to give the hounds a good run. Ernest had provided himself with a good pocket compass, so that he could steer as direct a course as the ground would allow to the point he had selected to round before turning back towards home.

"Let us go along over the smooth ground at a good pace—we shall save time to spare when we come to the difficult places," observed Ernest to Buttar, as they were waiting for the Doctor's signal to start. It was given—and away they went; steady at first, but gradually increasing their speed as they found that they could easily draw breath. They met with no impediments in the way. They easily leaped the brooks they encountered. The old couple in Ashby-lane stared at them, and wondered where they could be going, leaving little bits of paper behind them. Then they came to Ashby-downs: it was hot work toiling up the steep side, with the hot sun striking down on them; but when they got to the summit, a fresh breeze and a clear blue air revived their strength, and they went along merrily, every now and then looking back to try and catch sight of the hounds, judiciously dropping their scent in places where it could be seen, and not blown away by the breeze. They had several points to attend to. They had been especially charged by the Doctor to avoid trespassing on any private ground; they had to select an interesting course, and one not too difficult, at the same time with every possible variety of country.

On they went, making good play over the short smooth turf of the downs. At last they came to the cliff. Buttar was for descending again, and crossing the ravine where it opened into the plain country.

"No, no," said Ernest, "we shall increase our distance if we can manage to get down the highest part of the cliff. Let us try what we can do before we give it up."

Down the cliff they began to descend. There were plenty of craggy, rugged spots, which facilitated their descent, but in most places there was only room for one person to descend at a time, so, as in the instance of the stepping-stones, their pursuers had to form in Indian file. They easily reached the ledge. Below it the way was, indeed, difficult. At the very end, however, Ernest observed several points of rock jutting out. By climbing up to them he saw that he could drop down on a broader ledge, well covered with soft turf, and could then descend under the very ledge on which they were standing.

Buttar agreed to make the attempt, feeling certain that Lemon would find that or some other means of overcoming the difficulty.

Ernest clutched the rock, and got along bravely, followed by Buttar. "Take care that you do not sprain your ankle as you drop," cried the latter, as Ernest prepared to let go so as to descend to the ledge. He reached it in safety. He caught his companion in his arms so as to break his fall, and sprinkling some paper under the long ledge, they pursued their way. Once Buttar had to let down Ernest with their handkerchiefs tied together, while

Ernest again caught him. Safely they reached the bottom, and away they went across valleys, over streams, and up hills, never once dreaming of fatigue.

I need not follow them in the whole of their course. They were much delighted, on reaching a high mound, to see the hounds in hot pursuit of them, and still more when all the pack were assembled on the ledge trying to find a way down.

"I hope none of them will come to grief," said Buttar. "Do you know, I think that it would have been safer to have taken some other course: that is a difficult place."

"The very reason I was glad to find it," replied Ernest; "one of these days some of them may have a whole tribe of Red Indians or Caffres after them, and then they may be thankful that they learned how to get down a place of the sort. See! I think they are finding out the way. Let us push on." They rose up into view, and waving their caps, on they went. Next they found a descent, down which they trotted quickly, and then another cliff appeared before them; at the top some fine views were to be obtained. They did not hesitate; up they climbed Fairway Tower was in sight; a wide valley full of streams and rather difficult country was, however, between them and it. They pushed on along the downs; then they descended another steep hill, and on reaching the plain a rapid wide stream was before them. Ernest had expected to come down near a bridge, which he proposed crossing. He and Buttar looked at the broad stream with a puzzled expression. They were not quite certain whether the bridge was to the right or left. They decided on taking the left, going down the stream. At last they met a countryman. They inquired of him about the bridge.

"Oh; 'tis the other way, lads," he answered. "But, I say, young measters, bees you runnin' away from school in such a hurry?"

"No, no," answered Ernest, laughing. "We are running for the pleasure of making the school run after us. If we could get across the stream it may puzzle them to follow us. Can you show us any place where we may cross?"

"Yes; that I can," was the answer. "There bees a place with a sort of an island loike in the middle. There's a plank athwart one place, and a tree hangs over t'other. If ye be as active as ye looks, ye'll make no odds a getting over."

"Oh, thank you, thank you, my man, we shall be much obliged to you, and as your time is your money? here is what is your due," answered Ernest, handing the countryman a small coin. "But lead on; we have no time to lose."

"Noa, ma young ones, I'll no take your money. It's too much by half for just ten minutes' work. Come along though, if ye bees in a hurry," said the good-natured fellow, putting back the coin, and leading the way down the stream. "If so be when we gets wages, we never has them, ye know, till the work is done." He trudged on with his arms swinging before him, getting quickly over the ground, though his legs did not appear to move half so fast as those of the young gentlemen. He did not utter a word all the time, but seemed to concentrate all his energies in getting over the ground as rapidly as he could. Ernest and Buttar ran on by his side, dropping the paper here and there sufficiently thick to indicate their course. At last they reached the spot mentioned by the countryman. He showed them a narrow plank, partly hid by bushes, by which they crossed to a green island surrounded by willows, which hung over into the stream.

"A grand place for fishing, this," observed Buttar, as he looked into the dark, clear water which went whirling by in eddies, and here and there formed deep calm pools and little bays, in which they could not help feeling sure many a trout lay hid.

"No time to think about it, though," answered Ernest. "We will come here, by all means, another day and try what we can do. Let us now see how we are to get across the river. Lay the scent thickly, that the hounds may not be in fault, or they may lose it altogether and give the chase up in despair."

While they were speaking they were following the countryman through the reeds and grass, which was already high in that moist situation. He stopped at the base of a fine large willow, which they saw bent very much over the water, though the bushes prevented them from seeing how far. There were some notches in its trunk, and up these he climbed. They followed him closely, and saw him descend on the opposite bank by means of a knotted rope which hung from the end of one of the limbs. They were delighted with the plan.

"Capital!" exclaimed Buttar. "What fun it will be to have all the hounds come scrambling over the old trunk, and letting themselves down by the rope, one after the other."

The countryman looked at the speaker with a puzzled gaze. "The owndes!" he exclaimed. "They'll ne'er trouble the rope, I'm thinking." He evidently could not settle it in his mind that his young companions were not mad. Buttar and Ernest laughed heartily at his look of astonishment.

"We speak of our schoolfellows, who pretend to be hounds, and we are hares leading them on," exclaimed Buttar. The countryman clapped his hands and rubbed them together to express his delight at the notion, while he joined in their laughter at his mistake.

"Well, that there be a jolly good game, I do think," he exclaimed. "I loikes it, that I do—No, no—I'll not take your money, young measters. I gets a good day's pay for a good day's work, and that's all I asks, and all I wishes for." Ernest, on hearing this sentiment, put out his hand and warmly shook that of the countryman. "I like to hear you say that, friend. It is what all of us should alone desire, and I am sure the world would be much happier if everybody in it were like you; but good-bye, good-bye; I've no time to talk now. I should like to fall in with you and have a chat another day. It's a good bit off to Fairway Tower, which we must round before we turn homeward."

"You bees a free spoken young genl'man, and I'd lief have a chat we ye," answered the countryman; "my name is John Hodge, and I live in Lowley Bottom; ye knows where that is, I'm thinking."

"That I do; very glad. I'll come and see you, John Hodge; good-bye, good-bye;" exclaimed Ernest, as he and Buttar set off at full speed across a grassy willow-bounded field towards Fairway Tower, which appeared full in sight on the downs above them. They had thoroughly regained their wind during the time they had spent with John Hodge, so now they went away once more at full speed. They had a number of broadish ditches to leap, but they easily sprang over them, laughing whenever they pictured to themselves any of their followers tumbling in, a catastrophe they thought very likely to occur at two or three places, where the bank they had to leap to was higher than the one they leaped from.

Once more they reached the foot of the downs. These downs rose on the opposite side of the broad stream they had crossed. Looking along the course of the river towards the sea, it appeared as if the silvery thread of water had cut the green hills in two parts, and that then they had slipped away from it on either side, leaving a broadish expanse covered with meadows and copses, and here and there a corn-field, and a cottage garden, and a potato-ground, with its small, low, straw-thatched, mud cottage.

Up—up the smooth, closely cropped side of the steep hill they climb, with just as good a heart as when they started. Steep as it was, they scarcely panted an instant. Ernest was in capital training; that is to say, he was in the condition in which a strong healthy boy ought always to be. So, indeed, was Buttar; for neither of them ever ate a particle more of food than they required, they eschewed tarts of all sorts, and kept all their limbs and muscles in full exercise. May English boys never cease to practise athletic sports, and more especially systematic gymnastics!

The hare and his companion soon reached the top of the downs, and turning round, spread out their arms with open palms, and gulped down a dozen draughts of the pure fresh breeze, which would now be somewhat behind them, though they had hitherto had it chiefly in their faces, an important advantage which Ernest had taken into consideration when he selected the course for the day.

Note it, all you who may have to do hare. Get the wind in your face as much as possible during your outward course, in cold as well as in hot weather, but more especially in hot. In cold weather, however, it is important, as you will, if you have the wind behind you when going, get very hot, and you will be apt to get chilled when leisurely returning, or be prevented, from fear of it, of sitting down and resting. Not that such an idea of catching cold ever entered into the imagination of the two schoolboys. Along the ridges of the smooth downs they went merrily, gazing down into the valley below, and more than once looking round to discover if the hounds were following. Nowhere were they to be seen.

The foot of Fairway Tower was reached at last. It was the keep of a castle of very ancient date, built in the centre of a Roman encampment. The walls were of enormous thickness, allowing a staircase to wind up within them.

"Let us give them a good view of the sea," cried Ernest. Up the well-worn stone steps they mounted. Up—up they sprung, laughing merrily and cheering loudly when they reached the top. Few people, after a run of nearly fifteen miles, would have liked to have followed their example. The view, Ernest declared, repaid them. It was expansive, and it gave, from its character, a pleasing, exhilarating sensation to the heart as it lay at their feet basking in sunshine. On either hand were the smiling undulating downs, dotted here and there with flocks of sheep. Before them the country sloped away for a couple of miles till it reached the bright blue dancing ocean, over which several white sails were skimming rapidly. Inland there was a beautifully diversified country. There were several rich woods surrounding gentlemen's seats, and here and there a hamlet and a church spire rising up among the trees, and some extensive homesteads, the gems of an English rural landscape; and there were wide pasture lands, and ploughed fields already getting a green tinge from the rising corn, and many orchards blushing with pink bloom, and white little cottages, and the winding river, and many a silvery stream which ran murmuring into it; but I need not go on with the description. Ernest and Buttar drank in its beauties as they did the cool breeze which blew on their cheeks, and then they looked round to try and discover the hounds.

"I see them," exclaimed Buttar, after a long scrutinising search. "There they are, just coming out of Beechwood; they look no bigger than a troop of ants. Well, we have got a fine start of them—let us give them a cheer. They won't hear us, but they may possibly see us." Ernest agreeing to Buttar's proposal, they got to the top of the highest pinnacle, and taking off their hats they waved them vehemently above their heads, shouting at the same time to their hearts' content at the top of their voices, Hurra, hurra, hurra; once more, hurra! They did not expect, however, that the sound could possibly reach their friends, so they shouted, it must be owned, for their own satisfaction and amusement. Having shouted and waved their hats till they were tired, they agreed that it should be time to commence their homeward way. They accordingly prepared to descend from their lofty perch to the world below. They did not go down by the staircase, but by the rugged projections in the wall, where a wide breach existed, made either by the hand of time or by Cromwell's cannons in the times of the Cavaliers and Roundheads. They laughed very much as they stuck bits of paper into the crevices in the walls, and scattered them on every spot where there was a chance of their remaining. They were not long in reaching the bottom, for they were fearless climbers, and made little of dropping down ten feet or so to a ledge below them, provided they felt sure that they could balance themselves when there, and not go head foremost lower still, as careless climbers are apt to do. After this every step would bring them nearer home; but still they endeavoured to make the course as interesting as possible. Having taken a turn round the tower, and dropped the scent thickly in their track, off they again set. Along the upper edge of the downs they went at an easy jog-trot, and then when compelled at last, with regret, to leave the breezy hills, they took their way across a succession of fields where oats, and turnips, and mangel wurtzel were wont to grow, till they descended into the richer pasture and wheat-producing lands. Still they had many a stream and deep ditch to leap.

"How do you feel, old fellow?" said Ernest, after they had made good play for a couple of miles or more without stopping.

"As fresh as one of the daisies we are treading on," answered Buttar. "Do you know, Bracebridge, I never like treading on wild flowers; it seems such wanton destruction of some of the most beautiful works of nature. I feel all the time as a donkey who has got into a flower-bed ought to feel, — that I am a very mischievous animal. I would always rather go out of my way than injure them, especially such graceful gems as the wood anemone, or the wild hyacinth, or the wood sorrel, or primroses and cowslips. I feel that I could not restore one of the hundreds my careless feet have injured, even if my life depended on it."

"The same sort of idea has crossed my mind, I own," replied Ernest; "but then I bethought me, that they have been given in such rich profusion that, although hundreds or thousands may fall victims to our careless steps, as you remark, thousands and tens of thousands remain to show the glory of God's works, and that year after year they come back to us as plentiful and lovely as ever. But I say, old fellow, it won't do to stop and philosophise. We are hares for the nonce, remember, and the hounds are in hot chase after us. By the by, *apropos* to the subject, I remember reading a capital Irish story of Lover's, which made me laugh very much. For some reason or other, a fox walks into the cottage of a keeper, who is absent, and sits down on a chair before the fire, putting his feet on the fender, and taking up a newspaper, resolved to make himself comfortable. 'A newspaper?' exclaimed the Irishman to whom the story is being narrated. 'What did he want with that?' 'Faith! how else could he tell where the hounds were going to meet in the morning?' is the answer."

Buttar laughed heartily at Ernest's anecdote.

"Do you know that I cannot help feeling sometimes, as I am running along, as if I were really and truly a two-legged hare," observed the latter.

"Well, so do I," replied Buttar. "And when I have been doing a hound, I have so completely fancied myself one, as I have been scrambling through hedges and ditches, that I have felt more inclined to bark than to speak, and should certainly have claimed fellowship with a harrier had I encountered one."

"However that may be, as I do not feel inclined to sup on grass or raw cabbage, and should much rather prefer a good round of beef and some bread and cheese, let us now take the shortest cut home," observed Ernest, who was getting hungry.

"Agreed! agreed!" cried Buttar. "I don't think, though, that the hounds can be far behind us. It's my belief, when they come in, that they'll all declare they never have had such a day's run since they came to school."

The huntsman, and whipper-in, and hounds were left on the ledge of rock, looking out for a way by which to reach the bottom of the cliff. At last Tom Bouldon espied a bit of paper sticking in a crevice above where they were standing. He climbed up to it and seeing another, and another, clearly defined the path the hare had taken.

"Tally ho! tally ho!" he shouted.

"Tally ho! tally ho!" cried the huntsman, and sounded his horn.

In an instant, like shipwrecked sailors escaping from a wreck, all the boys were scrambling along the face of the cliff. Then they began to drop down, one after the other, fearless of broken limbs, and very soon they were assembled in the valley below. Once more they burst away in full cry. Across many a marsh they had to wade, and over many a stream to jump, into which more than one tumbled, and had to be hauled out by the rest. Indeed, had not Tom kept them up to their work, several of the hounds would have given up and turned back. Then Lemon cheered them on with his horn, and waved before them his flag, and, shouting together, they surmounted all difficulties, and seldom for more than a minute at a time lost the scent, till they came to the passage of the river. Here for a few minutes they were fairly puzzled. They got into the island, but how to get out again they could not tell. Round and round it they ran, till the scent was discovered by Lemon on the stem of the old willow.

"Tally ho! tally ho!" he shouted, springing along the leaning stem, and disappearing among the branches.

Tom whipped in the hounds, wondering what had become of their leader, till he was seen on the grass on the opposite bank, having come down, not having discovered the rope, rather more rapidly than he intended. Some had already descended in the same rapid way, coming down on all-fours, or with all-fours upwards, and there lay on the soft grass, kicking and sprawling in delightful confusion, before the rope was discovered. The rest got down by the rope, followed by the whipper-in, and then they all picked themselves up, and set off at full speed after the hare. I need not follow them. Continually this indefatigable whipper-in had to keep them up to their work, and very often had to help out those who had tumbled into ditches and trenches, or stuck fast in hedges.

"Well, I do declare we never have had such a run since I came to school," cried Tom, enthusiastically. "Bracebridge deserves a cup, that he does."

The sentiment was echoed by all hands, from Lemon downwards.

"Now, let us see if we can catch him before he reaches home."

Vain was the notion. The active hares kept well ahead of them, and when they reached the school, not a little tired, and as hungry as hounds should be, were found, seated at table, in clean dry garments, and enjoying a hearty supper. The two hares were speedily joined by huntsman, whipper-in, and hounds; and the Doctor and two or three of the bigger boys came in to superintend the feast, and to hear them "fight their battles o'er again." The hares said very little of their exploits; but it is surprising what wonderful accounts some of the hounds gave of what they had done, what hair-breadth escapes they had had, what hills they had climbed, what streams and ditches they had leaped.

Chapter Four
Ernest's New Friend

After the Easter holidays, several new boys came. One of them was called Edward Ellis. He had a remarkably quiet and subdued manner. The general remark was, that he looked as if he was cowed. He was certainly out of spirits. He spoke very little, avoided making friends, or, at all events, confidants, and seldom entered into any of our games. He seemed prepared to suffer any amount of bullying, even from little fellows, and if he was struck, he never struck again. He had been at school before, but he never said where. Probably, however, he had been there for some time, for he was already fourteen, though not big or strong for his age. With such a disposition and habits as I have described, of course he could not be a favourite with any one; at the same time, it could not be said that he was positively disliked. Ernest, seeing how solitary and melancholy he appeared, compassionated the poor fellow, and never lost an opportunity of speaking kindly to him. This conduct had its due effect, and Ellis took pains to show his gratitude.

Ernest had no little difficulty in defending his new friend, both from attacks made with the fists and those levelled with that still sharper weapon, the tongue. Ellis was much exposed to the latter, especially on account of his ungainly appearance and uncouth manners. Of course Blackall took especial delight in bullying him, as there was no fear of a retort, by word, look, or deed. This conduct especially excited Ernest's indignation, and he resolved to defend Ellis, at every personal risk, from the attacks of the bully.

"Oh, I have always been an unfortunate, unhappy fellow!" exclaimed poor Ellis one day, in the bitterness of his spirit, after he had been more than usually bullied. "Unfortunate I have been, and unfortunate I expect to be to the end of my days!"

"Oh, nonsense!" answered Ernest. "It is positively wrong to give way to such feelings. Just rouse yourself, and come and play like other fellows, and practise your limbs, and run and leap, and you'll soon get on as well as anybody else. Put yourself under the drill-sergeant and gymnastic master, and learn to dance, and you'll do as well as anybody."

"Me dance!" cried Ellis, with a doleful expression. "Tell me, Bracebridge, did you ever see a bear attempt to practise the Terpsichorean art. I should be very like the monster if I were to try it. But it is not that—there is something I cannot tell you about which makes me so unhappy, that I never expect to get over it. Nobody here knows anything about it, but some day they may, and then I shall be worse off than I am now."

"Well, I don't want you to tell me," replied Ernest, for he had an innate dislike to petty confidences. "But, I repeat, come and join us in our games. Just practise cricket, for instance, every day for a month or so, with single wickets, and you'll be able to join in our matches, and play as well as any one, I dare say."

"Oh, no! I've no hopes of myself. I'm sure I shall never play cricket," said Ellis, shaking his head.

"We'll see about that," observed Ernest, laughing at his friend's lugubrious expression of countenance. "But I'll tell you what you can do; you can play a game of rounders. It is not often that I play now, but I will get up a game for your sake."

Ellis was easily persuaded to accept Ernest's offer. They went out into the playground, and the latter was not long in finding plenty of players ready to join the game. Everybody was very much surprised when they saw Ernest select Ellis on his side.

"Why, Bracebridge, you'll never do with that fellow; he'll be out directly," cried several boys.

"Never mind; he'll play better than you suppose in a little time," was the answer. "Everybody must make a beginning."

Five of a side were chosen, and the ground was marked out. Five sticks were run into the earth, about sixteen yards apart, the lines between them forming the sides of a pentagon, with one stick in the centre. The centre was the place for the feeder.

"'Capital!' cried Ernest, clapping his hands at the success of his pupil. 'Run! run!—two bases at least.'"

"Those are what we call bases," said Ernest to Ellis, pointing out the spots where the sticks were placed. Then he drew a circle round one of them, which he pointed out as the "home."

Buttar, Bouldon, Dawson, and other fellows of the same age, were playing. Bouldon was on one side, Ernest on the other. The latter selected Buttar, and the former Dawson. They tossed up who was to go in first; Ernest won. He went in first; Tom had to feed him. Dawson kept a sharp look-out behind him, as did the other three players in different parts of the field. There is more science in the game than many people are aware of, though not, of course, to be compared to cricket, any more than the short bat which is used is to a cricket-bat.

"Now, Bouldon, give me a fair ball, you sly fox," cried Ernest, for Tom was notorious for his tricks and dodges of every sort. If a good hoax was played on the school, or on any individual, its authorship was generally traced to him. To do him credit, they were never ill-natured. He generally, when found out, bore his blushing honours meekly, and if not discovered, contented himself by laughing quietly in his sleeve.

"All fair and above board," cried Tom, bowling. "Look out!"

Ernest hit the ball a fine blow, and sent it flying away over the heads of all the out-players. Away he ran from base to base. He had already reached the third from the home—two distances more only had to be run—when Reynolds, a boy who could heave as far as any one in the school, got hold of the ball. One more run he thought he could attempt, for Reynolds could scarcely hit him at that distance. Reynolds, seizing the ball, rushed on with it. Ernest reached the fourth base. He wished to make Reynolds heave it; he pretended to spring forward; Reynolds threw the ball; Ernest watched its course, and as it bounded by him, he changed his feint into a reality, and reached the home. The next time he hit the ball still harder, and ran the whole round of the bases.

"Now, Ellis, you may have to go in before long," he sang out. "Don't attempt a rounder, though. Get to the first or second base easily; that will do. Come, feed away, Tommy."

Bouldon fed him, and though he sent the ball to a good distance, he only reached the fourth base. When he got there, he called out to Ellis to go in. Ellis seized the bat with a convulsive clutch, as if he was about to fight a battle with it, or was going to perform some wonderful undertaking. Even Ernest could scarcely help laughing at the curious contortions of countenance in which he indulged. However, remembering Ernest's advice, he kept his eye on the ball, and hit it so fairly, and with such good force, that he sent it flying away to a considerable distance.

"Capital!" cried Ernest, clapping his hands at the success of his pupil. "Run! run!—two bases at least."

Ellis did the distance with ease, and Ernest sprang into the home.

"Now look out, old fellow, to run right in, or, at all events, to the fourth base," he sang out to Ellis, whose spirits rose at his success; and he looked as eager as any one, and ready for anything. Tom tossed the ball to Ernest in a way somewhat difficult to hit, and when he struck it, he was nearly caught out. He, however, ran over a couple of bases, and Ellis stopped short at the fourth. This brought in a new player at the home. He sent the ball but a short way, and Ellis was very nearly struck out. The ball grazed him, but he was well in the home. Had he been struck out, he very likely would never have played well again. Tom now fed him. He hit the ball, and with all his might, and sent it as far as Ernest or Bouldon had ever done.

"Capital! well done, Ellis!" shouted many of the fellows, both players and lookers-on; and away he ran, and performed a whole circle.

Ernest determined to play his best, so as to keep Ellis in as long as possible. He was sure, from what he saw, that his success would give him encouragement, not only to play other games, but to mix more sociably with his schoolfellows. Ernest played capitally, but Ellis scored almost as many, to the surprise of those who fancied that he could not play at all. Few would have believed that he was the same awkward, shy boy, who was usually creeping about the play-ground, as they saw him, with a high colour and full of animation, hitting ball after ball with all his might, and cutting away round the bases. At last, one of their side was caught out, and Buttar went in. He was a good player, and added considerably to the numbers scored by his side. Still, as both Dawson and Bouldon were capital players, and so were most of their side, Ernest did his utmost to get as many runs as possible, at the same time that he wanted to make Ellis feel that he had himself contributed largely to the victory. Every time Ellis made a good hit, he praised him loudly, and certainly felt more pleasure than if he had done well himself. Poor Ellis had never been so happy since he was a child. He began to feel that, after all, he need not fancy himself less capable than his companions to enter into the usual sports of the school. At last, Buttar was struck out, and so was another player, and Ernest and Ellis alone were kept in. The latter could scarcely believe his senses, when he found himself the only person to help Ernest to keep up the game. Ernest was in the home; Ellis was on the base at the opposite side. He knew that he must run hard, or he would put Ernest out as well as himself.

"Now, Tom, two fair hits for the rounder," exclaimed Ernest.

The proposal was agreed to. Bouldon kept tossing the ball several times, but Ernest refused to hit. At last he hit, but did not run, and Ellis very nearly got out by attempting to do so. The next time he hit, and hit hard indeed. Away flew the ball further than ever, to the very end of the field.

"Now, Ellis, run! run!" he sang out.

Ellis moved his legs faster than he had ever before done, and shouted and shrieked with delight when Ernest made the round in safety. Thus the game continued. Ellis appeared to have a charmed existence as far as the game was concerned. Nothing could put him out. More than once his balls seemed to slip through the very fingers of those about to catch them.

"I say, Bracebridge, are you going to be out or not, this evening?" exclaimed Tom, getting positively tired of feeding.

"Not if Ellis and I can help it," was the answer. "We've taken a fancy to have a long innings, do you see?"

So it seemed, in truth; and the tea-bell positively rang while they were still in. By the custom of our school, a game of that minor description was then considered over; and the two new friends went into the tea-room together in a very triumphant state of mind.

"I told you, Ellis, you could do whatever you tried, just as well as other fellows," said Ernest, as he sat by him at tea. "Now I must show you how to play cricket, and hockey, and football, and fives, and all sorts of games. To-morrow we'll have a little quiet practice at cricket with single wicket, and I'll wager by the summer that you'll be able to play in a match with any fellows of our size."

Ellis thanked Ernest most warmly. He felt a new spirit rising in him— powers he had never dreamed of possessing coming out. He might yet stand on equal terms with his companions at school and with his fellow-men in the world.

"As I told you before, old fellow, what you want is a course of drilling. Our old sergeant will set you up and make you look like a soldier in a very few months. Just go and talk to the Doctor about it. He'll be glad to find you wish to learn. You'll like old Sergeant Dibble amazingly. It's worth learning for the sake of hearing him tell his long stories about his campaigning days— what his regiment did in the Peninsular, and how they drove all Napoleon's generals out of Spain and Portugal."

Ernest grew quite enthusiastic when speaking about Sergeant Dibble, with whom he was a great favourite. He succeeded in inspiring Ellis with a strong desire to learn drilling.

"Who knows but what after all I may one day be considered fit to go into the army!" exclaimed Ellis, after listening to a somewhat long oration in praise of Sergeant Dibble.

"I wish you would go into it," said Ernest. "I believe that I am to be a soldier, but my father will never tell any of us what professions he intends us for. He tells us we must get as much knowledge as we can obtain, and that we must perfect ourselves in all physical exercises, and then that we shall be fit to be bishops, or generals, or lord chancellors, or admirals, or aldermen, or whatever may be our lot in life. Of course, he is right. My elder brother came out Senior Wrangler at Cambridge, and pulls one of the best oars and plays cricket as well as any man in the University. If I can do as well as he has done I shall be content. He is now going to study the law, and then to look after the family property. I have to make my own way in the world somehow or other."

"Well, so have I to make my own way," observed Ellis. "I don't fancy that I shall ever have any property coming to me, and I thought that I should never get on, but always have to stick at the bottom of the tree; but do you know, that from what you have said to me, I begin to hope that I may be able to climb like others, if not to the top, at least to a comfortable seat among the branches?"

"Bravo! capital! that you will!" cried Ernest, who was delighted to find the effect his lessons were producing. He was not himself aware of the benefits he was reaping from having some one to watch over and assist. Ernest was undoubtedly very clever, but he was very far from perfect. He could not help feeling that he was superior to most—indeed, to all the boys of his own age at school. This did not make him vain or conceited in any objectionable way, but he was somewhat egotistical. He thought a good deal about himself—what people would say of him, what they would think of him. He was perhaps rather ambitious of shining simply for the sake of shining—a very insufficient reason, all must agree, if they will but consider how very very pale a light the brightest genius can shed forth when his knowledge comes to be measured with that which is required to comprehend a tenth part of the glories which the universe contains.

The half drew on. Blackall did not relax in his tyranny over the younger boys, though more than once it brought him into trouble. At last the Doctor heard of his bullying, and he was confined within bounds for a month, and had no end of impositions to get up. He promised amendment; but the punishment did not cure him, and in a short time he was as bad as ever. He began, as usual, upon those less likely to complain, and Ellis was one of his first victims. He seemed to take a peculiar delight in making the poor fellow's existence miserable, and every day he found some fresh means of torture. Ernest saw this going on day after day, and at last felt that he could stand it no longer. "I must get Ellis to stick up to him, or I must do so alone," he exclaimed to himself.

Although Ellis fancied that he could not play at games, he was very ingenious, and could make all sorts of things—little carriages of cardboard, with woodwork, and traces and harness complete, which he painted and varnished; and boats and vessels, which he cut out of soft American pine, and scooped out and put decks into them, and cut out their sails, and rigged them with neat blocks. Sometimes the blocks had sheaves in them, and the sails were made to hoist up and down, and his yachts sailed remarkably well and could beat any of those opposed to them. Then he made little theatres capitally, and painted the scenes and cut out the characters, and stuck tinsel on to them; and if not as good as a real play, they afforded a vast amount of amusement. These talents, however, were not discovered for some time.

We did not disdain to fly kites at our school, but they were very large, handsome kites, and we used to vie with each other in trying which could get the largest and strongest and most finely ornamented, and make them fly the highest.

Our French master, Monsieur Malin, was a great hand at kite-flying. He did not like cricket, or football, or hockey, or any game in which he might get hurt, because, as he used to say, "Vat you call my sins are not manufactured of iron. You *petits garçons* don't mind all sorts of knocks about, but for one poor old man like me it is not good." Had he been an Englishman, we might have despised him for not playing cricket or football, but we thought it was only natural in a Frenchman. As he played rounders, and prisoners' base, and hoops, and every game of skill, in capital style, and was very good-natured and ready to do anything anybody asked him, which he had it in his power to do, he was deservedly a very general favourite. It was great fun to hear him sing out, "Chivie! chivie! chivie!" when playing at prisoners base, and to see his legs with short steps moving along twice as fast as anybody else.

The weather was getting rather too hot for most of our running games which we played in the spring and autumn—with the exception, of course, of cricket, the most delightful of all summer amusements—when Monsieur Malin proposed a grand kite-flying match. Two different objects were to be tried for. There were two equal first prizes. One was to be won by the kite which rose the highest, or rather, took out the longest line; the other prize was to be given to the owner of the kite which could pull the heaviest weights the fastest. Two other prizes were to be bestowed, one on the handsomest kite, and the other to the most grotesque, provided they were not inferior in other qualities.

For two or three weeks before, preparations were being made for the match, and every day parties were seen going out to the neighbouring heath to try the qualities of the kites they had manufactured. Clubs were formed which had one or two kites between them, for the expense of the string alone was considerable. It was necessary to have the lightest and strongest line to be procured, which would also run easily off the reel.

Monsieur Malin was working away at his kite in his room, and he said that he would allow no one to see it till it was completed. Many of the bigger fellows condescended to take an interest in the matter, as did Lemon and Ernest and others, and even Blackall gave out that he intended to try the fortune of his kite. He stated that he should not bother himself by making one, but that he had written to London to have the largest and best ever made sent down to him. Many of the fellows, when they heard this, said that they thought there would be very little use in trying to compete with him. Dawson especially remarked that he should give up. "Blackall has everything of the best, you know, always in tip-top style," he remarked; "and you see, if he gets a regular-made kite from a first-rate London maker, what chance can any of us possibly have?" Blackall himself seemed to be of the same opinion, and boasted considerably of the wonders his kite was going to perform. Monsieur Malin smiled when he heard him boasting; Ernest said nothing, but looked as if he thought that he might be mistaken; while Buttar laughed and observed that Bully Blackall seemed to think that a large amount of credit was to be gained by buying a good kite. He might congratulate himself still more if he could buy at as cheap a rate a good temper and a good disposition.

Ernest, meantime, going on the principle he had adopted of doing his utmost to encourage Ellis, proposed to join him in the share of a kite. Ellis said that he should be very glad, and that he would undertake to make it himself.

"What! can you make kites?" exclaimed Ernest. "I never dreamed of that."

"Oh, I have made all sorts of kites, and know how to fly them well," answered Ellis. "I have the materials for one in my box now. I did not like to produce them, because the other boys would only laugh at me for proposing to fly a kite. I have ample line, though we may add another ball or two. All I want are two thin but strong laths, nine and eight feet long."

"What! are you going to make the kite nine feet high!" exclaimed Ernest. "That will be big, indeed."

"Yes; nine feet high, and eight from wing to wing," said Ellis.

"Why, what a whacking big fellow it will be!" exclaimed Ernest. "And I say, what a lot of paper it will take to make it!"

"Not a particle," answered Ellis. "It is all made of silk, which is lighter and stronger than any other material. Come with me to the carpenter's and get the laths, and we'll have it made by the evening, so as to fly it, if there is a breeze, to-morrow."

"I'll go with pleasure to the carpenter's; but if you are pretty certain that your kite will do well, do not let us fly it till the day of trial. It will astonish every one so much to see you come out with a great big kite, which, I doubt not, will beat all the others."

"Oh, no! I'm afraid that it won't do that. It will scarcely be equal to Monsieur Malin's, and probably Blackall will get something very grand down from London," answered Ellis, always diffident about anything connected with himself.

"We'll see," said Ernest quietly. "And now, as we have so grand a kite, let us go and see old Hobson about the carriage which we must make it drag. Any shape and any plan is allowable, remember, provided it can carry two. Now I have a design in my head which I think will answer capitally. You see old gentlemen and ladies steering themselves, with a person pushing behind, in an arm-chair. I propose having a sort of skeleton of a chair, with two big wheels and one small one in front, with a very long front part,—one seat behind for the person who manages the kite, and one in front for the steerer. There must be a bar in front with a block to it, through which the line must pass, and then I would have a light pole with a hook at one end, while the butt-end should be secured to the centre of the carriage. Suppose you were to sit in front and steer; I would sit behind and have a reel to haul in or let out the line, and with the pole and hook I could bring the kite on one side of the carriage or the other, as might be required to assist you to guide it. It is my opinion that we can make the carriage go on a wind, as yachtsmen say. That is to say, if the wind is from the north or south, we may make the carriage go east or west. Now, if other fellows have not thought of that, and the wind should change a few points, we may be able to go on in our proper course while they may be obliged to stop, and so we shall win the prize."

"Capital!" repeated Ellis, clapping his hands and hugging himself in his delight in a peculiarly grotesque way which always made his friend smile, though he determined some day quietly to tell him of the habit, and to advise him to get over it. "Capital!" repeated Ellis. "I've heard of something of the sort in Canada, where, on the lakes and rivers, what are called ice-boats are used. They are, however, placed on great skates or iron runners, and have sails just like any other boats, only the sails are stretched quite flat, like boards. They have a long pole out astern with an iron at the end of it, which cuts into the ice and serves as a rudder. They sail very fast, and go, I understand, close on a wind."

"What fun to sail in them!" cried Ernest. "I've often thought I should like to go to Canada, and that would be another reason. But, I say, Ellis, I fancy from the way you talk you know something about yachting. I'm very fond of it; you and I will have some sailing together one of these days."

Ellis said that he had frequently yachted with some of his relations, and that he should be delighted to take a cruise with Ernest when they could afford to have a boat. They talked away till they got to the shop of old Hobson the carpenter. He was a clever workman, with a natural mechanical turn, so he comprehended the sort of carriage they wanted, and willingly undertook to make it.

Chapter Five
Our Kite-Race

Towards the end of April, the rising sun ushered in a fine breezy morning, with every promise of a strong wind during the day. It was a half-holiday; but on grand occasions of the sort—for it was the day fixed for the kite-race—the boys were allowed to get up and begin lessons an hour earlier than usual. The Doctor always encouraged early rising, and he was, besides, anxious to show us that he took an interest in our amusements, by making such regulations as might facilitate them.

Ernest and Ellis had constantly been to old Hobson's to see how their carriage was getting on. "Never you mind, young gen'men, it's all right," was his answer for some days. "I won't disappoint you; but you see several has come here who wants such fine painted affairs, that I must get on with them. There's Mr Blackall, now, who has been and ordered a carriage which I tells him will take six horses to drag; but he says that he has got a kite coming which will pull one along ten miles an hour, twice as big as this, so of course I've nothing more to say."

A large flat case arrived in the morning of the race day for Blackall, just as we were going in to lessons after breakfast; so he had no time to open it. It was not as large as he expected, but still he was very confident that all was right.

Lessons over, we went in to dinner—and that meal got through, with more speed than usual, we all assembled to see the kites and the carriages which had been prepared.

The carpenters were in attendance with the vehicles they had got ready according to orders received. They were of all shapes and plans. Several, among whom was Blackall's, were very finely painted, but the greater number were mere boxes on wheels, put together at very little expense—which few boys were able to afford, even when clubbing together.

First appeared Monsieur Malin's kite; it represented a wonderful Green Dragon, twisting and turning about in the most extraordinary way—the tail of the kite being merely the small end of the tail of the dragon. It had great big red eyes, glowing with tinsel, and wings glittering all over, and a tongue which looked capable of doing a large amount of mischief. Loud shouts of applause welcomed the green dragon, as Monsieur Malin held it up like a shield before him, and moved about the playground, hissing, and howling, and making all sorts of dreadful noises.

Tommy Bouldon had joined a club, which produced a magnificent Owl, with a large head, and huge goggling eyes; and never did owl hiss more loudly than did their owl as it met Monsieur Malin's terrific dragon. They at last rushed at each other with such fury, that Tommy's head very nearly went through the owl's body, which would effectually have prevented it from flying at the match.

Lemon and Buttar had fraternised, and in front of them marched a Military Officer, magnificent in a red coat, vast gold epaulets, and no end of gold braiding and trimming, which glittered finely in the sun, while his richly ornamented cocked hat, set across his head, had on the top of it a waving plume of feathers, and a drawn sword in his hand shone in the sunbeams. He looked very fiercely at the dragon and the owl, as he did at everybody, for his eyes were large, and round, and dark.

The Dragon roared, and the Owl hissed at him, when he growled out, "I'll eat you," which produced loud shouts of laughter from both of them, while they quietly replied, "You can't."

After the General had shown himself, Ellis walked in, bearing a long thin pole, wrapped round, it appeared, by a flag. Ernest accompanied him, carrying a reel of fine but very strong twine. Some boys stared, and others laughed derisively, and asked if he thought that thing was going to fly. "You'll see—you'll see," he answered very quietly.

"Fly!—Dat it will—higher dan any of ours, I tell you, boys," observed Monsieur Malin, who had eyed it attentively.

Ernest and Ellis marched across the playground, into the field beyond, out of sight, and in less than two minutes returned, bearing aloft a magnificent Knight in silver armour, with a glittering shield on his arm, a plume on his helmet, and a spear in his hand. His visor was up, and his countenance, with a fine black beard and moustache, looked forth fiercely beneath it, while a band of roses, which was thrown over his shoulder, hung down and formed a very magnificent tail, glittering with jewels. No sooner did the gallant knight make his appearance than the derisive laughter and sneers were changed into shouts of applause. All were agreed that never had a more beautiful kite appeared.

"All very well," cried Dawson, who was expecting Blackall's kite to come forth, "but it is a question with me whether such a gimcrack-looking affair will fly."

Blackall had meantime been busily employed in unpacking his kite, which was to create so much astonishment, and do such mighty things. He undid the strings and brown paper, and laths, which surrounded it, with eager haste. A number of boys were looking on, all curious to see what was to be produced. Dawson was among the most sanguine, expecting that something very fine was to appear. At last Blackall was seen to scratch his head, and to look somewhat annoyed.

"Come, come, Blackall," exclaimed Sandford, one of the biggest fellows, and certainly no friend of his; "let us see this precious kite of yours. Out with it, man."

"Mind your own business, Sandford," answered the bully, sulkily. "I'll show the kite when I feel inclined."

"Ho, ho, ho!" replied Sandford, laughing; and knowing perfectly well that Blackall dared not retaliate, stooping down, he lifted the kite, and held it up to the view of the whole school. There was a picture of a big ugly boy daubed in the commonest ochre, and bearing evident marks of its toy-shop origin, though Tommy Bouldon and others declared that they recognised in it a strong likeness to Blackall himself. Blackall seemed to think that some trick had been played him, though it was very clear that the likeness was accidental.

"It's pretty plain who's got the ugliest and most stupid looking kite," said Buttar, as he passed by. "Very like himself. I wonder if it will fly."

"Yes, if it can find a small kite up in the sky to thrash," observed Bouldon. "But, I say, let us give three cheers for Blackall's toy-shop kite. I wonder if he will take it as a compliment."

A boisterous, if not a hearty, cheer was quickly raised, which barely served to cover a chorus of hisses and groans uttered by a number of little fellows, who had been in the habit of receiving gratuitous kicks and cuffs from their amicable companion.

There were several ordinary kites, remarkable chiefly for their size, being made of newspapers; but there were others contributing an ingenious variety of devices—bats, and frogs, and fish of curious shapes. The flying-fish especially looked very natural as they glittered in the sunbeams, only people could not help inquiring how they came to be up so high in the air.

At last all were ready to set forth; some pushed the carriages, and others carried the kites. Ernest and Ellis rolled up theirs, and carried it along very easily. The Doctor led the way, accompanied by two or three of the biggest fellows; but he would every now and then stop, and call up some of the smaller ones to have a talk with them.

The ground chosen for the trial of the kites was a high, downy table-land, with a fine flat surface. It was a very pretty sight to see all the boys, with their carriages and gaily-coloured kites, assembled together. There were nearly fifty kites, for many brought small kites, with which they had no intention to contend for a prize. All the masters, and several friends of the Doctor's and some of the boys, attended to act as umpires. At last everything was arranged.

The kite-flyers formed one long line, with the wind in their backs. The first point to be decided was the beauty of the kites. Lemon had his horn, which was to be used as a signal. He blew three shrill blasts. At the sound of the third, up they all flew, some starting rapidly upwards; others wavering about before ascending; a few refusing to mount altogether beyond a few yards off the ground. However, the greater number mounted rapidly, their brilliant colours flashing in the sunbeams. The spectators clapped their hands loudly, as a mark of their approbation, and then set to work to make notes, that they might decide when called on to declare on whom the prizes ought to be bestowed.

Monsieur Malin's Green Dragon came in for a large share of praise, so did the General Officer; but Ellis's Knight of the Silver Shield was decided to be the most elegant and beautiful of all the kites, and the owner was called forth to receive his meed of applause.

Many were surprised when they saw Ellis, with his awkward gait, shuffling out from among the crowd; and, more especially, when he announced himself, in a hesitating tone, not only as the maker, but as the designer of the Knight of the Silver Shield.

One kite went up some way, just sufficient to exhibit its ugliness, but wavered and rolled about in the most extraordinary manner, evidently showing that it was lop-sided. It received shouts, but they were not of applause, and they were accompanied by hisses, which the Doctor, however, repressed. The kite received in this unflattering way was Blackall's boasted toy-shop production. He was highly indignant, and walked about stamping with rage.

Buttar and Bouldon were much amused, and expressed a hope that he would expend his fury on his kite, and cut it to pieces. He drew out his knife, evidently with that intention, but he had not the heart to attack it.

"I'll tell you what it is, Bobby," said he to Dawson, who was standing by not a little disgusted, "it pulls terrifically hard, and in my opinion, if it is altered a little, and has a heavier wing put on the right side, it will yet do magnificently, and make all those howling monkeys change their tone. That dolt Ellis, and that conceited chap Bracebridge, will soon find that their finely-bedizened machine is cut out. My carriage is, I know, such a first-rate one, that it will go along with anything."

Dawson was in great hopes that Blackall was right, for he had staked his reputation, as he said, on the success of his patron and his imported kite, and he had no fancy to find himself laughed at. In what Master Bobby Dawson's reputation consisted he did not stop to inquire, and certainly anybody else would have been very puzzled to say.

The rest of the kite-flyers troubled themselves very little about Blackall and his ill success. They were all intent on making their own kites perform their best. After the kites had flown for some time, the Doctor advanced from the group of spectators and umpires, and summoned Ellis and Monsieur Malin, and, with an appropriate address, bestowed on them the two first prizes, complimenting them on their design, and the beauty of the execution.

And now the time arrived to try which kites could fly the highest. All were hauled in, and the boys stood as before in a row. The signal was given by Lemon, and up they went, soaring far away into the blue sky. This time Ernest had a kite as well as Ellis. It was a good large kite, with remarkably strong string. The device was that of a man-at-arms, with a gleaming battle-axe over his shoulder, or, as Ernest called it, the Squire.

"Why, Bracebridge! what do you expect that kite to do, eh?" exclaimed Lemon. "It is too heavy-looking to fly, and not large enough to drag a carriage."

"I hope that at all events he will do his duty, and prove a faithful Squire," answered Bracebridge.

"I wonder what he means?" said several boys who overheard him.

Away soared the kites; some of them appeared as if they would never come down again. The Green Dragon rose very high, and must have astonished the birds and beasts of the field, if it did not the human beings in the valley below. The Silver Knight also played his part well up in the skies, so did the General, and many others. Up, up went the Green Dragon, and high soared the Silver Knight; Excelsior was his motto; but high as he went, the Green Dragon went higher.

"Hilloa, Bracebridge, you and your friend should have chosen a different motto for your knight, for the Green Dragon is beating him, and the old Owl is not far behind," exclaimed Lemon, who, while manoeuvring his kite, found himself not far from Ernest.

"Stay a bit," answered Ernest, in a good-natured tone; "perhaps our knight may yet prove that his motto was not ill-chosen. We have not yet got to the end of our line."

Monsieur Malin kept easing out his line, and his monster went slowly upward, but it was evident that the weight of string it had already to bear was almost too much for it, and that it would not carry much more. It was a brave dragon, however, and in the French master's skilful hands, it is extraordinary how high it got up. At last it was evident that it was stationary, and required a great deal of manoeuvring to be kept at the height it had attained.

"Now, Bracebridge," cried Ellis, who had worked the Silver Knight up almost as high, "let me have your line."

"All right," answered Bracebridge, hauling down his kite till it was within thirty feet of the ground. "Hook on."

On this Ellis brought the end of his line up to Bracebridge, who fastened it to the string of the Squire, which immediately shot upward, while higher and higher flew the Silver Knight. He reached the Green Dragon, and floated proudly past him. Up he went, higher and higher, till a glittering spot could alone be seen in the blue heavens. Shouts of applause broke from the spectators.

"Now," cried Bracebridge triumphantly, "has not our knight chosen his motto with judgment, Excelsior? See, up he goes higher and higher."

Higher he did go, indeed; and in a short time the glittering spot was lost to view.

"We could easily get our Squire out of sight also, if we could find a line light enough and strong enough to bear the strain of the two kites together, but no string we have got here could bear the strain that would be put upon it," observed Ernest to those who came round to observe the wonder which had been wrought.

Some declared that it was not fair, and that they had no right to fasten the string of one kite to that of another.

"Oh! that's all nonsense, and you fellows know it well," answered Ernest. "The question to be decided is, which kite can reach the farthest from the earth, and ours has done so. Unless another gets higher, we shall win the prize."

No other kite got even so high as the Green Dragon, so the Silver Knight was most justly declared to be the winner of the prize.

"Froggy Malin's and those fellows' kites may fly high, but they will not be able to pull anything along," growled out Blackall. "Before they think that they are going to carry off all the prizes, let us see what my kite can do. He looks like a strong, tough fellow, who can pull hard at all events."

Dawson and a few of Blackall's admirers echoed these sentiments, fully believing that he did not boast without reason of what he would do.

The carriages were now brought forward from a chalk-pit, where they had been concealed, and formed a line in front of the spectators. Blackall's was certainly the largest, and not the least gay and gaudy, but more than one person smiled at the notion of its being dragged along by a single kite. None of the carriages could boast of much beauty, but some were very finely painted, and were admired accordingly. When Ernest brought out his vehicle, it was much laughed at, for it had such an odd, spider-like, skeleton look. Still the knowing ones acknowledged that it might have a great deal of go in it.

Most of the line of the kites was now hauled in and wound up. Ernest and Ellis got down the Silver Knight, and fastened some light lines to each of his wings, and brought them down to the carriage. Two or three boys stood round each carriage holding it. At a signal, given by Lemon on his horn, to prepare, they all jumped in. At another, all hands were taken off the carriages, and away most of them went at a fair speed. One did not move— it was Blackall's. Who could picture his wrath and indignation? He pulled and pulled at the line; the kite rose somewhat, but wavered about terribly: now it darted to one side, now to the other.

"Come along, Blackall, come along," shouted several of the racers, as they moved on, and left him trying all sorts of useless experiments to make the kite pull and the carriage move. Neither one nor the other could he accomplish. Shouts of laughter reached his ear, and he was conscious that they were caused by his ill success. This only increased his rage and bitterness. He stamped in his anger and impatience till he knocked his feet through the boards which formed the bottom of his carriage. He lost all command over himself. He hallooed; he shouted at his kite; and then he swore great, horrible oaths at the kite, and the carriage, and at the wind, till the voice of the Doctor sounded in his ear, ordering him sternly to get out of the carriage and drag it out of the way. He sulkily obeyed, and wound up the string of his kite, and betook himself to the background, trembling lest the Doctor should have overheard his expressions.

"I say, Dawson,—I say, Smith,—do you think the old one heard what I said?" he asked, as he was going off, and they stood, not liking to desert him altogether, and yet wishing to go on and see the fun.

"I believe you he did, my boy," answered Smith, who had but little of the milk of human kindness in his composition. "You spoke loud enough to be heard half-a-mile off."

"But I say, Bobby, do you think so? Did he hear me? By Jove, I shall get a pretty jobation if he did!" exclaimed the bully, appealing in a whining tone to Dawson.

The wretched, cowardly lad forgot that there was another—a great Omniscient Being—who, at all events, heard him; and that every evil word he had uttered had assuredly been registered in a book whence it would never be erased till the Day of Judgment, when it would be made known to thousands and tens of thousands of astonished and mourning listeners. But such an idea never crossed Blackall's mind. Had it, perhaps it might have prevented him from uttering the expressions of which he so frequently made use.

Fearful only of the immediate disagreeable consequences should the Doctor have heard him, he retired by himself from the ground; while Dawson, and the few other boys who had hitherto adhered to him, set off in pursuit of the racers.

With shouts of laughter the racers went on. At first the Green Dragon took the lead, followed closely by the Owl, for both the carriages were very light, and the kites were skilfully managed. Each of them had a second kite attached; for, unless there had been a very strong wind, one would scarcely have dragged them on. Monsieur Malin had selected two boys to manage his carriage, and he ran by their side to direct them; for his own weight would have been too great for it. The Knight and Squire followed closely on the first two carriages. They were flying, on starting, somewhat too high; but Ernest hauled in the lines, and the effect was soon perceptible. On went their daddy-long-legs, as he and Ellis called their car, and soon got up to the Owl.

"To-hoo, to-hoo, to-hoo!" cried the directors of the Owl, but the Knight and his Squire pulled away, and the Owl was left astern, and very soon the Green Dragon was overtaken. They, of course, were assailed with the most horrible hisses, and roars, and strange noises of all sorts; but these did not daunt the Knight and his Squire, who went bravely on.

"Excelsior! excelsior! Hurra! hurra!" shouted Ernest and Ellis, as their car took the lead. Gradually, but surely, it increased its distance from the rest. Monsieur Malin did his best to manoeuvre his kites; so did Lemon and the rest; but they could not manage to overtake the Knight and his Squire, though they hissed, and roared, and shouted with merry peals of laughter between the intervals, calling them to stop, and not go ahead so fast.

"Old Hobson did not deceive us," observed Ellis; "really this carriage goes along capitally."

"He has done us justice, certainly," answered Ernest. "But remember, Ellis, our success is entirely owing to your talent and judgment. You think too little of yourself. Now, hurrah! we shall soon be at the winning-post if the wind holds."

Never were there more merry or noisy racers; except, perhaps, in a donkey race, when the winner is the donkey which comes in last.

"Very easy to win that sort of race," some one will say.

Not at all, though.

In ordinary races, each jockey wishes the horse he rides to win; but, in donkey races,—which I hold to be superior to all others, whether at Goodwood, or Ascot, or Epsom,—each jockey rides his opponent's donkey, so each is anxious to get in before the other, and, if possible, to leave his own behind.

The wind blew fair; the kites drew capitally; the Green Dragon was, after all, not very far behind the Knight and Squire; and the Owl came too-hooing, close upon the Dragon's tail; while the General Officer seemed in a great hurry to catch the Owl, and kept singing out "Halt! halt! right-about-face," and other expressions evidently from a somewhat scanty vocabulary of military terms. The rest of the racers came up pretty thickly one after the other.

As they reached the winning-post, where one of the masters stood ready to mark the time of their arrival, there was a general shout for Blackall and his fat boy.

"Oh, he was last seen in the chalk-pit, hacking him to pieces with his knife, while he seemed inclined to treat his wonderful carriage much in the same way." A boy who had just come up gave this news.

A few expressions of commiseration were uttered by Dawson and others; but in their hearts no one really pitied the bully. How could they? What had he ever done to win the affection, or regard, or esteem of any one of his school-fellows? Certainly, to those with whom he associated and whom he patronised, he had ever done far more harm than good; and of this most of them were aware at the time, though they might not be willing to acknowledge it to themselves; and bitterly were they conscious of it before many years were past, when they reaped the fruits of his pernicious example. Several sunk into early and dishonoured graves: others lived, ruined in health and constitution, to bemoan the fate which their folly and vice had brought on them. But to return to our merry racers.

They were called up forthwith to receive their prizes. The most valuable were some serviceable fishing-rods, reels, lines, fishing-baskets, a couple of bows, and the various accoutrements required in archery, a good bat or two, and similar things valued by boys.

The Doctor made a very neat speech, and complimented them all on the skill and talent displayed both in kites and carriages.

"Especially I must compliment you, Bracebridge, on the beauty of your kites, and the skill with which you have managed them."

"Not me, sir, but Ellis deserves the praise," answered Ernest in a clear, loud voice, so that every one might hear. "He is a very clever fellow, sir, only he does not know it. He thought of the carriages and the kites, and, indeed, of every thing; I merely helped him. I joined him because I knew that by himself he would be too diffident to carry out his own plans. I was his assistant, that was all."

"I am glad to hear you thus speak of Ellis, but you equally deserve the prize, although you only aided him in carrying out his plans. I have, therefore, to present you with this bow, and all the equipments complete; and you, Ellis, with this fishing-rod, and all the accompanying gear."

Ernest, who was perfectly free from timidity, and always expressed himself well, made a very appropriate reply; and, at poor Ellis's earnest request, spoke for him also, and said a great deal more in his favour than he would have done himself.

Monsieur Malin seemed as much pleased at getting a prize as were any of the boys. A capital fishing-rod was presented to him; and he invited all who had rods to accompany him some day on a grand fishing expedition. Altogether, the kite-flying was most successful; and a stout old gentleman, one of the umpires, expressed a hope that next year they might all enjoy a similar treat; and that he was not at all certain that he should not try to get half-a-dozen kites and a carriage, with which he might join in the race. Several merry voices shouted "We hope you will, sir,—we hope you will." And that made him so enthusiastic that he promised, if he possibly could, to do as he had proposed.

They all went back to a capital, grand half-holiday tea, which was very different to the ordinary meal of bread-and-butter; and consisted of cakes, and sandwiches, and meat-pies, and sausages, and all sorts of substantial productions likely to satisfy the appetites of hungry boys.

The only person who did not enjoy the day was Blackall. He came back expecting every instant to be called up by the Doctor; but bed-time came, and he was not summoned. As he was on his way to his room he met Ellis, who was about to pass him without looking at him, or in any way taking notice of him.

"What do you mean by grinning at me, you young scamp?" exclaimed Blackall suddenly.

"I did not intentionally alter a muscle of my countenance," answered Ellis quietly. "Did you, however, address me?"

"If that's intended for impudence, take that," cried Blackall, dealing a heavy blow with his fist on Ellis's head. "I allow no young jackanapes like you to treat me with contempt."

"But if we feel contempt, how do you expect to be treated?" exclaimed a brisk, confident voice close at his elbow.

Blackall turned round to see who had dared thus to beard him. He saw Bracebridge standing close to him, in an attitude which showed that he was prepared for an attack.

"You want to get it, do you?" exclaimed Blackall, furiously, at finding his authority disputed by a boy of Ernest's size. "You shall have more than you expect."

"Now, run off, Ellis; run off," cried Ernest; "I'll tackle this fellow."

Ellis did not run, though Blackall let him go and advanced towards Ernest; but Ernest's undaunted bearing completely staggered him. He stood irresolute; while his opponent fixed his eye boldly on him. He feared some trick. He thought that some big fellow must be behind, ready to back up Bracebridge; or that he knew the Doctor was coming. He judged of other people by what he knew himself to be. He had no conception of the existence of the spirit which animated Ernest.

"Well, what are you going to do?" said Ernest, as he stood with clenched fist before him. "If you are going to strike me, do it at once, and get it over. I have no wish to stay here all night, waiting to be attacked by you."

While Ernest was speaking, Blackall was considering what he would do. At last, seeing no one coming, he plucked up courage, and made a dash at Ernest, who, springing aside, adroitly, warded off the blow.

Poor Ellis, meantime, stood by, trembling with agitation. He knew from sad experience that the bully hit very hard; and every blow he saw aimed at his friend he felt as if it had hurt him ten times as much as if it had been struck at himself.

They were in one of the many passages leading to the bedrooms, through which neither the masters nor servants often passed, so that Blackall knew that he was pretty secure from interruption. Ernest was aware of the same fact. He cared nothing at all about the thrashing he should get, and was only anxious to save Ellis. Ellis, however, would not move, and Blackall looked as if he would thrash both of them.

Still more angry at being baulked of his revenge, Blackall again struck at Ernest, and tried to catch him, but in the latter object he did not succeed, though he hurt Ernest's arm, so that he could with difficulty defend himself; and now blow succeeded blow with considerable rapidity.

Bracebridge disdained to fly, and as he could not hope to return the blows with much effect, he contented himself at first with standing on the defensive, waiting his opportunity to hit his powerful opponent in the eye or face, where he might leave a mark not easily effaced. He knew that if he succeeded, he should still further enrage the bully; but he also knew that it was very likely to prevent him from ever attacking him again. As Blackall hit out, he sprang back along the passage, then suddenly stopping, he leaped forward again, and put in the blow he desired.

Blackall's eyes struck fire, but he was too well accustomed to the use, or rather the misuse, of his fists to allow his opponent to escape him. Ernest was again retreating. Blackall caught him under his arm, and was about to inflict the most severe and disagreeable of punishments, by gibbing him, when poor Ellis, who had hitherto stood trembling at a distance, in obedience to Ernest's directions, could bear it no longer; and, throwing himself forward, leaped on Blackall's back, and held his arms with all his might and main, butting away at the same time, like a ram, with his head, and kicking furiously with his long legs, biting, it was said, the bully's ears and cheeks. However that may be, Blackall was compelled to let Ernest go, for the purpose of shaking off his new and ferocious assailant. This was not very easily done, for Ellis had remarkably long and strong arms, and held on like a vice. Ernest seeing this, resolved to bring the bully to terms.

"I say, Blackall, if Ellis lets you go, will you promise faithfully not to hurt him in any way, by word, look, or deed?" exclaimed Ernest.

Blackall did not deign to reply, but continued his impotent efforts to shake off his old man of the woods. He jumped and leaped, and backed against the walls, but to no purpose; he could not manage to get rid of his burden.

"Well, what is your determination?" asked Ernest again, advancing in a threatening attitude towards Blackall, on whom he could now, had he chosen, have inflicted a very severe punishment. "Will you promise faithfully, by all you hold sacred, not to touch or hurt Ellis in any way for this?"

"I should think you had better try to make a bargain for yourself first," said Blackall.

"Not I!" said Bracebridge, proudly; "I can stand a thrashing far better than Ellis. I am pretty well accustomed to your lickings, and they don't hurt me much. Therefore, again, I ask you, will you promise, or will you not?" As he spoke, he doubled his fists, and advanced on Blackall, whose face was completely exposed to an attack, while Ellis kept battering away at his head, and grasped his arms tighter than ever.

What might have been the consequences I do not know; Bracebridge, in all probability, would pretty severely have handled the bully, and, his anger being excited, would have left some marks not very easily eradicated on his countenance: when a light was seen in the passage, and a quick step advanced towards them. Bracebridge disdained to fly, and Blackall could not, so they waited the result.

"Ah! vat you garçons do there?" exclaimed Monsieur Malin, for it was the French master, holding up his candle. "Let me see! Ah, I understand! You, Blackall, are one very bad boy. You go to bed now. Bracebridge, Ellis, you come with me."

Ellis on this jumped off Blackall's back, and glad he was to do so, for his arms were beginning to ache terribly with his exertions.

Blackall sneaked off, vowing vengeance in his craven heart on his adversaries; and the kind-hearted Frenchman led the other two away, and urged them to keep clear of the bully. When, however, he heard how the affair had taken place, he was very much inclined to go and inform the Doctor, to try and get Blackall expelled, but they entreated aim not to do so, and declared that they did not fear him, and would not run the risk of thus injuring his prospects.

"Ah, you are brave garçons, brave garçons!" exclaimed Monsieur Malin.

At all events, they were true, right-feeling English boys.

Chapter Six
Our Military Exercises

Bracebridge had to press his advice on Ellis more than once before he could induce him to apply for leave to drill and to learn fencing and the broadsword exercise. All these sort of lessons were classed among the extras, so that the Doctor did not insist on the boys learning them unless by the express wish of their parents. If they themselves wished to learn them, they had to write home and get leave. This system, I fancy, made these branches of education far more popular than they would otherwise have been. The several masters, knowing that the number of their pupils depended on the interest they could excite in their respective sciences, did their utmost to make them attractive. They generally succeeded.

Monsieur Malin would, at all events, have been popular. He was a gentleman by birth and by education, of polished manners, and very good-natured, and as everybody liked him, everybody wished to learn French. Old Dibble, our drill-sergeant, was very unlike him in most respects, but still he won all our hearts. He was a kind-hearted man, and had an excellent temper, and he took great pains to teach us our drill and to make us like it. He was the very man to turn us all into soldiers, and, as Bracebridge had said of him, he never grew weary of recounting his deeds of arms to all whom he could find ready to listen. He was a tall man, somewhat stout, with a bald patch on the top of his head, and grey hair and whiskers, a thoroughly soldier-like hooked nose, and fine piercing grey eyes. Good-natured as he was, he would stand no nonsense or any skylarking; and we all agreed that when he was in the army he was certain to have kept all the men under him in capital order.

Our dancing-master was Mr Jay. He was a proficient in his art; and though he might not have been able to jump as high or to spin round on one leg as long as an opera-dancer, he was able to teach us to dance like gentlemen. He was also a professor of fencing and gymnastics, and a very good instructor he was. He understood thoroughly what the human body could do, and what it might do advantageously. He also taught boxing.

The Doctor was a great encourager of all athletic exercises, and allowed all the boys who wished it to take lessons in boxing once a week for half-an-hour at a time. The greater number availed themselves of the permission, and most of the school were very good boxers. The result was that, as a rule, we were a most peaceable set of boys, and I believe that fewer quarrels took place than among any equal number of boys in England. We had a riding-master, who used to come every Saturday with five or six ponies, and give us lessons in a paddock attached to the school-grounds. The Doctor used to say that his wish was to educate our hearts, our minds, and our bodies as far as he had the power, and that he found from experience that the greater variety of instruction he could give us, the more perfectly he could accomplish his object. He himself gave us instruction in swimming. I have described the pond in the grounds. He used a machine something like a large fishing-rod. A belt was fastened round the waist of a young swimmer, and by the belt he was secured to the end of a line hanging from the rod. The Doctor used to stand, rod in hand, and encourage and advise the boy till he gained confidence and knew how to strike out properly. He was anxious to prevent any one from getting into a bad way of striking out, for, as he used to say, it was as difficult to get rid of a bad habit as to acquire a good one. He was, therefore, always waging a deadly warfare against all bad habits from their very commencement, not only with regard to swimming, but in every other action of life. As soon as a boy had learned to strike out properly, he turned him over to the instruction of one of the bigger boys, who had especial charge of him in the water. He had always four or five boys whom he had taught to swim thoroughly well, and he made them swimming-masters. They benefited by having to give instruction to others, and by learning to keep their tempers. Nothing, perhaps, tries the temper so much as having to teach dull or inattentive boys. Blackall had been made one of the swimming-masters, but at the commencement of the bathing season the Doctor called him up, and without a word of explanation told him that he thought fit to dismiss him from the post. He lost, in consequence, several privileges attached to the office. To a person of Blackall's character, the mode of his dismissal was a considerable punishment. It showed him that the Doctor was aware of some of his misconduct, but of how much he was still left in ignorance, and he had to live on in fear that some more severe punishment was still in store for him. I am glad to say that there were very few other fellows at all like Blackall in the school. There were, of course, some few bullies and blackguards, or who would speedily have become so if left to their own devices, and there were cowards, and boys who carelessly told an untruth, or were addicted to the too common vice of prevarication. There were also vicious boys, or who would have been vicious had they not been watched and restrained. These were exceptions to the general rule.

The Doctor's system, embracing the law of kindness, answered well, and brought forth good fruits.

"Come along, Ellis," said Ernest, one Saturday afternoon, when he found his friend busily working away at the model of a vessel he was cutting out of a piece of American pine; "there's Sergeant Dibble in the playground; I'll take you up to him, and tell him that he must turn you into a soldier before the holidays. He'll do it if you obey his directions." Sergeant Dibble was found in the middle of the playground, surrounded by a number of boys, who were listening eagerly to one of his stories with which he was amusing them till the hour to commence had arrived.

"The reason why we conquered was this, young gentlemen," he was saying. "Every man, from the highest to the lowest, knew his duty and did it. If they didn't know it and didn't do it, Lord Wellington sent them about their business, no matter who they were. Remember that when you grow up. Your duty, I take it, is to do your best in whatever station you may be placed; what you are certain will produce the best results and forward the objects in which you are engaged. It is not enough to say, 'Such were my orders;' you must try and discover the spirit of your orders. Above all things, you must never be afraid of responsibility. Never be afraid of being found fault with when you know that you've done what's right. I was going to tell you how we crossed the river Douro, in Portugal; how we surprised Marshal Soult, and how Lord Wellington ate the dinner which had been prepared for him and his staff. We very nearly made him and his whole army prisoners, and we followed them up so closely that they had no time to rest till they were clear out of Portugal; but the hour is up. Fall in, young gentlemen; fall in!"

Ernest took this opportunity to go up to the Sergeant and to explain that he would find Ellis a very willing though, perhaps, a very awkward pupil, and begged that he would treat him accordingly, and not suppose that his awkwardness arose from carelessness or idleness.

Sergeant Dibble looked at Ellis for a few moments. "No fear, Master Bracebridge," he answered; "I've made a first-rate soldier out of far worse materials. If he's the will, he'll soon get them long arms and legs to do their duty. It's rather hard work to get a person who has no ear to march in time, but that's to be overcome by perseverance, and the eye must be made to do the work which the ear cannot. Fall in, Master Ellis, if you please."

Ellis had no notion of what falling in meant, so he shuffled about from place to place, looking up inquiringly at the Sergeant. "Take your place, I mean, in the awkward squad, Master Ellis."

"That's where I shall always have to be," thought poor Ellis. "Which are the awkwardest squad, Sergeant?" said he, looking up. "It strikes me that I should go there."

Whatever Ellis thought of himself, there were several other boys just as awkward, or at all events as unapt to learn military manners. Little Eden was one of them, that is to say, he always forgot what he had learned during his previous lesson. Gregson was another. He was not awkward in his movements, but while instruction was going forward he was always thinking of something else. One reason that Bracebridge succeeded so well in whatever he undertook was, that he had the power of concentrating his attention on whatever he was about; in the school-room or play-room, in the cricket-field or on the parade-ground, it was the same. It was his great talent. He had many other talents, and he also had, from his earliest days, been well trained. Had he been an only son, he might have been spoiled, but he had many brothers, and his temper had been tried, and he had been taught to command himself, and while he relied on his own energies for success, to obey his elders and to treat all his fellow-creatures with respect. Sergeant Dibble very soon pronounced him his best drill. The awkward squad had been standing by themselves for some minutes, looking very awkward, indeed, when Sergeant Dibble exclaimed —

"Fall out, Mr Bracebridge, and take charge of that squad. Exercise them in the balance step, and put them through their facings."

Ernest, not a little proud, obeyed, and while the rest of the young soldiers were marching up and down, taking open order, wheeling to the right or left, and going through a variety of manoeuvres, he placed himself in front of the boys I have described, with others, making altogether about a dozen. His first aim was to awaken them all up. "Attention!" he exclaimed in a sharp tone, which made them all spring up suddenly. He then explained very clearly what he wanted them to do, and put himself in the required attitude, taking care that they all did the same. Very few could not do the balance step. Chivey and other hopping games had taught them that. He kept them at it a very few minutes, and then telling them to practise it by themselves, went on to teach them their facings, explaining the object of each movement. He did it all in so patient and good-natured a manner that every boy in the squad expressed a hope that Bracebridge might be set to teach them again.

"I'll tell you what we will do; we will work away every day in the week, and when Sergeant Dibble comes next week we will show him what we can do." The idea was taken up enthusiastically, and even the least apt of the squad made great progress. In two or three weeks they were fully equal to those who had been drilling all the half. Sergeant Dibble was delighted, and foretold that if Master Bracebridge went into the army he would distinguish himself.

"I don't know what I am to be," replied Ernest; "I know that I am to do everything I am set to do as well as I can."

There were some twenty boys or more who were very far from perfect in their drill in the larger squad, and Sergeant Dibble managed to persuade them to put themselves, during the week, under Ernest's instruction. Some few, at first, kicked at the notion, but finally all agreed to obey his orders on the parade-ground during one hour every day. Others, of their own accord, joined, and in a short time he had quite a large army of volunteers. He spared no pains to perfect them. He got the Sergeant to bring him a "Manual of Drill Instruction," and every spare moment he spent in studying it attentively.

In a few weeks Ernest's squad surpassed that composed of the older boys in the accuracy and rapidity of their movement; and Sergeant Dibble, when he came, expressed his astonishment and delight on finding what could be done when all set to work with a will to do it.

Ernest, too, gained great popularity, and many who had before rather envied him now frankly acknowledged his talents and excellent qualities. He himself also behaved very well. He did not set himself up above the rest in consequence of what he had done and the applause he had gained, but the moment the drill was over he became like one of the rest, and took his hat, or his fishing-rod, or his hoop—though, by the by, he was getting rather out of hoops—and went off shouting and laughing with all the merry throng.

The greatest possible change was worked in Ellis. He no longer looked like the same boy. The alteration in his appearance was almost as striking as that which takes place in a country clown caught by a recruiting sergeant, half drunk at a fair, as he rolls on, looking every moment as if he was going to topple over, from public-house to public-house, and when he has been under the drill-sergeant's hands for a couple of years, and is turned into the trim, active, intelligent soldier. At first, few who saw poor Ellis's awkward attempts could possibly avoid laughing. How he rolled from side to side; how he stuck out one foot, and changed it again and again, finding that it was the wrong one; how, when the word "to the right-about" was given, he invariably found himself grinning in the face of his left-hand man, unless by good chance the latter had made the same mistake as himself, when he became suddenly inspired with the hope that he had, for a wonder, hit off the right thing. He soon found his hopes disappointed by being summoned to repeat the movement, with a caution to do it correctly. Then, on receiving the order to march, he nearly always started off with his right foot instead of his left, and when he did put out the left, he quickly changed it to the right, under the impression that he must have made a mistake. Still his perseverance was most praiseworthy. Bracebridge had assured him that in time he would become a good soldier if he wished it, and a good soldier he resolved to be, whether he followed up the profession or not. He read as hard as he had ever done, and found time to manufacture all sorts of things, and yet no one practised more than he did drilling, and games, and all sorts of athletic exercises. Before the change I have described was perceptible, the half was nearly over, and the summer holidays were about to begin. I have, in mentioning it, run on somewhat ahead of events. Ernest had advised him to learn to dance and to fence.

"Come, come, you are joking now, old fellow," was his reply, in his former melancholy tone of voice. "I may learn any rough affair, like drilling and gymnastics, and, perhaps, the broadsword exercises, and learn enough to cut a fellow's head off; but to hop and skip about to the sound of a fiddle, or to handle a thin bar of steel so as to prevent another fellow with a similar weapon running his into me, is totally beyond my powers. I know that I could not, if I was to try ever so much."

"So you thought about gymnastics, and so you thought about drilling, and yet you have succeeded very well in both. Remember the motto of our Silver Knight. Push on up the hill; work away at one thing, and then another. It is extraordinary how much may be learnt in a short time, if people will but give their minds to what they are about. I know a good number of things, and I can do a good number of things, and yet I have not spent more hours of my life with a book before me than have most boys of my age; but then, when I have had a book before me, I have been really busy, getting all I could out of it; I have not sat idling and frittering away my time as so many fellows do. I don't fancy that I cannot do a thing because it is difficult; I always try to find out where the difficulty lies, and then see how I can best get over it. I like difficulties, because I like to conquer them. This world is full of difficulties, which it is the business of men to conquer. A farmer cannot get a field of corn to grow without overcoming difficulties. He must dig up or plough up the ground; he must get rid of the weeds; he must trench it, and after a time manure it; and this he must do year after year, or it will not produce abundantly. And so it is throughout all the works to be done in this world: then why should we expect to get knowledge, to cultivate our minds, to get rid of the weeds growing up constantly in them, without labour, and hard labour, too? Now, I dare say, my dear fellow, you think that I am talking very learnedly, or you may say, very pedantically; but I do not even claim originality for my views. My father pointed them out to me and my brothers long ago. He threw difficulties in our way, and stood by till we overcame them, telling us it was the best practice we could have in the world. I cannot tell you how much we owe to our father. He is the wisest man I ever met. I dare say there are many cleverer people; men who can talk better, and have done more, and have written more, and who are thought much more of in the world; but my brother and I agree, for all that, that he is the wisest, and if not the most talented, which we don't say he is, that he makes the best use of the talents he has got. You must come and see him one of these days; I would say at once; but I think that you will like him, and that he will like you better by and by. I wrote to him about you, I must confess that, and he put me up to some of the advice I gave you. My brothers and I always write to him just as we write to one another; indeed, we generally pass our letters on to him, because we know that he likes to hear everything that we are doing. We have no secrets from him, as I find some fellows here have. We always go to him for advice about everything. He often tells us to act as we think best, and to let him know what we have done. Sometimes he tells us that he thinks we have acted very judiciously; at other times he tells us that, from the judgment he has been able to form, we ought to have done differently. He has never kept us in what might be called leading-strings; but has placed the same confidence in us that we do in him—that is to say, he knows we want to do what is right. Depend on it, Ellis, there is nothing like having the most perfect confidence between your father and yourself. I assure you that I should be miserable if I had not, and if I did not believe that he is the best friend I have on earth, or ever shall have."

Bracebridge said a great deal more to the same effect. Indeed, whenever he got on the subject of his father's excellences, he was always enthusiastic. Not without ample reason, I believe, for Mr Bracebridge was a man possessed of very rare qualities; and Oaklands, his place, was one of the most delightful houses to visit at in the country, or probably, in all England; that is to say, young men and boys, and indeed young people, generally, found it so. Ernest knew that it would do poor Ellis a great deal of good to go there. From what he could make out, Ellis's father and mother were advanced in life and great invalids, and Edward, their only son, had been considerably over-petted and over-coddled, though, as they had a good deal of sense with regard to many important matters, they had not spoilt him. They had corrected him as a child when he deserved it, and watching the growth of bad propensities, had endeavoured to eradicate them before they had attained any size. They were themselves very shy, diffident people, and thinking little of themselves, thought very little of their son, and brought him up to think very little of himself. Certainly, if they erred, they erred on the right side.

Ellis was not weak; he was not a boy at all likely to be imposed upon by a bad person; his principles were, as far as could be seen, good, and his sympathies appeared to be always on the right side. Thus he was undoubtedly particularly fortunate in falling in with a boy like Ernest Bracebridge, whom he could admire, and who could, at the same time, enter into his feelings, and take an interest in him. Still Ernest did not think that he was doing anything out of the way in encouraging him. There was something so natural and unpretending about his character, and so free was he from anything like conceit or vanity, that he was scarcely conscious that he was superior to his companions; or, if he was conscious of the fact, that it was anything on which he should be justified in priding himself. Of one thing I am sure, that he had not found out that, by his own force of character and talents, he had already become one of the most popular boys in the school, and that, had he made the experiment, he would have had more followers than any boy even in the first class. The way he had tackled Blackall the evening of the kite-race had become known, though neither he nor Ellis had talked of it; and this gained him many admirers, especially among those over whom the bully was accustomed to tyrannise. At last Blackall began to be twitted with it, even by the fellows of his own age. It became at last a joke among his compeers to ask him how his ears were—how he liked to have an old man of the woods on his back, and how he could allow himself to be thrashed by a fellow half a head shorter than himself, and so much younger. He dared not attack either Ernest or Ellis openly, but he resolved to take his revenge on them as soon as possible. He had not long to wait for an opportunity. Before our drilling lessons were over, Sergeant Dibble used to arm us all with basket-hilted sticks, which served the purpose of broadswords; and, forming in two parties on opposite sides of the parade-ground, we were ordered to advance and attack, and defend ourselves, delivering or receiving so many cuts each time the two lines passed each other. Blackall, who prided himself on being a good swordsman, thought this would be a fine opportunity for inflicting a severe revenge on Bracebridge, whom he dared not now bully as formerly, and kick and cuff whenever he met him.

"Now, young gentlemen, prepare for the broadsword exercise," the Sergeant sung out in his clear, sharp voice. "Fall in line; fall in!"

Ellis had begun to learn the broadsword exercise, though it was a sore trial to him, for he found great difficulty in recollecting the proper guards or strokes, and he was always receiving some severe cuts across the head or shoulders or legs, and getting into trouble by giving the wrong strokes, and making his opponents, who were not prepared for them, suffer accordingly. Bracebridge had hit upon a plan to save him somewhat from this, by taking him as his opponent; and when he saw him making the wrong stroke, he was ready with the proper guard; and when he saw that Ellis had not his right guard, he either hit him softly, or hit at the guard presented to him. This was very good practice to Ernest, though it made Sergeant Dibble sing out, every now and then—

"Mr Bracebridge! Mr Bracebridge! can you never remember to listen to the word of command, sir? When I say cut two, I often see you cut four; and when I say third guard, you are apt to use the first or second guard. How is this, sir? Mr Ellis, you are not attentive either, sir, permit me to observe. When I say defend, draw up the hand smartly, and from the first guard. Be smart!—second guard! third guard! Remember, if you have a big, ugly fellow, with a sword sharp enough to divide a bolster, who happens to wish to cut your head off, he doesn't stop to consider which is the right guard to make, or thrust to deliver. He'd whip off your head before you had time to look round, and then what would you think of yourself, I should like to know?"

Ernest never replied, while exercising, to these or any similar remarks, but he and Sergeant Dibble soon understood each other, and the Sergeant was convinced that Ernest was a better swordsman than he had supposed.

"But, Mr Bracebridge, it will never do to let Mr Ellis go on in that way. Now that he has a little more confidence, we must make him run his chance with the rest," he urged. "A few cuts with a hazel stick won't do him any harm, and will make him open his eyes a little."

To this, of course, Ernest agreed, and the present day was one of the first poor Ellis had to look out for himself.

Blackall had meantime watched Ernest; and hearing him found fault with, and seeing him and Ellis make a mess of it, as he thought, he held his swordsmanship in very low estimation. This made him confident that he could do what he liked with him. It required some management to get placed opposite to him, but he succeeded, and felt highly delighted at the thoughts of the revenge he was about to enjoy.

"Draw swords, gentlemen;" sung out Sergeant Dibble. "Both parties advance. Mr Jones's party assault with the second cut; Mr Smith's defend with the second guard. Now hit hard and sharp, gentlemen. If the proper guards are up you can do no harm." Blackall was in the Jones's party, and purposed fully to carry out the order. Bracebridge saw that he was opposite to him, and assumed a look of perfect indifference. The bully expected to see him turning pale and looking alarmed. "March!" sung out the Sergeant. "Double quick!"

On rushed the two squadrons, for so they could not help fancying themselves, and, as I believe, the Sergeant for the moment fancied them also. They met with a hostile clash. Blackall, not knowing that the Sergeant's eye was on him, shifted to the third cut, hoping to give Ernest a severe blow across the legs, but Ernest's eye was as quick as his, and catching the movement of the arm, he had the third guard ready to receive the blow.

The Sergeant made no remark, but kept a watch on Blackall's movements, "Very well, gentlemen; very well!" he exclaimed. "Now let Mr Smith's party assault with the fourth cut. Bravo! performed with perfect precision." And so he went on. Each time, however, that Jones's division had to assault, he saw that Blackall endeavoured to take some undue advantage of Ernest, who with equal regularity contrived quietly to foil him. Ernest kept his eye on his opponent's, but said nothing, and in no other way showed that he was aware of his evil intentions. Blackall at length began to lose his temper at his own failures: he ground his teeth and turned savage glances towards Bracebridge, who met them with a quiet look, free, at the same time, from scorn or anger. Not once did Blackall succeed in inflicting a blow, and though Ernest at last might have bestowed several very severe ones, he rightly refrained from so doing.

"I know perfectly well that even had he hit me, I ought not to have hit him back," he said to himself; "much more then ought I to refrain when he has not succeeded in his object. I should like to try the plan of heaping coals of fire on his head. I might soften him, but I should have less hope with him than with any one. I will try. It matters not what may happen to me, but I am resolved, at the same time, I will not let him go on bullying any fellow whom I can defend." When the drill was over, Sergeant Dibble called up Ernest.

"I saw it all, sir," he said. "You did capitally. I never saw a young gentleman keep his temper as you did. Why he wants to hurt you I don't know, but I will put you up to a trick or two which will place him in your power. You are getting on famously with your fencing. He piques himself on being a first-rate fencer. He is not bad; and he does very well when he fences with Mr Jay, or any one he knows. Now, though I do not teach fencing, I can fence; and, what is more, I have learned several tricks which people do not generally know. I once saved a wounded Frenchman's life and took him prisoner, and nursed him as I ought to have done, and then I found he was a master of the science of defence and attack. I never saw a man who could use a small sword as he did. Well, as a mark of his gratitude, he taught me all he knew, and, especially, how to disarm an opponent. It is simple, but requires practice. There is no one in the fencing-room; come with me there and I will show it to you. Practise the trick till I come again, whenever you have an opportunity, either by yourself or with a friend you can trust, like Ellis or Buttar. I'll answer for it that you will be perfect in a couple of weeks at most. If you lead Blackall to it, he is certain to challenge you before long. Disarm him three times running, and I do not think that he'll ever wish to attack you again in any way."

Ernest could not resist the offer the Sergeant made him. He thought that the knowledge might be of the greatest importance to him during his life, so he at once went with the Sergeant into the fencing-room. "You see, Mr Bracebridge," observed his instructor, "if you had a real sword in your hand, you would give your opponent such a cut round the wrist that he would probably be unable to hold a weapon again for many a month afterwards."

Ernest set to work at once in his usual way, and Sergeant Dibble taking great pains to instruct him, he quickly acquired the trick.

"You see, sir," observed the Sergeant, "though a foil does not cut, the button, if the leather is off, as I often see is the case, will give a very ugly scratch round the wrist, and if this is repeated two or three times, a fencer will rather stand clear of the man who can do it. Just do you try it on Blackall, and you'll see if my word don't come right."

After the Sergeant was gone, Ernest thought over what he had said. He did not, however, half like the idea of taking the advantage which had been given him over Blackall.

"No, no!" he exclaimed to himself. "I'll tell him beforehand what I am going to do. If I was going to engage with him in mortal combat, the matter would be different; I should feel as if I was going to commit a murder; but now I feel as if I was going to inflict on him a very deserved punishment and take down his pride a little." So Ernest set to work, and practised the trick Sergeant Dibble had taught him. After a day or two he took Buttar and Ellis into his confidence, and they all practised it together. Ellis, however, could not manage to accomplish the turn of the wrist in a way to be effective, but Buttar, who had resolved to be a soldier, and took a deep interest in all military exercises, was never weary in practising it. When Sergeant Dibble came again, he told Ernest that he would be perfect in another week, and complimented Buttar also on his proficiency.

Ellis, meantime, was making great advances in the use of the broadsword, and the Sergeant assured him that if he would go on and persevere, he would very soon be far superior to many idle fellows who now sneered at him, and would not practise unless the master was present.

Chapter Seven
A Fishing Expedition

"I say, Bracebridge, we must try our new rod before we break up," said Ellis, one Saturday, just before the boys were going in to dinner. "It's a capital afternoon for fishing, cloudy and soft. I'll see about bait if you will promise to come. Buttar and Bouldon say they will, and so will Gregson; so we shall be a jolly party, and shall gain something even if we don't catch fish." Ernest, who always appeared to have more spare time than any one else, consented to go, provided he had half-an-hour's reading after dinner, to get up some work. Ellis had learned to be almost as eager as his friend in anything he was about. He now hurried off to send Jim, a lame boy, who was allowed to go on errands for the young gentlemen, to prepare the baits for the fishing-party. They all assembled at the appointed hour, with capital rods in hand, with the exception of Gregson, who declared that he always made his own rods, and that his, though uncouth in appearance, would catch as many fish as all the rest put together. The young fishermen had very little excuse for not catching fish. There was a large pond, about two miles off, with a clear full stream running into it. In the stream were trout, grayling, roach, and dace, and the pond was full of fine carp, and tench, and perch, while occasionally the other fish from the stream condescended to swim into it. The fishing belonged to a gentleman in the neighbourhood, who took a great interest in the Doctor and his school, and always allowed a dozen boys at a time to fish there. They had to go to the Doctor or one of the masters for leave, and as seldom more than a dozen wished to go at a time, it was not often that any were disappointed. Off they set, with their fishing-rods over their shoulders, singing away as merrily as crickets. There were one or two ponds and streams in the way, where they proposed to try their fortune for a few minutes, as it was reported that sometimes very fine fish were caught in them. The first they came to was a quiet dark pond, shaded by trees. Gregson declared that he thought it must be full of fish, and he was considered an authority on such matters. Ellis, who knew also a good deal about fishing, rather doubted that such was the case.

"Come and try," said Gregson; "there is no great harm in doing that, at all events." Gregson prevailed, and no one perceived a quiet chuckle in the tone of his voice. He persuaded them all to fish with very small hooks and red worms, which he gave them. They had not fished long before Bouldon exclaimed, "I've a bite, I've a bite!" His float began to bob; down it went, and up he whisked his rod. "A fine fish," he cried out; "but, hillo, it has legs—four legs, I declare! Why, it's a monster; a terrible monster. Hillo! Ellis, Gregson, Buttar, come and help me. Will it bite, I wonder?" Gregson ran laughing up to Bouldon to see what was the matter.

"Why, it is a water-newt!" he exclaimed. "A harmless, curious little creature—there, don't hurt it! It has not swallowed the hook. I'll put it into my basket and take it home. It will live in a tub of water for a long time. Look! it is something like a lizard, but it has a flat tail made for swimming. What curious little feet and legs! Now, though the newt has four legs, it lays eggs; and to guard them from injury, wraps them up in the leaves of water plants, with its four paws. When the young newt is hatched, it is very like a tadpole. It is like a fish, for it breathes through gills; but as it increases in size the gills go away and the front legs appear, and then the hind ones. In a frog-tadpole the hind legs appear first, and then the front ones."

"Curious sort of fellows," observed Tom Bouldon, who had been listening attentively to Gregson's account; "but, I say, I thought fellows, when they grew bigger, took to gills instead of throwing them aside."

"Oh! Tommy, Tommy, what a pun!" was the general cry.

"What a good pun, or what a bad one?" asked Bouldon with perfect simplicity. "But, I say, Gregson, are there any other fish but your friends, the newts, in this pond, do you think? because if there are not, I vote we move on."

"I never heard of any; but I wanted a newt, and so I proposed that we should fish here."

On hearing this, there was a general proposal that he should be left behind to catch newts by himself; but he promised faithfully to show them where the best fish were to be caught, if they would forgive him. On these conditions he very easily obtained pardon for his trick.

"I say, did you ever catch a fresh-water lobster?" asked Gregson. No one had, and no one believed that there was such a thing. "I'll soon show you one," said Gregson; and when they came to a shallow stream with highish banks, pulled off his shoes and stockings, tucked up the sleeves of his shirt and the legs of his trousers, and was soon busy feeling under the banks, just below water.

"Why, he has got one; he has indeed!" shouted Bouldon, as Gregson produced, by the antennae, a crayfish, which, to prevent himself from being bitten, he caught by the back; its claws, though they stretched wide open, as if they had the cramp very badly, being utterly harmless.

"This is a Crustacea," cried Gregson, holding him up in pride; "and if not a lobster, it may well be called one. I have often caught two or three dozens of them, and found them capital for tea or breakfast. In my opinion, if a person has his senses about him, and will but study natural history, he would be able to live entirely on the herbs and fruits of the field, the birds of the air, and the animals of the earth and water."

"Ho, ho! a pretty sort of existence that would be!" exclaimed Bouldon. "I suppose you would have us to eat grass, like sheep or cows, or snails, or vermin, or tadpoles."

"No, no! Tom, but I will undertake to place a capital dinner before you; and, except the trouble of catching the animals, it shall cost nothing beyond a halfpenny, which I will expend in mustard and pepper. I cannot grow the pepper, so I shall buy a farthing's-worth of that and a farthing's-worth of mustard seed, which I would grow, and could then give you mustard to eat, and also a salad."

"What would you do for salt?" asked Buttar.

"I would make that very quickly by the seaside. A few pails of salt-water thrown into any clean hollow of a rock would soon evaporate and leave some excellent salt," answered Gregson. "Then I would give you several sorts of fish, and crayfish, and, if I can get to the sea, fish of all sorts, and lobsters, and crabs, and shrimps, and oysters, and every variety of shell-fish, and sea-weeds also, some of which are excellent and very nutritious; but I can do very well without going to the sea. Of animals in England there are not many; but I can snare rabbits, and so I could hares, but that would be poaching, and therefore I cannot give you hares; but you shall have all sorts of birds—larks, and blackbirds, and sparrows, and young rooks, and wildfowl, and many others; and then there is no end of vegetables. Nettle-tops, when well boiled, are excellent, and so are a number of other plants which are looked upon as weeds; and you have no idea of the number of roots which grow in the fields, and hedges, and hill-sides, which are fit to eat. Then, to give flavour to our birds and rabbits, I can find mushrooms in abundance, and, indeed, several flavoury seeds and roots. While I think of it, I can do without pepper; we have some native pepper. I can make several teas which have a very nice taste, and I can produce very fair coffee from the root of the dandelion. If I was in Canada, I could manufacture excellent sugar from the maple-tree. Here I could make it out of beetroot, but it would be troublesome. I can give you as a dessert some delicious strawberries, and raspberries, and filberts, and I could get plenty of chestnuts, and no one would accuse me of stealing them; indeed, with a little consideration and trouble, I could place before you a first, second, and third course, which ought to satisfy the taste of the most fastidious. For my own part, I do not object to frog's legs and snails; and if I was hungry, and could get nothing else, I would eat a snake without hesitation; but I do not ask others to entertain my views."

"Oh, oh! Greggy, you cannibal! you would eat grubs and caterpillars, I suppose? Why, you are no better than an Australian savage," exclaimed Bouldon, with a look of ineffable disgust.

"That is the worst of you, Gregson, you go into extremes," observed Ernest. "We tried once, at home, for curiosity's sake, just the dinner you describe, and a very good dinner we had, though it was more suited to a Frenchman's than an Englishman's taste. My father says that if people studied the subject, many more things would be found fit for food than are now used. For instance, if two people were cast on shore on an uninhabited island, or were travelling through the wilds of America or Australia, one might starve from ignorance of what was fit to eat, while the other, from having a thorough knowledge of botany and natural history generally might find an abundant supply of nutritious food. When fruits are not in season, there are nearly always roots to be found under ground, and various herbs, and even the leaves, and gum, and stems or bark of trees. The inhabitants of Terra del Fuego live on mushrooms which are found growing on the stems of the evergreen beech; indeed, I might multiply instances without end. The naturalist not only knows that such things exist, but, from having studied their habits, knows exactly where to look for them. I have often read of poor fellows starving in the midst of plenty, simply from their ignorance that food was close around them. Others have been afraid to eat what they found for fear of being poisoned. I tell you what, Greggy, I think that you are perfectly right, only you should take care not to disgust people by talking of being ready to eat things for which they may have an antipathy. We know that locusts, and sea-slugs, and bird? nests, are considered great delicacies in some countries, and so are dogs by several people, and really I do not see why a dog should not be as delicate as a pig."

"Well! I declare that it is next door to cannibalism to eat a dog, man's faithful friend and protector," cried Buttar, who was more of a sportsman than any of the rest of the party. "I would sooner starve than eat my old dog, Ponto."

"I am not at all an advocate for the practice of dog eating," said Ernest. "But I do argue that civilised and educated people, as we profess to be, should obtain a far greater knowledge of the productions of the earth than we possess." Gregson was glad to find himself so well supported, and the rest finally agreed that they would get books and try and pick up some knowledge on the subject.

"Books are all very well, and very important indeed; but they alone won't do; you must study and examine for yourselves. Books will, by themselves, never give you a practical knowledge of natural history." This conversation lasted till the merry party arrived at the stream where they proposed to fish. They all set to work, each in his own way. Ernest was the only fly-fisher of the party. There was a light breeze which just rippled some of the deep pools in the stream, and as he walked up it, passing his companions one after the other, he seldom passed ten minutes without getting a rise and catching a fish.

"Hillo, Gregson," said Bouldon; "I thought you, with your stick, were going to catch more than any of us. There's Bracebridge far ahead of you already; you'll be beaten, old fellow."

"Wait a bit," answered Gregson quietly. "My fish have not begun to bite yet. I am thinking of trying the pond for an hour or so. I ground-baited it as I came by, and I have no doubt I shall catch something." Bouldon, who was the worst fisherman of the party, in consequence chiefly of his want of patience, accompanied Gregson in the hopes that he might benefit by the ground-bait.

"What is it you put in?" he asked. The young naturalist showed him some balls which looked like balls of clay with some red seams, but they were composed of clay and bran, and gentles, and red worms, and one or two other ingredients, which Gregson averred would attract all sorts of fish. "You must not interfere with my sport, but you shall have a spot to yourself; and I'll answer for it before long that you will have plenty." Gregson himself, as he spoke, threw in his line, and as Tom looked on, caught several perch and roach in rapid succession.

"Oh, I can't stand that; I must go and see what I can do," exclaimed Bouldon, moving on.

"Very well, just go a little on this side of that willow," said Gregson; "you will find a deepish hole there. Throw in your ground-bait, and before long you are very likely to get some bites. See; I've caught another. What a whacking big perch! Three pounds' weight, I should say. I'll have him out soon; don't stay for me, I can tackle him." This success of Gregson's made Bouldon still more anxious to be off to try and catch some fish. Hitherto he had got nothing. Having thrown in all the ground-bait he had got, he baited his hook with the full expectation of catching a basket-full. He cast in his line and stood patiently watching his float. It would not bob. He altered the depth of the hook several times; the worm wriggled, as at first, untouched. He began to grow very impatient.

"This will never do," he muttered; "I must shift my ground till I find the fish more inclined to be caught." He looked round towards Gregson, who was pulling up fish as fast as he could. "His basket must be already nearly full, and I have not caught even a wretched gudgeon."

On this Tom went round the pond, throwing in his line here and there with the same want of success. At last he got a bite; "A big fish," he thought to himself. "I'm sure it is; hurra! perhaps my one fish may weigh as much as all Gregson's and Bracebridge's together." He hooked his fish, which after one or two tugs, poked his nose to the surface just to see who was at the other end of the line, which somehow or other had got hold of his lips.

"A grand, magnificent pike!" shouted Tom with delight, letting go his reel as the fish began to pull, and darted off into the centre of the pond. Bouldon stood ready to turn him as soon as he began to slacken his pace. Never had he felt so eager about catching a fish, for never had he held a bigger one at the end of his line. It would have been better for him had it been much smaller. There was a quantity of weeds in the pond; and numerous large flat leaves of the beautiful white water-lily floating near, moored to long tough stems, among which he was in a dreadful fright that the fish would get, when he felt sure it would contrive to carry line and hook and float away. The pike, if pike it was, seemed fully aware of the advantage it possessed, and darted about in every direction.

"The hook must have caught the very edge of the upper lip, or it would have bitten through my line long ago," thought Tom. "What can I do? I wish Gregson were here to help me. He would know some dodge to get this fellow on shore. I'm sure I don't. Hillo! Greggy! Ellis! Do come and help me. Any of you fellows there?" He dared not for a moment turn his eye away from the water, lest the fish should take the opportunity of getting off.

"Hillo! does no one hear? Hillo, I say! Come, my good fellows, lend a hand to land this monster!" No one answered. The fish had run out with the whole of his line; the rod was bending almost double. He advanced to the very edge of the pond; he thought that he might give a little more scope by going to the right hand, where there was what he supposed to be a projection of the bank. So there was, but it was only of grass, and had nothing under it. He put his foot on it; the fish pulled harder than ever; he never dreamed of letting go his rod, and over he went, the impetus of his fall, and the pulling of the fish, carrying him a considerable distance from the shore. His head went under water, and he got a good quantity of it in his mouth; but at last he came up to the surface, spluttering and blowing, and trying to strike out, but still, like a true Briton, keeping fast hold of his rod. He now shouted out with all his might, his shout becoming a sharp cry for help, for he felt very truly that life was in imminent danger. The water was deep; he had thick heavy shoes and trousers on, and he could not make up his mind to lose his rod. For some time he positively swam away from the shore, not knowing what he was about, but fortunately at last he found out what he was doing, and tried to get back. His heart sank within him when he found how far off he was from the land. His clothes were pressing him down, and the long slimy stems of the weeds began to twist and turn round his legs. "Oh, I shall be drowned—I shall be drowned!" he cried out in an agony of fear. "Help— help!—help, oh help!" he shouted, struggling to keep himself above water. His eye looked on either side of the pond. He saw some one approaching the spot where he had stood, but coming leisurely, and evidently not aware that he had tumbled into the water. "Help, help;" he again shouted, and he felt that in another minute he must go down, for the more he attempted to approach the shore, the more his legs became entangled by the fatal weeds. He thought that he recognised the gaunt figure of Ellis.

"Oh, if it had been Bracebridge now! he swims so well, he might have got me out," he thought to himself; but he had very little confidence that Ellis would help him. Just then his last cry must have reached the ear of the person approaching, for he set off running towards the spot as fast as his legs would carry him. Bouldon began to hope once more that he might be saved. Then he saw that it was Ellis.

"Keep up, keep up!" shouted Ellis; "I'll be with you." He disencumbered himself of his basket as he ran, and the moment he reached the spot he threw off his shoes and his jacket, and, rod in hand, having broken off the hook from his line, plunged into the water without an instant's hesitation. All the time, however, he shouted, "Help! help! help!" He swam out bravely towards Bouldon, poking his rod before him till the end reached his struggling school-fellow. "Catch hold of this—catch hold of this!" he sang out lustily. Bouldon heard him, but his senses were becoming confused, and he could not exert himself to reach the point of the rod. Ellis swam on still further, but he saw the weeds, and he knew that, should his legs once become entangled in them, he should be unable to help his friend, and should probably lose his own life.

"Oh! come nearer, come nearer!" gasped out poor Bouldon, making vain efforts to get free.

Ellis, against his better judgment, generously made the attempt. He instantly felt that he, too, was among the weeds. He tried to get back. His only consolation was to see that Tom had got hold of the end of his rod. Ellis exerted himself to the utmost. Move forward he dared not; but throwing himself on his back, he lifted up his legs, and endeavoured to disentangle them from the weeds which were round them. At last he felt that he could strike out with them; and paddling with one hand at the same time, he gently pulled on his rod, so as to tow Bouldon towards him. The weeds had, however, got so completely round poor Tom's legs, that Ellis found that he was not moving him.

"I'm sinking, I'm sinking!" Tom cried out.

Ellis struck away with all his might. "Hold on to the rod, whatever happens, that's all," he cried out, tugging and tugging away. "I'm moving you, I'm moving you!"

So he was, but it was only so far as the weeds would allow him to go. Tom had followed his example, and thrown himself on his back. Just then a shout was heard, and soon afterwards Ellis caught the words he had been himself using, "Keep up, keep up!—never fear!" He thought it was Bracebridge's voice; so it was. He was up to them in an instant.

Now, Bracebridge, by his father's advice, never went out on any expedition without a supply of stout twine. Producing some from his fishing-basket, he fastened one end of it to a drooping branch of the willow-tree, which overhung the pond, and the other on to his own rod, and, having thrown off his clothes, he boldly plunged into the water, knowing that the weeds would have much less power over his naked legs, than if he had kept on his trousers. He reached poor Tom with the end of his rod just as he was sinking. Tom grasped it convulsively, and Ernest holding on to the part of the line made fast to the tree had sufficient force to drag him out from among the weeds. Ernest, meantime, told Ellis to try and get to shore, so as to be able to help him to draw in Bouldon. Ellis was not long in doing so; and climbing up the bank, he hauled in the line Ernest had so thoughtfully made fast to the tree. In a short time, by careful pulling, Bouldon was hauled clear of the weeds, and Ernest was able to take hold of his arm, and to support him while Ellis towed them both up to the bank. By this time Bouldon was unconscious, but, notwithstanding, he still with one hand held fast hold of the butt-end of his rod, and the rod had evidently something else at the other end of it. They drew him up the bank still holding on his rod.

"Ellis was not long in doing so: and climbing up the bank, he hauled in the line Ernest had made fast to the tree."

The change of atmosphere from the warm water of the pond, perhaps, to the cooler air, revived him, and opening his eyes he looked up at Bracebridge.

"You, Ernest! I thought it was Ellis. Is he safe?"

"Yes, yes; all right, old fellow!" answered Ellis.

"Oh, thank you, thank you! Then do try and get my fish on shore," were the first words exchanged between the party when they had got safe to land.

"It's a whacking big pike, that I know," cried Tom. "Oh! Bracebridge, don't let him go; that's all."

"I only hope no stranger will come near and find me, like a picture in the 'Boy's Own Book,' fishing *in statu quo*," said Ernest, laughing, "But quick, Ellis, bring the landing-net; I shall have him directly, I believe."

There was a broad laugh as Ellis put the net under the fish—for fish there undoubtedly was. "Why, Tommy, your big pike has turned into a perch after all," cried Ernest; "a good-sized one though. But how did you come to fancy it a pike?"

"Because he pulled so horribly; and when I saw his big jaws above water, I thought nothing but a pike could possess such a pair of gills," answered Tom, with much simplicity.

Ernest and Ellis laughed heartily at Bouldon's pike. Ellis took off his clothes, and wrung them dry, and assisted Tom, who was getting rapidly well, to do the same; and while Ernest put on some of his garments, he lent the remainder to clothe his companions, while theirs were drying. They very quickly got their fishing gear to rights again, and were soon, as eager as before, engaged in their sport.

The disturbance they had made in the water had not frightened away the fish, and they each of them caught several large perch. When they at last got their clothes dry enough to put on, and worked their way up to where Gregson was fishing, they found that he had actually filled his basket completely full; fulfilling his promise that with his old stick, as he called it, he would catch more fish than all the rest put together. He bought his hooks, though he could make them; but the rod, line, and float he had entirely manufactured himself, as he had all the rest of the gear, and thus he certainly had reason to be proud of his achievements.

He was horrified when he heard how nearly two of his companions had lost their lives, while all the time he had been so close at hand. When, however, they were joined by Lemon and Buttar, and Bouldon described the way Ellis had come to his rescue, everybody was loud in their praises of him except Ernest. He said nothing at the time, but as they were walking home, he took Ellis's hand, and pressing it warmly, remarked, "You have behaved very gallantly to-day, my dear fellow. I was certain that when the opportunity offered, you would do so. No one could have done better, or shown more coolness or courage. Had it not been for you, Bouldon would have lost his life; of that I am certain. He was almost gone when I came up."

"Why, Bracebridge, I considered that you saved both our lives," exclaimed Ellis, in a tone of surprise at hearing himself so praised. "Had you not come up, we should both have been lost."

"Oh! I only used a little judgment, and followed one of the many bits of good advice my father has given me from time to time," said Ernest. "I neither ought nor will take any of the credit which belongs to you; so pray, my dear fellow, do not talk of what I have done."

Ellis, however, argued the point; but Ernest took care that the way he had behaved should be thoroughly known and well understood by all the boys, as well as by the Doctor.

The fishing-party had a very pleasant walk home, and seldom had fuller baskets of fish been brought to the school.

That evening, after prayers, the Doctor called up Ellis, and, placing him on his right hand, said that he wished to compliment him, among all his companions, for his bravery and coolness, which had enabled him to have the inestimable gratification of saving the life of a fellow-creature, a school-fellow, and a friend; "and," added the Doctor, turning to Ernest, "I feel that you, Bracebridge, deserve not less credit for the generous way in which you have acted in the matter."

Ernest did not obtain less credit, and Ellis found himself in a very different position to what he had before held in the school.

Chapter Eight
Trials of Edward Ellis—A Game at Golf

The summer holidays were over, and nearly all the boys had collected at school. Most of them loved their homes; but really our school was so pleasant a place, that very few regretted returning to it. Several new boys came. One of them was called Andrew Barber. He was somewhat of a noisy overbearing character, and showed from the first a strong disposition to bully, and to quarrel with those who did not agree with him. He had, however, a box full of valuables, and a couple of bats, a set of wickets, and two first-rate footballs, and a set of hockey-sticks, so that with a pretty large class he was rather popular. Dawson very quickly made up to him, and Blackall condescended to allow him to cultivate his acquaintance. I write about him from recollection. Perhaps when he first came, the defects I recollect in his character may not have been so apparent. Bracebridge came back quiet and gentlemanly as ever. He had not been idle during the holidays. It is extraordinary how much he had seen, and done, and learned. He had been reading pretty hard both Greek and Latin, and Mathematics. He had made a tour through the manufacturing districts, the commencement of a series his father promised to take him, to show him the true source of English wealth. He had had a very pleasant yachting expedition, and had learned a good deal more about a vessel, and how to sail her, than he had before known. He had become a proficient in archery, and had filled a book full of sketches. Then he had read through a History of France, and made a synopsis of the work, as well as two or three biographies; and he had fished and ridden, and botanised and geologised, and seemed to have seen and talked with a great number of interesting people. Even Buttar, to whom he gave this account of himself, was surprised; and yet Buttar was one of the hardest readers in the school.

"How I can possibly get through so much, do you ask?" said Ernest. "Why, I will tell you. I am never idle. I always arrange beforehand what I want to do, and when I am at work, I give all my mind to that work, and never allow myself a moment to think of anything else. I have the gift, and a valuable one it is, I feel, of being able to concentrate my thoughts on the particular subject in which I am engaged, while I never allow them to be drawn off by anything else. I believe that my mind is so constituted that I should do this of my own accord; but my father has strongly urged on me the importance of the habit, and I accordingly practise it systematically. Whenever I find my mind wandering away from the subject on which I am engaged, I bring it back forcibly, just as if it were a truant, or a deserter from his colours. Some people can think of two things at the same moment; but my father says it is much better to think of one thing well at a time, as likewise to do one thing well; so, as you may have observed, I never attempt more. The consequence of this system is, that I gain some credit, more or less, for nearly everything I undertake."

"Indeed, you do," exclaimed Buttar enthusiastically. "I wish that I were like you; but my thoughts are constantly wool-gathering, whatever I am about. Now, Ellis is like you. He can keep his mind fixed on his work, whether mental or physical; and see how rapidly he has got on. I wonder when he is coming. It is extraordinary how I took to liking that fellow; I quite long to have him back among us."

"He wrote me word a few days ago that he expected to be here to-morrow. He tells me that he looks forward to coming back with great pleasure, though formerly it was always with pain and dread that he approached the school."

"I am glad of it," remarked Buttar. "There is a good deal in that fellow. I did not fancy so at first, but I am now convinced that he could beat most of us at anything he tries. He is a right honest good chap into the bargain. I hope that he will be here soon."

Poor Ellis would have had his spirits much raised, had he been aware how those whom he most esteemed among his schoolfellows talked of him.

The Doctor made a rule of examining all the boys when they returned after the holidays, to ascertain what progress they had made during the time. They had also a holiday task; but they all, except the very idle ones, found it a very easy matter.

Ernest found himself at once put up a class, and the very first day he went up, he took a good place in that class. Bracebridge could not be otherwise than a favourite with the Doctor, and with all the masters. Monsieur Malin especially liked him. He took so much pains to acquire French, and to pronounce it properly, and would repeat words over and over again till he had caught the right sound: then he at once understood the necessity of attending to the idioms of the language, and did not fancy that he was speaking French when he literally translated English into French, as did most of his companions. He moreover (and the Frenchman fully appreciated his delicacy) never allowed a smile to appear on his countenance, however absurd the mistake his master might make when speaking English.

Monsieur Malin was a great linguist, and took a pleasure in imparting a knowledge of his attainments to Ernest, who in that way began to study Italian, German, and Spanish, and found, to his surprise, a wonderful ease in picking them up. He always carried in his pocket a little book, in which he entered the words he wished to learn. When he walked out, he used to learn as many of these words as he could remember. One day he devoted to one language, one to another, and he found that he acquired all three with very little more exertion of mind than was necessary to learn one. He had learned Latin and Greek with his father in the same way, and at an early age he had had a very large vocabulary; indeed, there was scarcely a word in English which he could not readily translate into those languages when he came to school. In consequence, directly he learned a rule of grammar, he was able to apply it. Other boys, following the old system, went hammering and hammering away at their grammar without understanding it, and without being able to apply its rules, and lost their own time and patience, and that of their unfortunate masters.

However, I am not writing an account of the lesson hours of my schoolboy days, but rather of the play-hours. At the same time, I believe that they are more connected, and the importance of the latter is greater than some people are apt to suppose.

Bracebridge, Buttar, Bouldon, and Gregson were waiting to welcome Ellis when he got down from the coach, which passed through the village, half-a-mile from the house. They all, as they walked home, had a great deal to say, and a great deal to tell him. Each one was eager to describe where he had been, and what he had done in the holidays, and to know all that had happened to Ellis during the same period. They then had to tell him of all the changes which had occurred at the school.

"We have loads of new fellows," exclaimed Bouldon. "There is Milman, and Bishop, and Lloyd, and Taylor, and a fellow named Barber, and Cooper, and Lindsay; and there are five or six little fellows, whose names I don't know, and several more are coming, and they say two or three big fellows, who will be especially under the Doctor. A capital increase for one half, though, to be sure, several have left in the upper class. It shows, however, that the school is getting up."

"I know that I wish one fellow had left," said Buttar. "The school suffers in consequence of him. I wouldn't have a younger brother of mine come as long as he is here, that I know, to be bullied by him; to be kicked, and cuffed, and abused is bad enough, but to hear him talk—to have to listen to his foul language and stories, and all sorts of ideas which come into his abominable mind, is infinitely worse."

"You are right, Buttar," exclaimed Bracebridge, warmly. "That fellow Blackall and his tongue is a pest to society. If he simply bullied he could do very little harm; but, I say, what is the matter with Ellis? how pale and wretched he looks!"

"Bracebridge," said Ellis, coming round to him hurriedly, "who is this fellow Barber? Where does he come from? Do you know? Oh, tell me!"

"From Doctor Graham's at Hampstead. I know for certain. He told me so this morning," replied Bracebridge. "But, my dear fellow, what is the matter with you?"

"Oh, Bracebridge, you'll know too soon," Ellis gasped out. They had dropped a little behind the rest of the party. "Yet you'll not think ill of me. You'll not believe what he says, will you? Promise me that, without proof, without better proof than he can give. However it may appear, I am not guilty; indeed I am not."

"What are you talking about?" exclaimed Ernest, thinking that poor Ellis had gone mad. "I have never heard a word against you. Nobody has said anything of which you might complain. Had anyone, I would not believe him, and I am sure your other friends would not. Everybody who really knows you likes you, trusts you, and believes you to be an excellent fellow. You have taken some fancy into your head. Get rid of it, do."

"It is no fancy, indeed it is not," said Ellis, more calmly. "Perhaps I was wrong to say anything about the matter. I know that there is a French saying, *Qui s'excuse s'accuse*. I'll not excuse myself more than I have done to you. Should anything be said against me, I may rest sure of your friendship at all events. More I do not desire."

"Indeed, my dear fellow, you may. Whatever others may say, I will not believe you capable of doing anything of which you need be ashamed," said Ernest, warmly pressing his friend's hand.

"Thankyou, thank you!" replied Ellis; "you make me feel less miserable. Still your friendship will be sorely tried. Of that I am certain."

Ernest, during all the time Ellis was speaking, was debating in his mind whether or not he was labouring under some strange hallucination. "Whatever it is that you fear, do not talk about it," he said, as soon as Ellis had ceased speaking. "It will do no good, and can only make people think things which are very likely far from the truth. I would advise you not to talk even to me about it. Come and have a good game of cricket, or take a turn at fencing, or broadsword, or come and learn golf. There is a Scotch fellow, Macgreggor, who has come this half, and has undertaken to teach us, and it has become all the rage. It's a capital game for summer, and gives one plenty of exercise. One game or the other will soon knock all such notions out of your head."

Poor Ellis smiled faintly as he replied, "I am afraid not, but I will try to follow your advice. I will keep up my spirits, and perhaps matters will turn out better than I have a right to expect. I should like to learn golf, if you are doing so. I have once or twice seen it played at Blackheath, and I should think that it would suit me better even than cricket."

"That's right, that's right," said Ernest. "I say, you fellows, Ellis has a great fancy to join us in learning golf. He is like me; he dislikes the same routine of games year after year, however good they may be. We'll get Macgreggor to give us a lesson this evening. He seems to be a very good-natured fellow, though he is so big and old."

Macgreggor was a private pupil of the Doctor's, who had lately come to prepare for Cambridge. He was a good specimen of a Highlander, who had never before been south of the Tweed. He spoke strong Scotch, but not broad Scotch; that is, Lowland Scotch, with the full forcible expressions which are to be found in such abundance in the language. He was a truly honourable, high-spirited fellow, and most kind-hearted and generous. Had Blackall's misdeeds come to his notice he would have doubled him up, as our Yankee cousins would say, in no time. The rest of the party willingly agreed to the proposal. As soon as they reached the house, Ellis had to go and present himself to the Doctor, who was struck by his grave and pale countenance.

"My dear boy, what is the matter with you?" asked the Doctor kindly.

"Nothing, sir; nothing," was the answer. "It is not because I am sorry to come back to school, because I am very happy to find myself here."

The Doctor looked pleased, and he knew that Ellis was not a boy to make a set speech for the purpose of paying a compliment. He was glad to find also that he had not spent his holidays in idleness, but had studied quite as hard as was wise, and had read a number of useful works.

"You have done very well indeed," said the Doctor. "If every boy would follow your plan, and read attentively a good history during the holidays, they would become very fair historians at a small expense of labour, and they would save their time which is now, in most instances, so miserably squandered. Most boys during their school-life have from fourteen to sixteen holidays, each about six weeks in length—in fact they are idle for two whole years of the most valuable period of their existence for acquiring knowledge. During that time they might acquire a thorough knowledge of the history of the whole world."

Ellis thanked the Doctor for his advice, and said that he would follow it, and try to persuade some of his schoolfellows to do so likewise.

Dinner was over, so some was sent in for Ellis, and then he and his friends set off, with Macgreggor and several other boys, to the neighbouring heath, where they were to play golf.

Macgreggor had brought with him a supply of golf sticks or bats, which he generously distributed among those who wished to play. He soon fixed on Bracebridge as being likely to prove one of the best players, and told him that he should be his opponent on this occasion, although he had received only three or four lessons from him.

Ernest chose Buttar, Ellis, and Knowles, who played already very well, and Macgreggor took Bouldon, Gregson, and Jackson, another not bad player, considering that he had only just taken a golf stick in hand. As the ground over which they had to play was very irregular, they marked their three holes in a triangle about a quarter of a mile apart.

"See, Ellis, what a beautiful golf stick Mac has given me," said Bracebridge, showing his golf club. It was a formidable-looking weapon, about three feet long, formed of ash, curved and massive towards the end, which was made of a lump of beech, the handle being neatly covered with velvet. The thick end of the club was loaded with four ounces of lead, and faced with hard bone. Altogether no weapon could have been designed better adapted for hitting a small ball with a powerful stroke. The golf ball itself was very small, not bigger than a small hen's egg. It was formed of white leather, which had been soaked in water, and stuffed full of feathers by means of a stick till it became perfectly hard. It was afterwards covered with four coats of fine white paint to increase its hardness.

"You observe, Ellis," said Bracebridge, "the great object is to get a ball both hard, light, strong, easily seen, and which will not be the worse for a wetting. All these qualifications are possessed by this little fellow. Why golf has gone out so much in England, I don't know. Two centuries ago it was a fashionable game among the nobility; and we hear of Prince Henry, eldest son of James the First, amusing himself with it. In those days it was called 'bandy-ball,' on account of the bowed or bandy stick with which it was played. We now only apply the term bandy to legs. Still farther back, in the reign of Edward the Third, the game was played, and known by the Latin name of *Gambuca*. Now, are we all ready?"

Macgreggor, who had just come up with his companions, replied that all his party were ready to begin. Each side was accompanied by two boys, carrying a number of other clubs, one of which was of iron, and some were shorter, and some longer, to enable the players to strike the ball out of any hole, or rut, or other place in which it might have got.

"These extra clubs are called putters, and the men who carry them cads, or caddies," Ernest remarked to Ellis. "This heavy iron club is, you see, to knock the ball out of a rut, which would very likely cause the fracture of one of our wooden clubs. Now you understand all about the matter. Follow me; I'll tell you what to do when Macgreggor is not near; otherwise, though he is playing against us, he will advise us what to do."

The ball was thrown up, and the game began. Macgreggor had the first stroke. He sent the ball a considerable distance towards the nearest hole.

Ernest had then to strike his ball. If he struck it very hard it might go beyond the hole, which would have thrown him back; and if he did not send it as far as the ball first struck, Macgreggor's party would have had the right to strike twice before his would again strike the ball.

Ellis at first thought that there was nothing in the game, but he soon perceived that there was a good deal of science required, and that nothing but constant practical experience could make a person a good player. He, however, as Bracebridge was doing, gave his mind entirely to it, and by listening to the remarks made by Macgreggor, he learned the rules and many of the manoeuvres golf players are accustomed to practise. He very soon got deeply interested in the game, as did, indeed, all the party; and perhaps had they been asked at the moment what they considered one of the most delightful things to do all day, they would all have pronounced in favour of playing golf.

Golf is a most difficult game to describe. I should liken it, in some respects, to billiards on a grand scale, except that the balls have to be put into holes instead of pockets; that they have to be struck with the side instead of with the end of a club, and that there is no such thing as cannoning.

Bracebridge sent his ball very cleverly a few yards only beyond Macgreggor's, which called forth the latter's warm approval. Then Gregson struck the ball, and sent it but a very short distance. Buttar next sent theirs nearly up to the hole, and Bouldon then going on, and being afraid of going beyond the hole, sent it not so far, as Buttar had struck their ball.

"Two, two," shouted Bracebridge. "Now, Knowles, hit very gingerly, and let me see if I cannot send our ball in."

Knowles rolled the ball within a few feet of the hole, and Ernest, who, in consequence of Bouldon's miss, was now allowed to strike, guided by his correct and well-practised eye, sent it clean into the hole, to the great delight of Macgreggor, who was pleased at having so apt a pupil.

Bracebridge now took his ball out of the hole, and struck it on. Macgreggor, however, was not long in catching him up, but Tom Bouldon was a great drawback to Macgreggor. He had not calmness enough to play the game well. He was continually missing the ball, or sending it beyond the hole, while Macgreggor, and Bracebridge, and Ellis especially, always considered how far it was necessary to send it, and took their measures accordingly.

Few games show the character of a person more than does that of golf, although all, more or less, afford some index to those who are attentively looking on. A boy, when playing, should endeavour to keep a watch over himself as much as on all other occasions, and he should especially endeavour to practise that very important duty of restraining his temper. Boys are too apt to fancy that they may say and do what they like, and often they abuse each other, and make use of language of which, it is to be hoped, they would be ashamed when out of the playground.

While the game was going on, and drawing near its completion, Bracebridge being ahead, a number of boys came out to see what was going forward. From their remarks, there was not much chance of the game becoming popular. There was not enough activity and bustle in it to please them. It was not to be compared for a moment with cricket, or rackets, or football, or even hockey.

Among the spectators were Blackall and Dawson, and the new fellow, Barber. His eye was ranging over the heath. Ernest and his party were then at a distance, playing up towards the last hole.

"Well, to my mind, after all, it is only like a game of marbles, played with a little leathern ball instead of a stone, and a stick instead of one's knuckles," sneered Blackall.

Dawson echoed the sentiment. "How that fellow Bracebridge can find anything to like in it, I do wonder," he remarked. "In Macgreggor, who has been brought up to it, it is a different affair."

"Hollo! who is that fellow?" exclaimed Barber, as the players drew near.

"Which do you mean?" said Dawson. "That natty-looking fellow, who is taking the ball? He's a genius; and if you were to take him at his own valuation, there is not such another fellow in the school, or perhaps in the world."

Dawson never lost an opportunity of having a fling at Bracebridge, who had passed so rapidly by him in the school, and had beat him at all their games.

"No, no; I mean a lanky-limbed, long-faced fellow, who looks as if his face was made of butter. I think I know him," said Barber.

"Oh, you mean that miserable wretch Ellis," snarled Blackall. "He's a fellow born to be licked. He is of no other earthly use. I'll give you leave to thrash him as much as you like; it will save me the trouble, and I shall be much obliged to you."

It might well save Blackall trouble; for had he ventured to touch Ellis, he knew full well that he should have got into it.

"Yes; if Ellis is his name, I am certain it is him," observed Barber, as Ellis drew nearer. "He was at my last school, and I wish you fellows joy of him."

"Why, do you know anything against him?" asked Blackall, eagerly, thinking that he might have the satisfaction of annoying Bracebridge, and Ellis's other friends.

"Oh! you know we never say anything against a fellow out of school, however bad he may be," said Barber, looking virtuous. "All I can say is, he is not the sort of chap I should choose for my associate. He may have altered, you know. Few fellows remain always the same. When I see a fellow get into rows, smash windows, screw off knockers, and show that he has some spirit, I always have hopes of him; but that fellow was always a sneak, and, in the end, proved something a great deal worse. I'll not say anything more about him."

"Oh, I wish you would!" said Blackall. "If there is anything against a fellow, I like to know it. I am rather particular in my company; and though I do not associate with him now, I might be tempted to do so if he came back some week with a box full of grub, or with anything else worth having."

This sally of wit was fully appreciated by his auditors, who laughed heartily, or I should rather say loudly, at it.

Poor Ellis meantime had been so intent on watching the game, that he had not observed their approach, till the voices reached his ear. He looked up, and then he saw Barber watching him, with a sneer on his countenance. He recognised him at once as his old school-fellow.

Bracebridge was standing near. "I'll go and speak with him at once," he said quietly, "It may be that he will not think it necessary to repeat the vile story that was told of me at our former school. If I pass him by as a stranger, it will make him more inclined to think ill of me."

Ellis acted according to the impulse of the moment. He walked up to Barber, and, putting out his hand, said, "Don't you remember me, Barber!"

"Perfectly," said Barber, with great emphasis, and a sneer on his lips. "One remembers people sometimes whom one would rather forget."

"What do you mean, Barber?" said Ellis. "You are not so cruel, so unjust, as—"

"Put what construction you like on my meaning," answered Barber. "I am a straightforward fellow. I say what I think; and of all the characters I have ever met, I hate most that of a canting hypocrite. I never trust such an one. You know best what such a fellow is capable of doing."

Ellis stood by listening calmly, but not unmoved, to this cutting speech. He turned pale and red, and seemed to have difficulty in drawing his breath. He looked for a moment imploringly at Barber, but saw only a sneer on his countenance; so gulping down all the feelings which were rising in his bosom, and which, had he allowed them to break forth, would not have tended to harmony, he turned away and rejoined Bracebridge, who was waiting for him.

"There he goes," sneered Barber. "Just like him. Had any fellow spoken to me as I did to him, I would have knocked him over with my golf club; but he did not even move his hand as if he would have struck me."

After hearing these remarks, Blackall, Dawson, and other boys of that set, thought Barber a very fine spirited fellow, and came to the conclusion that Ellis was not only a regular sneak, but that he was probably a convicted thief, or liar, or something fully as bad, if not worse. He said nothing after rejoining his friends, but his spirits sank lower than Bracebridge had ever before seen them. He seemed incapable even of doing his ordinary lessons in the way he had been accustomed to get through them. Even the Doctor and the masters observed the change. By degrees, too, many of the boys with whom he had been accustomed to join in their various games began to look shy at him. One declined to play with him, and then another, and another, till at last he found that he was cut by the whole school, with the exception of the three or four friends who generally sided with Bracebridge—Buttar, Bouldon, Gregson, and little Eden. Poor fellow! it was a sore trial. Whatever the fault of which he had been guilty, he had long ago heartily repented of it. Of that, at all events, there could be no doubt. It seemed hard that he should be compelled to suffer, supposing even that he was guilty, when a new sphere was open to him; and the better disposed boys, even though they mostly went with the tide, could not help feeling that Barber had acted in a very ungenerous way in bringing tales from one school to another, and in injuring the character of one who had always proved himself so harmless and kind-hearted a fellow.

Bracebridge did not hesitate to show his opinion of Barber on all occasions, and took every opportunity of marking his regard for Ellis, and in showing his disbelief of the tales current against him. Thus the last half of the year drew on, and winter was once more approaching.

Chapter Nine
An Attempt to Introduce
Fagging—A Game at Hockey

The half-year sped on much as usual. Not a gleam of sunshine burst forth to dispel the clouds which hung lowering over the fair fame of poor Ellis. He was either too proud or too indifferent as to what was said of him to take any notice of the various tales—different versions of the same story—flying about the school to his discredit. Now and then Bracebridge heard of them, but he invariably replied that he believed them to be utterly false, and he always treated the boy who ventured to begin to narrate them to him with the scorn which a tale-bearer deserves. The tales at last reached the ears of the masters, but in so indefinite a form that they could take no notice of them, much less report them to the Doctor; but they had the bad effect of making them look upon poor Ellis as a black sheep, and of inducing them to treat him with suspicion. Wrong motives were assigned to all he did, and, with one exception, no one spoke kindly or encouragingly to him. The exception was Monsieur Malin. Ellis's clever contrivance with the kite and carriage had won his regard; and though, to be sure, his reasoning might have been very incorrect, he could not fancy that so ingenious a boy could have been guilty of the conduct alleged against him, and which had brought him into such general disrepute. He talked the subject over with Bracebridge, who was delighted to find that Ellis had so powerful a friend. Monsieur Malin determined, therefore, to support Ellis. He called him up one day, and asked him if he would like to learn French.

Ellis said, "Yes, of him; if he could get leave."

"Well, if you cannot get leave, I will teach you myself in the play-hours, or at any odd times. You stay in so much, and play so little with the other boys, that you will not mind that, I know," he said, in a kind encouraging voice. "You will learn soon, I know, and then we will walk together, and talk French, and you will learn more rapidly than any one else."

"Thank you, sir! indeed, thank you!" said poor Ellis, the tears coming into his eyes. "It is very kind to take so much trouble with a person like me. I will do whatever you tell me."

"Then write home, and get leave to learn, and I will tell you what you shall do in the meantime," replied the French master. "Get into your head as large a vocabulary of words as you can collect. Put down in a little pocket-book the French and English of everything you can think of. Thus: write down, a boy, a man, a book, a desk, and I will show you how to pronounce them properly. Here is a book; accept it from me; I got it on purpose for you. Now write down a boy; now the French, garçon. The *c* you hear is soft. Roll the *r* well in your mouth. Repeat it frequently." Monsieur Malin made him write down numerous other words, and repeated them over to him frequently till he had caught their exact sounds. "Now, my boy, you have learned your first French lesson," he observed. "Every day add as many words as these to your vocabulary. Begin with the substantives; go on to the adjectives, next the verbs; then study the construction of the language; the simple rules of grammar; and lastly, in the same manner that you have learned single words, collect the idioms of the language. Read constantly aloud, and learn by heart interesting portions of modern French writings especially the speeches of the best orators of the present day, and I can promise you that in a very short time you will become a very fair French scholar."

Ellis saw the wisdom of Monsieur Malin's advice, and implicitly followed it. Bracebridge helped him, and they in a short time were able to converse together. In the meantime Ellis got leave to learn French, and some of the boys were very much surprised, and rather indignant, to find him put in one of the upper classes.

"That's the fellow who pretended that he did not know French, and has all the time been listening to us, and overhearing all we said," remarked Blackall, whose own knowledge of the language was so limited that, at all events, it would have puzzled a Frenchman to have comprehended him. "It's just like the sneak," he continued. "I wonder how a chap like Bracebridge can patronise him, or how a big fellow like Lemon can condescend to speak to him."

Though these remarks, as it was intended they should, reached the ears both of Ernest and Lemon, they took no notice of them, and thus they did Ellis no further harm. It is very sad that I should not have to recount the pleasant sayings and doings of my schoolfellows; but as in the world the worst actions of people often come most prominently forward, so they do at school, and generally make the deepest impression. I know, however, that even at this time there were many pleasant things said, and amusing things done; that there was much good fellowship among us; that we entered into our games with thorough heartiness; that we made very satisfactory progress in our studies, and were generally happy and contented. Indeed, the school was thoroughly well-conducted and ably ruled. The dark spots I have been picturing arose entirely from the bad tempers, dispositions, and ill-conduct of those ruled. So it is with this world at large. It is admirably ordered, beautifully fashioned, ruled with unbounded love, regularity, and justice. Men, and men alone, have made all the blots and stains to be found in it; they have caused all the irregularities and disorders which abound; all the misery, all the suffering, all the wretchedness; we see they have themselves and themselves only to blame; that is to say, man alone is at fault; man, and sin which man introduced, beguiled by Satan. But up, boys! Do not suppose that you are to yield to this state of things; to say that so you find them, and that so you will let them be. No; far from that. You are sent into the world to fight against them, to overcome them, to strive with Satan, the prince of sin and lies, and all abominations, with all your might and main. It is a glorious contest; it is worth living for, if we did but understand it aright. The knights who went out, as we are told of old, armed cap-à-pie, to do battle with enchanters, and dragons, and monsters of all sorts, had not half so glorious, so difficult, so perilous a contest to engage in. The writers who invented those fables had, I suspect, a pretty clear notion of what is the true destiny of man. The enchanters were the spirits of evil; their necromancies the works of Satan; the dragons and monsters, the ills, the difficulties, the obstacles to all good works which have to be overcome. It was not the fashion to speak out great truths plainly in those days, as it has happily become at the present time; and so philosophers who held them wrapped them up in fables and allegories, the true import of which only the wisest and most sagacious could comprehend. The great truth that all men are sent into this world to work, to fight, to strive with might and main, the Doctor tried to impress on his pupils. He found it difficult, however, to make them understand the matter. Many of them thought that they knew better than he did on that subject. Some of them had been told at home, by ignorant servants or injudicious friends, that they were born heirs to good fortunes; that they were to go to school, and be good boys, and get through their lessons as well as they could, and then they would go to Oxford or Cambridge, because most gentlemen of any pretension went there; and then that they would be able to live at home and amuse themselves for the rest of their lives. Of course, such boys thought that what the Doctor was saying could have nothing at all to do with them, and could only refer to the children of poor people, who had nothing to give them. The Doctor, suspecting what was in their thoughts, surprised them very much by propounding the doctrine that no one was exempt from the rule; that all mankind, from the sovereign on his throne to the peasant in the field, are born to labour—to labour with the head or to labour with the hands, often with both; or if not, strictly speaking, with the hands, at all events with the mind and body.

"And what, think you, is the labour all men ought to engage in? What is the great present object of labour?" asked the Doctor. "Why, I reply, to do good to our fellow-creatures, to ameliorate their condition by every means in our power."

No boys took in these truths more eagerly than did Bracebridge and Ellis. They talked them over and over, and warmed with the glorious theme. To the former they were not new. His father had propounded the same to him long ago, but the Doctor's remarks gave them additional strength and freshness.

"It is grand, indeed," exclaimed Ernest, "to feel what victories we have to achieve, what enemies to overthrow; that if we do our duty we can never be entirely defeated; and that, though success may be delayed, we must be victorious at last; that there can be no hanging down of the hands, no lassitude, no idleness, no want of occupation through life, no want of excitement. I don't care what grumblers may say; I maintain, with my father, that this is a very glorious world to live in, with all its faults; and still more should we be grateful that we are placed in it, when we remember that it is the stepping-stone to eternity."

Ernest was, perhaps, somewhat beyond his years in his remarks, but it must be remembered that he was an unusual boy, and that there were not many like him. Still he was but a boy. Anybody observing him would probably have remarked that he was a good-looking, intelligent boy, but might have failed to discover any super-excellencies in him. Indeed I think that I have before remarked that he owed his success at school to the fact, that all the talents he possessed by nature had been judiciously cultivated, and allowed a full and free growth. Certainly no boy stood higher in the estimation both of his master and schoolfellows. He could not help discovering this, and he resolved by all means to maintain and deserve their good opinion. He had sometimes a difficult task in keeping to his resolution.

I have said that Blackall for some weeks had appeared to be much less dictatorial and inclined to bully; but by degrees his former habits returned with greater force, from having been put under some restraint for a time. Ellis and Eden, and even Bouldon and Buttar, came in for a share of his ill-treatment; so did a new boy, John Dryden by name, a sturdy, independent little fellow, who, for his size, was as strong as he was brave, but, of course, could not compete with a boy of so much greater bulk and weight.

A considerable number of fellows vowed that they would stand this conduct no longer; yet what could they do? Blackall alone might have been managed; but several big fellows had united with him, and had taken it into their heads that they should like to introduce fagging. They got, indeed, two or three fellows—Dawson, Barber, and others—to undertake to be fags, just to set the system going, those young gentlemen hoping very soon to become masters themselves. They talked very big about the matter; they thought it would be a very fine thing: their school was first-rate as it was, and if fagging were introduced it would be fully equal to any public school. Of course, the affair was to be kept a great secret. There could be no doubt that the Doctor would approve of it ultimately, but at first he might be startled; though he never hesitated to introduce any alterations which were improvements, he might possibly look upon fagging without that reverence which it deserved as a time-honoured institution. He could not fail to acknowledge that fagging was a very good thing; but then his school was not a public school, however first-rate it might be as a private establishment; and he might not wish to make it like a public school. Thus the important subject was discussed for some time, till at last it was decided that it would be wiser to begin quietly, at the same time in due form. The big fellows who had resolved to be the masters determined to draw up a paper, which the intended fags were to sign, agreeing to do duty and to serve their masters as fags, according to the custom established at all public and first-rate schools. Barber, Dawson, and other advocates of the system, signed the precious document willingly enough, and they managed to get some twenty other boys to do the same.

But when it was shown to Buttar and Bouldon, they turned it over and over, and asked what it meant.

"Oh, don't you know?" exclaimed Dawson. "It's a plan we have got up for becoming a public school."

"I'll tell you what," answered Buttar, bursting into a fit of laughter, "I look upon the affair as a bit of arrant tom-foolery; and so you may tell the donkeys who drew it up."

Dawson grew very red; but he had a respect for Buttar's knuckles, and so he held his tongue. Bouldon had, meantime, recognised Blackall's handwriting, and having a considerable amount of contempt for those whose signatures were attached, he exhibited it in an unmistakable, though certainly an unrefined manner, by holding up the paper, and spitting into the middle of it. Then he folded it up, and crammed it into Dawson's pocket. Dawson and he had had a set-to fight a little time before, and though Dawson was the biggest fellow of the two, he had ultimately declined continuing the combat. The action performed by Bouldon was equivalent to a declaration of war to the knife with Blackall and all the big fellows who supported the system he wished to introduce. Dawson turned redder than ever, and looked very fierce at him; but Tom closed his mouth, planted his feet firmly on the ground, and doubling his fists, said—

"You'd better not attempt it, Dickey; you know me now."

Dawson did know him, and so he blustered out—

"You're a beastly fellow, that I know; and so I'll go and tell Blackall what you say."

"Go, Dickey, and say I sent you," cried Bouldon; and, undaunted by the threat which had been uttered, he bestowed a parting kick of very considerable force on the portion of Dickey's body then turned towards him. Dawson ran off, vowing vengeance.

"You shouldn't have done that, Bouldon," said Buttar, who was a very gentlemanly, refined fellow. "The actions were expressive, and could leave no manner of doubt as to what our course of action must be; but perhaps we might have succeeded better had we left them in doubt, and waited till they commence operations."

"I dare say you are right, Buttar," said Bouldon; "but, in truth, all my English spirit was roused within me at the preposterous notion of those few big fellows proposing all of a sudden to make slaves of the rest of the school. However, what is to be done now?"

"Let us go and talk to Bracebridge, and hear what he says," said Buttar.

They soon found Bracebridge, and told him all that had occurred. He was just as indignant as Tom was, and he could not help laughing at the way in which he had exhibited his feelings, though he agreed with Buttar that a less demonstrative mode of proceeding might have been wiser. He was decidedly of opinion that immediate steps should be taken to put a stop to the proceedings of the big fellows, and that a counter-resolution should be drawn up, and sent round for the signature of those boys who had resolved not in any way to submit to fagging. He and Buttar immediately went into the school-room, and drew up the paper which they considered met the object. It was very temperate, and couched in the most simple language, as such documents always should be to be effectual. It ran, as far as I remember, much in the following words:—

"We, the undersigned, understanding that an attempt is being made by some of the big boys to introduce a system of fagging into the school, bind ourselves to resist such a proceeding by every means in our power, and under no consideration to obey any boy who may order any of us to fag for him."

"That will do," observed Bracebridge. "The sentence might be better rounded, but the document is short and explicit. We will see what effect it will have. Let Dawson have a sight of it before it is generally signed. Here, you and I will sign it, to show from whom it emanates. They will not begin to try on their tricks upon us, I suspect. They will not know who else has signed it; and we will put the little fellows up how to act, as circumstances may show us to be most advisable."

"Capital!" exclaimed Buttar, affixing his signature in a clear bold hand to the document. "Would it not be better to tell Lemon what we have done?"

"I think not," said Ernest. "The resolution emanates from us, so let us carry it out. There is nothing like independence and freedom of action to ensure success. Lemon will not wish to make anybody fag for him; but being a big fellow, he may not see the matter in the same light we do. If we bravely resist the attempt, he is much more likely to assist us in crushing it at the end, than if we were to go whining to him now for aid and advice."

Buttar agreed in this point also with Ernest, and undertook to let Dawson immediately have a look at the document. Dawson said he should like to show it to some of the big fellows.

"Catch a weasel asleep, and draw his teeth," answered Buttar. "No, no, Dickey! You may take a copy of it in pencil, and show it to anybody you like. You may say also, that all the school, with the exception of a few miserable sneaks, like some who shall be nameless, will sign it and stick by it. And now, just go and tell the fellows what you have seen."

Off went Dawson with the copy of the protest to his masters. They laughed scornfully.

"That upstart, conceited young monkey, Bracebridge, is at the bottom of all mischief," observed Blackall; and the opinion was echoed by two or three other fellows.

"I'll tell you what," said Blackall; "the only way will be to begin fagging at once, and to crush this proposed rebellion in the bud. We must parcel out the boys of the lower classes, so that each of us may have four or five fags a-piece. You see we have already each of us got a willing fag. They shall be head fags, and assist to keep the rest in order. We'll tell them that, and then they will help us to bring the rest under subjection."

Blackall's plan was willingly assented to by the rest of the big boys who had entered into this conspiracy against the liberties of their younger schoolfellows; and minor details being arranged, they considered everything ripe for carrying out their plans. All this time neither the Doctor nor masters suspected that anything out of the way was taking place. During the school hours matters went on in their ordinary routine. Some of the boys, who had been thinking over what was to be done, were less attentive than usual, and had more faults in their exercises. Games were got up and carried on by the boys with their accustomed spirit. Hockey and football had now come in. The Doctor did not prohibit any games, but he insisted that all should be played with good temper; and a few he only allowed to be played in the presence of a master. Hockey was one of these, and consequently it was not often played, except when a large number could join in it together. A great game of hockey was to be played one Saturday afternoon in November. Blackall came forward as the chief on one side. He called over the names of a number of boys, but only a few of the younger ones joined him. He remarked that they were entirely Dawson's companions. Another big fellow stood up to lead on the opposite side, but so few consented to play that he was obliged to throw up his leadership. Then Bracebridge, urged by several standing round him, stepped forward, and he instantly had forty or fifty boys ranged under him. Those who had previously ranged themselves under the other big fellow, Haddon, went over to Blackall.

The sides were now more equal, but still Blackall had not enough on his side. He cried out for followers, but still no one would go over to him. Bracebridge had at last to send off some of his side to make both parties equal. There were thus about forty on each side. Everybody knows what a hockey-stick is like. It is a tough fellow, made of oak or crab-apple tree, and turned up at the end in a crook, flattened somewhat at the convex side. It is a formidable weapon, and it is very disagreeable to receive a blow from it on the shins. In some places a cork bung is used, but I have always seen and played with a light ball made on purpose, and covered with leather. We were very particular at Grafton Hall about our hockey balls. Though late in the year, the weather was fine, so we played in the cricket-field. It was a fine wide extent. A line drawn twenty yards in advance of the hedge on either side formed the respective boundaries. It was nearly due north and south. Ernest's party were on the north side, and their goal consequently on the south side of the field. Bracebridge and Blackall tossed up to settle which side was to begin. "Heads!" cried Ernest. The shilling came down with the head up. It was considered low by the big boys to employ halfpence on such occasions. Blackall looked daggers at his opponent. Bracebridge took the ball, and placed it about a third of the distance away from his line. His side were arranged behind and on either hand of him. He planted his feet firmly, and lifting his stick above his head, cried "Play!" and, looking first at the point to which he intended to send it, gave a steady blow to the ball. Blackall and his side watched its approach, and rushed forward "to take it up," or, in other words, to impede its progress, and to send it back in the direction whence it had come. They were boldly met by Ernest's party, who once more "took up" the ball and drove it energetically back.

All Ernest's party were young boys. Few were more than a year or two older than he was, and scarcely any were taller or more active; indeed, he was the acknowledged best player of his set. On Blackall's side, on the contrary, were a number of big fellows, and all those who had undertaken to act as fags, as well as other hangers-on and chums of the big fellows, patronised especially by them because they were well supplied by injudicious friends at home with hampers of cakes and game, and hams and tongues. I've heard people say, "I'll send poor Tom a basket of good things, because it will enable him to gain the friendship of some of the bigger boys." Now, I will tell those silly friends that it will do no such thing. It will make some of the worst boys make up to him as long as his grub lasts, or while they think that he is likely to get any more; but they will do him much more harm than good, and their friendship he will not get. No; send a boy to school fitted as much as he can be, and let him win friends and work his way onward by his own intrinsic merits; but never let him think of buying favour with gifts of any sort. But we are in the middle of a game of hockey. It was, however, necessary to explain the class of boys who were ranged on either side. Those hockey-sticks looked formidable weapons as they were flourished about in the hands of the opposing parties. Again Blackall's party met the ball; a dozen hockey-sticks were at it, and one boy, calling off the others, struck it so clear a blow that he nearly sent it up to the goal across Ernest's line. However, he, Buttar, Bouldon, and some other of the most fearless and active boys rushed at it with their sticks, regardless of all the blows aimed at them by their opponents, and drove it back again into the middle of the ground. Then on they flew to drive it back still farther. Both parties met in the centre. There was a fierce tussle. The hockey-sticks kept striking each other, but none struck the ball. Blackall had gone farther back to catch the ball, should it be driven past the front rank of his party. Ernest had retired behind his friends for the same purpose. His eye, however, never left the ball. He saw a stick uplifted which he thought would strike it. So it did, and the ball came flying towards him. His quick eye saw it coming, and with unerring aim he struck it over the heads of both parties, who, not knowing what had become of it, broke asunder, and enabled him to pass between them. He reached the neighbourhood of the ball at the same moment that Blackall, having seen it coming, got close up to it. They eyed the ball, and they eyed each other for some moments; their eyes flashed fire.

"Out of my way, you rebellious young scamp!" shouted Blackall, irritated by what he considered Ernest's daring coolness. Ernest did not even look at him, but threw himself into a position to strike the ball. His eye was at the same time on Blackall's stick. He saw him lift it to strike, not the ball, but him. He had not learned the use of the single-stick for nothing, and throwing himself back, he warded off the blow, and then, quick as lightning, struck the ball, and sent it past his cowardly opponent. Blackall, not in the least ashamed of himself, attempted to repeat the blow while Ernest was unable to defend himself; but before his stick descended another actor had come into the field. It was Ellis, who had been close at hand, and now springing forward, he interposed his own stick, and saved his friend from the effects of the blow, drawing, of course, all Blackall's rage upon himself. Had any body seen his countenance, they could not have failed to observe the smile of satisfaction which lighted it up as Blackall showered heaps of virulent abuse on his head.

"Go on, I don't fear you; remember that," said Ellis quietly; and then hurried on, in the hopes of assisting Ernest to drive the ball on to the goal. The keen eye of Monsieur Malin, who was the master on duty on that afternoon, had observed this little piece of by-play. He noted it, but said nothing at the time. It required all Ernest's activity and the energetic support of his party to make head against the big, strong fellows of the opposite side. When he had very nearly driven the ball home to the goal, several of them threw themselves before him, and drove it some way back again; but Buttar, Bouldon, Gregson, and some others had now come up, and even little Eden rushed heroically in to stop its course and to drive it back, so that Ernest might once more get it within the power of his unerring stick. The big fellows of Blackall's party had rushed on, separating widely, and not observing, or rather regarding, little Eden, whom had they seen they would not have supposed daring enough to attempt to hit the ball. He did not hit it very far, certainly; but yet his stroke was one of the most important which had been given, for it enabled Tom Bouldon to send it up very nearly to the goal. Ernest saw it coming. He sprang forward; and almost before it had stopped, his stick had caught it and sent it triumphantly over the line. The big fellows were astonished when they saw how and by whom they had been defeated. Blackall especially was enraged.

"That young scamp, Bouldon, and that little shrimp, Eden, ought not to be allowed to play. There is no guarding against their sneaking, underhand ways," he observed. I believe, indeed, he made use of still more opprobrious epithets, with which I do not wish to defile my pages. Even some of his own side laughed at his anger, but still no one thought of rebuking him.

"Never mind, we'll beat them well the next turn," answered Rodwell, a big, good-natured fellow, on his side. "Now, young Bracebridge, you, sir, look out for yourself. We are not going to let you run over the course in this way again."

"Oh, we are not afraid of you; we shall do our best to win again, at all events," said Ernest, taking up the ball, and walking off with it to his side of the ground. "Now look out, old fellows."

"What's that the impudent young scamp says?" exclaimed Blackall. "We'll pay him and his sneaking set off before long, so let him look out."

Ernest heard what was said, but took no notice of the remark. He appeared to be entirely absorbed in considering in what direction he should drive the ball. He eyed the position of the various players, both on the other side and on his own. He called Bouldon up to him, and whispered various directions to him. Bouldon ran off, and immediately several of his side changed their places.

"Ah! that boy was born to become a general," observed Monsieur Malin, who was looking on at the game with deep interest.

The opposite side were rather astonished. They were not accustomed to so systematic a way of playing, still less to see directions issued by one boy so implicitly obeyed by others. They could not make it out. Ernest lifted up his stick, and struck the ball. Off it flew in a direction away from all the best players on the opposite side, but some of the most active of his party ran on, and hitting it before them, one after the other, drove it right through the ranks of their opponents. So quickly did one striker succeed the other, that none of Blackall's boys could get a stroke. He ran to the rescue, but this was one of the many occasions, as he frequently found to his cost, when mere animal strength could avail but little. The ball was carried on, struck rapidly past him, followed up by relays of Ernest's friends, and finally sent by Buttar, accompanied by a loud cheer from all his side, over the boundary. Such a victory could not have been expected under ordinary circumstances, had even the big boys been the conquerors, but the latter were doubly astounded, till Rodwell sang out—

"Bravo, young Bracebridge! You have had a lucky chance, but we'll lick you soundly next time, so look out."

"Chance! yes, it was only chance," repeated Blackall, glad to find a plausible excuse for his defeat. A third round was to be played, but the younger party were so cocky that they proposed having four rounds. To this, of course, the others were too glad to consent, under the belief that they could at all events make it a drawn battle; while Ernest's friends gloried in the hopes of beating their big opponents three to one.

Blackall having observed that Ernest placed his men according to a certain plan, thought he would do the same. He, therefore, with not a small amount of pretentious formality, ordered the boys on his side to look out in different directions, and to follow a certain course. Some went where they were told, but others proceeded to where they themselves considered that they should be better placed, and instead of obeying the orders of their leader, acted according to their own judgment, which, to do them justice, was fully as good as that of Blackall. Bracebridge watched the proceedings of his opponents, and smiled as he pointed them out to Buttar. He very soon made his own arrangements. Blackall thought that he was going to act precisely as he had done in the previous game. He had no such intentions. Handing the ball to Bouldon, he told him to strike it up, while he, Buttar, Ellis, Gregson, and several others went scattering up before him. The big fellows looked at him, and gathered thickly in his front. They took no notice of Ellis, who was away to the right. Bouldon looked towards Bracebridge; then, turning suddenly, struck the ball in the direction of Ellis, who followed it up ably as it came by him, and turned it towards Buttar. Buttar had in the meantime broken through the big fellows and though several of them, hurrying on, tried by reiterated blows to stop it, he carried it once more successfully up to the goal. Blackall and some of his party literally stamped with rage at the idea of being beaten three times running by the younger boys, "At all events, that puppy Bracebridge had nothing to do with the affair this time," he exclaimed, showing the feeling which animated him.

Ernest's party cheered again and again—they could not help it. Both sides agreed to play out the fourth game. Ernest managed his friends equally well as at first, but his opponents were more alive to his tactics. The battle was very hotly contested; several times he got the ball nearly to the goal, and it was again driven back. This game had already taken as long to play as the other three—defeat would be almost as honourable to the younger party as victory—they kept up the game by sheer activity and good play; not that the bigger boys played ill, but they wanted combination and a good leader. Blackall had now completely lost his head and his temper. Once or twice when Bracebridge came near he felt very much inclined to strike him, but Ernest watched his eye, and was very quickly out of his way. At last, Blackall found himself with the ball directly before him; he lifted up his stick, expecting to strike it right ahead up to the goal. He looked at the point before him to which he intended to send the ball, and he looked at his stick, and he looked at the ball, but he did not look on one side—had he done so, he would have perceived Bracebridge springing along with his stick ready to strike. Strike he did too, and away flew the ball out of Blackall's very clutches. Blackall's rage now burst forth—twice he struck Ernest across the shins, and though the latter managed to break the force of the blows, he was much hurt. Then the bully lifted up his stick and struck Ernest on the arm more than once. He was about to repeat the blow on his victim's head, and the effect would have been very serious, when he felt his own ears pulled lustily.

"Ah, you big coward—is dat de vay you play your games? I'm ashamed dat any boy at de school vare I teach should behave so," exclaimed the voice of Monsieur Malin. "If I do not take you instantly before de Doctor it is because it is too bad to tell him of, so I will pull your ears myself. Bah!"

Right heartily did the good-natured French master tug away at the bully's ears till they were red to the very roots. He knew that he himself was doing what in spirit was prohibited, for no master was allowed to strike or punish a boy. He might have argued that pulling the ears was not striking, and that punishing meant flogging or caning. Blackall on another occasion might have resisted, but now he felt that he had been guilty of so cowardly an action that no one would support him, so he submitted tamely to the infliction.

"Go, get out of de ground, you shall not play—you are not worthy of it," continued the French master, pulling him away by the before-spoken-of appendages of his head.

Meantime the games went on. Ernest, though much hurt, tried to exhibit no symptoms of his suffering. He and his friends strove hard, but the big fellows resolved not to lose this last game as they had done the others, and finally by strenuous exertions drove the ball up to the goal. Never was a game at hockey at our school more hotly contested. A great deal came out of it.

Chapter Ten
The Bully's Punishment

That game of hockey caused a great deal of ill-feeling among the less generous and most ill-disposed of the big fellows towards the younger ones who had so thoroughly beaten them. Blackall bullied more than ever, and several others imitated his example. They had also already begun to carry out their precious scheme of fagging. Some of the little fellows thought it very good fun at first to obey a bigger one, provided he did not order them to do anything very difficult, or likely to bring punishment down upon themselves. Grown bold by impunity, the faggers resolved to divide the boys of the classes below them among themselves as fags by lots. Of course it was the very worst plan that could have been devised; indeed, tyrants generally do form very clumsy and very bad schemes for keeping those weaker than themselves in subjection. The younger boys might willingly enough have served older friends who had been kind to them and had protected them, but it was preposterous to suppose that without force they would obey any big boy who might choose to order them. It was some time before this scheme became known to Ernest Bracebridge and his friends. As he never listened to the tales and tittle-tattle of the school—indeed, he found that the current stories were generally absurd exaggerations of the truth— he might have remained some time longer ignorant, had not Bouldon come to him one afternoon, after school, in a state of great indignation, saying that Blackall had called him up and ordered him to go to a shop two miles off, to buy him a tongue, some rolls, and other eatables.

"When I expostulated, he had the audacity to tell me that I should clean his shoes if he wished it," exclaimed Tom, with a savage laugh. "And what do you think? that I was his fag, that I was awarded to him, and that he intended to work me thoroughly? I asked him by whom I was awarded to him? He replied, by a vote of my seniors and betters; and that if I did not work willingly I should be compelled to serve him by force. I don't remember what I said at first—I know that he called me an impudent young scamp for my pains; I concluded by telling him that I should consult you and Buttar and other fellows, and that if you consented to be fags, I should not have a word to say."

"You were perfectly right—I am glad you said so," observed Ernest. "Find Buttar, and Ellis, and Gregson, and we'll talk the matter over. We'll mention the subject to Lemon; I know full well that he will not wish to fag any boy, yet perhaps for the sake of a quiet life he may not be inclined to interfere with the plans of the other big fellows. However, I do not want him to interfere; whatever we do, we should do ourselves; fortunately, we are well prepared for the emergency. We number fifty fellows staunch and true. Go round and tell them to be prepared—that something is going to happen. That will put them on the alert. When Blackall finds that you have not obeyed his orders, and that he will have to go supperless to bed, he will probably attack you. Tell Eden to watch you—never for a moment to lose sight of you, and directly he sees Blackall attack you, to come up and tell me—I'll have all our fellows ready, and we'll rush to the rescue."

"Oh, excellent," exclaimed Bouldon, rubbing his hands; "I wish that he'd just begin trying it on. Won't I aggravate him by what I say and do; I'll tell him my mind more than he ever before heard it in his life."

"No, no, don't enrage him; that's not right," observed Bracebridge; but Tom, as he went off, shook his head as if he intended to follow his own ideas on the subject.

While Bouldon, followed at a distance by Eden, strolled about the playground and fields as usual, hoping that Blackall would meet him, Ernest went round to a number of boys who had combined with him to resist any aggression which the big fellows might make upon their rights, and told them to keep together, some in the gymnastic court, and the rest in the fencing-room. Meantime he and Buttar, and a few others on whose judgment he most relied, met together and consulted as to the best course to pursue under the present emergency.

"I've an idea," said Buttar; "let us get some ropes and bind our tyrant. He dare not interfere with me now, but I am determined that he shall not treat others as he treated me."

Some ropes were easily found which had been used to lash up their play-boxes. Ernest and Buttar were to be the leaders. Ernest went to the fencing-room to take command of the boys there; Buttar to the gymnastic court. They did not remain there idle. One company began twisting and turning and leaping on the poles, while Ernest got his followers to practise with their basket-sticks and single-sticks. Then he proposed a drill, and they all fell in and went through their exercises with as much precision as if Sergeant Dibble himself had been present. They marched and wheeled, and formed in close order and extended order, and various other simple manoeuvres, in very good style. While they were thus engaged, Eden rushed into the room, exclaiming, "Blackall has caught Bouldon, and is half-killing him; he says that he will teach him to disobey his orders. Haste—haste, or I really believe he will do him an injury. I never saw a fellow in such a rage."

No one needed a second summons. Bracebridge put himself at the head of his companions, who kept their ranks, and, marching out in good order, they met the party in the gymnastic court, whom Eden had likewise summoned.

"Double quick march," cried Bracebridge; and the two bands rushed on towards the extreme end of the grounds, where Eden told them the bully had encountered poor Tom. The spot towards which they were hurrying was separated from the rest of the grounds by a thick coppice. Several tall trees grew about it, and it was by far the most secluded place in the grounds. It was a favourite resort in the summer time of some of the more studious boys, who went there to read, and, at other seasons, Gregson and a few other boys, who were fond of the study of natural history, used to go there to search for specimens, as Tom Bouldon used to say, of bird's nests, beetles, bees, and wild flowers. Blackall, also, and two or three of his class, occasionally retired there, but neither to read nor to study natural history, but to smoke and to drink, when he could procure liquor. Bouldon ascertained that he had gone there on this occasion, and, anxious to bring matters to a crisis, went round that way, passing directly in front of him.

Blackall, who was sitting alone by himself, looking at the grass, saw his shadow slowly pass along before him. Lifting up his lack-lustre eyes, they fell on Tom. He immediately started up, and seized him by the collar. "Ah, my fine fellow, I've caught you at last, and all alone. I wanted to find you, and now I'll pay you off with a thrashing which you will remember to the end of your days."

Bouldon looked up and down to see if anybody was coming to his help. He had missed Eden, who had, however, seen him through the trees in the hands of Blackall, and then scampered off as fast as his legs would carry him, his imagination somewhat supplying the particulars of the thrashing which had not even yet begun. Bouldon struggled hard to release himself when he found that Blackall had got hold of his collar, for he had no wish to become a martyr unnecessarily, as he knew from experience that his persecutor hit very hard and cruelly whenever he had the power.

"I'll give you a chance yet," said Blackall. "Will you fag for me, or will you not?"

"Most certainly not," answered Tom, firmly. "I'll see you at Jericho, and ten thousand leagues further, rather than lift a finger to obey one of your commands. There, you've got my answer."

"Then take that," exclaimed the bully, bestowing a thundering lick on poor Tom's ear. "How do you like the taste of that? Will you obey me now?"

Blackall generally played with his victims as a cat does with a mouse before destroying it.

"Not I," answered Tom briefly, compressing his lips.

Another heavy box on the ears followed close upon this answer.

"Will you now?" again asked Blackall.

"No," bawled out Bouldon.

Several cuffs and blows now descended on his head and shoulders. Again Blackall asked him if he would fag. Bouldon did not deign to answer.

"Do you hear me? Are you deaf?" thundered out the bully.

Bouldon made not the slightest reply to this question either by word or look. The consequence was that the bully began striking away at him right and left, till Tom felt that he was getting very severely punished, and he could not help wishing that some relief was at hand. He struggled as much as his strength would allow, and at last, forgetting all the rules of prudence, he broke away, and instead of endeavouring to escape, he clenched his fists and struck at the bully in return. The consequence was, that he was soon knocked down on the grass. He was not very much hurt, so when he saw Blackall about to kick him, he sprang up in time to avoid the blow.

"Ah, you arrant coward, to think of kicking a fellow half your size when he is on the ground!" he exclaimed, standing at a distance, however, so that he might have time to leap out of Blackall's way. Under any circumstances he would not have deigned to run; that is not the fashion of any English boys I have ever met. On the contrary, he was anxious to keep near Blackall, and to spin out the time till his friends could arrive to his assistance. He would particularly have wished them to find him on the ground, and Blackall engaged in kicking him. Of course Tom's look, and attitude, and words very much increased the exasperation of the latter, who now, springing after him, caught him again by the collar, and began pummelling him with all his might about the ribs and head, till his face was one mass of bumps and bruises. Still Bouldon would not cry out for mercy, or give in. Whenever he had an opportunity he broke away from his persecutor, and once more stood on the defensive, returning, when he could, blow for blow. He was soon, however, again knocked down with a blow on the forehead, which almost stunned him. He saw the bully advancing with his foot to kick him.

"Oh, don't, don't; you'll kill me," sang out poor Tom, who really did dread the force of the big fellow's heavy shoe, given with the full swing of his leg.

Blackall heeded him not, and would have executed his barbarous purpose, had he not that instant felt a heavy load fall down on his back, and a pair of arms encircling his neck. He had once before been treated much in the same manner, but who or what his present assailant was he could not tell. The nails were long, and the hands not a little grimy, while the knees of his assailant kept pressing his ribs in a most unpleasant manner. Blackall's look of horror showed that he fully believed that he had been seized by a big baboon, or some monster who might strangle him.

"Now at him again, Tom, and don't let him go till he has promised never to attack you more," said a voice, which Blackall recognised as that of Gregson.

However, Tom was this time too much hurt to get up, and he lay moaning on the grass, anxiously wishing that some one would come to his rescue. Gregson had, it appears, been up in a tree hunting for young squirrels and various insects. He had remained a spectator of the fight for some time, thinking that he could not do much good by his interference. When, however, he saw how hard it was going with Tom, he resolved to go to his help. Descending a tree, he climbed along one of the lower branches, from the end of which he had easily dropped down on the bully's back. There he clung, like the old man of the sea who clung to the back of Sinbad the sailor. But, as I have said, Blackall was a very powerful fellow, and after he had got over his terror at this sudden assault, he used every means to get rid of his assailant. He could not shake him off; and Gregson did not flinch from all the pinches and blows behind his back which he received. At last, Blackall bethought him of backing against a tree. Unfortunately for the young naturalist, one with some stout branches grew near, and Blackall backed up to it, till he bumped it with such force that he very nearly broke both his back and his head, and he was very soon fain to let go. No sooner was he on the ground than the bully vented all his fury on him, and knocking him over with a blow of his ox-like fist, kicked and cuffed him till he was even in a worse condition than Bouldon.

"I'll teach you to play your pranks on me, you young scoundrel," he exclaimed. "However, you could not have chosen a better place, for there is no one likely to come here to interfere with us, and I intend to pay you both off in a way you will not fancy, let me tell you that. My fists are rather heavy, so I do not intend to use them, lest I should kill you outright, but I have a colt about me, of which you shall now have a taste." Saying this, the bully pulled out of his pocket a piece of hard rope, covered from one end to the other with hard knots. Seizing poor Gregson, who lay on the grass even more hurt than Bouldon, Blackall dragged him along, and placed him near his friend, and then flourishing his formidable colt, was about to make it descend first on the back of one and then on that of the other of his victims, when a loud shout arrested his arm, and, looking up, he saw from both ends of the glade a strong body of boys, in military order, advancing towards him.

"Hold your hand, you big coward. If you dare strike either of those fellows, well not leave a particle of skin on the flesh of your back, let me tell you," shouted a voice in a loud tone.

One of the parties was led by Buttar, the other by Bracebridge. The latter had spoken. Buttar uttered a similar caution; but Blackall, seeing that only younger boys composed the approaching bands, and fancying that they would not venture to interfere with him, resolved for very pride not to desist from his purpose, and down came his weapon on the backs of the two prostrate victims of his tyranny. It was equivalent to a declaration of war to the knife.

"Others passing a rope round his body he was speedily tripped up and hauled down to the ground."

"On, on, on," shouted Bracebridge and Buttar.

Their followers required no second appeal.

"Remember what I told you," shouted Ernest—"Each man to his duty."

The bully turned round and gazed, first on one side and then on the other, at the approaching bands. He was observed to turn pale, even though he flourished his colt above his head, and uttered loud threats of vengeance against any who might dare to approach him. A scornful laugh was the only answer he received, as the two bands advancing in double quick time completely surrounded him, and then with a shout threw themselves upon him. Some seized his neck, others his arms, and others his legs, in spite of his kicks and blows, while others passing a rope round his body he was speedily tripped up and hauled down to the ground. He swore, and shouted, and threatened more loudly than ever.

"Gag him, gag him," suggested Buttar. "Don't let the fellow talk blasphemy."

"I'll half murder you some day for this, you Buttar, you," cried the bully, glaring fiercely at him.

"Pooh, pooh," was all Buttar deigned to reply. "Here, quick, a handkerchief, and that piece of wood."

The materials for the gag were handed to Buttar, and though the bully made several attempts to bite his fingers, he succeeded in most effectually fixing a gag in his mouth. Still Blackall struggled furiously; but though not one of his assailants was half his size, they succeeded in dragging him to a tree, to the trunk of which they secured him with the rope they had passed round his waist. Then they lashed his hands as if he was clasping the tree, with his face to the trunk, while his ankles were placed in a still more uncomfortable position.

"He cannot abuse us, or kick, or strike, but he can see," suggested some one.

The hint was forthwith taken, and he was quickly blindfolded.

"We will draw lots to settle who is to colt him," said Ernest. "You understand, my friends, that it will be better he should not know who have been his executioners."

Lots were forthwith drawn with some ceremony. Four boys were chosen, and they, nothing very loth, began to flourish the very weapon with which he had just been striking their friends.

When Ernest and his party came up they found Bouldon and Gregson on the ground, both of them so much hurt as to be scarcely able to rise. Ernest with two or three other boys, having seen Blackall safely secured, went to attend to them. They got water from the pond and bathed their temples, and undid their shirt collars, and in a little time set them up on their legs. As may be supposed, the first use they made of their restored strength was to go and watch the proceedings taking place with regard to Blackall. Their feelings revolted at the thought of thrashing one who had been so lately ill-treating them. They felt that had they done so, they would naturally be accused of being influenced by vindictive feelings; whereas they wished that he should understand that; the thrashing he was receiving was a lawful punishment for the cruelty he had so long inflicted on others. The boys who had been selected as executioners set to work very much in the fashion of young boatswain's mates on board of a man-of-war. After one had given five or six strokes another came on, till at last some one declared that he had fainted. So he had, but it was chiefly through rage and indignation. However, they took the gag out of his mouth, but the first use he made of his restored power of speech was to abuse and threaten them so dreadfully, that they came behind him and again clapped the gag into his mouth. In vain he struggled. He was too securely bound to get free. Ernest had learned, as every boy should, how to knot and splice properly, and was unlikely to allow any slip knots to be made. When Blackall showed that he was completely recovered, the boys who had been appointed to flog him, once more made ready to go on with the operation, but Ernest stopped them. His feelings revolted at thus punishing a school-fellow, however richly he might have deserved punishment, who had been rendered so utterly helpless.

"Stay," he cried out. "He has had enough to show him what we have the power of doing, and the pain he has suffered may teach him in future not to inflict pain on others. Take the gag out of his mouth, and let us hear if he will promise to behave properly in future towards all the younger boys of the school, to beg pardon of Bouldon for his unwarrantable attack on him, and especially that he will promise to abandon his absurd attempt to fag any of the boys of the school. You hear what has been said, Blackall. Will you consent to these terms? Take the gag out of his mouth and let him answer."

Blackall had heard every word that was said, and had he been wise, he would have yielded to the force of circumstances; but instead of that, he began as before to abuse and threaten Ernest and Buttar, and all the boys whose voices he recognised, and to declare that he had a perfect right to fag one and all of them if he chose.

"The gag! the gag! Treason! treason!" was the reply, accompanied by loud laughter from all the party.

The gag was quickly produced; but as Blackall found it being adjusted, his courage, or rather his obstinacy, gave way.

"What is it, do you say, that you want of me, you fellow?" he asked, in a very much humbled tone.

Ernest repeated the terms he had before proposed.

"As to that, I do not mean to say that I am not ready to agree to your terms," he replied; "only just mark me, you fellows. I don't think that I am a greater bully than others, and if you fancy that I am going to agree not to lick a fellow who is impudent, you are mistaken. I'm not going to promise any such thing. Fagging is not in vogue, so I'll give that up for the present, but I don't know what other big fellows will do."

This speech of the once formidable bully was received with loud shouts by most of the younger boys, but Ernest, who knew something more than they did of human nature, did not put much confidence in what had been said, still he saw that it would be politic to release him while he remained in that humbled humour.

"Very well, Blackall," said Ernest; "we are all glad to hear what you say, and we intend to rely on your promise; but remember that we are all united to resist aggression, and that the moment you break your promise, we shall take steps to punish you. Now release him."

In obedience to the orders of their leader, some of the boys cast off the lashings which secured their prisoner to the tree, but they wisely took care to keep him blindfolded to the last, that he might be unable to injure them. His hands and legs being set free, they all hurried back to their ranks, where they stood in two compact bodies as before, bidding defiance to any attack he might venture to make on them.

"You may take your handkerchief off your eyes and go free," said Ernest.

Hearing this, the humbled bully began pulling away at the handkerchief round his eyes, much to the amusement of the lookers-on, for he had considerable difficulty in untying the knot, and getting it off his head. His first movement showed clearly that he was much inclined to break the articles of peace, but when he saw the formidable array of boys drawn up on either side of him, with Bracebridge at the head of one party, and Buttar at that of the other, discretion prevailed, and with a sulky, downcast look, he turned round and walked away across the fields in an opposite direction to that which he saw the hostile armies were taking. Ernest suppressed the commencement of a cheer in which his supporters very naturally showed an inclination to indulge.

"Let him go, and treat him with the silent contempt he deserves," he observed. "He has got a lesson which he will not easily forget; but at the same time we shall all do well not to trust him. He will not let the matter pass without trying to revenge himself on some of us."

Blackall heard the first part of Ernest's remarks. He turned round as if to give vent to his feelings; but not finding words to express himself, he stamped with his foot, and continued on in the direction he was going.

"I wonder whether he will go and complain to the Doctor of the thrashing we have given him," exclaimed Bouldon, as they were marching homeward. "I certainly did not expect to see him take it so tamely. I expected that he would have fought and struggled to the last, like the rover's crew the song talks about. Instead of that, he struck his colours in a wonderfully short space of time."

"Oh, those bullies are always white-livered rogues," observed Buttar, "so are nearly all the tyrants one reads about in history. Conscience makes cowards of them all. Depend on it that he will hold his tongue, and neither tell the Doctor nor any of his own special chums."

It was to be seen whether Buttar was right. The boys who had not united with Ernest were surprised to see so many of his friends marching about in order the whole afternoon; and even when tea was over, never less than five or six of them were together. They looked about for Blackall, but he did not make his appearance. The elder boys were excused from coming in to tea on half-holidays, so there was nothing remarkable in this, and none of his friends seemed to notice his absence. Of one thing all Ernest's companions felt certain, that no attempt to fag them would succeed while he remained at school.

Chapter Eleven
Blackall's Revenge and its Results

Everybody remarked the sullen angry expression which Blackall's countenance bore after the event I have just described. When any of his associates talked to him about fagging, he frowned, and, putting out his lips, declared that there was no use attempting to coerce the young scamps, for that the advantage to be gained was not worth the trouble it would cost. This was very true, but at the same time it was not an opinion anybody would have expected from him. Whenever he met Bracebridge, he always looked at him with an expression of intense dislike, which he was at no pains to conceal.

The Christmas holidays were now approaching, and a long course of bad weather kept the boys in more than usual. They consequently amused themselves with their indoor exercises. Their broadswords and foils were constantly in their hands during their play-hours.

One day Ernest and Buttar were fencing together. They had been at first equally matched, but Ernest was never content unless he was perfect in every exercise he took up, and so he had practised and practised, and thought the matter over, till he could beat his friend thoroughly. Buttar took his defeats very good-naturedly.

"I cannot manage as you do, old fellow," he used to observe. "You always contrive to send my foil flying out of my hand when I fancy that I am going to play you some wonderful trick at which I have been practising away for the whole of the last week."

A match was just over when Blackall entered the fencing-room. His eye fell on Ernest. Just then something called Buttar out of the room, and Ernest was left without an antagonist.

"Come, young gentleman, you are both good fencers. Try a pass of arms together," said Mr Strutt, the fencing-master. "Oh, you must not draw back; I shall fancy you are afraid of each other if you do. Come, take your foils and begin."

Blackall hesitated. He had not exchanged a word with Ernest since the day he had received his flogging, and he hoped never to have to speak to him again.

"Perhaps Blackall would rather not fence with me, sir," observed Ernest to the fencing-master.

"Oh, nonsense, nonsense. Take up your foil and begin," was the answer he received.

"I am ready to fence with you. Come here in this corner of the room, out of the way," said Blackall suddenly.

Ernest followed him. He remarked that there was a peculiarly evil look in his eye. He did not, however, unfortunately, observe what he was about with his foil in the corner.

"Now, young gentlemen, attention," cried Mr Strutt to some of his pupils, whose exercise he was superintending, and the words Quarte, Tierce, Seconde, Demi-circle, Contre de Quarte, Contre de Tierce, and so on, were heard resounding through the room.

"Come, let us begin, and have no child's play," exclaimed Blackall with vehemence, throwing himself into the attitude to engage. He made several rapid passes, which Ernest parried dexterously. As he did so, he observed that his adversary's foil had no button on it. Still he thought that it was the result of accident; and as he had very little fear of Blackall's hitting him, he did not deign at first to take notice of it. Something, however, he observed in the expression of his opponent's eye made him doubt the wisdom of this delicacy.

"Blackall," he cried out, parrying a desperate thrust at his breast, your foil has no button. "Were you to hit me, you might injure me very much."

"What care I?" answered Blackall. "I'll pay my debts, depend on that. Take that—and that—and that!" As he spoke he lunged rapidly at Ernest, who as rapidly turned aside the point of his weapon. Still Blackall was no bad fencer, and Ernest had the greatest difficulty in defending himself. Now he had to guard against a straight thrust, now against a disengagement, now the beat and thrust, now the cut over the point, and now the double. He saw that it would be too dangerous to attack himself; indeed, his only wish was to disarm his adversary, and then to refuse to fence with him any longer. This Blackall seemed to suspect, and to be on his guard against, while his aim was too clearly to wound, if not to kill, his opponent. Ernest under these very trying circumstances kept perfectly cool. He had parried every thrust which Blackall had made, but the latter at length pressed him so hard that he had to retreat a few paces. Once more he stood his ground, and defended himself as before. As he did so, suddenly he felt his foot slip, and, while he was trying to recover himself, Blackall pressed in on him, and sent his foil completely through his shoulder. One of the boys had just before dropped a lump of grease, which had been the cause of the accident. Ernest felt himself borne backwards, and, before any one could catch him, he fell heavily to the ground. The blood flowed rapidly from the wound; a sickness came over him, and he fainted. Blackall pretended to be very much grieved at what had occurred; but the fencing-master, looking at him sternly, asked him how it was that he could use a foil without knowing that the button was off.

"And what is the meaning of this, let me ask?" he said, stooping down, and with his knife hooking out the end of a foil from a chink in the boards. "The point was broken off on purpose. You have tried to kill that young lad there. I know it; and I shall take you before the Doctor, and let him judge the case."

"What makes you say that?" asked Blackall, turning very pale. "Why should you suppose I should wish to hurt Bracebridge?"

"I know it—I know it," was the only answer he got, while Mr Strutt with several of the boys was engaged in lifting Ernest, and binding up his shoulder to stop the bleeding. Blackall knelt down to assist, but the fencing-master sternly ordered him to stand back.

"I will not trust you," he exclaimed. "You are a bad fellow! I believe it now. I see it all clearly. I ought not to have allowed such an one as you to fence with him. If he dies, you will be his murderer; remember that. You shall know the truth from me, at all events." Thus did the excitable but kind-hearted fencing-master run on.

As he and some of the boys were about to lift Ernest off the ground, to carry him upstairs, Monsieur Malin came in. When he had ascertained the state of affairs, he immediately sent off Buttar to summon the surgeon who attended the school, which it seemed no one else had thought of doing. The presence of a medical man would, he knew, save the Doctor a great deal of anxiety. Having done this he walked up to Blackall, and put his hand on his shoulder.

"Things do not take place in this school without my hearing of them," he remarked. "Mr Strutt thinks you wounded Bracebridge on purpose. I believe that you are capable of any crime: but come with me to the Doctor; we will hear what judgment he pronounces on the subject."

Blackall would gladly have got away or shrunk into himself; but when he found that he had no channel of escape, he seemed to screw up his courage to face out boldly the charges brought against him.

It is a very unpleasant subject. I would rather not have had to describe Blackall and his misdeeds; but as his character is so odious, I hold him up as a warning to some not to imitate him, and to others to avoid, and on no account to trust to or to form any friendship with such a person when they meet him.

There was in the house a strong-room, in which occasionally very refractory boys were locked up. Confinement in it was looked upon with peculiar dislike, and considered a great disgrace. It was furnished with books and slates, and pens, ink, and paper, and the boy who was put in was always awarded a task, which he had to perform before he was let out. Any of the masters might put a boy in there, and incarceration in this place was the only punishment they were allowed to inflict on their own responsibility.

"There, go in there; translate and write out for me these five pages of English into French, and learn these fifty lines of Racine," said Monsieur Malin, as he put Blackall in, and, locking the door, took away the key. "I will report your conduct to the Doctor, and hear what he has to say to it."

Blackall was left in a great fright. He did not know what part of his conduct might be reported, and he felt conscious that he was guilty of many things which, if known, would cause him to be expelled. He knew also that Monsieur Malin would not excuse him his task, so he tried to get through with it; but all his efforts were in vain. He could do nothing, and his thoughts would turn to the act of which he had just been guilty. "I did not want to hurt him—I did not want to kill him," he said to himself; but each time that he said so conscience replied, "You did; you know you did. Cowardly mean-spirited revenge induced you to commit the act, and it shall not go unpunished."

The Doctor was not told of what had occurred till the medical man had arrived and examined Ernest's wound. He had him at once put to bed, and washed and dressed the wound, and then he gave him some cooling medicine, but he said that he must see him again before he would pronounce on the matter. He might not materially suffer, but it might prove to be a very dangerous wound. This report got about the school. Buttar, Bouldon, and poor Ellis, and many other boys, were deeply grieved when they heard it. During the evening there was much anxiety and excitement in the school.

It was generally reported that Blackall had endeavoured to kill Ernest; then that the wound had assumed a very dangerous aspect, that the surgeon was very anxious about him, and that there was very little hope of his recovery.

When the Doctor appeared in school in the evening his countenance was very grave, and he seemed grieved and anxious. He spoke very little, and it was observed that while he was reading prayers his voice faltered.

There were many sorrowful young hearts in the school that night; for another sadder report than the first got about, and it was believed that Ernest Bracebridge—the clever, the brave, the spirited one, whom all then acknowledged to be without a rival in the school—was dead.

Naturally, the late attempt to introduce fagging was discussed, and the part Bracebridge had taken in suppressing it was openly spoken of. Thus, not only did all the boys in the school learn all about it, but it came to the ears of the masters, and, finally, to those of the Doctor himself. Monsieur Malin had heard of it before, but he had judged it best to let things take their course. The Doctor, having gathered all the information he thought necessary, collected several witnesses, among whom were Buttar, Bouldon, and Ellis, and summoned Blackall into his presence.

Blackall appeared, led in by two of the masters. He heard all that had to be said against him, and a full account of his barbarous treatment of Bouldon and Gregson, and the flogging which followed.

"I do not excuse Buttar, nor do I poor Bracebridge, for their conduct on that occasion. It was their duty to come and complain to me, and not to take the law into their own hands; but I am fully willing to believe that they acted under mistaken notions. However, I do not wish at present to say anything more against them; but there stands one whose whole conduct I so severely condemn, that I can allow him no longer to be an inmate of this school. To-morrow morning I shall publicly expel him. Retire till then to your respective rooms."

Although on ordinary occasions the Doctor had a great flow of language, he was very brief when any serious matter was under discussion, as if he was afraid to trust his feelings in words. No one in the school had an opportunity of again speaking to Blackall. He was supposed to have passed the night in the solitary room, as it was called. The next morning, after breakfast, he was brought into the school-room between two of the masters, and there in due form publicly expelled the school.

"Sir," said the Doctor, "from the numerous charges brought against you, and which you do not attempt to disprove, you will, if you do not alter your conduct, be a disgrace to any community in which you may be found.

You have been constantly guilty of drunkenness and tyranny, blasphemy and swearing, idleness, and utter negligence of all religious and moral principle. I deeply regret that I was not sooner informed of your conduct; and I humbly acknowledge that I am much to blame in not having more minutely inquired into the character of every boy under my charge. I trust that you are an exception to the general rule, and that there are no others like you. Lead the unhappy lad away."

Soon after this a post-chaise came to the door; Blackall with one of the masters was seen to get into it, and from that day forward no one ever heard anything positively about him. His conduct was undoubtedly worse than that of any of his companions. The way he had been punished utterly put a stop to anything like fagging, and even brought bullying into very great discredit.

I have not mentioned Ernest Bracebridge since he had been wounded in so cowardly and treacherous a way by Blackall. The reports which flew about the school proved to have been somewhat exaggerated. The surgeon very naturally ordered that he should be kept quiet, but he had not said that there was any danger. He speedily stopped the bleeding, though, at the same time, he thought it safest to sit up with him, to watch that the wound did not break out afresh and allow him to bleed to death. In a few days even the slightest danger which might have existed was over; and in the course of a week he was able once more to resume his place in school. The Doctor had a good deal of conversation with him with respect to his conduct towards Blackall; and though he acknowledged that there were many extenuating circumstances, still, he pointed out, that he, as master of the school, would not allow the law to be taken out of his hands and exercised by another, however great the provocation.

"The same reasoning, remember, Bracebridge, holds good in society," he observed. "Private individuals must never take upon themselves the execution of the laws while a duly elected authority exists. Happily, in England, a man need only bring his complaint before a magistrate, and he is nearly certain to obtain ample justice. Remember that, my dear boy, whenever you are tempted to take the law into your own hands. If you yield to passion, or to your feelings, you will be acting against the laws both of God and man; and do not suppose that it is a light thing to do that."

Ernest thanked the Doctor for his advice, and promised to remember it. Only a couple of weeks remained now before the holidays were to begin — those jolly Christmas holidays which, to boys living in the country, generally afford so much amusement.

The conversation Ernest had had with the Doctor made him feel more inclined to confide in him than he had ever done, and he resolved to open his heart to him about Ellis, who, in spite of his excellent conduct, and his quiet amiable manners, was as much as ever mistrusted by the boys in general. Barber, especially, turned up his nose at him, and never failed, when talking with his own particular chums, to throw out hints that, when Blackall was expelled, it was a pity the Doctor did not clear the school of Ellis, and other canting hypocrites like him. More than once these ungenerous remarks had been repeated to Ernest. He talked the matter over with Buttar, who agreed that they ought not to be allowed to go on unnoticed.

"If Ellis has done anything really disgraceful, he should explain his conduct to us, who have so long supported him through thick and thin," observed Buttar. "For my part, I believe that he ever was what he now is, a highly honourable good fellow; and if so, he ought to be defended, and his character placed in a proper light before the whole school."

"I have been long thinking the same," said Ernest. "I would do anything to serve him; and the life he is now leading is enough to ruin him in health and mind. He looks thin and careworn—like an old man already."

That very evening Ernest went to the Doctor, and very briefly told him all about Ellis; how fast he was improving, and how happy he had become, till Barber came to the school and spread reports against his fair fame.

The Doctor asked Ernest what the reports were. Ernest told him.

"Poor fellow! how very unfortunate," he remarked. "When he came here, his father sent me a letter from his former master, saying that he had been accused of stealing some money from another boy; but that, though the evidence against him was very strong, and apparently conclusive, he fully believed him guiltless of the offence. His father, who came to me on purpose, assured me that his son was altogether incapable of committing the crime of which he was accused; at the same time, that he thought it right to mention the circumstance to me, to account for his low-spirited and retiring manner. I appreciated the father's motive, and accepted the charge of his son, not supposing that any boy from the lad's former school would come here to accuse him. I have watched him narrowly, and I feel sure, from what I have seen of him, that he is, at all events, now a most unlikely person to commit the crime of which he is accused."

"I am very glad indeed, sir, to hear you say this," replied Ernest. "I would myself stake much on Ellis's honour; but how are the other boys to be convinced of this, when one who professes to be a witness is among them, and constantly repeats the tale?"

"I must think about it," observed the Doctor. "I may show my disbelief of the truth of the accusations brought against him by honouring him on every fitting opportunity; but unless he can disprove the tales uttered against him, I fear the less generous boys will continue to believe him guilty. However, I have said I will consider the subject. And now, Bracebridge, believe me, I thank you for having introduced the matter to my notice."

After this conversation, Ernest became much happier about Ellis. For the Doctor, also, a much warmer regard and respect arose in his heart than he had ever before felt. He had from the first looked upon him as a kind, sensible, and just man; but he did not suppose that there was any sympathy between him and his pupils. He knew that they came to school to be taught, and that it was his duty to teach them; but he was not aware of the deep interest which he took in their eternal as well as in their temporal welfare; how he employed his best thoughts and energies for that purpose; how much toil and pains he had taken to bring the school into its present condition; and how much it grieved him to find that, with all the pains he had taken, there was so much to correct and arrange. The Doctor, however, knew the world, and that in no human institutions can perfection be attained—nor can it be expected that they should be without faults; but he knew also that by care and attention those faults may be decreased, if not altogether got rid of, and he did not despair.

Ernest, as I was saying, had never before this thoroughly understood the Doctor. Now he did, and he found him a kind, sympathising, affectionate friend. Indeed, in my opinion, unless a man is this to his pupils, he is not fit to be a schoolmaster. Neither can a parent, unless he is his children's friend, expect to command their love and obedience.

Ernest now discovered the Doctor to be very like his own father in many respects, and therefore placed unbounded confidence in him. He gladly opened his own heart to him, and with the frankness of a warm-hearted boy, told him all his thoughts, and hopes, and wishes.

The Doctor had always liked Ernest, and felt great satisfaction at watching his rapid progress; but now he discovered qualities and talents which he had not before surmised, and from that time he placed the most perfect confidence in him, and the interest Ernest excited was as great as if he had been his own son.

At the end of the year prizes were given, and, in spite of his accident, Ernest carried off several. One of the performances which invariably created the greatest interest was the speech-making. The speech given to Ernest's class was that part of Julius Caesar where Cassius endeavours to persuade Brutus to join the conspiracy against Caesar. Buttar also spoke very well, and took the part of Brutus. All the neighbourhood were collected on the occasion, and a sort of stage was erected at one end of the play-room, which was ornamented with boughs of holly and other evergreens, and flags and coloured lamps.

Altogether, it was a very pretty spectacle. Instead of painted scenes, a bower of evergreens and flags was erected on the stage, in which the boys performed their parts.

Some of the bigger boys gained a good deal of applause, for the Doctor taught his pupils not only Greek and Latin, but what he looked on as of not less consequence—to write and speak their own language correctly and fluently.

Many who could scarcely express themselves so as to be clearly understood when they came to the school, had by the time they reached the upper classes become quite eloquent, and were able to write their themes with correctness and precision. Not much was expected from the younger boys, but when Ernest began to speak, the attention of all the guests was arrested: not a whisper was heard; and when he concluded, a loud and continued applause burst forth, and even his school-fellows agreed that he had surpassed himself. Buttar also gained a fair share of the applause bestowed on his friend, and he was not jealous that he did not gain more. No one listened more attentively than did Ellis, for he had declined to speak, though urged by Ernest to do so, and tears rushed unbidden into his eyes at the success which Bracebridge had obtained.

"I tell you, you fellows, that there is not a fellow like him!" exclaimed Tom Bouldon, clapping his hands vehemently. "He is as good, and brave, and clever as any fellow in the world. I always thought so, and now I am certain of it, and don't mind saying so."

Happily these remarks did not reach Ernest's ears. Gratifying as they must have been, they would have proved somewhat dangerous, even to a mind so well balanced as his was. He knew that he had achieved a success, but he was well aware that, after all, it was not a very great one, and that he had many more far far greater to achieve before the victory would be won.

I must not forget one of the amusements which generally terminated the winter half of the year. It was a grand race on stilts. There was a wide extent of flat meadow land in the neighbourhood, intersected with narrow ditches full of water. This was the ground selected for the sport. It was something like the Landes in the south of France. Monsieur Malin had introduced the amusement.

Boys when they first came to the school, who had not been accustomed to walk on stilts, were surprised at the height of those used, and the rapidity with which the older fellows walked along on them. Many of them were ten feet high. The resting-place for the feet was a piece of wood flat on the upper surface, with a strap to it which could be fastened round the feet or not. The upper ends of the poles were held by the hands, with the shoulders pressing against them. By this mode a boy could leap off his stilts without risk. Some are used which do not reach above the knee, round which the end is secured by a strap, but a fall with these may prove a very serious matter, and the Doctor would not allow them to be used.

It was good fun on stilt day to see the greater part of the school mounted up high above the ground, and striding away at a rapid rate over the fields; to hear the shouts and shrieks of laughter, especially if any unfortunate wight put the end of his stilt into a ditch deeper than he expected, and, unable to draw it out again, dropped on his nose. Monsieur Malin generally led the party, and no one cheered and laughed more than he did. This year it was arranged that a steeple-chase should take place; so it was called; but in reality it was not a steeple which formed the goal, but a low object—a white gate, which could only be seen from an elevation; therefore the boys with the highest stilts were the best able to keep it in sight.

Fancy upwards of eighty boys collected on a fine clear frosty afternoon, mounted up five or six feet off the ground, some even more, stalking away as fast as they could go over the fields, shouting, and laughing, and hallooing to each other.

As usual, Ernest was one of the most active. He and Buttar took the lead, but they were closely followed by Tom Bouldon, who was very great upon stilts. The exercise suited his temperament. He had been at the school ever since Monsieur Malin introduced them, and so he was well-practised in their use. He thus had an advantage Ernest did not possess. He went steadily on across hedges and ditches, and across ploughed fields, and moist meadows and marshes, till he overtook Buttar, and then he came up with Ernest, who was beginning to fag, and then he went ahead, and finally got in at the winning-post half a field's length before anybody else.

Two days after that the school broke up, and the boys, in high spirits at the anticipation of the amusements they were to enjoy, started off in all directions to their respective homes.

Chapter Twelve
The Christmas Holidays. Skating and other Winter Amusements

Ernest liked his school very much, but he had good reason to love his home still more, for such a home as his—or rather its inhabitants, which constituted it his home—was well worthy of all the affection of his warm affectionate heart. His father and mother were so wise and sensible and kind, so just and so indulgent. The expression of their countenances and their general personal appearance at once showed that they were above the ordinary run of people; yet, noble as they looked, none but the base and evil-disposed were afraid of them. It was a pleasure to see the smiling faces and the affectionate looks with which they were received as they walked about the village, where they and their ancestors for several generations had lived before them. Often and often they might be seen simply, and, if the weather was bad, roughly, dressed; going from cottage to cottage, with a basket of medicines, or provisions and clothing, for those poor neighbours who were, they well knew, utterly unable to obtain them for themselves. Their daughters followed their example. No more sweet, amiable, and yet refined, girls were to be found in the country. Their brothers declared that no such girls existed in the world; and yet, though they could do all sorts of things, and ride, and fish, and even play cricket with them on a pinch, they were not in the slightest degree proud or conceited. They could sing and play, and when they went to balls, which was not very often, no young ladies appeared to greater advantage, or were more lively or graceful. They were admired, and yet fully respected, by all who knew them.

I have described what Ernest was. His brothers were his equals in most respects. His eldest brother was a very fine young man, and had taken high honours at Cambridge. He was an excellent specimen of an English gentleman of the nineteenth century. Free from all affectation and pedantry, still his whole nature seemed to revolt from anything slangish or low. No oaths, nor anything which would be considered one, nor any cant expressions, ever escaped his lips. Yet he was full of life and spirits, the soul of every society in which he moved. He had numerous friends, and so mild and quiet was his disposition that he seldom or never made enemies; or rather, I may say, if he made an enemy, he quickly got rid of his enmity. All his brothers looked up to him, and loved him heartily.

"My brother John says so and so," or "My brother John did so and so," was a constant phrase of theirs, and it was always something good he had said or done. He was at home, and so were indeed all Ernest's brothers. One was in the navy—Frank. What a light-hearted and merry fellow he was. He had seen some hard service, had been highly spoken of in a dispatch, and had a medal on his breast. He was a gallant, true-hearted sailor, and was as much liked by his companions afloat as his brothers were by theirs on shore.

Such were the inhabitants of Oaklands. The house itself was a fine old substantially-built edifice, with thick walls, standing on a gentle elevation, and overlooking a wide extent of country. The grounds which surrounded it were large, and contained woods, and shady walks, and fishponds, or rather lakes, and ornamental flower gardens, and rich velvety lawns, and kitchen gardens.

A short time before the holidays, Mr Bracebridge had written to his son, desiring to have the addresses of several of them. What was his reason for doing this, his father did not tell him.

The holidays began. What a happy Christmas-day the whole family spent together! It was spent as Christmas-day should be spent—in affectionate family intercourse, and not in a wild gaiety which is calculated to drive away all thought and recollection of the great and glorious event it is intended to celebrate on that day. How happy everybody was both upstairs and downstairs; what long yarns Frank spun of his adventures in many lands, and his hair-breadth escapes; how he made them laugh at some of his stories, and cry, if their hair did not stand on end, at others, so exciting or so full of horror did they appear. I should like to repeat some of them, but I have not time to do so now. Of course everybody was wishing for a frost, that they might have skating.

"Oh, how delightful it will be!" exclaimed the midshipman. "I have not put on a pair of skates for the last five years. I have seen ice enough and to spare in the shape of icebergs, and floes, and fields of ice, but that is not the sort of ice suitable for skating. A big, thundering iceberg is a wonderful thing; we nearly got run down by one, or rather we nearly ran into one, if the truth must be said, when I was in the 'Stag,' only, of course, we always lay the blame on anything but ourselves; so in this case we blamed the iceberg for getting in our way, as if it had not just as much right to be there as we had, and as if it had not been our business to get out of its way. We were going round Cape Horn, and the master thought fit to make a considerable offing, and to keep away to the southward. It was my watch on deck. We had a fair wind on our starboard quarter. Jim Holdfast, whom I took out with me, and who promises to turn out a prime sailor, was forward. It was a pitchy dark night. We could barely make out our hands held out before us, and as to seeing across the deck, that was impossible. We had three reefs in our topsails, and though it was not blowing very hard—that is to say, a man might open his mouth without fear of having his teeth blown down his throat—we were running at the rate of nearly eight knots an hour through the water. By the way the stern of the ship lifted, and then by the feeling that she was gliding away downward into the depths of some watery valley, we knew that huge mountainous seas were rolling up astern of us. I frequently looked astern to try and make them out, but I could only hear their loud surge or slush (I must coin a word), as they broke close to our taffrail. Now and then, by keeping my eye on the sky, a vast ominous darkness came up between me and it, and that I knew from experience was a giant billow, big enough, if it once broke over us, to swallow up us, or a ship ten times as large. My watch was nearly out. I was thinking that I should not be sorry to get below, and go fast asleep. Now, 'you gentlefolks of England, who stay at home at ease,' will, I dare say, fancy that no one could go to sleep under such circumstances; but for us sailors it would never do if we allowed a gale of wind or any such trifle to keep us awake when it was not our watch on deck. The officer of the watch had just ordered eight bells to be struck, that is to say, it was the end of the first watch, or twelve o'clock at night, when a voice from forward shrieked out—for it was not an ordinary hail, but a cry which showed that life or death depended on the words being heard.

"'Iceberg ahead! Port the helm!—port—port—luff—luff! Ease away the weather braces—haul taut the lee braces!'

"I recognised the voice as that of Jim Holdfast. I do not think the second-lieutenant, who had the watch, was aware who was speaking, but he was a sensible fellow, and instead of being angry, as some officers would have been at finding anybody venturing to give an order instead of themselves, he repeated it, and discovering that it was obeyed, hurried forward to ascertain more clearly if possible the state of things. I looked out to leeward. There rising, as it were, out of the ocean was an indistinct mass of luminous matter (I can call it by no other name), out of which proceeded a cold chilling air, piercing to our very marrow. High, high above us it seemed to tower. The seas roared against its base. Not a man on deck but held his breath, for no one knew what was next to happen. We were terribly near to it. The sea, as it dashed up the sides of the icy rock—for there was no doubt it was an iceberg—came toppling back in showers of foam, and deluging our decks. As the ship heeled over to the breeze, her mainyard, I verily believe, grazed the iceberg. Had she been a few feet nearer to it, perhaps, I may say, a few inches, I do not believe that the gallant little sloop or any one on board would ever again have been heard of. The watch below had been called, and they came tumbling up in a great hurry, not knowing what was the matter. I could tell by the exclamations of a few near me that they wished themselves anywhere but where they were. The dear little ship flew on, and in another minute the iceberg was left astern. Then a cheer from all hands arose, and I believe many returned sincere, though silent, thanks to Him who had so mercifully preserved us. We hauled our wind and stood to the northward, for we had no fancy to encounter another of those big ice mountains in that dark night, not but what we knew that even then we might still run against one. You see, our sailor philosophy is to do our very best, and then not to trouble our heads more than we can help as to what are to be the consequences. When the excitement had calmed down, inquiries were made as to who had seen the iceberg, and so promptly given the order to 'port the helm,' through which the ship had undoubtedly been saved. Jim Holdfast, when he heard the inquiries made, was in a great fright, thinking that he was going to be punished, or well rowed at all events; and he never would have confessed that he had ventured to give the order, had not I gone to him and insisted on his coming forward, and saying how he had seen the iceberg, and had known that, unless what he had ordered was done, the ship would be lost. The next day the sea went down, and we were able before night to haul up permanently on our course for Valparaiso, the capital of Chili. Well, after breakfast I got Jim to come aft with me to the captain, who, with most of the officers, was on the quarter-deck.

"'I've found the culprit, sir,' said I. 'Here's the man who first discovered the iceberg, though he had never seen one before, and —'

"'And gave the order which saved the ship, and all our lives,' said the captain, interrupting me, and smiling pleasantly. 'Holdfast, my man, you did a most seaman-like thing. I shall at once give you a higher rating, for you have shown yourself thoroughly deserving of it.'

"I never saw a fellow so thoroughly astonished. He pulled away a lock of his hair, till I thought he would haul it out by the roots, for he, of course, held his hat in his hand; and he scraped away with his foot, and said that he didn't think he had done anything out of the common way, and it was only his duty, and that sort of thing; but there was nothing like affectation in what he said. Still more astonished was he when the captain continued—

"'You shall come to my clerk every day, and perhaps he will give you some instruction which may be useful to you. If you go on as you have begun, I may hope some day to see you on the quarter-deck.'

"The captain said a good deal more to the same effect. As I was saying, Jim was astonished. He said very little in return, but only pulled away harder than ever at his hair. Though before that time I should not have supposed that he had a spark of ambition in his soul, I after this observed a marked change in his demeanour and character. I suspect his eye was never off the quarter-deck. When not on duty, he was always reading and writing, and talking on nautical subjects. He was neater, and cleaner, and more active than before; at the same time that he was just as respectful as ever to all above him. He came home with us, and as soon as the ship was paid off, he went of his own accord to a nautical school to learn navigation, to enable him to do which he had saved up every farthing of his pay. Now, I say that Jim has set an example which many young gentlemen would do well to follow. If our captain gets a ship soon, he will take him with him; and when he hears how he has been employing his time on shore, I am very certain that he will keep his eye on him, and advance him if he can."

Everybody present had listened with intense interest to Frank's account of his ship's narrow escape from destruction, and this of course encouraged him to continue his narrations on subsequent evenings; but as my readers are not his brothers and sisters, and father and mother, who might possibly be somewhat prejudiced in his favour, I will not repeat them.

The young men and boys were all looking out eagerly for a frost; and every night they went out, one after the other, to ascertain whether the smell of the air gave indications of one having set in. Who does not know that peculiar clear, fresh feeling, so invigorating and exhilarating, which the air has when a frost has begun? Night after night, however, passed, and still the frost did not commence; but as the atmosphere grew colder and colder, everybody believed that their hopes would not long be delayed. Skates, which had long lain dormant in tool-chests and cupboards, were got out and polished. Skating shoes or boots were greased, and straps were repaired. At last Ernest, in high glee, rushed in among the family circle assembled around the drawing-room fire one evening, and declared that a right honest frost had, without the slightest doubt, set in, and that in two days he felt sure the ice would bear. The anticipation of the pleasure they all so much enjoyed put them into great spirits; and if either of the younger ones had been asked what he considered the greatest misfortune that could happen to the world, he would very likely have replied, a thaw. When, however, they had exhausted the subject, or at all events the patience of their hearers, their eldest sister proposed that those who were not engaged in any manual employment should read or tell a tale. The proposal was cordially welcomed. Frank gave for his share of the evening's amusements a further account of his adventures; then a tale was read; and at last Charles,

Ernest's second brother, who had lately returned from Germany, undertook to give a terrible ghost story which he had heard in that country, and which, as he said, had the advantage of being entirely true, though he was not disposed to quarrel with those who would not believe it.

"Is it an ancient or modern story, Charles?" asked Ernest; "I have no fancy for modern ghost stories. They all end in so ridiculous a way that one feels vexed at having taken the trouble of reading them."

"Oh, this is a true antique tale," said Charles; "but you shall hear it. Is everybody ready to attend? Well, then. Once upon a time—"

"No! no! no! Don't begin a story in that old-fashioned, obsolete way," exclaimed Ernest. "I never can fancy that a story is worth hearing when it begins with 'Once upon a time.'"

"Heave ahead! and let us hear what it is about," cried Frank. "Leave out the 'Once upon a time.' We are all ready. Just plunge at once into the story—don't give us a long-winded prelude, that is all."

"Very well, then; I will leave out the objectionable expression, and will begin at once by telling you all about the hero and his exploits up to the time my story commences. So once more. Listen—listen now! Here goes:—

"Kurd von Stein was a gallant and adventurous knight; he cared not how far he wandered, nor what danger lay in his path. He had travelled to all lands, and in all climates, defending ladies from insult, and the defenceless from oppression. His love of adventure led him through wood and wild, over mountains and across seas; but it was in the night that he loved best to ride forth, when the soft moon shone on the silvery lake and quiet forest; when the stars gazed calmly on the earth, as if seeking to penetrate its future, and mourning over its past; when the hoot of the owl and the cry of the beast of prey were the only sounds to be heard, besides the tread of his own charger, when he left the forest glade for the more beaten track.

"The Castle of Jauf, whose grey ruins may still be seen on a wooded height in the high country of the Rhine, was at that time a stately pile, with battlements, towers, and walls of massive strength; but it was uninhabited even then, and in the country round strange tales were told of sights and sounds which issued from it, not only at night, but even during the day. Spirits were said to hold their meetings there, and the place was shunned by all mankind.

"Sir Kurd, however, knew nothing of these tales; he had come from a great distance, and beyond inquiring his way, and ordering his necessary food, had held no communication with the peasantry, whose dialect was with difficulty understood either by his servant or himself. As he came within some hours of Jauf, he desired his servant to proceed to the castle of a baron whom he had met in the wars in Belgium, and who lived at no great distance, while he himself turned into the forest in hopes of meeting with some adventure. On he rode, through the pleasant oak woods, and by many a wild crag; but he at last found that he had wandered out of the direction he meant to have taken, and had no idea where he was, or which way he ought to turn to find his friend's castle; but he comforted himself with the old proverb, 'that every road leads to Rome, and even out of the labyrinth you will reach your destination.'

"The last ray of sunset had disappeared as Sir Kurd entered a wide valley, and faintly through the deepening gloom descried a large building, standing on a height at its further end—it was the Castle of Jauf. His horse was tired, and he himself both weary and hungry; he therefore determined on going to the castle, and asking for food and shelter for the night. He rode slowly up the hill on which the castle stood; but as he came near the walls, the darkness increased so suddenly that it was with difficulty he found the entrance to the court. He called loudly, but no servant appeared at his summons. His shout was given back by a dull echo from the walls, within which night and solitude alone seemed to reign. The court was full with long grass; he led his horse across it to a tall silver pine, whose outline he could faintly trace through the darkness, bound him to it, and then sat down to rest. After a little time he looked up,—and see! A light shone from one of the windows! He rose quickly, found a door, and felt his way up the narrow spiral staircase. At the top of the staircase was a door, which he opened, and found himself in a large baronial hall; but he hesitated to advance when he saw that the only person in it was a girl, who sat by the long table. She wore a black dress, and a string of large pearls confined her soft brown hair; and her attention was so absorbed in a large book which was open before her, and which she read by the light of a lamp, that she did not seem to be aware of the knight's entrance. She was very lovely, and her expression told of a gentle heart; but she was pale as a cloud, and some deep sorrow seemed to have robbed her cheek of its roses.

"'Noble lady, I greet you well,' said the knight, at length.

"She looked up, and thanked him silently by a gentle inclination of her head. He continued:—

"'In my journey through this wood I have lost my way; may I ask for some food and a night's lodging?'

"She rose, and with noiseless step left the hall, returning presently with two dishes, one of venison, another of wild fowl; these she placed on the table, and again retiring, brought a goblet of sparkling red wine. Having arranged everything, she signed to Sir Kurd to eat, accompanying the sign with a sad smile. He very willingly accepted her invitation; and though he found that both bread and salt had been forgotten, his modesty prevented his asking for them. It seemed strange, too, that not a single word had escaped the maiden's lips, and he dared not speak to her. But the spirit of the generous wine, which came from the sunny hills of Burgundy, began to assert its power over him, and prompted him to speak as follows:—

"Much-honoured lady, may I be allowed one question?"

"She bent her head.

"I suppose you are the daughter of the house?"

"Again she bowed.

"'And who are your parents?'

"She turned to the wall of the apartment, on which hung many portraits of knights and ladies; and pointing to the two last, she said, in a voice so soft, so melodious, that it seemed like the sighing of an Aeolian harp—

"'I am the last of my race.'

"'Here,' thought Sir Kurd, 'this may turn out as good an adventure as ever knight met with in an out-of-the-way part of the world. To be sure, they sometimes won a princess, sometimes a wicked fairy; but this maiden pleases me, and it is a splendid castle. Ah, poor thing! no doubt it is grief at the loss of her parents which has paled her cheek. Perhaps I may find means of comforting her.'

"He advanced, took her hand, and said—

"'Believe me, lady, I grieve to hear that death has so early robbed you of your parents; but ladies require the protection of knights. Have you— pardon the liberty I take—have you chosen one to make you happy?'

"She shook her head. He continued, modestly—

"'In that case, may Kurd von Stein—whose name may have been heard even here as that of a trusty Knight of the Empire, and as having distinguished himself in many wars—may Kurd von Stein offer you his heart and hand?'

"A gleam of pleasure lighted up the pale face of the girl; such a one as you may have seen pass over a meadow when the moon shone suddenly from behind a cloud. She rose, and from a cupboard brought two gold-rings, set in black, and a wreath of sweet rosemary, (See Note 1.) which she twisted amongst the pearls in her hair. She signed to the knight to follow, and went towards the door. As he passed down the hall, he wondered that neither male nor female attendants were to be seen; but at that moment the door was thrown open by two old men in full holiday suit. Their robes were white, and richly embroidered with gold; their black barettes had large silver ornaments. They placed themselves on either side of the knight and lady, and with them descended the long flight of stairs, on which Sir Kurd's step alone was heard; the others seemed rather to glide than walk.

"Sir Kurd began to feel very uncomfortable; he did not like the style of thing at all, and half repented of having pledged himself; but it was now too late to retract, and an irresistible power seemed to draw him onwards. The old men led them to the castle chapel. Lights already burned on the high altar; monuments of gleaming white marble, ornamented with weapons and golden inscriptions, rose on all sides. It was before one of these that the lady stopped; the iron figure of a bishop rested on it; the eyes were closed, the hands folded. She touched the figure; it instantly rose, and the eyes sparkled, as you may have seen the northern lights sparkle through the keen air of a winter night. He went to the altar, and standing before the bridal pair, said, in a deep and solemn voice—

"'Say, Sir Kurd von Stein, will you wed with the noble and honourable Lady Bertha von Windeck?'

"As the leaves of the aspen and tremulous poplar shiver when a chilly breeze touches them, so trembled the knight as the lady passed her arm round him. He tried to say—he did not quite know what; but he could not utter a sound, his very blood seemed curdled in his veins. Hark!—the crowing of a cock. A storm swept through the chapel, and the castle trembled to its very foundations. In an instant all had vanished, and Sir Kurd sank down in a swoon. On coming to himself, he lay—where? Amongst the long grass in the castle court, under the spreading branches of the silver pine, and by his side stood his faithful charger, while the cold grey light of morning began to appear in the east.

"'Was it a dream? Did I really see these awful sights?' said the knight to himself; and still the cock crew on.

"Sir Kurd mounted his horse, quickly left the castle, and, without looking behind him, rode towards the spot where the cock was yet crowing. He soon reached a hospitable farm-house, standing amongst the meadows in the valley, by the side of a clear stream. Here he dismounted, just as the sun rose, and while partaking of a hearty breakfast, of which he stood in great need, he related to the farmer all his adventures of the past night, who, in his turn, told many others of the same sort. Sir Kurd found that his servant had been unable to reach the castle to which he had sent him, and had spent the night at the farm; so they soon after started together, the knight feeling most thankful to be rid of his ghostly bride."

Charles's story met with perhaps more applause even than it deserved. He confessed that it was a very free translation of a German tale he had read somewhere, but it was not admired the less for all that.

Two days after this a carriage drove up to the door, and out of it stepped Buttar and Ellis. Ernest knew nothing of their coming. It was a surprise his father wished to give him. The boys were delighted to meet each other, and kept shaking hands till they nearly dislocated each other's wrists. Buttar, who had come from a distance, had picked up Ellis on the way. The parents of the latter were glad to have him with a companion like Ernest, from whom, from his account, they believed he could reap so much benefit.

Not long after another carriage arrived, and great was the delight of all parties when Lemon and Tom Bouldon's faces were seen looking out of the window.

"This is jolly!—how delightful!—how capital!—what fun!" were some of the exclamations which escaped the boys' lips as they shook hands with each other.

"And the frost has begun here, as I suppose it had with you," added Ernest. "And the gardener says he is certain that the ponds will bear to-morrow, and if they do, we shall have some magnificent skating. There is not a particle of snow on the ice, and when it set there was a perfect calm, so that it is as smooth—as smooth—what shall I say?—as ice can be. Oh, we shall have some first-rate skating, and hockey, perhaps, and sleighing also, such as people have in Canada. John has had a sleigh built, such as he saw when he went over there in the last long vacation. He proposes to drive young Hotspur in it. We shall fly over the ground at a tremendous rate if he does. There isn't a horse in the country like young Hotspur for going. My pony, whom we call Larkspur, is first-rate of his sort; but when I am riding out with any one mounted on young Hotspur I feel just as if I was on board a small yacht with the 'Alarm' or one of those large fast racing cutters in company. You have all brought your skates I hope. If you have not, I dare say we have some spare ones which will fit you. We have had them given to us at different times, and most of my brothers have outgrown theirs, so that I have no doubt we shall find enough. Oh, Ellis, do you say that you cannot skate? Never mind, you will soon learn. You have learned many things more difficult. I'll undertake that you will be quite at home on your skates in the course of a week."

So Ernest ran on, as he conducted his friends round the house, to exhibit to them its numberless attractions, and to show them their rooms.

They could not fail to be pleased, for the house, although not fitted up with anything like luxury, contained within itself abundance of objects to afford amusement and instruction to the inmates when confined by bad weather.

There was a first-rate library, in the first place, and a very interesting museum, illustrating all parts of the world. The articles in it were well arranged, and every one had a clearly written and full description attached to it. The articles from each country were placed together, and the countries were arranged according to their respective quarters of the globe. There were good maps, and many pictures illustrating the scenery or habits and customs of the inhabitants. Many hours might be passed profitably in it, which is not often the case with museums. At all events, I have never found that I could carry away much information from one. At the same time, I own that I think very likely I may have a more correct notion of the forms of animals, and of the shape of boats and buildings of foreign countries, than I should possess had I not visited the British Museum, and others of less note. The most advantageous way of visiting a general museum is to go with a definite object each time, and to attend exclusively to that object. I have never seen a museum better arranged than that which had been formed by Mr Bracebridge, aided by his sons, who were great collectors for it, and accordingly took a warm interest in its success. However, not only studiously disposed people found amusement in the house. There was a billiard table, and foils, and boxing-gloves, and single-sticks, and basket-sticks, and implements for all sorts of less athletic games at which ladies can play.

"Why, Ernest, you live in a perfect paradise of a home," exclaimed Buttar, as at last they reached the sleeping-rooms which Mrs Bracebridge had appropriated to her young guests.

"My father and mother make it so," said Ernest, enthusiastically. "They regulate everything so well, and yet we have such perfect liberty. Our father trusts us entirely. He tells us that there are certain things which he does not wish us to do—sometimes he gives us his reasons, and very good ones they are; at other times he gives no reason, but simply says we are not to do certain other things, and we know that his reasons are good, so we do not think of doing them. Frequently he leaves us to act according to our discretion, and gives us only general rules for our guidance."

Buttar could thoroughly appreciate the advantages his friend possessed, for they were advantages of no ordinary kind, and were the cause of the superiority he possessed over the greater number of his companions.

What a merry evening that was on which the boys arrived! Lemon had met Charles Bracebridge in Germany, though it was only just before the holidays he discovered that Ernest was his brother. He now came more especially to visit him. He was of a more suitable age than Ernest for a companion.

There was a Christmas-tree loaded with really useful prizes, so that all the boys were glad enough to obtain some of them, and their distribution caused great fun; then they had a most uproarious game of blindman's buff. Some of them dressed up in all sorts of costumes, so that when they were caught, the blind man could not tell who they were.

Bouldon made a capital blind man. He rushed furiously here and there, over everybody and everything, never minding where he went, shrieking with laughter all the time, but keeping his hands well out before his head, so that he ran no chance of knocking it against the wall. More than once Tom came head over heels down on the ground; but amid the shouts of laughter, in which he himself heartily joined, having stood on his head for a minute, he leaped up, and made a desperate dash at some of the players. At last he caught Buttar, who also made a very amusing blind man, and though he suffered several mishaps, never for a moment lost his temper.

Among Buttar's very many good qualities, a fine temper was one. Nothing ever put him out, though he was often much tried. He was good-tempered by nature, but he was also good-tempered from principle. He knew how wrong it is to lose temper, and he despised the frivolous excuses often made by people for doing so. The game of blindman's buff lasted a wonderfully long time. At last the ladies began to think that it had become almost too boisterous, and Lemon, who was a capital hand at starting games, proposed the game of "baste the bear."

"What's that?" asked Buttar. "In all my experience I never heard of that game."

"I'll show you, then. Who knows it? Do any of you?"

Tom Bouldon acknowledged that he did.

"Very well, Tom; you must be the first bear. I'll be your keeper," said Lemon. "Properly speaking, everybody ought to draw lots as to who should be bear, and the bear selects his keeper. However, we will suppose that preliminary got over. All the rest of the company are to tie their handkerchiefs into knots, with which to baste the bear. Now, I, as keeper, will fasten a rope round the waist of the bear, leaving a scope of about five feet. We take our position within a circle of about five feet in diameter, in the centre of the room. Here the circle is easily formed by tacking a little red tape down to the carpet. If I, as keeper, touch anybody without dragging the bear out of the ring, that person must become bear, and may select his keeper; or if the bear catches anybody by the legs, and holds him fast in the same way, he must take the bear's place. Now we are all ready. Very well, then, hit away with all your might."

Tom looked very lugubrious as, taking up his position, he saw the preparations making for his basting.

"Oh, oh, oh! Don't, kind gentlemen, hit hard," he cried out in piteous accents; and then in a deep tone he added, "if you do, to a certainty I'll catch hold of some of you, and make you rue the day."

Nothing daunted by Tom's threats, the party began to attack him vigorously; but they ran no little risk of being caught by Lemon, who sprang out on them to the full length of the rope, now and then almost pulling Tom out of his line; Bouldon also was very active, especially when any of his schoolfellows came near him. He growled and roared in a very wild-beast-like way, sometimes springing at Ernest, sometimes at Buttar or Ellis. Frank, the midshipman, also came in for an equal share of his attentions, and he seemed to consider that he was much on a par with him. The moment Frank understood the game, he played as vehemently as anybody. He said that it was a capital game, and that he should introduce it on board the next ship he joined. In spite of all his activity, Tom got many a hard lick, and still he remained a bear. At last he pretended to be so weary of his exertions, that he could not attempt to capture one of his tormentors. Those who were acquainted with Tom best, and saw his eye, knew that he was not to be trusted. The midshipman, however, was not up to him, and rushing in, found himself grasped tightly round the knee by the seeming half-sleeping bear.

"I thought that I should catch you, Frank," cried Bouldon, shouting in triumph. "Now please go and turn into a bear, and take care that you don't get into a butter boat."

Frank had therefore to become the bear. He chose Ellis as his keeper. Never was a more extraordinary bear seen. He stood on his head; he jumped about with his feet in his hands, and rolled round and round as a ball; and when anybody came near to baste him, he jumped and kicked about in so wonderful a way that no one could hit him. Every one also saw that he was very likely to catch them if they ventured near.

At last Charles, the narrator of the German ghost story, got caught, and he chose his brother John as his keeper. They tried to catch one of their sisters, or some of the eldest of the family, but were very glad at length, so pestered were they by Bouldon, to catch him, when in a daring mood he ventured near them. Thus the game went on, and many other games succeeded, till bed-time at last arrived, and the boys exclaimed with one voice, "Well, we have had a jolly evening!"

> Note 1. A wreath of rosemary is worn by the dead in many
> parts of Germany.

Chapter Thirteen
Christmas Holidays and Winter Amusements

"Hurra! it was a terrific frost last night! the ice bears, and the gardener says we might drive a coach and six over it," exclaimed Ernest, rushing into Buttar's and Bouldon's room. "Up! up! Let us breakfast, and go down and try it. Get up, do, and I'll go and tell the other fellows. John has been getting his sleigh ready, and harnessing young Hotspur; so I don't doubt he intends trying the ice to-day."

Soon all the merry party were assembled in the breakfast-room. Just before nine Mr Bracebridge made his appearance, followed immediately by the rest of the family, and read a chapter in the Bible, and Morning Prayers. Then, when everybody had selected their places, he advised them to apply themselves to the cold viands, under which the sideboard literally groaned. With wonderful rapidity, eggs and ham, and brawn, and veal pie, and tongues, disappeared down their throats, mingled with toast, and rolls, and muffins, and slices from huge loaves of home-made bread, and cups of coffee, and tea, and chocolate. Bouldon did great execution among the viands, and he did not allow his modesty to stand in his way. At last breakfast was over, and then gimlets, and bradawls, and spare straps were in great requisition, to enable them to fit on their skates before they went to the pond. Some had spring skates, which were very quickly put on, the spring, which was between the sole of the boot and the sole of the skate, keeping all the straps tight, at the same time without any undue pressure. John Bracebridge was celebrated as a first-rate skater. His skates were secured to a pair of ankle boots, which fitted him exactly, and laced up in front. He put them on at the pond. There are two objections to that sort of skate. One is, that the feet get chilled from putting on a cold pair of boots, and if a person is skating away from home, he may not be able to find anybody to take care of his shoes.

"Are all the skates ready?" cried Ernest.

"All! all!" was the answer.

"Then don't let us lose more time of this precious frost," he added. "Remember, it may very speedily be over; so let us make the best of it we can."

In a laughing, merry body, with skates in hand, they hurried down through the grounds to the pond. It might well have been called a lake, for it was an extensive and very picturesque sheet of water, almost entirely surrounded by trees, with now and then an opening bordered by a plot of grass, or a bend of the grand walk which ran round it. Here and there was an island with a few birch-trees or willows growing on it, and over the trees could be seen, rising in the distance, a downy hill, now sprinkled with some snow which had fallen the night before the frost regularly set in, and which had thus not affected the surface of the lake. At the lower end the ground fell, and a long stream-like serpentine channel could be seen winding away, in one place overhung by trees, and in others between green meadows, till lost in the distance. The lower part was, in the summer, the favourite resort of anglers, for it contained some of the finest tench to be found anywhere in the neighbourhood.

No time was lost by those accustomed to skating in putting on their skates. John and Charles Bracebridge and Lemon had soon theirs ready, and rising on their feet, off they struck like birds about to fly, and away they went at a rapid rate, skimming over the smooth mirror-like expanse. Ernest longed to follow, for he had his skates on, and skated almost as well as they did; but he saw Ellis sitting down, having just cleverly enough put on his skates, but unable to move on them.

"Come, Ellis! up on your feet, my dear fellow, and lean on me," he exclaimed, gliding up to him. "Take this stick in your right hand. Be sure that you can stand on your feet; your ankles are as strong as those of other people, and your skates are as well put on. Look at Buttar, and Bouldon, and me. You will be able to skate as easily as any of us with a little practice. There is no necessity why you should tumble down. You can balance yourself off the ice perfectly, on the gymnastic poles, and in other ways. Now, hurra!— off you go!"

" Away went Ernest, fleet as the wind, holding his right hand up before him to balance himself."

Ernest knew that Ellis required all sorts of encouragement, so he said more to him than he would to any other boy. Ellis at last got up; his ankles slipped about a little, but he was anxious to follow his friend's advice. In a short time he felt that he could stand firmly on the ice; then he slipped about, pushing one skate before the other. First he helped himself on with his stick, and then he balanced himself with it, and in an incredibly short time could move about so as to feel little fear of falling.

"Now," exclaimed Ernest, "I have set you on your feet, I'll go and take a skim over the surface. Remember, the more you practise, and the faster you throw away fear, the sooner you will be able to do the same. Good-bye!"

Away went Ernest, fleet as the wind, holding his right hand up before him to balance himself, and disdaining any stick for the purpose. He did not stop to hear Ellis utter his thanks and regrets at having kept him so long from commencing the graceful exercise in which he so much delighted.

Ernest certainly did not enjoy it the less from having first performed a good-natured action for his friend. He, and Bouldon, and Frank looked on with admiration as he went gliding away over the ice; so easily, so gracefully he moved, now inclining to one side, now to the other, moving on apparently without the slightest exertion.

"There is not another fellow like him in the universe," exclaimed Bouldon, enthusiastically. "It will be a happy day when he is the cock of our school; and that he soon will be, for he could, if he chose, thrash many fellows twice his size already."

"I'm glad to hear you say that," answered Frank, not less warmly. "Ernest was always a pet of mine; we never quarrelled when we were together. I wish that I could have him to go to sea with me. He's just the fellow to be a general favourite in the navy, and to get on in it, too. He must do that."

Ellis could scarcely trust himself to speak, but he was not the less pleased to hear his friend thus eulogised. He knew that he thought him superior to anybody else, but he was not aware that he was held in such high estimation by his own family. Buttar and Lemon, coming up before the subject had been changed, added their own meed of praise to that which the others had awarded. Meantime Ernest, unconscious of what was being said, after circling the pond with what is called the forward roll, changing it to the Dutch—so denominated because it is the movement employed by the Dutch peasants as they skate over their canals and lagoons on their way to market—then began making figures of eight, the spread-eagle, the back roll, not to mention many other figures and evolutions, which perfectly astonished Ellis as he looked at them. Frank had not skated for a long time; but, undaunted, he soon had on his skates, and away he went, furiously on, as if he had suddenly been converted into a battering-ram. So fast did he go that he could not stop himself, and overtaking a stout gentleman, who was going deliberately along, before he could beg him to get out of his way he ran right up against him, and the consequence was, that he and the stout gentlemen came to the ice together, making a very considerable star, and a noise which was still more terrific. First there was the sudden crash and rending asunder of the thick ice, and then the noise went rolling and mumbling away to the other end of the pond.

"Hallo! young gentleman, we shall be in! we shall be in!" cried the stout gentleman, in an agony of fear.

"I can swim, if we are," answered Frank, scarcely refraining his laughter. "But beg pardon, sir; my skates ran away with me—they did indeed; and if I hadn't fallen foul of you, they would have carried me right across the pond. I'll help you up, though. You are not hurt, I hope."

"Not much, I believe. I came down on you, and you formed a soft cushion," answered the stout gentleman, good-naturedly. "But as to helping me up, do not, I pray you, attempt it on any account; we shall both of us go in if you do. Let us both roll away in opposite directions from the crack before we attempt to get on our feet. See how I manage."

As the stout gentleman spoke, he began slowly to roll himself over and over away from the centre of the star, and Frank imitating him, they were both of them soon again on their legs. Frank was going off again at full speed, having once more repeated his apologies for his carelessness, when the stout gentleman stopped him.

"We must not leave others to fall into the danger from which we have escaped," he cried out. "I observed, just now, some triangles with labels on the top, marked cracked and dangerous. We will get one and place it over the spot."

"I'll go and get the sign-posts you speak of," said Frank. "Don't trouble yourself, sir."

"Then I will keep guard round the spot, to prevent any unwary person from approaching it," said the stout gentleman.

Frank, on his return, found him going round and round the star.

"By to-morrow, I daresay, the wound will have healed," he remarked. "By pressing it gradually down, as I have been doing, the water will have risen into the interstices and have frozen the broken pieces together."

"I hope, sir, that I shall not be so clumsy again. I may not always meet people ready to take a knock-down so good-naturedly as you have done," said the midshipman.

Frank and the stout gentleman became great friends after this, and Frank obtained from him many useful hints about skating. Meantime, several other people assembled on the lake, which now presented a very animated spectacle. Frank having come back to see how Ellis was getting on, found Ernest with him, giving him some further instruction, from which the pupil was much benefiting.

"Well, Ernest," said Frank, "we have not had a skate together for a long time. What do you say to a race round the pond? I have got the use of my legs, I find, pretty well, but I don't think I could come any of those twists and turns, and spread-eagle kind of things."

Ernest said that he should be delighted to race his brother Frank, but advised him to curb his impetuosity.

"Oh, never fear! I've no other notion of going ahead but by putting on all the steam. My engines don't work at half-pressure," answered the midshipman. "Who'll start us? Buttar, will you?"

"With all my heart," answered Buttar. "Now get in line. Remember, the course is right round the pond, in and out into all the bays, and between all the islands. Now, once to make ready, twice to prepare. Once, twice, thrice, and—" Frank was so eager, that he was off almost before the word was out of Buttar's mouth—"away!"

Off went the racers, the rest of the party following, but making short cuts so as to observe their proceedings. The contrast between the two brothers' style was very amusing. Ernest's was all science or art, which enabled him to move gracefully along without any apparent exertion. All he did was to keep his hands waving slowly, to expedite his movements as he swept round an island or into a bay, and to preserve his balance. Frank, on the contrary, had very little skill or science. All he did was by sheer muscular power, with a determination to keep his legs, and to go on ahead. The skates went deeply into the ice as he struck out, and he seemed rather to be running than skating, with such rapidity did he put one foot before the other. All the time his arms were in violent motion, while he flourished a stout oak stick, thick enough to fell a buffalo, and at the top of his voice kept shouting and shrieking with laughter, calling on Ernest to heave-to for him, or to port or starboard his helm, or to keep along in shore, and not attempt to make short cuts.

Ernest was very much amused at his nautical brother's mode of proceeding, and he could not help suspecting that Frank was assuming a considerably greater amount of roughness than he really possessed. However, Ernest found that he had to skate his very best to keep ahead of him, when going in a direct line, though he beat him hollow whenever they had to make turns between the islands and the mainland, or to pass along the sinuosities of the bays. Still it seemed surprising, considering the little practice he had had, how perfectly at home Frank was on his feet. Ernest made a remark of that sort to him.

"Not a bit surprising, old fellow," he answered. "It is simply because I know the skates can do the work I put them to. A fellow who has learned to stand on the deck of a ship, rolling her guns in the water, and pitching bows under, and has had to furl top-gallant sails with a hurricane blowing in his teeth, can easily do anything of this sort, if he has the mind to do it. I am not like you, Ernest; you see I have been scorching under tropical suns, while you have had time to practise the art of skating."

They could not, however, talk very much as they went flying round the pond. Buttar and Bouldon, and Ellis and others sung out, "A race, a race, a race!" and attracted the attention of the rest of the people on the ice, who all stopped skating to look at them. It seemed still a doubtful point which would get in the first. Perhaps Ernest had not gone as rapidly as he might, that he might give Frank the pleasure of keeping up with him. There was a long clear run nearly from one end of the pond to the other. They were just about to do it. Ernest was a little ahead of Frank, so that he could turn his head over his shoulder to talk to him. Ernest came gliding smoothly on. "Skurry, skurry, skurry; clatter, clatter; ez–z–ez," came Frank. I cannot better describe the noise made by his skates. Utter fearlessness was evidently the secret of his power. On he came, as little fatigued, in spite of all his exertions, as when he started.

"Heave-to, old fellow, I say; heave-to! Give us a tow, then, for I see how it is; you intend to keep ahead, though how you do it I can't tell," he continued to cry out as he approached the end of the pond, where Buttar and the rest stood ready to receive them. Ernest, as might be supposed, came in first, and gracefully wheeled round after he had touched Buttar's hand. On came Frank, hurrahing and shouting, "Second in, at all events." Touching Buttar's hand, on he went. Was the bank to stop him? Not it. Up it he went, across the gravel walk, through the bushes, and down a bank into a meadow below, where was another piece of water, across which he shot, and then over another walk into the long canal pond, down which he went, shouting and laughing louder than ever.

"Our race is to the end of the ponds, Ernest, remember that. Ponds, old fellow! why don't you come on?"

Tom Bouldon, delighted, went after him, as did two or three other boys from the neighbourhood who were not skating; but Ernest was afraid of spoiling his skates, by giving them such rough usage, and left Frank to enjoy his fun, and to boast that he had beaten him in the long run. It was some time before Frank returned, his exploit causing a great deal of amusement to all present. Some time before this a fire, with a large screen of matting to keep off the wind, had been seen to blaze up, and now a horn sounding, the party on the ice assembled round it. They found servants roasting potatoes under the ashes, which were served out with plates of salt, and butter, and toast, to all who asked for them, while at the same time hot punch was handed about to the visitors.

"Capital stuff this!" cried Tom Bouldon, smacking his lips, after he had quaffed a glass of it, and, turning to Buttar, "I wish that the Doctor would provide us with something of the sort in an afternoon in cold weather. It's warm lemonade, with a little wine in it, I suspect. I'll take another glass of it, if you please."

Of course the servants handed Tom as many glasses as he asked for. Buttar took two or three. Away they skated. At first Tom got on very well, but in a few minutes he declared that the ice had become more slippery than ever, and that he had the greatest difficulty in keeping his legs; at the same time, that he felt a strong inclination to push on ahead.

"I say, Buttar, I believe that I could race the wind. Come, let us try; I don't mind what I do," he exclaimed, as he skated on furiously. "I don't mind what I do—do you?"

Buttar himself felt rather excited, but he suspected the cause, and recommended Tom to come and sit down with him on the bank till they became more composed. It was fortunate that they found out in time the strength of the punch, or they might have been, as some of the visitors to the pond were, by their own imprudence, completely overcome.

Tom was very glad that he had escaped committing himself, and much obliged to Buttar for warning him. He had bully Blackall's career before his eyes to warn him of the effects of drunkenness, and dreaded by any chance being led into it. He more than once went up to the fire for a hot potato, but each time the punch was offered him he wisely declined taking it. By the end of the day everybody declared that never was known so perfect a first day of skating. Most of the party, except the more practised skaters, were not a little stiff and sore from the exertions and tumbles. Ellis could scarcely move a limb, and Frank declared that he felt as if he had been fighting away the whole day. They had, indeed, been on their feet from half-past ten in the morning till nearly dark.

The next day much the same scenes were enacted.

After luncheon, a jingling of bells was heard, and young Hotspur appeared, drawing an elegant American sleigh. John Bracebridge, who was driving, dashed fearlessly on to the ice. The steed seemed delighted to have so slight a weight after him. The sleigh—so it is called in Canada and throughout America—had a seat in front for the driver, and an easy sloping one behind for two passengers. A handsome fur rug hung over it behind, almost reaching the ground, while there were two or three buffalo skins, in which those in the carriage might effectually wrap themselves up. Instead of having wheels, the carriage was placed on runners, two skates as it were, made of iron, with a frame-work lifting the body of the carriage about a foot, or a foot and a half, from the ground, and giving it a very light appearance. The harness was ornamented with little silvery sounding bells, and fringe, and tufts of red worsted, which made the whole turn-out look very gay. It gained universal admiration, and two ladies were easily persuaded by John Bracebridge to get into it, and to be driven round and round the pond.

"You may fancy yourselves transported suddenly to Canada, and whisking away over the Saint Lawrence," he observed, turning round as he drove on; "only I assure you that so smooth a piece of ice as this is rarely found to drive over. In Lower Canada especially, the sleighs are driven on the roads over the snow; but the old-fashioned French Canadian sleigh, used by all the country people, is so low that the front part sweeps the snow before it, and thus ridges are quickly formed all across the road. Another sleigh following has to surmount the ridges, and of necessity digs down on the opposite side, and scoops out more of the snow. Sometimes, also, they slide off either on one side or the other, and thus a succession of hills or waves, as it were, are made with slides, which send the sleighs nearly off the road on one side or the other, and make the driving away from the larger cities very far from pleasant. About Quebec, however, the roads are kept in good order, and sleighing is there a very agreeable amusement."

As young Hotspur could not go trotting round and round the pond all day, John at last drove him home, and then Frank proposed a game of hockey on the ice. He had provided a supply of sticks and a ball, and the proposal was welcomed with applause. The people present were not long in forming sides. Charles undertook to lead one side, Frank the other. Frank got his stout friend to be on his side, but he generally chose boys. He got Ernest and all his schoolfellows, except Lemon, who joined Charles, and there were several other boys who skated pretty well, and, as he said, looked plucky. A person must know how to balance himself well to play hockey on skates, otherwise, after having struck the ball, he is very likely to allow his stick to swing round, and to bring him over. There were twenty people on a side, big and little; but the shorter ones had decidedly the advantage, and ran away with the ball whenever they got up to it, driving it before them before any of the opposite party could overtake them. Ernest gave his brother some useful hints, from which he profited. The same tactics which Ernest had often employed at school Frank brought into play. The chief point in his plan was to keep three or four boys together, one to follow up another. If the leader missed, then number two ran in; if he failed to strike, then number three, and so on. The stout gentleman also turned out to be a capital player. He went on the "sure and steady wins the race" principle. Quietly yet rapidly he glided about after the ball, and when he got up to it, never failed to strike it, and to strike hard too. His exertions indeed mainly contributed to the success of Ernest's side, which triumphantly gained the day. Several games were played, and each time Ernest's side was victorious, though the defeated party took it very good-humouredly. Charles, however, observed that he had received several lessons from his opponents, and that he thought they would not find him so easily beaten again.

"Don't be too sure of that, Charlie," sung out Frank. "We also intend to-morrow to play twice as well as we did yesterday. Our motto is, 'We'll fight and we'll conquer again and again.'"

The morrow came, and a great game of hockey was the absorbing amusement of the day; even young Hotspur and the sleigh failed to attract so much interest. The stout gentleman was in his glory. He appeared with a hockey-stick of his own manufacture, and in garments which, if not graceful, precluded any of the youngsters from catching hold of his tails. There were the same sides as on the previous day, with several additional players; but none of them were very good, nor did they add much to the relative strength of each party. Ernest was the first to place the ball on the ice to strike it. The instant his stick descended, and the ball went whirling away over the smooth glass-like surface of the ice, Frank, followed by Buttar, Bouldon, and Ellis, darted forth with tremendous speed in the hopes of reaching it before any of the opposite party, and of driving it home; but before they could strike, Charles and Lemon were up to it, and sent it flying back again. The stout gentleman, however, who had only moved slowly on, saw it coming, and gliding up as it slid on towards him, struck it a blow which sent it two-thirds of the way across the pond once more. Frank, Ernest, and Buttar were up to it, Bouldon and Ellis keeping a little way behind them: Frank struck the ball, and sent it flying on, but it was into the midst of their opponents, who quickly drove it back again, when Bouldon, skating up, prevented it getting between Charles and Lemon, who stood prepared to drive it up to the goal, if, as they hoped, they could elude the vigilance of the stout gentleman. He, however, was not asleep, and watching their movements, as Tom Bouldon observed, as keenly as a boa-constrictor, glided swiftly up to the spot where they had driven the ball, and sent it spinning back, till once more Frank and Ernest got it within their power. Thus the game continued fluctuating; but finally, after many a bandy here and there, and many a tussle between the opposing parties, not a few upsets and other catastrophes, it was sent up to Ernest, who struck it a blow which sent it flying along between everybody, nobody being able to stop it up to the goal.

The next game was, however, still more severely contested; and at last, by desperate struggles, was won by Charles' party. Ellis had made wonderful progress in skating, thanks to Ernest's lessons, and his own resolution to overcome all difficulties. Of course, he got several severe tumbles, but he always picked himself up and went away again as if nothing had been the matter. In a short time he overcame all fear, and obtained the complete mastery over his feet.

"I should like to have your friend Ellis with me at sea for a few months," said Frank to Ernest, as they watched him tumble down and get up again, and go several times in succession to practise on the outside edge, undeterred by failures. "I like the fellow's spirit, and I am sure that there is a great deal to be made out of him."

"I am sure there is," was the reply. "At the same time, he is really so talented, and so good-hearted and humble-minded. He is one of my greatest friends. He trusts me, and I trust him, and that is, I suspect, the true secret of friendship."

Another day, Frank, taking a hint from John's sleigh, rigged out one with ropes. It was little more than a wide plank on runners, with seats for two people. The boys harnessed themselves to it, and invited the visitors to the lake to come and be dragged along. They had many applications for the honour, and it was a source of great amusement. No one seemed weary of dragging the sleigh, or of being dragged in it. Round and round the pond they went, often at so tremendous a pace that those being dragged shrieked out with terror; but their alarm could not have been very great, for when they were asked if they would go on again they never refused, or if they did, it was to let some sister or friend take their places. The next day three similar sleighs appeared, but they were covered with cloaks or rugs, and each had a flag of a different colour flying in front of it. As each sleigh required several persons to drag it, nearly all the gentlemen skaters were in a short time turned into horses, while the ladies were all eager to be dragged along; so away they all went, skating round and round the lake, and those who looked on could distinguish where their friends were by the colour of the flags. Sometimes they raced, and then the excitement was tremendous. However, one of the sleighs was upset, and the passengers thrown out, and the skaters sent here and there, some on their backs, and some on all-fours, to the alarm of those at a distance, and to the great amusement of those near, and who knew that no one was hurt. Mr Bracebridge, after this, prohibited racing with sleighs, for fear of accidents of a more serious character.

It is impossible to describe minutely all the amusements of those memorable Christmas holidays. A fortnight passed away, and though the glass-like appearance of the ice had somewhat disappeared, owing to the innumerable cuts its surface had received from careless skaters, the skating was continued with unabated ardour. Then came down a heavy fall of snow, which completely covered the ponds with a thick coat. Passages, were, however, swept across the ice, but the interest of skating was somewhat diminished. More snow followed, and then, except on small patches and walks which, with some exertion, were kept clear by the gardeners, there was no room whatever for skating. Notwithstanding this there were abundant sources of amusement. The younger guests were fortunate in having so good a master of the revels as Frank, the midshipman.

"Hurra, boys, a bright idea!" he exclaimed, one morning at breakfast, when some of the party were lamenting the destruction of the ice. "We'll build a castle of snow; not a puny little affair, but a castle with high walls and parapets, and a deep ditch and outworks, such as cannot be captured without hard fighting. However, as we don't really wish to kill each other, instead of cutlasses and bayonets, and swords, and pistols, and all those sorts of deadly weapons, we will use good honest snowballs. We'll build the castle first, and choose sides afterwards, so that no one will know whether they are going to defend or attack it, and no one inclined to be treacherous will leave any weak places. There is a high mound in Beech-tree meadow, which will make a capital foundation, and save a great deal of labour. Who is for it?"

Of course, all the younger guests were delighted with Frank's proposal. Mr Bracebridge also entered into it. "You shall have the assistance of all the gardeners, who can do nothing during this weather," he observed; "I will tell them also to engage half-a-dozen men thrown out of work; they with their barrows will much expedite the operation."

"Thank you, papa; thank you, sir," exclaimed the boys; and as soon as breakfast was over most of them jumped up ready to go to the scene of action. Ernest, however, said that he had his holiday task to go through, and that he must give one hour to that while he was fresh, and before he allowed his thoughts to be occupied with the amusements of the day. This reminded Buttar and Ellis that they had their tasks, to which they had as yet paid very little attention. Bouldon was inclined to think this proposal to study a very slow proceeding, as he had been in the habit of not looking at his task till the last week of the holidays, and often he did not finish off learning it till he was on his way to school. Now, however, as Ernest and others set the example, he began to think that he ought to do something.

"Very well," observed Frank; "we will not start for an hour and a quarter; that will give you time to get out your books; and if you all read hard, you will do something. I'll go to school, too, and rub up my navigation."

Ernest, followed by his guests, accordingly repaired to the study. Tom Bouldon, on looking into his portmanteau, found that, by the most unaccountable negligence, as he said, the servant had not packed up any of his school-books, but had put in instead a copy of "Robinson Crusoe," "Tom Cringle's Log," and the "Boy's Own Book." However, Ernest and Ellis between them were able to supply him; so Master Tom, having no excuse for idleness, set to with a will, and was surprised with the progress he made, and the satisfaction it afforded him.

"Well, I really think I will do a bit of my task every day till it is finished," he exclaimed, as Frank, pulling out his watch, told the party that time was up, and that they might set off for the scene of action.

When they reached Beech-tree Meadow, they found a quantity of snow already collected from a distance in the neighbourhood of the mound. On one side, a little way off, was a miniature castle, which Frank said he had got up early in the morning to construct, so that everybody might see what they were about. The model was much admired, and Frank acting as architect, the work proceeded with wonderful rapidity. Some carried the snow; others acted as masons, and piled it up and smoothed it off, he, standing in the middle, aiding and directing. A circular tower of fully twenty feet in diameter was quickly raised, and fully fifteen feet high, and finished off at the summit in a castellated form, with a parapet; and then there was an outer wall with a deep ditch; between them and the tower was a gateway, and a bridge, constructed partly of snow and partly of planks, led to it. It really had, when finished, a very imposing appearance, and looked as capable of resisting a foe as one of the Martello towers which guard the coasts of Great Britain.

Frank had, in the morning, despatched an invitation to all the boys he knew of in the neighbourhood to come and join in the sport, and by the afternoon a large army was collected. Everybody was too eager in the work to go in to luncheon, so it was brought out to them. At last all was ready. Lemon undertook to be the leader of one party; of course, Frank acted as general of the other. Ernest, and Buttar, and Ellis were on Frank's side; Bouldon, with Charles, and some of the other Bracebridges, joined Lemon. There were besides some twenty or more boys on either side, so that there were fully fifty combatants. They tossed up as to which side was to defend and which to attack the castle. Lemon got the first choice, and undertook the defence of the place. A flag on a pole was hoisted in the centre, and till this was hauled down the castle was not to be considered as captured. As soon as these preliminaries were arranged, all hands set to work to manufacture snowballs. Several piles were made at short distances surrounding the castle. These might be captured by a sortie. There were also flags on staffs stuck about which might be taken. On the outworks of the castle and on the walls were several flags. Piles of snowballs were placed inside the castle walls, and there were also heaps of snow out of which others could be manufactured. Lemon had brought his horn, and the besieging army had a couple among them, which had a very fine effect.

Frank, having marshalled his troops, formed them into three divisions, which were to attack simultaneously on different sides. Ernest led one, Buttar another, and Frank commanded the third party in person. These arrangements were made out of sight of the castle; and, to give more effect to the attack, the army marched through the woods sounding their horns, which were answered by a note of defiance from the castle.

"It is getting somewhat cold," exclaimed Buttar, who was practical in his notions. "The fellows inside must be colder still, waiting for us. All our valour will be frozen up. Let us begin to warm up our blood."

"Certainly, Colonel Buttar," answered Frank, laughing. "A very sensible remark. On, brave army to the attack! Death or victory! Don't mind the snowballs. Turn your heads into battering-rams, and your pockets into arsenals, and the place will quickly be ours. Now, Colonels Bracebridge and Buttar, lead round your men to the positions allotted to you."

"Too-too-too!" sounded the horns louder than ever, and the three divisions burst at the same moment out of the woods, and advanced to take up their positions near where their ammunition had been piled up, of the existence of which the defenders of the castle were supposed, till that moment, not to be aware.

"Too-too-too!" again sounded the horns, and while a sentinel remained to guard each pile of snowballs and their respective flag-staffs, the rest of the army, having loaded themselves with ammunition, rushed bravely to the attack. Then began a regular snow-storm. The besiegers and besieged pelted away with tremendous energy, till the former were covered with snow from head to foot, while the latter could scarcely show their faces above the walls. Under cover of this heavy fire, or rather snow-storm, Ernest attempted to cross the bridge, which had been allowed to remain, and to force the door. He was followed closely by Ellis and two other boys: but they were almost overwhelmed with the heaps of snow showered down upon them. Still they battered away with their fists and shoulders, as they were unprovided with other weapons; but the door would not yield. In fact, it had been completely blocked up from within, so that no force could have opened it. Meantime, Buttar, by Frank's directions, was shelling the castle from a distance; but as this produced no effect, and only supplied the besieged with ammunition, he was ordered to draw near to assist in a general escalade. Frank's plan of dividing his forces had prevented the besieged from making a sortie. He now ordered a general escalade. Scaling ladders were not to be used, but the backs of the combatants were to serve for the purpose. No sooner was the order given than, rushing up together, with masses of snow they filled up the ditch; and then one sprang on the back of the other, and others mounted above them; then Ernest, seeing a good ladder formed, climbed up it to the top, though he was nearly knocked over by the shower of snowballs which assailed him; the top of the castle, also, was so slippery that he had the greatest difficulty in getting hold of it, and his position was anything but pleasant. Meantime, Tom Bouldon, one of the besieged, who was burning to distinguish himself, seeing all the rest of the party engaged, telling Lemon that he had a dodge, and to look out for him, slipped over the parapet amid a shower of snow, so that he was unseen, and then, climbing up the side of the ditch, scampered off to get hold of one of the standards of the enemy, the sentinel left to guard it having deserted his post that he might join in the attack. He seized it, and was hurrying back, scarcely restraining a shout of triumph, when Ernest saw him.

"Tom, you traitor, let go that!" he sung out; but as he was mounted on the backs of four other boys, and fighting away at the top of the wall, he could not enforce his commands.

Tom, hearing him, scuttled away to the other side, where Buttar was endeavouring to effect a breach. Two boys made chase after him, but he got up to the wall before them, and throwing the flag into it, he sprang up on the backs of some of the besiegers, who did not find out in time that he did not belong to their party; and Lemon being on the watch for him, lent him a helping hand, and got him safe into the castle. Then he seized the flag he had brought so gallantly off, and went round the castle walls, waving it in the faces of the besiegers, and crowing as lustily as any young cock. Frank, when he discovered what had been done, felt like a general who has unwarily allowed his camp to be attacked; and now, seeing that the other two standards were unprotected, sent back a guard to each.

It may appear strange that Bouldon should have so easily got into the castle; but in his case he had a friend to help him, while in the case of the besiegers everybody was opposed to them. So strong was the castle, and so manfully was it defended, that it appeared as if it would effectually hold out to the end of the day.

Time after time Frank returned to the assault, and as often he and his troops were tumbled over into the ditch. This, also, was Ernest's fate; indeed he at last gave up all hopes of taking the castle in the way proposed. Telling the rest of his followers to continue pelting away with all their might, he called Ellis to his councils. Ellis at once advised an attempt to undermine the walls. He had run his head into a soft place, and he thought he might get through. The idea was a bright one. Ernest immediately went round and got some men from Frank and Buttar, to assist by the warmth of their snowballing to cover their proceedings, and then he and Ellis set to work to bore their way through. The other two commanders were all the time to keep up a series of incessant assaults, which might fully occupy the attention of the enemy. No one within the walls suspected what was taking place. They went on firing away with their snowballs as furiously as ever. No one seemed wearied. There was something very inspiriting in the work. It was far pleasanter than real fighting, because all the combatants might hope to live to fight again, for whichever side fortune might declare itself.

Lemon seemed to think, at last, that things were growing rather tame, so he seized his horn and began "too-tooing" away with all his might. It was answered more loudly than before by the horns of the besiegers, followed by a hotter shower of snowballs than ever sent by them into the castle. While Lemon and his followers were busily engaged replying to it, they found their legs seized by Ernest and Ellis, and several other boys, while Frank, mounting on the backs of some of his troops, leaped over the parapet on the opposite side. Lemon was so astonished that he knew not what order to issue. Buttar—a messenger being sent to summon him—came round with some followers to the same side, and forced his way with them through the hole. An attempt was made to throw the daring besiegers over the walls; but they kicked and shoved against them so furiously that a large breach was effected, up which the rest of the assailants poured; while Ernest and Ellis, overcoming all opposition, forced their way up to the standard, and seizing the flag-staff, hauled it down at the moment that one side of the castle fell with a tremendous crash, leaving it utterly defenceless. Lemon's horn sent forth a long wail of despair, while the other horns sounded notes of triumph, and the castle was declared to be truly and gloriously won.

"It is not your first military triumph, and I hope will not be your last," said Ellis to Ernest, as they were marching homeward.

"Nor yours either, and I hope will not be your last. If I go into the army, my great delight will be to find that you are going also."

When the boys reached the house, all the visitors from the neighbourhood found that they were expected to dine and spend the evening. The combatants did ample justice to the fare set before them, and it was announced that a conjuror would make his appearance in the evening, to astonish them with his wonderful performances. Ernest and Bouldon disappeared directly after dinner. Ernest said he had to go and make preparations for the conjuror, and Tom, putting his hand to his heart, said that he felt it his duty to go and help him. When the boys came up from dinner they found one end of the large drawing-room, in which there was a deep recess, fitted up as a theatre, and in the centre a table, at which sat a man with a huge pair of spectacles, a long white beard and moustache, a high conical cap, covered over with all sorts of strange hieroglyphics, and many other curious devices. Round his head was a turban. He wore a tight green waistcoat, a red silk flowing robe over it, while a handsome sash bound his waist, in which was stuck an ink-horn, a wand, a huge knife or dagger, a pistol, and several other articles. Altogether, he was a somewhat formidable-looking character. By his side appeared, when the curtain drew up, a curious-looking clown, with a huge face, with all sorts of twists and curls in it, great big ears, a cock-up nose, and a short stumpy beard. This extraordinary physiognomy was covered with a high cap, which had a tassel and bells. He wore also a party-coloured waistcoat, huge full breeches of all the colours of the rainbow, hose of yellow, and long shoes with rosettes of vast size. He stood forth a veritable clown or jester of bygone days.

The magician rose. He seemed to be a very tall man, and contrasted strongly with his attendant, who was one of the roundest, shortest, most punchy-looking little men ever seen. A symphony was played on a piano behind the curtains, during which the magician waved his wand, and then in a deep voice he explained that he was about to perform a series of wonderful and unaccountable tricks, which no one had ever equalled, or was ever likely to equal while the world lasted; on which the clown clapped his hands and nodded his head in approval, exclaiming, in the oddest squeaking voice imaginable, "Certainly, certainly; my master speaks the truth; who can doubt him? If anybody does doubt him, let him take care of me."

The conjuror hemmed, and, waving his wand, took up a pile of halfpence. "Now, ladies and gentlemen, you see these halfpence, and you see this cap. The cap I will place on the table, and taking the halfpence in my left hand, as you see, I will pass them from under the table into the cap. Heigh, presto, fly!" Sure enough, he lifted up the cap, and there were the halfpence. "Now I will pass them back again into my hand—listen." One after the other they were heard dropping into his hand, and when the cap was lifted they were gone. Then he put a die on the table, and covering it with his cap, sent the halfpence back to take its place. There they were. He covered them up; they had disappeared, and the die took their place.

He next produced a round tea-caddy. He asked a lady for a cambric handkerchief. Several were tendered. He took one, and put it into the caddy. Drawing out one end, while examining it by a candle to observe its texture, it caught fire. It had burnt a good deal before he could find the cover to put it out. No sooner had he done so than, pronouncing a few magic words, he opened the canister, and presented the handkerchief uninjured. Loud applause followed. "Now, ladies and gentlemen," he said, holding up a large silk pocket-handkerchief, "examine this handkerchief. It has no double lining. It is a plain simple handkerchief. Watch me narrowly. I throw it over the table. I hold it up. See what comes forth." A whole stream of filberts fell from the handkerchief. "Here, Placolett, take them to the company," said the magician, and the round-faced dwarf, with many odd twists and bounds, handed them round. Again the magician spread the handkerchief, and this time produced a still larger quantity of sugar-plums, sufficient, it seemed, to fill a hat. They also were handed round. Once more the handkerchief was spread, and produced a number of bouquets of beautiful flowers, some real and some artificial. These in like manner were distributed among the young ladies present.

"Will any lady lend me a plain gold ring?" asked the magician. One was handed to him by Placolett. He held it up between his finger and thumb. "Presto, fly!" he exclaimed, and threw it into the centre of the room. Everybody tried to catch it, but could not. It had vanished. Placolett hunted about, and at last found it under a cushion at the furthest corner of the room. Again he handed it to his master, who invited a little girl to take it; but before it reached her fingers it had disappeared, and Placolett, as before, hunting about, found it in the heel of a boy's shoe. Now Placolett collected a dozen pocket-handkerchiefs from the company, and the magician tied them up in a handkerchief, which he placed on the table. He ordered Placolett to bring him a basin and a jug, meaning, of course, that the jug should contain water, but there was none, so he sent Placolett again to fetch it, and ordered him to bring some soap. Meantime he threw some black balls up to the ceiling, which never came down again; and then he swallowed a mustard-pot, a salt-cellar, and a pepper-box; and then he took three cups and three balls, and made the balls pass under the cups, so that each cup had a ball under it, and then he brought them all together under one cup merely by waving his wand over them; and finally some twenty cups in succession appeared out of one of them. At last Placolett came back, bringing some water, but it was cold instead of hot, and there was no soap, and then an iron was wanted. Before he went for them, his master made him borrow two hats. One the magician placed above the other on the table. Then he took one of his magic cups, and showing that there was nothing in it, turned it upside down. He lifted it, and, lo and behold, there was a walnut inside! This he put into the hat, and as often as he lifted the cup there was a walnut, which, like the first, he transferred to the hat. At last Placolett came back. "Now," observed the magician, "the hat is half-full of walnuts. Heigh, presto! pass through the upper into the lower hat," he cried, and lifting the upper hat, that was found to be empty, while the lower one was half-full of indubitable walnuts, for the guests cracked several which were handed to them by Placolett.

"Now, ladies and gentlemen, you gave me some handkerchiefs," observed the magician. "I shall have much pleasure in washing them for you." Saying this, he took the bundle on the table, and emptied its contents into the basin, and then began washing in a very unartistic, rough way, evidently tearing them; and one, before wetting it, he held up to the candle, and carelessly set it on fire. Then he spread a blanket, and took them out, and began ironing them; but the iron was too hot, and he was evidently singeing them horribly. "Never mind," he exclaimed, "I have a magic ironing machine, which will do the work in a moment." He produced a box, with a handle like a churn, put the wet half-singed bundle in, and giving one turn of the handle, produced the handkerchiefs all washed, neatly folded and scented, and sent them round by Placolett to their owners.

It would be difficult to describe all the clever tricks he performed. He put a ring into a handkerchief, and it disappeared. He passed an awl through a piece of wood and Placolett's nose, and then put a piece of whipcord through the hole, working it backwards and forwards, to the dwarfs evident agony; and then he produced a funnel, which he held at a boy's elbow, and by pumping away with the other arm, at last a stream of wine flowed out. Then he put a large die on the table, and covered it with a box and then with a hat. He lifted up the hat and then the box, and the die was gone. He produced it, however, from under the table, through which it had evidently gone.

I will not speak of many other minor tricks which he performed with cards and other things, which elicited a fair share of applause. He next borrowed a sovereign, and produced an apple, which he sent round to the company. He begged some one to mark the sovereign, which was given back to him. He put it on the table, and covered it with a red cup. Then he took a knife, and holding up the apple, cut it in two, when the sovereign was found to be in the middle of it.

"Ah, I forgot; I have still a trick or two more," he remarked. "Here is a bottle. Will any lady like port, or sherry, or claret, or whisky, or brandy, or liqueur?" Some said one thing, some said another, and Placolett handing a tray of small glasses, he filled one after the other with whatever was asked for. Once he let the bottle drop, but it was not broken, as he was able to prove by handing it round to the company. Then, after considering a moment, he showed a large glass bowl full of ink. He took some of the ink out with a ladle, and put it into a plate, which he showed to the company. Then he covered up the bowl with his silk handkerchief, and on lifting it the ink had disappeared, and the bowl was seen to be full of clear water, with gold and silver fish swimming about in it.

"One exhibition more," he remarked; "and, ladies, wind up your nerves for a dreadful catastrophe. Here is a pistol, powder, and bullets. Examine them. Will any one load the pistol? See that the powder is genuine." It was done. The magician took the pistol, and put in some wadding. Then Placolett took it back, and some gentleman having marked three bullets, put them in one after the other. More wadding was then put in, and rammed down. "Who will fire?" asked the magician, holding up a plate at arm's length. Scarcely had the smoke cleared away when the magician handed the plate with the three marked bullets rolling about in it.

Everybody was expressing surprise at the interesting performance they had witnessed, and wondering where the magician had come from, when he and Placolett, with many bows, retired behind the curtain. Directly afterwards it was opened, and who should appear but Ernest and Tom Bouldon, while the magician and his attendant had disappeared.

Even Christmas holidays must have an end. The guests went back to their respective homes, all declaring that they had never enjoyed themselves so much as they had on this occasion since they first went to school.

Chapter Fourteen
Return to School—A Grand Game at Football

"Here we all are again," exclaimed Tom Bouldon, as he shook Ernest, and Buttar, and Ellis, and his other friends by the hand, as they first met at school after those memorable Christmas holidays. Of course they had a great deal to talk about; the fun they had had at Oaklands, and what they had all done afterwards; then they had to discuss the changes in the school; the qualities of the new boys who had arrived, and what had become of the old ones who had gone away.

Barber had got back, and was as conceited as ever, and as supercilious towards his old school-fellow Ellis, who still seemed always strangely cowed in his presence. In many respects Barber, unhappily, bade fair to rival Blackall. He was not so great a bully, but then he had not the power of being so, as he was not so strong, and not so high up in the school. However, he seemed fully inclined to exercise his bullying propensities towards poor Ellis, and though he did not strike him, he never lost an opportunity of attacking him with the words which wound far more than sharp knives.

"This must never be," exclaimed Ernest, one day, when he had accidentally heard Barber abusing Ellis, and the latter had walked away without retorting or attempting a defence.

"Your friends, my dear Ellis, must for their own sakes, as well as for yours, insist on your taking notice of what that fellow says, both of you and to you. We must bring him to an explanation, and clear up the mystery. We are certain, as I have often assured you, that his treatment of you is undeserved; and why should he go on insinuating all sorts of things against you, and not dare to speak out?"

"Oh, do not push things to extremities," answered Ellis, and the tears almost came into his eyes. "That can do me no good. Barber does not act generously towards me, but I think that he believes that he has the right to abuse me; and if he really thought me guilty of the crime of which I am accused, he would certainly be right in not associating with me."

Ernest was not satisfied with this reply, and Ellis's behaviour afterwards was so strange, he thought, towards him, that when he and Buttar talked the matter over together, they could not help allowing a shade of suspicion to creep over their own minds that all was not right. They tried not to let Ellis discover it, but he was too keen-sighted and sensitive not at once to perceive that their feelings towards him were changed, and that made him, in spite of all they could do, retire more than ever away from them and into himself.

The weather continued so cold that the ordinary games could not be played with any satisfaction, and none but those requiring a good deal of bodily exercise were in vogue. Lemon, and some of the more actively disposed fellows, determined to get up a game of football, though it was generally played at our school late in the autumn. There were plenty of boys ready to join in it, but the chief question was to decide who should form the sides. A number of the older boys were thought of, but they were not popular, or not active enough, or did not care enough about the game. At last it was decided to offer the command of one side to Ernest Bracebridge. It was a high honour, considering the time he had been at school. He could not, nor did he wish to refuse it. He consulted Buttar, who of course agreed to be on his side, whom they should select. They asked Bouldon, and Gregson, and several others among their immediate friends, and then began to pick out others on whom they could depend, and who generally played with them. Neither of them mentioned Ellis. It was the first time they had neglected to ask him to join any game that was to be played since he had become what they called one of them. He happened to pass by, and heard them calling out the names of those invited to play. He stopped a moment, looked towards Ernest, and then turned away.

"I say, Buttar, do go and try and find him," said Ernest, in a low voice, relenting in a moment. "Ask him—press him to join us."

Buttar gladly set off on the mission; but though he looked in every direction, and inquired of everybody he met, Ellis was nowhere to be found.

"It cannot be helped; I wish that we had from the first asked him to join us," remarked Ernest, when Buttar returned to him with his report.

"Of whom do you speak?" asked Selby, a biggish and very gentlemanly boy.

"Of Ellis," said Buttar.

"Oh, we are much better without him," answered Selby. "There cannot be a doubt that he is not a satisfactory person, and you two fellows lose caste a good deal by associating with him. The idea is that he imposes on you; not that you believe he has been guilty of an act of dishonesty, and still consent to be intimate with him."

"An act of dishonesty!" exclaimed Ernest, with astonishment. "I cannot believe that."

Buttar repeated almost the same words.

"There can be no doubt about it. I heard the story this winter from a fellow who had been at the same school with him, and whose veracity I cannot doubt. He told me that Ellis was always looked upon as a very quiet, rather sawny sort of a fellow, without any harm; that he kept much to himself, and had no intimate friends. He was also always poor, and spent no money in the way other boys were in the habit of doing.

"There was another boy at the school who had always a good deal of money, sometimes as much as three or four pounds in his purse at a time. He was a very good sort of fellow, so he was thought, but rather soft. Ellis and he became intimate, and were looked upon as great friends, till on one occasion Arden, on going to his desk, found that his purse was gone, and, as he declared, with five pounds in it. A hunt was instituted in every direction; the masters were told of the loss, and the boys began to suspect each other. Soon it was whispered about that one of the boys was the thief. It was very extraordinary that just at this time Ellis appeared to have a good deal of money in his possession. He spent more than he had ever before done. Certainly, in two or more instances it was by giving it in charity. He bought also a microscope and some books, which another boy said that he had heard him remark he wished to have, but had not the money to buy them. These of themselves were suspicious circumstances; and many said that they thought Ellis must have taken the money. Some days afterwards suspicion grew into certainty when, on the master ordering all the boys to get up from their seats, that the school desks might be examined, a purse was found in Ellis's, which on being held up was claimed by Arden as that which had held his money. Ellis appeared to be struck dumb when he heard this. He stammered out that he had that very morning picked up the purse in the road near a hedge, and that he had intended going round to discover whether it belonged to any of the boys at the school. As it was empty, he knew that it would not be of much consequence, and that he had forgotten to make the inquiries he proposed. Of course everybody believed this to be a very lame defence; but the master inquired into the matter, and to the surprise of the boys said that he was satisfied, and that Ellis had fully accounted to him for the way he had become possessed of the money and the purse. The boys seemed to think that the master was more easily satisfied than he ought to have been, because he did not want to lose a pupil; at all events, Ellis was looked upon as a thief, and sent to Coventry. This treatment affected his health, and he was soon afterwards removed by his friends from the school. That is all I know about the matter."

"I am glad we did not ask him to play football," exclaimed Buttar. "The story is a very ugly one. I do not like the look of things."

Ernest gave a look of reproach at Buttar. "I am far from convinced that poor Ellis was guilty of the theft imputed to him," he remarked; "knowing him as I do, and as you ought to know him, Buttar, he acted on the occasion just as I should have expected him to do. However, while such stories are going about, it is certainly better for his sake and ours that he should not play in any of our games."

"Certainly," said Selby. "If he cannot offer us a proper explanation, I for one should object to play with him. But never mind him at present. It is high time that we should get ready for our game. Have you prepared the football, Bracebridge? It was your business to do so, or to get it done."

"Oh, I can do it very well myself," said Ernest, "I have two first-rate new ones hanging up in the play-room; they only want refilling. Come with me, and we will douse them in the pond." Two large footballs, but very flaccid-looking, were brought out, and by tying a stone and a line to them they were both very soon thoroughly soaked. He then took them out, and brought them into the house. First he took one, and undoing the lacing which confined one side, he drew out a flaccid bladder. "This is the sort of football we use here," he said, holding it up to Selby. "It cannot be easily rendered unserviceable by thorn, nail, or spike of any sort. If the bladder is injured, its place can be supplied for a few pence, and the leather casing will last for years. This is my blow-pipe," he added, producing a piece of tobacco-pipe. Undoing the mouth of the bladder, round which a piece of string was tightly fastened, he inserted his pipe, and very soon filled it with air. Before this, however, he had put back the bladder into its case. Having completed the filling of the bladder, he tightly laced up the ball so as to completely enclose it. "You see," he observed, "should this get pricked, even while we are playing, I can easily stop up the hole by forming a neck, and tying a piece of thin string round it. Buttar, do you take charge of the other ball in case it is wanted. It is high time for us to be on the ground, to see that the goals are properly erected."

Ernest, Buttar, and Selby on this hurried off to the park field where the game was to be played. The Doctor allowed football to be played, on the understanding that it would immediately be prohibited should one boy intentionally kick another; and two of the masters were required to be present to see that the game was carried on properly. The goals were about a hundred and thirty yards apart. They were formed of two upright poles, eight feet from each other, with a cross-bar to secure them at the top. The aim of the players was to pass the ball through their opponents' goal, and, of course, to prevent it from being passed through their own.

Ernest could not help feeling proud when he found forty boys ranged under him, many older and bigger than himself. He forgot for the time all about poor Ellis as he ran with one of the big footballs in his hand to the ground where the game was to be played, followed by those who had placed themselves under his leadership. Lemon and his party were there before him. Some of them, it must be owned, rather looked down upon him as a young upstart, and expected an easy victory. Lemon, however, when he consented to have him as opponent, knew well that he was one not to be despised, and endeavoured to impress upon his followers the necessity of playing their best.

"Those youngsters are sharp, active little fellows," he observed. "You must keep your eyes about you, and your legs going, or they will get the better of us, depend on that."

Ernest, on his part, addressed the boys on his side, and pointed out to them that those with whom they were about to contend were big and strong, and practised players, and that they could only hope to beat them by activity, watchfulness, and the exercise of their utmost skill.

These principles of action Ernest had learned from his father; they were such as his own mind eagerly grasped, which he brought into practice in his subsequent career, and which were the main cause of his success.

Lemon and Ernest tossed up for the first kick. Ernest won. With the ball raised high in his two hands, he walked rapidly into the middle of the ground. The sky was blue, the air keen and cutting; a brilliant glow of exuberant health sat on the cheeks of nearly all the players. A few only, who had begun to fancy themselves men, and to smoke and to drink, and to imitate other vices of lawless and ignorant youths—no longer boys, and yet unworthy of the true manhood they are assuming,—looked pale. There was a strange mixture of heights and sizes assembled together; big fellows, like Lemon, Selby, Barber; and little ones, like Eden, Dawson, Jones, Tomlinson, and others whose names have not hitherto been mentioned. Ernest, Buttar, Bouldon, and Gregson came between the two sets as to size, but not far distant from the older ones as to intelligence and the respect in which they were held. Bouldon would by himself have been classed differently, but from associating so much with steady first-class boys—first-class as to estimation—by showing that he really wished to do right, he gained a good character among his superiors.

"All ready!" sung out Ernest; and letting the ball drop, he kicked it with all his might in the direction of Lemon's goal.

Now the opposite party rushed in, and sent it flying back over his head and the heads of several standing behind him; but Buttar and Gregson had fully expected this, and were prepared accordingly to defend their goal. They met the ball hopping along in full career, and sent it back so far that, before anybody could rush in, Ernest had been able to give it an expediting kick, and to send it very close up to his opponent's goal. Now there was a general and terrific rush up towards Lemon's goal, and his followers found that they had good reason to dread the impetuosity and courage of the smaller boys. Ernest had chiefly selected his side from among those who possessed most pluck and endurance. Fearless of kicks, overthrows, or crushes, on they dashed at the ball. Now and then a big fellow like Barber would try and get a kick at it; but immediately he was met by a dozen sharp-moving toes, which struck away so desperately that he could never get a fair kick. For a long time the ball kept moving backwards and forwards near Lemon's goal, the attention of all his side being required to prevent it from being kicked through it. Several times it rose into the air, but was speedily sent back again; yet no one on Ernest's side could manage to send it back over the heads of their opponents. Buttar and Tom Bouldon were always in the midst of the *mêlée*. More than once Bouldon was overthrown, but he always picked himself up, and however much damaged, postponed, as he said, an inspection of his wounds till the game was over. Ernest, as in duty bound, had to avoid a *mêlée*, that when the ball came out of it he might be in a position to direct the movements of his party. Gregson never got into one intentionally; but when he did, he showed that he was as steady and fearless as any one; but his tactics were to keep moving about, to be ready to assist his chief, or to take up the ball when it approached the goal. Some called him the sluggish player; but Lemon's party found it difficult enough to send the ball through the goal when he was to be found anywhere near it. Dawson and three or four other big fellows had got the ball between them, and were pushing it forward triumphantly, having completely overwhelmed Ernest and his immediate supporters by sheer strength, and were fully expecting to drive it without impediment through the goal, when Gregson, who had been standing a little on one side, saw them coming. Only little Eden and some other small boys were near, but they, one and all, if not for the honour of the game, were ready to risk anything for the sake of Bracebridge. Gregson called them. They all saw what was required of them. Gregson rushed in, fully meeting the ball; with a swinging leg, he gave it a lifting kick, and sent it right over the heads of his opponents. The little fellows rushed in behind them, and began to kick on the ball. This compelled the big fellows once more to separate, and again to retrograde so as to front it. Gregson, Eden, and their companions threw themselves impetuously on it. One after the other went over it, till the ball was hidden under a heap of boys. Barber, and some others, dared not kick, or they would have done so; and while they were lifting up their opponents to get once more at the ball, Ernest, Buttar, Bouldon, and others came up to the rescue, and once more the ball was banded backwards and forwards as furiously as ever. For long the fortune of the day appeared as doubtful as ever. I have observed that big boys never play so well, when opposed to others evidently smaller, than themselves, as they do when their antagonists are of the same age and strength as they are. This, perhaps, was one of the secrets of Ernest's success in all the matches he played. He chose his side for cleverness, and activity, and daring, and, what was more, they all trusted in him, and were ready to do anything he ordered. Every now and then there was a loud shout and a tremendous rush, and finally the ball would come out of the *mêlée* and, left in the power of a few trusted players, could be seen flying backwards and forwards between them, each side watching for a favourable opportunity to drive it at once home to the goal. Now, at length, Ernest has got it. It was sent to the extreme right of the players. This was done by a dodge of Gregson's. He was invaluable for any movement of the sort, and staunch as steel. Onward Ernest kicks the ball; his side rush in to prevent the approach of their opponents, who have mostly been led off to the ground. A few only are fully aware of what is about to occur. A few rush on desperately to stop the progress of the ball; but the young ones are too energetic and too quick for them. They urge it on; the rest stand for an instant aside, to let Ernest give a last kick. It is a grand effort of strength and skill, and the ball flies through the goal, amid the shouts of all his side, echoed by the applause of the spectators.

Lemon and many of his supporters took their defeat very good-naturedly, and with sincerity congratulated Ernest and his side on their success. A few of the less amiably disposed were somewhat sulky, especially among those of his own size; so was Barber, who was afraid that he should lose the influence he wished to obtain from being beaten by the younger boys. This was only one of several games. Ernest was not always successful; twice his side were beat thoroughly, but they made up for it afterwards, and in the end won more games than the bigger boys, much to the surprise of the latter, who could not tell how it had occurred. Some, like Barber, said that there must have been some underhand play, and abused Lemon as the cause of their defeat. Lemon at last heard some of their remarks.

"If big fellows will smoke, and booze, and over-eat themselves, how can they expect to be as active and wide-awake as little fellows, who have not begun such follies?" he remarked quietly. "It matters little, let me assure them, what such fellows say of me."

Both Ernest and Buttar had thought a good deal about the matter of Ellis. After a lengthened consultation, when their hearts relented towards him, they resolved to press him once more to join their games; but he resolutely refused.

"No," he replied. "You have believed me guilty, or you would not have treated me coldly. I do not blame you—far from it. If you heard the story about me, as I know it has been repeated, you could not have done otherwise, unless you had thought right to believe my word before that of others. Should the time ever come when I can, to your satisfaction, prove my innocence, we will then be on the same terms as before."

"Oh, but we do believe you innocent, Ellis," said Ernest. "Not a shadow of doubt remains on my mind that you are so, and I am sure Buttar thinks as I do."

"Very well," answered Ellis, with unusual coldness; "I rejoice to hear it. I have taken my resolution. I cannot bear fluctuations of friendship. If I am ever able to prove my innocence, as I ought to have endeavoured to prove it long ago, I trust that we shall stand on the same footing that we did before."

Nothing any of his friends could say after this altered the resolution Ellis had formed of not playing in any of the games with the other boys, or of associating on intimate terms with any of them. Still he himself was far from idle in his play-hours. He was a constant exerciser on the gymnastic poles, and never failed to practise, when he could, both with the foils and broadsword. He also took lessons regularly in dancing and drilling, and seemed anxious to perfect himself in all athletic exercises.

However coldly others had treated Ellis, there was one person who ever turned a deaf ear to the stories told of him, and never for a moment altered his conduct towards him. That was Monsieur Malin. From the time Ellis had begun to learn French of him he had become his firm friend. Some believed that Ellis had confided to him the circumstances of his past history; but the less generous could not understand how he had managed to secure the regard of the French master, and fancied that he had invented some tale to gain his sympathy.

Thus the half-year drew on; the cold weather at last passed away. Spring commenced, the flowers bloomed, the leaves came out on the trees, the birds began to sing, the fish to dart and leap out of the water. Ernest and Buttar were reminded of a visit they promised, long, long before, to pay to John Hodge. They agreed to make it a fishing expedition, and to try their luck in the wide stream they had crossed on that day memorable for their hare hunt. They invited Gregson to accompany them. They wished to ask Ellis, but the moment school was over he had disappeared, and had not even waited for dinner. To absent himself he must have obtained leave from the Doctor; so they set off without him. They were very merry. Gregson was excessively amusing, with his quaint anecdotes about animal life and the adventures which had happened to him.

"I would rather go elephant and lion hunting for a year than become prime minister of England," he observed, laughing. "Nothing could compensate me for not being allowed to live in the country,—the largest fortune would not, had I to spend it in London; and I should prefer Australia or New Zealand, or the wilds of the Cape Colony, or Natal, or the backwoods of Canada. Still I am a Briton, and wherever I might go I should like to live under the flag of old England."

Ernest and Buttar echoed the last sentiment.

"But," said Ernest, "for my part I should not wish to live without the society of my equals in knowledge and intelligence. In my opinion, the interchange of ideas and information is one of the charms of existence. In that way we get, in the most agreeable manner, at the pith and marrow of books, at the opinions of other people, and at what is going forward in the world: don't you think so, Buttar?"

Buttar, though a clever fellow, had not as yet thought much about the matter. He remarked, however, that if he could get information by talking, or rather by hearing others talk, that it would be much pleasanter often than having to pore over books. But that was not what Ernest meant. "Ah, but there must be a fair exchange of ideas and information, to make social intercourse as pleasant as it is capable of being. You must give as much as you take."

"Well, I never before thought of that," remarked Gregson. "I have never yet fallen in with people willing to talk of my favourite subjects. Perhaps if I was to meet them I should enjoy their conversation as much as you suppose you would those of literary characters or other well-informed persons."

"Oh, I am not alluding to literary characters, as you call them," said Ernest. "I mean well-informed, intelligent, unprejudiced persons; or, what would be still more agreeable, would be to collect people who have devoted themselves to different branches of science, and who are yet fully capable of understanding each other's peculiar subjects."

So the schoolboys talked on as they walked briskly towards the scene they proposed for their sport.

"But do not let us forget Hodge," said Ernest. "Hereabouts he dwells, I believe. Let us inquire at this cottage." An old woman came forth from the door where they knocked, and told them that John Hodge lived better nor a quarter of a mile down the road, and he, poor man, was sure to be at home, for he had met with an accident, and, she had heard say, was very ill, and had been out of work for many a long day. They thanked her and hurried on.

"Ought we to go and trouble him?" asked Buttar.

"Certainly, he may want assistance," was Ernest's thoughtful reply.

A little child pointed to a neat cottage door. That was where John Hodge lived. They knocked, and were told to come in. They started back with surprise on seeing Ellis seated on a chair, reading earnestly to the man they had come to see, while a woman stood by, with her apron to her eyes, and five small children were playing about the humble brick-floored room. How changed was poor Hodge! Thin and pale in the extreme, with an expression of care on his countenance, he sat propped up in an old oak chair. It was evident that he could not move, or indeed breathe, without pain. Ellis was so absorbed in his occupation that he did not perceive at first the entrance of his schoolfellows. They stopped at the threshold, unwilling to interrupt him. He was reading the Bible, and having read some verses he began to explain their meaning. At last he finished.

"Sit down, young gentlemen, sit down, pray," said Mrs Hodge, offering them some three-legged stools, which she wiped mechanically with her apron.

Her words made Ellis look up. The colour came into his cheeks when he saw the new-comers. They nodded kindly to him, and then explained that they had come in consequence of an invitation they had received long ago, and that they were sorry to find their host in so bad a state. John Hodge said that he recollected them, that he was glad to see them, but he made no complaint, or spoke even of the cause of his illness. After they had sat and talked a short time, Ellis got up to go away; Buttar and Gregson accompanied him, but Ernest lingered behind, and taking out the contents of his purse, offered it to the dame.

"Thank ye kindly, sir," she replied, motioning him to keep it; "but that young gentleman has given us all we want for some time. He says he gets it from his friends; that we are not robbing him; and we couldn't be taking it from you or from any one, unless we wanted it very badly. Ah, sir, if ever there was an angel on earth he is one; of that I'm certain."

"Well, well, when you do want you mustn't mind taking it from me. I owe your husband some money as it is," answered Ernest, putting out his hand to the poor woman, and then to Hodge. He took up the children, and gave a kiss to a little rosy boy, who smiled in his face, and then saying he would come back soon, turned after his companions. He felt much gratified at hearing such an account of Ellis. At once an idea struck him. In the story Selby had told him about Ellis, it appeared that one of the causes of suspicion against him was his being possessed of a considerable sum of money. Might not that have been given to him for the purpose of being bestowed in charity, as he undoubtedly had lately been furnished with funds for the same object? Ernest, though not over precipitate usually, at once jumped at this conclusion. It was very delightful to be able to think so, and the conviction that he had wronged Ellis in his thoughts caused him to be doubly anxious to make ample amends without delay, and this added considerably to the warmth of his manner when he overtook him. He pressed him, as Buttar and Gregson had been doing, to accompany them on their fishing excursion. At length he said that he should like to go, but pleaded want of rod and fishing-tackle.

Gregson laughed. "Oh, I can supply you with all you require," he observed. "My rod you can have, and I can replace it with one to suit my purpose in ten minutes. I have two spare tops, and tackle enough to fit out a dozen fishermen. Come along, you have no excuse."

Ellis agreed, and with light steps the party proceeded towards the broad stream they had fixed on. The day was warm and slightly overcast, and the water was not too clear, so that they had a fair prospect of success. They were not disappointed. Never before had they caught so many fish. They kept pulling them up one after the other. Many were very fine trout. Ellis had never caught such in his life before. They all agreed that fishing was one of the most delightful of occupations. Their hearts as they walked homewards opened more than ever towards each other. Ernest at last spoke out:—

"Ellis, my dear fellow, we have been doing you great wrong,—that is, Buttar and I,—I don't think Gregson has. We were certain that you were very sorry, and were quite changed, but we thought you might have been guilty of the thing they talked about; now we are certain you were not. The money you were known to possess was given you for a good object—to bestow in charity. One proof of your guilt falls to the ground."

"Oh, Bracebridge, I am glad to hear you say so," answered Ellis. "You are right. I promised not to say from whom I received it, and so I could not. No one accused me to my face. The Master knew that I was innocent. What could I do? I now feel sure that all will turn up right in the end. I am so happy."

Chapter Fifteen
The Summer Holidays—A Picnic and its Consequences

An event which made us all very sad took place at the end of that half-year. I remember it as well as if it were yesterday. It was the departure from the school of Monsieur Malin; yet for his sake we ought not to have been sorry. He was going to quit a position which was undoubtedly very irksome to a gentleman, and to return to La Belle France to take possession of a property which had unexpectedly been left him. He announced the fact to each of the classes as they came up to him during the morning, and all heard the information with signs of evident sorrow. Ellis burst into tears.

"Going away, Monsieur Malin; you, my kindest friend, going!" he exclaimed, and his whole look and manner showed that he had an affectionate and grateful heart.

The feeling was infectious. A number of the little fellows, who did not even learn French, and had very little to do with Monsieur Malin, cried. Some, however, had reason to be sorry at his going away, for often had his watchful eye saved them from being bullied by the big boys; they, too, felt that they were about to lose a friend and protector. Why, it may well be asked, should the French master have gained so much more influence among the boys, and be so much more generally liked than any of the English masters? It was simply because he exhibited so much more sympathy for others. He made himself one of them. It was not that he now and then played a grand game of cricket with them, but that he entered into all their minor sports and amusements. He could show them how to make models of all sorts; he manufactured carriages with cardboard, or cut out boats, or carved animals in wood, or made little grottoes with shells; indeed it is impossible to describe all the ingenious things he could do, and how kindly and patiently he taught the boys how to do them. It made some of the English masters quite jealous when they observed the sorrow which Monsieur Malin's departure caused among the boys. The Doctor remarked upon it, and said that it was the best compliment any master could desire to have paid him, and he trusted that whoever succeeded him might as richly deserve it.

"Bracebridge, I wonder that you are not more sorry than you appear to be at Monsieur Malin's going," observed Buttar, the day that the event was announced; "I thought that you were always one of his greatest favourites."

"I believe that there are no fellows like him better than I do," answered Ernest; "I am very, very sorry, for my own sake, that he is going; but really, when we come to consider that he is going away from the bother, and trouble, and noise of a school, to go and live on a beautiful property of his own, in a delightful climate like that of France, I cannot but be truly glad to hear of his good fortune. He has been telling me all about the place, and how happy his mother and sister will be to go and live with him; and he has invited me, during some holidays, or when I leave school, to go and pay him a visit; and when I told him that I was afraid he would forget me, he assured me that he would not. Really he is a kind-hearted, good-natured fellow, and I do feel excessively happy at his good fortune."

Buttar agreed that Ernest saw the matter in its true light, and so did Ellis, and then they bethought them how they could show him their regard. Unfortunately, as it was the end of the half, none of them had any store of pocket-money remaining; so one proposed offering him a penknife, and another a pocket-comb, and a third an inkstand; indeed, there was no end of the number of small gifts which Monsieur Malin had pressed upon him. He was in a dilemma about the matter.

"You see, my dear young friends, that I do not like to refuse, and I do not like to deprive you of these things; yet I am truly grateful to you for this mark of your regard. What I will do is this; I will make a list of your names, and of all the things you desire to give me. You shall keep the articles, all of which you can use, but I could not; and I will keep the list, and when I look at it, I shall be fully reminded of you all, of your generosity, and of your kindly regard towards me."

Monsieur Malin had to go away a week or so before the school broke up. Just about that time Ernest wrote home, giving an account of the story he had heard about Ellis, of the injustice that he felt that he himself had done him, of the strong evidence he had discovered in his favour, and consequently of his wish to make him all the amends in his power. By return of post he received a letter from his father, enclosing one to Ellis, warmly inviting him to spend a portion of his holidays at Oakland Ellis could not fail to be gratified, as were his parents, who gave him leave to accept the invitation. Buttar's family were spending the summer in the neighbourhood; and curiously enough, Tom Bouldon and Gregson had been invited to visit some friends living not far off. The schoolfellows thus found themselves near together during the early part of the summer holidays. No long time passed before they all met. How they did talk of fishing expeditions, of cricket-matches, of boating, of pic-nics, of riding, of archery meetings, of bathing, of sports of all sorts, in the water and out of the water, on sea and on land! Ellis talked a great deal of yachting also, but they were too far from the sea to have any hopes of indulging in the amusement. He was much more at home in a boat than on horseback, for riding was not an accomplishment which he had enjoyed any opportunity of practising. One of the first amusements which Mrs Bracebridge had arranged for her young guest, and the other friends of her son, was a pic-nic to Barton Forest, a large and picturesque wood in the neighbourhood. There were long open glades, and green shady walks, through which the deer alone were in general wont to pass, except on such an occasion as that at present in contemplation, or when an adventurous couple strayed into its retired precincts. I ought to have spoken of the cordial way in which Ellis was received, not only by Mr Bracebridge, but by Mrs Bracebridge and all the family, and the wish they exhibited of placing him at his ease, and making him quite at home. He showed how much he valued their kindness by looking far more lively and happy than he had done for a long time. The day of the proposed pic-nic broke bright and fair, with every prospect of the continuance of fine weather. Several families joined in it from far and near, and all sorts of vehicles were put in requisition: barouches, and pony carriages, and gigs, and even carts and waggons. The merriest, and certainly the most noisy party, went in a long spring waggon, and to their charge were entrusted several hampers, containing part of the provender for the rural feast. Ellis, Bouldon, Buttar, and others were of this party. Ernest, with his brother Charles, rode, and frequently came up alongside to have a talk with their friends. The boys gave way heartily to the excitement of the scene; they laughed they sang, they shouted to their heart's content—no one hindering them. Never, perhaps, have a merrier party ever collected in a waggon. Tom Bouldon, and one or two others, only regretted that they had not pea-shooters with them, as he said, to pepper the passengers in their progress, but Ellis cried out against this.

"No, no!" he exclaimed; "it may, or may not, be all very well on a high road, where people expect such things when they see a parcel of schoolboys together, and if they don't like it, will not stand on ceremony about heaving stones in return; but in a country district they take us for young gentlemen, and would never dream of throwing anything at us in return. The cottagers would only wonder what had come over us—perhaps would think us gone mad; at all events it would be very cowardly to attack them."

Buttar agreed with Ellis, and they soon won over the rest to their view of the case. They, however, found plenty to amuse them as they drove along. The early days of the holidays are generally very jolly days—all the fun is to come; the amusements in store are almost uncountable; and though they may have been disappointed during a former summer, they are sure, so they think, not to be this. If they are, they will make amends for it next year. At last the pic-nickers reached the ground. Carriages drove up, and ladies and gentlemen, the fathers and mothers, and elder brothers and sisters of the schoolboys. Some ladies and gentlemen came on horseback and ponyback, and several even, besides the boys, in waggons, while the provisions and servants arrived in spring-carts and dog-carts, and altogether there was a very vast assemblage. It was arranged that, having walked about a little, and seen some of the views which the wood afforded, and some old ruins within its borders, the party should dine, and then that various sports should take place, pony races, archery, quoits, nine-pins, skittles, throw-sticks or batons, single-stick; indeed, more than I can well remember; while swings were hung up between the trees, and two or three long planks had been placed on some felled trees, to serve as see-saws, so that all ranks and ages could find amusement. Never were better arrangements made. People may wander the world around and not find more pleasing, heart-enlivening scenery than England affords—scenery more rich or full of fertile spots, or which should make its inhabitants grateful to Heaven for having placed them in such a land. There were fields already waving with corn, and bright green meadows full of fine cattle, some grazing, others standing under trees chewing the cud, or in shallow bends of the river, or in reedy ponds; there were sheep scattered thickly over sunny hills, and still further off downs; and there were copses of hazel, and alder, and willow, and woods of beech, and oak, and birch, and tall elms dividing fields and orchards innumerable, among which peeped many a white-washed cottage; and here and there were pretty hamlets, with their village green or common; there was a bright sparkling stream, swelling as it advanced into the dimensions of a river, and high hills, and valleys, and glens branching off in all directions.

"A fair and truly attractive scene," said Ellis, turning to Ernest, who cordially agreed with him as they gazed at it together.

A gentleman who stood by turned round and watched the countenance of the speaker. "That is not a common boy, I am certain," he observed to a friend. "He is capable of doing much in the world, and I suspect will do it."

Ellis could not help hearing the last remark, and it gave him great encouragement.

Now came the time to prepare for the rural banquet. It was great fun unpacking the hampers, and carrying their contents to the tablecloths which had been spread on the grass. What number of chicken-pies, and veal-pies, and rounds of beef, and hams and tongues, and cold chickens and veal, and fruit-tarts and pies, and cakes of all shapes and sorts, and what heaps of fruit, strawberries and gooseberries, and currants and raspberries! indeed there was no lack of anything; and what was most wonderful, nothing was forgotten, and there was a fair proportion of each joint or dish. I have been at a pic-nic where, from want of a preconcerted plan, everybody brought veal-pies, or chicken-pies, or hams, and there was no bread, or salt, or mustard. Somebody had a French horn or cornopean, and at its sound people came trotting pretty quickly in from all directions through the woodland glades and up the avenues leading from the ruins, or bypaths coming from the side of the stream. The long drive and the exercise they had since taken had given them good appetites, and none lingered behind. The boys, especially, were in good time, and in the course of a few minutes everybody was seated in every possible attitude convenient for carrying food down their throats. Not that anybody sat quiet many minutes together. Somebody was always jumping up to help somebody else, or to go in search of some tongue for their chicken, or some chicken for their tongue, or for a glass of ale or wine, or for a piece of bread, or for some mustard or salt; indeed it seemed wonderful how many things were wanted to make out a dinner which are procured with so much ease in a dining-room, as things of course, that no one ever thinks about them. In this way the first course lasted a long time. Just at the end of it the servants brought some dishes of hot potatoes, which had been cooked gipsy fashion, and then several people began again for the sake of eating them. The tarts and fruit-pies were very good, but the juice of some had run out, and one or two had been tumbled into, and Tom Bouldon, in jumping across the tablecloth, had stepped exactly into the middle of one of them, splashing his trousers all over with currant juice, and considerably damaging the pie itself. It was in consequence the last consumed, but a facetious gentleman helped it out to the people who sat at the further end of the tablecloths, and knew nothing of the catastrophe. Then there was champagne, which some of the boys in their innocence called very good gooseberry wine, greatly to the disgust of the gentleman who brought it: the truth being, however, that they liked gooseberry wine just as much as the finest champagne to be procured. Healths were drunk, and toasts were given, and sentiments and speeches were made, which, if not very witty, caused a good deal of merriment and laughter; and at last the dinner part of the pic-nic came to a conclusion. Then, of course, the servants had to dine, which they did at a little distance from the spot their masters had chosen, and seemed to enjoy the fun, for they also drank toasts in ale, made speeches, and laughed heartily at all their jokes. The ladies and gentlemen, meantime, walked about, or sat down and admired the scenery, and the boys got ready for their games. Targets had already been erected. After the grown-up people began to get tired of looking at the views, the gentlemen marked off the distance, and the ladies taking their bows, shooting began. Ernest, Buttar, and some of the bigger boys joined them, but they soon voted it very slow work, and Bouldon proposed taking a roving expedition.

"We have not much time, so let us be off at once," said Ernest. "Nine shall be the game. Are you all provided with blunt-headed arrows? That is right. Twelve a-piece we should have. Let us take half-an-hour's turn round the wood, and then be back for the races. By that time the servants will have the dinner things cleared away and the ponies saddled for racing."

Away went the party whom Ernest had enlisted right merrily. First they fixed on an old oak-tree for their butt, and at a word given by Buttar, who was chosen leader, every one shot from the spot where they were standing. Some shafts hit the tree, others just glanced off, and others flew altogether wide of it. Buttar had his note-book out, and the distance each shaft had fallen from the tree was measured by the length of the bows, every boy measuring with his own, and noted in the book. They again ran on. "Halt!" said Buttar. "That elm, the third from the gate, shall be our target. Shoot!" Every one shot his best, but Ernest and Buttar only hit; Bouldon's arrow glanced off; no one else struck the tree. The distances being measured and noted, on again they went. A white post at a considerable distance was next fixed on as the mark. Ellis hit it, Ernest went near, and the shafts of the rest of the party flew wide or short of it.

"Ah, I calculated the range," observed Ellis. "I shot my arrow with a considerable curve, for I saw that the mark was further than my bow could send it at point-blank range."

"Why, Ellis, you will make a good artillery officer," said Buttar, laughing. "Whenever we shoot with sides, I shall know who to choose. I had no idea you were a scientific archer."

"I very seldom have shot before, but directly I got a bow I began to study the subject, and to learn all that has been said about it," answered Ellis. "I always read what I can about it when I begin anything which is new to me."

The half-hour spent in roving passed very quickly away. Those who had never shot before in that way agreed that it was far more amusing than shooting at a target, and that they found they learned to measure distances much better in the former than in the latter way. When they got back they found a variety of other sports going on. Some of their friends were playing quoits. It is a capital game for exercising the arms. Two iron pins or hobs were stuck in the ground, about eighteen yards apart. Quoits, as everybody ought to know, were derived from the ancient game of discus. They are circular plates of iron, with a hole in the centre, one side being flat and the other rounded. The game is played often with sides. The aim of each player is to pitch his quoit on the hob, or, if he cannot do that, as near it as possible, the parties throwing from one hob to another. Charles Bracebridge and Lemon were playing on opposite sides when the archers came up. First Charles threw. One quoit was close to the hob, and the other quoits he sent were within a few inches of it, and of each other. Then Lemon threw. His first quoit was just outside Charles', but nearer than any of his other quoits, but his other quoits fell outside the rest. Thus both only counted one. Had a second quoit of Lemon's fallen close to Charles' first, Lemon would have counted two, though his other quoits might have fallen to a greater distance. The nearest, it will be understood, count and cut out all outside them. The servants were amusing themselves during the interval with skittles and nine-pins, so that everybody of the party, high and low, old and young, were engaged; and in that I consider consists the chief zest of a pic-nic of the sort. Sometimes a pic-nic may take place at a spot of peculiar interest, where the party may find abundant matter of amusement without games of any sort; or in other instances people merely meet in a pretty spot, to dine in a pleasant unrestrained way in the open air, and generally manage to become better and more quickly acquainted than they can at a formal dinner-party. The boys, however, were most interested in the proposed pony races, and a general cry of "The race!—the race!—the race!" rose among them. It was echoed by others, both ladies and gentlemen, and all the ponies, and horses, and, we may say, four-legged animals the party could muster, were brought forth. As the race was entirely impromptu, no arrangements had before been made. It was first settled that everything was to run. The larger riding-horses were to have a longer distance to run, and were not to start so soon as the others; the carriage-horses came next, then the ponies, then the cart-horses, and lastly the donkeys. One very big, stout gentleman, who pleaded that he was not fit to be a jockey, and that his horse would run away with a lighter weight on him, undertook to clear the course. That was settled. Then came the question as to who were to be the riders.

"All the boys, except a few of the little ones," cried a sporting gentleman. "Of course they can all ride. Come up, youngsters. Mount—mount! let us see what you can do. You must have your proper colours. We can find scarfs and handkerchiefs enough to fasten round your caps."

No one liked to say that he could not ride. Much less did Ellis, though he had only mounted a quiet pony's back a few times in his life: still he thought that he could manage to stick on for a short distance, and was unwilling to confess how little experience he had had.

"I congratulate you, Ellis," said Ernest, nodding to him when he saw him mounted. "You seem to have got hold of a clever little animal. He'll go, depend on that. If I had not my own little Mousey to ride, I should like to have had that pony. He belongs to Mr Seagrave, does he? Oh! he always has good animals. If you do not win, you'll be in one of the first, I'm pretty certain of that." So Ernest ran on.

Buttar came up and congratulated Ellis in the same way, and gave him a hint or two how to sit and manage his steed, which he saw that he wanted.

"Ah, ah, capital, capital!" exclaimed Tom Bouldon, as he rode up on a big carriage-horse. "Really, Ellis, you are to be envied. That is just the little beast I should like to have had. How I am ever to make my fellow go along I don't know. You won't change, will you?"

Ellis laughed. He certainly did not wish to change. At the same time, had it not been for the observations of his friends, he felt that it would have been wise not to have ridden the race at all.

Instead of a bell, a horn was used to guide the proceedings. The horn sounded, and the steward of the course requested the spectators to arrange themselves on either side of a wide, open glade, at the further end of which there was a clump of trees. Round this clump the racers were to go, and to come back to a tree near where the party had dined, which was to represent the winning-post. The next thing was to place the racers at their proper distances. All were at last arranged. Ernest, Buttar, and Bouldon, who could ride well, were in high glee, and it must be confessed that they thought very little about poor Ellis. The gigantic steward of the course having ridden over it, to see that all was clear, retired on one side, and taking his horn, blew a loud blast; that was for the donkeys to start. Away they went, kicking up their heels, but making good progress. Two blasts started the cart-horses, three the carriage-horses, four the ponies. They, of course, afforded the chief amusement. Whips and heels were as busy in urging them on as if the safety of a kingdom depended on their success. The riding-horses came last. The owners had entered them more for the sake of increasing their numbers than for any wish to beat the rest, which they believed they could easily do. Away, away they all went; if not as fleet as the racers at the Derby, affording far more amusement, and as much excitement, in a much more innocent way. The pony on which Ellis was mounted did not belie the good opinion Ernest and the rest had formed of him. As soon as the horn, the signal of the ponies to start, was sounded, off he set, and very soon distanced all, except Ernest's and Buttar's steeds, which kept up close behind him.

"Bravo," shouted Ernest, delighted at his friend's success. "Keep him up to it, and you'll win the prize. I knew you'd ride well when you tried."

Ernest was, however, not quite right in his conjectures. Ellis stuck on very well, but as to guiding the pony, he had no notion of it. As long, however, as the donkeys, and cart and carriage-horses, were before them, he went very well, but they were caught up before they reached the clump of trees round which they were to turn. They reached the clump, but Ellis, to his friend's dismay, shot past it. The pony's home lay in that direction, and seeing a long green glade right before him, he got his bit between his teeth, and away he went, scampering off as hard as he could lay his feet to the soft springy grass. Ellis held on with all his might. He in vain tried to turn the pony's head. He felt that he was run away with, and had lost all control over the animal.

Ernest saw the pony bolt. At first he was inclined to laugh. Then he recollected with dismay that there was a very steep hill just outside the wood, and a little beyond it a deep chalk-pit, with precipitous sides, down which he feared that the pony, if it became alarmed by anything, might in its excitement plunge. How to stop Ellis was the question! To follow him he knew would only increase the speed of the pony. There was, he remembered, a short cut to the precipice through a green narrow path to the right. Without a moment's hesitation he galloped down it. Buttar, divining his object, followed. The rest, not seeing where they had gone, fancied that they had turned the clump, and continued the race.

Mousey, Ernest's pony, behaved magnificently. On he galloped, as if he knew that a matter of importance depended on his speed. Some boys running out of the wood fancied that he was running away, and, clapping their hands, tried to turn him aside, but he heeded them not. The wood was at length cleared. Ernest looked up the road to his left, in the hopes of seeing Ellis coming along it, but he was afraid that he had already passed. On the ground were the marks of hoofs, which looked, he thought, very like those made by a pony at full speed; so he and Buttar galloped along the road they thought he must have taken. Down the steep hill they went at full speed, keeping a tight rein, however, on the mouths of their little steeds. They thought they made out poor Ellis in the distance.

"He sticks on bravely, at all events," cried Ernest. "He's a fellow to be proud of as a friend. Oh! he must not come to harm."

Away they went. They thought that they were too far off to frighten Ellis's pony, and as Ernest knew the country well, he hoped that they might still overtake him by cutting across some fields. The gate leading into them was shut, so they knew that Ellis had not gone that way. A boy was sitting whistling on a stile hard by. Ernest asked him if he had seen a young gentleman on a pony going fast along the road. He nodded, made a sign that he was going very fast indeed, but showed that it had never entered his head to try to stop the pony. Ernest forced open the gate without waiting for the lout to do so, and they galloped through and along over the turf. There were two or three slight hedges, but they forced their way through them. The road, after winding considerably, crossed directly before the path they were taking. They heard a horse's hoofs come clattering along the hard road. They were just in time to be too late to meet Ellis. He passed them a moment before they could open the gate. His cap had fallen off; his hair was streaming wildly, and he was holding on by the mane with one hand, though he still tugged at the rein with the other. He saw them. He did not shout or cry for help, but his eye showed that he understood their object. Now was the most dangerous time. They were approaching the chalk-pit. If they followed too close they might frighten the pony, and produce the catastrophe they were anxious to avert. With great presence of mind they pulled suddenly up, and Ernest believed that their so doing had the effect of decreasing the speed of the runaway pony. They then trotted slowly on, till they trusted that Ellis had passed the point of extreme danger. Once more they put their ponies to their full speed. They almost dreaded to approach the spot, lest what they feared might have occurred. Ernest rode close to the brink of the pit. To his joy, there was no sign of the pony having gone near it, and they thought that they saw him in the distance. On they pushed after him.

Ellis himself, when he found that he was run away with, determined to do his best to stick on, hoping that by going up some hill or other the pony might be brought up. He forgot how high the forest was situated, and that it was chiefly downhill the pony would have to go. He did stick on, and bravely too, but very frequently he thought it would be in vain, and that he must be thrown off. He felt happier when he saw the attempts made by his friends to overtake him, even though they failed to accomplish their object.

At last Ernest despaired of catching the runaway, when he saw him at the commencement of a long straight road, with no short cut to it, by which he could hope to get ahead of Ellis. Still he and Buttar pursued. Ellis went on, how many miles he could not possibly tell; he thought a great number. He was getting very weary; his knees ached; so did his shoulders. The road was picturesque, overhanging with trees. There were houses ahead—a village, he thought. A boy in a field heard the pony coming along the road. He had on a white pinafore. As he jumped over the gate, it fluttered in the pony's face: that made him start, and poor Ellis was thrown with considerable violence against some palings on the opposite side of the road. His foot remained in the stirrup. On he was dragged, when a gentleman, hearing the cry of the little boy with the pinafore, came to the gate at the moment the pony was passing, and caught his head. The little country-lad came to assist, and held the pony while the gentleman disengaged Ellis's foot, and carried him into his cottage, which stood near the road. Not long after, Ernest and Buttar rode by.

"Are you companions of a young gentleman whose pony ran away just now?" asked a voice from the shrubbery.

They said yes, and were requested to come in.

"He is not materially injured," said a lady, who had spoken to them as they dismounted. "My husband has gone off, however, for a surgeon, a clever man, who lives near, and my son is sitting by him while I came out to watch for you. His great anxiety was that you should not miss him. Now we will go in."

They found Ellis already in bed. He complained of a great pain in the neck, and shoulder, and head, and the lady seemed to fear that he might have dislocated his shoulder, and received a concussion of the brain, and injured his spine.

Ellis, however, seemed not to be alarmed about himself, and only expressed his regret that he was giving so much trouble.

After a little time the surgeon came, and pronounced that no bones were either dislocated or broken, though the patient had been terribly shaken, and ought not to be moved, but said that he thought that in a day or two he would be all to rights.

The gentleman and lady, who said that their names were Arden, begged Ernest and Buttar to remain with their friend; but at last it was arranged that Buttar should ride back, to announce what had become of the other two, and that Ernest should remain to help to look after Ellis.

In the evening, when Ellis went to sleep, the rest of the party, with the exception of Mr and Mrs Arden's son, who sat watching by his side, were in the drawing-room.

"You are not a stranger to us," said Mrs Arden to Ernest. "We have the pleasure of knowing your family; and, if I mistake not, my son and your companion are old friends. My son thought so when he saw him, but was afraid to ask, lest he should agitate him. The meeting is most fortunate. My son, who was at school with him, has long been wishing to find him, but he could not discover his address. He was the means of causing a most undeserved suspicion to be cast on your friend's character, though he had the satisfaction of knowing that his master fully exonerated him. It must be acknowledged that there were suspicious circumstances against Edward Ellis, but my son felt sure that he was altogether incapable of the act imputed to him."

Mrs Arden then told Ernest all the circumstances which he had already heard from Selby.

"Now comes the part of the story most grievous to my son. Many months afterwards, he discovered the money he had lost in the secret drawer of his desk, where he put it that he might carry some silver in his purse. The silver he spent, and he has no doubt that he dropped the purse when pulling out his knife and some string from his pocket, exactly at the place where it was found."

Ernest was overjoyed at hearing this. "I am certain Edward Ellis would consent gladly to be run away with a hundred times, and have his collar-bone broken each time, for the sake of hearing this," he exclaimed, warmly.

After a time Henry Arden came down, and expressed his sorrow at his carelessness, and earnest wish to make all the amends in his power; and Ernest told him that the best amends he could make would be to come to school, and thoroughly to exculpate Ellis by telling the whole story. This he promised to do, and when Mr and Mrs Arden heard an account of the school, they declared their intention of sending their son to remain there permanently.

I need not describe the heartfelt satisfaction of Ellis, when he got better, at meeting his old school-fellow, and hearing from him the explanation of the mysterious circumstance which had so long really embittered his existence. Those were truly happy holidays, and he looked forward eagerly to the time when he might return to school, and lift up his head among his companions without a sense of shame, or the slightest slur attached to his name.

Chapter Sixteen
Eton and its Amusements

Edward Ellis felt very differently to what he had ever before done when he returned to Grafton Hall. He was one of the first. His particular friends had not come back, but the other boys, not knowing what had happened to him, could not help remarking the change. He walked with a firmer step, he held his head more erect, and seemed altogether a changed being; yet he was at the same time the like good-tempered, kind, gentle, generous-minded fellow he had always been. In a few days the whole school were collected, and Ernest, and Buttar, and Bouldon and others welcomed him with even more than their usual cordiality. A new boy also had arrived, —it was said, indeed, several had come, for the school was rapidly increasing; they had been seen and judged of, but this one had not made his appearance. At last it was known that he was an old school-fellow of Barber's and Ellis's. The morning after his arrival he entered the school-room, holding by the hand of the Doctor, who led him up to his desk.

"Silence, boys," said the Doctor; "I have to introduce to you a new pupil of mine, but before he takes his place in the school he has made it an especial request that he may endeavour to make amends for a great wrong he was unintentionally the cause of inflicting on one who has for some time been your school-fellow—Edward Ellis. He will now speak for himself."

On this Henry Arden, in a clear distinct voice, repeated the account I have already given of the cause which led to the suspicion that Ellis had stolen his purse; blaming himself, at the same time, for his own neglect and stupidity.

"Since then I find," he added, "that the money of which he was possessed was entrusted to him by a wealthy relative, who had formed the highest possible opinion of his integrity and judgment, that he might distribute it as he thought fit among objects of charity. From henceforth I hope that you will all think as highly of Edward Ellis as those who know him best do. Three cheers for Edward Ellis!"

Three cheers were given, the Doctor leading, and three hearty cheers they were, such as the Doctor delighted to hear his boys give on fit occasions.

Ellis tried to get up and speak, but his heart was far too full. After two or three brave attempts he was obliged to sit down.

"Bracebridge," he said, "do you get up and tell them all I feel. You know." Ernest got up, and made a very fitting speech for his friend, which was loudly applauded, and then three cheers were given for Ernest, as the "Favourite of the School." Ernest himself was somewhat taken aback at this, but he was very well pleased, and replied in a way which gained him yet further applause. From this time Ellis made still more rapid progress than before, and many people thought him not much inferior in talent to Ernest Bracebridge. He got up several steps, one after the other, but his success did not make him less humble than he had ever been. Out of doors, he made as great progress in his amusements. Cricket was now in, and in that finest and most interesting of English manly games he soon gained considerable proficiency. He used to play, and then only occasionally, with two or three small boys at single wicket; now he entered boldly into the game, and played whenever he could. Ernest, who was becoming one of the best players in the school, always got him on his side when he could. Soon after the commencement of the half there was to be a game between the six best players in Ernest's class and five others from any class except the highest, whom they might choose on one side, and five of the second class and six others from any other class below them. No school in England could boast of a better cricket-field than did that of Grafton Hall. It was, too, a lovely day when that game was played, and there were a good many spectators. Ernest and Ellis, Buttar, Bouldon, and two others of their class, together with several good players from other classes, formed their side. They were all resolved to play their best, and to fear nothing. They had the first innings.

"Now, Ellis," said Ernest, "you remember our first game at rounders. You thought you could do nothing with that, but you tried, and did as well as anybody. So you can with cricket. You have had fair practice, you know the principles, and you have no vices to overcome."

"I'll do my best, depend on that," answered Ellis, resolving to exert himself to the utmost. He had thought over and thoroughly studied the principles of the game, and as his eye was specially correct, he played far better than many who had infinitely more practice. To make a good cricketer, a person must have physical powers for it; he must study the principles of the game; why he should stand in certain positions, and why his bat should be kept in a particular way; and also he should practise it frequently, so as to make his hands and arms thoroughly obedient to the will. Buttar and Bouldon first went in. They made some capital hits. Bouldon scored twelve by as many runs from four hits in succession.

"Bravo, Tom!—bravo, Bouldon!" resounded on all sides. Bouldon got into high spirits; he felt as if the whole success of the game depended on him, that he could work wonders. He made one or two more capital hits, but every instant he was growing vainer and more confident. He began to hit wildly; to think more of hitting far than of where he sent the ball, or of how he guarded his wicket. Proper caution and forethought is required at cricket as well as in all the other affairs of life. A ball came swiftly and straight for his wicket. He hit it—off it flew, but the watchful eye of one of the other side was on it, and ere it reached the ground it was caught. Tom threw down his bat, and declared that he was always out of luck; that having done so well he hoped to have stayed in to the end. Another boy took his place. He also did good service to his side, but at length was bowled out. Buttar, who always played coolly, remained in. He got several runs, but seldom more than two at a time at the utmost. Ernest now went in. He had become a first-rate cricketer. He possessed strength, activity, eye, and judgment, all essential requisites to make a good player. Great things were therefore expected from him. He, of course wished to do his best. He quietly took up the bat, weighed it for a moment, and finding that he had a proper grasp, threw himself into the position ready for the ball. His first hit was a telling one. Often had he and Buttar played together, and they well knew what each could do. They ran three without risk. They looked at each other, to judge about trying a fourth one, but it was too much, they saw, to attempt. Had they, Ernest would have been out. Hit after hit was made, several, however, without getting runs, for the field was exerting itself to the utmost. If they could put these two players out quickly they might win easily; if not, they would have a hard struggle to beat them. Buttar played capitally, but at last he was growing weary, and a new bowler was sent in. The very first ball he delivered came curling round, and sprung in between the wicket and his bat, and down went his stumps. A very good player succeeded him, who, though he did not get many runs off his own bat, enabled Ernest to get them. He, however, after doing very well, made an imprudent run, and he was stumped out. Still Ernest kept in, and it was Ellis's turn to take the bat. All his former awkwardness of gait was gone. He stood well up to his bat. His first stroke showed that he was no despicable opponent, and he got four runs. This awakened up the field again, who had been expecting soon to get in. The two played capitally, and made their runs rapidly and fearlessly. They knew that the opposite side must play well to score as many as they had done. It was fine to see the two friends hitting away, and crossing each other as they made one run after another, almost insuring the success of their side. However, the best of players must be out at one time or the other. Ernest was caught out, and ultimately Ellis was run out by the next player who went in. At last the other side got their innings, and played well; but when the game was concluded it was found that Bracebridge's side scored thirty more than they had done,—an immense triumph to the lower class.

His success did Ellis a great deal of good, and he now made even more rapid progress than before, both in and out of school. It was the last time either he, or Ernest, or Buttar played in that class, for by Michaelmas they got another step, and by the Christmas holidays Ernest and Ellis got into the first class, distancing Buttar and Bouldon, who were only in the second. This rise was of the very greatest benefit to the school. The two first were now above Barber, and thus were able to exercise a considerable influence over him and fellows of his sort. They could look down also on Bobby Dawson, and several others who were inclined to patronise them when they first came to school. They also received all the support they could desire from Selby and other gentlemanly if not clever boys like him, and from warm-hearted enthusiastic ones like Arden and Eden. They completely, in the first place, put a stop to anything like systematic bullying. Of course, they could not at all times restrain the tempers of their companions, or prevent the strong from oppressing or striking the weak when no one was present. Bullies and tyrants, or would-be bullies and tyrants, are to be found everywhere; but when any little fellow complained to them, they never failed to punish the bully, and to bring to light any act of injustice, making the unjust doer right the wronged one. They did their utmost to put a stop to swearing or to the use of bad language. They at once and with the exertion of their utmost energy put down all indecent conversation; and if they found any boy employing it, they held him up to the reprobation and contempt of their companions. Falsehood of every description, either black lying or white lying, they exhibited in its true colours, as they did all dishonest or mean practices; indeed, they did their very utmost to show the faults and the weak points of what is too generally looked on as schoolboy morality. The system of fudging tasks, cribbing lessons, deception of every sort they endeavoured to overthrow. Some people might suppose that they undertook far more than they could perform, but this was not the case; all they undertook was to do their best. They did it, and succeeded even beyond their own expectations. Of course they at first met with a great deal of opposition. They knew well that they should do that. Some fellows even asked them for their authority in acting as they presumed to do.

"Here is our authority," answered Ellis, the colour coming into his cheeks and his eye flashing. He lifted up a Bible which he held in his hand. "We are ordered to do all the good we can in this world: we are doing it by trying to improve the character of the boys in the school. We are ordered to exert our power and influence to the utmost to do good: all the power and influence we possess we are exerting for that purpose. You see we are doing nothing strange; only our duty."

Some few of the boys sneered at Ellis behind his back for what he had said, but they were the meanest and worst boys in the school. No one uttered a word before his face; the greater number applauded him, and wished they could follow his example.

It is impossible to describe the various events which took place at Grafton Hall during the time Ernest was there. He gained more and more the good opinion of the Doctor, and of all the masters, and at length reached, more rapidly than any boy had before done, the head of the school. He gained this distinction by the employment to the best advantage of a bright, clear intellect; by steady application to study; by an anxious wish to do his duty; by never losing an opportunity of gaining information; and more especially, by not fancying himself a genius, and that he could get on without hard reading. Those were very happy days at Grafton Hall, both for him and his immediate friends, as also for the boys below him.

Another Christmas passed by, and another summer drew on. It was understood that he would leave at the end of another half. As the boys rose to the top of the school at Grafton Hall, they had many privileges and advantages which, of course, the younger ones did not possess. They had separate sleeping-rooms, where they might study, and they enjoyed a considerable amount of liberty. One day Bouldon came into Ernest's room in high glee.

"Come along, Bracebridge; it's all settled! You are to go, and so is Ellis. We are to be back in four days; but we will enjoy those four days thoroughly."

"I have no doubt that we shall," said Ernest quietly, looking up from his desk. "But where are we to go?—when are we to go?—what are we to do? Tell me all about it; you have not done so yet."

"To be sure I have not! How stupid of me!" said Bouldon, laughing. "I forgot that you did not know anything about a plan I formed long ago. You know that I have a brother at Eton—a jolly good fellow—a year older than I am. There is not a better brother in the United Kingdom than my brother Jack. Well, for the last two years, I should think, he has wanted me to go down to see him while he's at school; but as our holidays are much about the same time, I've not been able to manage it. Lately, he has been writing home about it; and, at last, he has persuaded our father to get leave for me to go from the Doctor, and to invite two friends. I fixed on you at once, and it was a toss up whether I should ask Buttar or Ellis; and I thought that the trip would be more novel and amusing to Ellis than to Buttar. The Doctor did not give in at first; but then he said you were both of you deserving of reward, and that if you wished to go you might. Of course, you'll wish to go; you'll enjoy it mightily."

Ernest thought that he should, and so did Ellis, who was quickly summoned to the conference; and the Doctor having been prepared to grant their request, gave them leave directly they asked it, giving them only some sound advice for their guidance during their stay among strangers. In high spirits they all set off for London, and were soon carried by the Great Western down to Eton. Tom had told his brother when to expect them, and Jack Bouldon was at the Windsor Station ready to receive them. He fully answered the description which had been given of him.

"I'm so glad you are come!" he exclaimed. "We have a fine busy time of it—lots to do. I've luncheon for you in my room. We are to dine at my tutor's, to meet our father, you know, Tom; and after it we'll go and see the boating. I belong to a boat; but I have sprained my arm, and mustn't pull, which is a horrid bore. Come along, though."

It is extraordinary how quickly Ernest and Ellis became acquainted with their new friend, and how fine a fellow they could not help thinking him, though he was scarcely older than either of them. They had not gone far when Jack stopped in front of Layton's the pastry-cook's.

"Come in here, by the by," he exclaimed, pulling Ernest by the arm. "I ordered some refreshment as I came along; we should not be able to do without it, do you see."

The visitors required but little persuasion to enter, and as soon as they appeared a supply of ices and strawberry messes were placed before them.

"No bad things!" they pronounced them.

"No, indeed!" said Jack, carelessly. "They slip down the throat pleasantly enough. We don't patronise anything that isn't good at Eton, let me assure you."

All present fully concurred in this opinion, the food they were discussing being a strong argument in its favour; but at last the strawberry messes came to an end, and they continued their walk into Eton. Although the town itself did not exactly excite their admiration, they expressed their pleasure when they saw the college buildings, and the meadows, and the rapidly-flowing clear river, and the view of Windsor Castle, rising proudly above all, a residence worthy of England's sovereigns.

"Now," said Jack Bouldon, "come along to my tutor's. You'll want some rest before the fun of the day begins."

His tutor's house was a very comfortable, large one, not far from the college gates. Jack ushered them into his room. He was not a little proud of it. It was all his own, his castle and sanctum. It was not very richly furnished, but it looked thoroughly comfortable. There was a turn-up bedstead, and washhand-stand, which also shut up, and prevented it having too much the appearance of a bedroom. A good-looking, venerable oak bureau served to hold most of the occupant's clothes, below which, in the upper part, were his cups and saucers; and in the centre his writing materials. In one corner was a chest, containing a quantity of miscellaneous articles too numerous to name; and in another was a cricket-bat and fishing-rod, while the walls were adorned with some prints of sporting scenes, one or two heroes of the stage, and another of the Duke of Wellington; a table, an arm-chair, and three common chairs completing the furniture of the apartment.

"You are cozy here, Jack," said his brother, throwing himself into a seat, and pulling Ernest into the arm-chair. "There's nothing like independence!"

"As to that, we have enough of it, provided we stick to rules," answered the Etonian. "However, I don't find much difficulty in the matter. I like my tutor, and he is very considerate, so I get on very well."

"But, I say, Jack, what do you do? How do you amuse yourselves all the year round," asked Tom Bouldon. "You Eton fellows seemed to me, as far as I could make out, to do nothing else but play cricket and boat. All other games you vote as low, don't you?"

"Not at all," answered Jack. "Let me see. At the beginning of the year, between Christmas and Easter, we have fives. You know how to play it. We have very good fives-courts. We play fifteen up. Then we have hockey; that's a capital game. You play it at your school, don't you? But, after all, there is nothing like making up a party to go jumping across country. It is rare fun, scrambling through hedges, tearing across ploughed fields, leaping wide ditches and brooks, and seeing fellows tumbling in head over heels. Then we have running races in the play-fields, of about a hundred yards, which is enough considering the pace at which fellows go. Better fun still are our hurdle races; and a fellow must leap well to run in them. But the greatest fun of all are our steeple-chases, of about two and a-half miles, over a stiffish country, let me tell you. There are no end of ditches, streams, and brooks with muddy banks, into which half the fellows who run manage to tumble, and to come out very like drowned chimney-sweepers. Those are all good amusements for cold weather. From Easter to the end of July is our great time for games. Of course, cricket and boating are the chief. You understand that our playing-fields are divided between different clubs. Every fellow subscribes to one or the other of our clubs. The lowest is called the Sixpenny; that belongs to the lower boys; they are, you will understand, all those in the upper school below the fifth form. Then there is the Lower Club, to which those in the fifth form belong who are not considered to play well enough in the upper club. Only, of course, first-rate players can belong to that. It is the Grand Club to which the eleven belong, and those who play equally well, and will some day become one of them. There is another club called the Aquatics, which belongs exclusively to the members of the boats. Cricketing is fine work; but, for my part, I like boating even better. Here, before a fellow is allowed to go on the river, he is obliged to learn to swim. It is a very necessary rule, for formerly many fellows lost their lives in consequence of being unable to swim. There are numerous bathing places on our river devoted to our especial use, and at each of them is stationed, with his punt, a paid waterman belonging to the college, whose sole duty it is to teach the boys to swim. Twice every week during the summer one of the masters in turns examines into the swimming qualifications of the boys, and he gives a certificate of proficiency to those whom he considers can swim well enough to preserve their lives if capsized in a boat. After a boy is qualified he is allowed to boat on the river. The masters generally make him swim thirty-five yards up and down the stream, and then about ten across it, round a punt, and back again to the point from which he started. Some fellows very quickly do this, if they are strong and not afraid; in fact, if they feel that they can do it. Others never gain any confidence, and if they were capsized could do very little to help themselves. In most cases, the first thing a fellow does when he wants to begin to boat is to agree with some chum to take a boat between them. This costs them five pounds for the summer-half. It is called a lock-up, because when it is not being used it is supposed to be carefully locked up in the boat-house. Sometimes fellows who do not care so much about boating, and don't want to give five pounds, pay a smaller sum, and take any chance boat which may be disengaged. The boats we generally use are called tubs, tunnies, and outriggers. Besides these there are 'The Boats' especially so called. There are seven of them, all eight-oared. Anybody can join these who is in the fifth form. There are three upper and four lower boats; that is, three belong to the upper and four to the lower fifth form. Each has her captain, who fills up his crew from the candidates who present themselves. The higher boats have, of course, the first choice, according to their rank. Each crew wears a different coloured shirt from the others, and have different coloured ribbons on their straw hats. On grand occasions, as to-day, we all appear in full dress, and a very natty one I think you will agree that it is."

Ernest and Ellis listened attentively to the description, and could not for the moment help wishing that they also were Eton boys. Luncheon was soon over, for the ices and strawberry messes had somewhat damped their appetites. Then they went out into the playing-fields, where a cricket-match was going forward. Jack Bouldon pointed out some of their crack players with no little pride.

"There's Jeffcott; he's at my tutor's," he observed. "The tall fellow with the light hair; he's just going in. Did you see how beautifully Strangeways was caught out? See! Jeffcott is certain of making a good hit. I knew it! He'll get two runs at least. There's Osbaldiston, the fellow who is in with him. It's worth watching him. He's even a better player than Jeffcott, though he is still so young. There! I knew it! What a grand hit! Run! run! three times, you'll do it! Capital! He's at my tutor's. A first-rate fellow, and expects to be one of the eleven next half."

So Jack Bouldon ran on, his companions heartily joining in his enthusiasm. Then they went back to his tutor's, as dinner was to be early, to be over in time for the boating in the evening. They there found Mr Bouldon, who expressed himself much pleased at meeting Ernest and Ellis, as friends of his son's. Dinner they thought the slowest part of the day's amusements, and were very glad when the time came for them to repair to the Brocas. That is the name given to the field by the river whence the boats start.

The Brocas presented a very gay and animated appearance as the crews of the boats, and the other boys, and the visitors began to collect from all directions. As Jack Bouldon had said, the costume of the boats' crews was very natty. It consisted of a striped calico shirt of some bright colour; white trousers, with a belt round the waist; a coloured necktie, to suit the shirt; a straw hat, and a ribbon round it to match, the rest of the dress; silk stockings, and pumps with gold buckles. The ribbons round the hats had the name of the boats on them, with some appropriate device, and generally a wreath of flowers worked on them. Nothing, indeed, could well exceed the neatness and elegance of the boating dresses; so Ernest and his friends agreed.

The crews now quickly took their seats in the boats. They went about the business easily, as if they were going to take part in a naval review rather than in any serious engagement. The boats, as they were ready, began to leave the Brocas, the lowest boat going first, and laying off in the stream till all were ready. Then a signal was given, and away they started, the highest boat leading, and the rest in order taking one turn up and down before the Brocas, that the spectators might have the opportunity of admiring them.

At about three miles from Eton is a place called Surly. Here a repast, on tables spread in the open air, was prepared for them; and as the boats' crews were expected to be not a little thirsty after their long pull, some bottles of champagne were provided for each boat. After the boats had been sufficiently admired by the spectators on the Brocas, off they started, as fast as the pullers could bend to their oars, with long and sweeping strokes towards Surly, accompanied by a boat with a band of music playing enlivening strains.

Jack Bouldon, though he could not pull himself, had secured a boat for his father and his friend, and a crew to man her; and as soon as the boats had gone off, they all jumped into her, that they might follow and see the fun. Each boat had her sitter jealously guarding the exhilarating beverage.

They were not long in reaching Surly. The crews landed, and lost no time in seating themselves to enjoy their cold collation, or in quenching their thirst in the hissing, popping, sparkling champagne. The viands were quickly despatched and thoroughly relished, aided by music and champagne, and good appetites; and then toast after toast succeeded in rapid succession, all drunk with the greatest enthusiasm,—"The Queen," and "Floreat Etona," however, calling forth even a still greater amount of applause. Capacious as champagne bottles may be, their contents will come to an end; and this consummation having occurred, once more the crews embarked in their boats and commenced their homeward voyage, music, fun, and laughter enlivening the way.

It was dusk as they approached Eton, where, in the centre of the river, a vessel was moored, whence, as they began to pull round her, burst forth a magnificent display of fireworks. Then the crews of the boats stood up, and, waving their hats, cheered vociferously. Up went the rockets, surrounding them, as it were, with a sparkling dome of fire, and afterwards, in succession, burst forth Catherine wheels, spiral wheels, grand volutes, brilliant yew-trees, and showers of liquid fire, and a number of other productions of the pyrotechnic art too numerous to describe.

The boats continued pulling slowly round and round the vessel all the time of the exhibition, producing a very pretty and enlivening effect.

As Jack Bouldon and his friends walked back to his tutor's, of course he enlarged on the excellencies of Eton, and the amusements of the school.

"Oh, I wish that you would come back at the end of the half, and see our pulling matches, and swimming and diving matches! We have several of all sorts. We have a grand race between two sides of college, the upper and lower boats. Then there is a sculling sweepstakes, open to all the school. The prize is a cup and a pair of silver sculls, which the winner holds for a year, and on giving them up has his name inscribed on them; so that he has the honour of being known ever after as a first-rate sculler. Then there is a rowing sweepstakes for a pair of oars, which is also open to all the school; and each of the houses have their own private sweepstakes, when they draw lots for pairs. The distance we row is about two and a-half miles. Now I must tell you about the swimming matches which we have at the end of the half. There is one prize for the best swimmer in the school, and another for the best swimmer of those who have passed that half. In the diving matches we dive for chalk eggs, and out of fifteen thrown in, I have seen as many as twelve brought up. I have brought up nine myself, and I cannot boast of being first-rate. Another prize is given to the boy who takes the best header from a high bank; and those are all the prizes given. We have another grand day, called Election Saturday, the arrangements for which are very like to-day. The chief difference is, that the eight are chosen out of all the boats, and row by themselves, in their dress of Eton-blue shirts, and blue hat-bands and ties, as I have described to you."

It was nearly half-past ten when the boys got back to Jack's tutor's, and he had to leave them, while they went to the inn with Mr Bouldon, who had undertaken to see them off the following morning, on their return to Grafton Hall.

They all declared that they never had enjoyed so amusing a day as that spent at Eton.

Chapter Seventeen
Conclusion

"Had anybody told me when I came to this school that three years would so rapidly pass by, I would not have believed them," said Ernest, addressing Ellis, Buttar, and Bouldon, as the four old friends were walking up and down the playground, ready to form for proceeding to church the last Sunday they were to spend together at Grafton Hall before the summer holidays. "I should have been glad to have remained here another half, or even a year, but my father wishes me to read with a tutor whose exclusive occupation it is to prepare fellows for India; so I am to go to him in a few weeks. I intend to read hard, for I am resolved not to be idle wherever I go."

"Oh, I envy you!" exclaimed Bouldon, "for I know that you will get on; and I wish you may, that you may come back again safe and sound to old England."

"Oh, I must not think of coming back for years, I fear," answered Ernest. "The less one calculates in that way the better. I suspect that people are too apt to neglect the present when they allow their thoughts to dwell too much on the future. The great thing is, as my father says, to do our duty during the present, and to enjoy life as it was intended that we should enjoy it, and to allow the future to take care of itself. I do not mean to say that we are to neglect the future, but that we are not to fancy always that the future is to bring forth so much more happiness than the present time can afford. You understand what I mean, or rather what my father means. Now, Gregson is an example to the point. See how happy he always is. He is happy in doing his lessons, because he gives his whole mind to them; and though his talents are not brilliant, he always does them well. Then the moment they are done, he turns to his favourite pursuits. Then he is as happy as he can desire to be in this life. He is not idle for a moment; every book he opens on natural history gives him pleasure; every walk he takes he finds something new and delightful. The birds of the air, the beasts of the field, the creeping things on the earth and under the earth, the trees, the flowers, their numberless inhabitants, all are matters of intense interest to him. He cannot look into a horse-pond without finding subjects for study for days together. Every stream is a mine of wealth; and as for the ocean the smallest portion affords objects the study of which is inexhaustible. Depend upon it, that it would be worth living for the sake of enjoying the study of natural history alone. Then see what vast fields of interest does each branch of science exhibit. The more I inquire into these matters, the more convinced I am that life ought to be a very delightful state of existence, and that it is our own fault if it is not so."

Thus Ernest gave expression to his opinions. He laid considerable stress on mental occupation, but he did not altogether forget that man is susceptible of a very considerable amount of physical enjoyment, which he is too apt, through his own folly, to lose. It is not often that lads of Ernest's age think as he did, nor is it often that those who do have listeners so ready and eager to imbibe his opinions.

The signal was given, the boys fell into order, and marched off to church. It is matter for thought, and solemn thought too, when one feels that one is visiting a place of interest for the last time; but there should be something peculiarly affecting when one kneels for the last time in a place of worship where one has knelt for years, and offered up our prayers and petitions, and sung our songs of praise, to that great and good Being who is our life, our protector, our support, united with many hundreds of our fellow-creatures. Perhaps with not one of them may we ever kneel or pray again, but yet one and all of them we shall meet at that great and awful day when we stand before the judgment-seat of Heaven. How shall we all have been employing ourselves in the meantime? What will then be our doom? How vain, how frivolous will earthly ambition, wealth, or honours appear!

Such thoughts as these passed rapidly through Ernest's mind as he sat and listened to the good, the kind, and faithful minister of the parish.

Ernest had many last things to do before he left school. He had to play his last game of cricket, to climb the gymnastic pole for the last time, to take a walk over his favourite downs, to pay many last visits to rich and poor alike. John Hodge was not forgotten. The assistance given by Ellis, and him, and Buttar helped the poor man along till his strength returned, and once more, to his great satisfaction, he was able to resume work. Ernest could not feel altogether sad: that would not have been natural; and yet he was truly sorry to part from his friends and schoolfellows, and from the old familiar scenes he had known so long. He had, however, plenty of work to keep his mind employed. There were examinations to be gone through, speeches to be made, and prizes to be bestowed. The parents of the boys, and the residents in the neighbourhood who took an interest in the school, were invited to attend. All the examinations which admitted of it were *vivâ voce*, and took place in the lecture-halls, to which the visitors repaired as they felt interested in the subject, or in the boys who were undergoing their examinations. Several people followed Ernest through the whole course of his examinations, and were much struck by the clear, ready way in which he replied to all the questions put to him, and the evidence he gave of having entirely mastered all the subjects he had studied. All those capable of judging were convinced that, numerous as were the subjects he had studied, he was in no way crammed, but was thoroughly grounded in them all.

After the examinations, the visitors and the boys assembled under a large awning, which had been spread for the purpose. At one end was a raised platform, where several of the most influential gentlemen, many of them clergymen, and others, as well as the head-master, took their seats with the boys of the first class, while the rest were arranged below. First an oration was spoken by several boys, candidates for a prize, to be bestowed on the best orator. Ernest, Buttar, Ellis, and several others tried for it. All spoke well, but Ernest was found to have double as many votes as any other boy. Then the gentleman who had been placed in the chair got up, and expressed his approbation of the system on which the school was managed, and his satisfaction at finding the very great progress it had made; and he concluded—"I consider those boys truly fortunate who are under such a master, and in so delightful an abode." Then the names of the boys who had gained prizes were called over, and one after the other, with looks of satisfaction, ascended the platform to receive them. Ernest came down literally loaded with prizes. He looked surprised as well as pleased. He was first in everything. The reason that he was so was simple enough. He had bestowed the same attention and energy on all the subjects he had studied; he had given them his entire mind; all his talents had been employed on them; consequently, he could scarcely fail to obtain a similar success in all.

The prizes consisted chiefly of books, mathematical instruments, and drawing materials. After they were distributed, the chairman once more rose, and congratulating Ernest on his success, complimented the Doctor on having educated so promising a pupil and on the admirable discipline of the school itself.

The visitors and boys repaired to the large dining-hall, where a handsome dinner was spread.

"Why, Doctor, you have given us a magnificent feast," exclaimed Mr Bouldon, who had come to see his son. "I suspect you youngsters don't get such a dinner as this every day."

"But indeed we do," shouted out Tom Bouldon. "Ask the Doctor; he'll not tell you an untruth."

"Your son states what is the case," replied the Doctor, "except, perhaps, with regard to quantity—we have certainly the same quality of food every day, and served in the same way. My object is to make my boys gentlemen in all the minor as well as in all the more important points of breeding. I believe that it is important for this object to give them from the first gentlemanly habits which can never be eradicated. They all, I hope, love their homes for their domestic ties, but for no other reason do I wish them to prefer any place to their school. The result is, I rejoice to say, that we have no Black Monday at Grafton Hall, and that I see as happy, smiling faces in most instances at the commencement of a half-year as I do at the end of it, when they are about to quit me."

Ernest had never made an impromptu speech before, but he could not now resist the impulse he felt, so rising, he exclaimed—

"What the Doctor says, ladies and gentlemen, is very true. I, as the head of the school, and just about to leave, may assuredly be considered good evidence. He has made the school a happy home to us all; he has made us like learning by the pleasant way in which he has imparted knowledge to us, at the same time that he has shown us the importance of working out most branches of it for ourselves. He has invariably treated us justly; and while he has acted towards us with strictness, he has also never failed in his kindness under all circumstances, and at all times. He has always been indulgent when he could, and has done everything to insure our health, our comfort, and amusement; I cannot say more. It is my belief that Grafton Hall is one of the happiest and best schools in England, and that Dr Carr has made it so. Heaven bless you, sir."

Amidst thundering rounds of applause from all his schoolfellows Ernest sat down. The Doctor was very much affected at the way Ernest had spoken. The party at last broke up. The next day the boys went home, and Ernest found himself no longer, properly speaking, a schoolboy. Still he was in no hurry to shake off his schoolboy's habits and feelings. After spending a few weeks at home, he went down to his new tutor at Ryde, in the Isle of Wight. The house stood high up, overlooking Portsmouth and Spithead, where England's proud fleets are wont to assemble at anchor. It was the yachting season, and the place was full of visitors.

The day after his arrival he went out, and one of the first people he encountered was Ellis. The friends were delighted to meet. The latter soon explained the cause of his being there. His father and mother had come to Ryde, and had secured a very nice little yacht for him, small compared to the large vessels which form the navy of the different clubs, but quite large enough to sail about in every direction on the waters of the Solent.

"It was one of my favourite amusements," said Ellis. "In truth it was the only one, till you taught me to like cricket and other games at school. Now you must come and learn about yachting with me."

Ernest said that he should like it much, but that he must read hard with his tutor.

"The very thing to help your reading," pleaded Ellis. "Ask him, and if he is a sensible man he will tell you that if you take a trip now and then on the water it will refresh your brains, and you will be able to read all the better for it."

To Ernest's surprise, his tutor fully agreed with the advice Ellis had given him, and it was not long before he found himself on the deck of the "Fairy." Such was the name Ellis had given to his yacht. Scarcely had Ernest stepped on board than he set to work to make himself acquainted with all the details of the vessel. The use of the helm and the way the wind acts on the sails he understood clearly. He had studied theoretically the principle of balancing the sails with the wind, and also the mode in which the water acts on the hull. He had read about leeway, and headway, and sternway; and now that he had an opportunity of examining the practical working of these theories, he hoped to master the subject thoroughly, so as never to forget it, and to be able, when called on, to make it of use. At first the old sailor, who acted as the master of the yacht, and for that matter crew also, for there was only a boy besides, seemed inclined to look on Ernest as a green hand, and to turn up his nose at him. Ernest, however, did not show that he perceived this, and went about very quietly, gaining all the information he required.

"What is this rope called?" he asked of the old man while Ellis was below, before he got under way.

"The main sheet, sir," was the answer.

Ernest made no other remark, but he examined where one end was secured; he ran his eye along it from block to block, and calculated how much of it was coiled away.

"These are the shrouds, I know; and this?" he asked.

"The backstay, sir," replied the old man.

He underwent a thorough examination.

"And this, I see, must be the topmast backstay; and this the forestay; and that the topmast stay. Is it not so?" he asked.

Thus he went on, rapidly learning not only the names, but the uses of all the ropes, and of everything on deck. By the time Ellis returned on deck he was surprised to find that Ernest had already made himself at home on board, and, as he said, was ready to lend a hand to pull and haul if required.

"The tide will soon have made, and we shall be able to get to the westward," said Ellis, looking about him. "We'll set the mainsail, Hobbs, and be all ready for a start."

Preparations were accordingly made to set the mainsail. The throat was hoisted nearly up; the peak was half hoisted; then the jib was bent on, and hauled out to the bowsprit end.

"Come, Ernest, bowse away on the bobstay," cried Ellis.

Ernest was for a moment at fault, but when he saw his friend hauling away on a rope forward, he took hold of it, and soon guessed its object.

"Let us tauten the bowsprit shrouds a bit," said Ellis. Ernest knew what that meant. The jib was hoisted and bowsed well up, then the backstays, and the topmast-stays were tautened. "Now, Hobbs, go to the helm; we'll get the foresail up." Ernest helped Ellis to hoist away on the fore-halliards; the old master overhauled the main sheet while Ellis overhauled the lee-runner and tackle. The throat he settled a little, that is, he let the inner end of the gaff drop a little, and then he and Ernest gave all their strength to hoisting the peak of the mainsail well up. The mainsail now stood like a board; the wind was light, so the gaff-topsail was set, and then, as Ellis wished to cast off-shore, he watched till the wind came on the port or left side of the foresail. Instantly he let go the moorings, and the Fairy's head turned towards the north, or across channel; the jib sheet was hauled in, so was the main sheet; the foresail was let draw, and the little vessel, feeling the full force of the breeze, glided swiftly along through the sparkling waters.

Ernest clapped his hands. "Oh, this is truly delightful," he exclaimed, after they had been skimming along for some time, enjoying the view of Spithead, where several large ships were at anchor; of Ryde, climbing up its steep hill; of Cowes, to the westward, and the wooded shores of the Solent extending in the same direction as far as the eye could reach. The wind freshened up again, and they had a magnificent sail, looking into Cowes harbour and standing through the roads, where some dozen fine yachts were at anchor, and some twenty more cruising about in sight. They passed Calshot Castle on the north, and beat on till they sighted Hurst Castle, at the entrance of the Solent passage to the westward, while the little town of Yarmouth appeared on the island shore, and Lymington on the mainland.

"The wind is likely to fall towards the evening, and if you young gentlemen wishes to get home before night, we had better be about," said old Hobbs, looking up at the sky on every side.

Although Ellis was very fond of anchoring whenever he felt inclined, or the tide and wind made it convenient, and of sleeping on board, or of keeping under way all night, Ernest was anxious to get back to read during the evening; the helm was therefore put up, the main sheet was eased away, and the "Fairy" ran off to the eastward before the wind.

Ellis was at the helm. "As we are in a hurry, we will make more sail, and see how fast the little barkie can walk along; Hobbs, get the square-sail on her."

"Ay, ay, sir," was the reply; and the sail being hauled up from forward, was bent on to its yard, and soon being swayed up, presented a fine wide field of snowy canvas to the breeze. Thus the little craft bowled along, till once more she approached her moorings off Ryde. Then the square-sail was taken in, and the jib being let fly, Ellis put down the helm, and shot her up to the buoy, which old Hobbs, boat-hook in hand, stood ready to catch hold of and haul on board.

"I have never enjoyed a day more," exclaimed Ernest; "now I must go home and read as hard as I can to make up for lost time."

"You will read all the better, as I said, and come as often as you can; we will do our best to get back so that you may not lose all the day." This was said by Ellis as they parted.

The next time Ernest came down to sail in the "Fairy" he found Arden, whom Ellis, having met at Ryde, had invited to join them. Arden was a very nice little fellow; the only and treasured child of his father and mother, and had always been delicately nurtured; too delicately, I suspect, for he had been prevented from engaging in many of the manly exercises which are so important in fitting a boy to meet the rough usage of the world. He could thus neither climb nor swim, and as Ellis said, was very much like a fish out of water on board a boat, though he was very unlike one in the water. He was, however, now anxious to remedy some of his defects, and finding sailing pleasant, was glad to accompany Ellis whenever he asked him.

The old schoolfellows got on board, as merry and happy as lads who feel conscious that they have been working hard and doing their duty can be. Those, I hold, who are viciously employed and neglecting their duty can never be happy. The wind was from the same quarter as the last time Ernest was on board, though there was rather more of it. The "Fairy" having been got under way, stood over to the north shore, and then tacked and stood towards Cowes. As she bounded buoyantly over the waves, the spirits of the three schoolfellows rose high. Ernest added considerably to his stock of nautical knowledge, while Arden was exercising his muscles by climbing up the rigging, hanging on to the shrouds by his hands, and swinging himself backwards and forwards. All this time the breeze freshening, the gaff-topsail had just been stowed; old Hobbs was at the helm, and Ellis himself was to windward, when Arden, in the pride of his newly-acquired accomplishment, as he was running forward on the lee-side, as he said, to take a swing on the shrouds, his foot slipped, he lost his balance, and before he could clutch a rope, over the slight bulwarks he went, head foremost into the water. Ernest was sitting on the same side of the little vessel. Quick as thought, before Ellis, who had been looking to windward, knew what had happened, or Arden could cry out, Ernest sprang overboard. He knew that every instant would increase the difficulty of saving his friend: he threw off neither shoes nor jacket; there was no time for that. Arden came to the surface, and stretching out his arms towards him shrieked out, "Save me, save me! O my mother!" Ernest struck out bravely through the water towards him, while the little cutter flew on; it seemed leaving them far behind: such was not the case, however. Old Hobbs giving a look behind his shoulder to see where they were, put down the helm, that he might put the vessel about as rapidly as possible, and heave-to, while Ellis could jump into the punt to their rescue.

Ernest had no time to consider what was to be done; his first aim was to get hold of Arden and to keep his head above water. The poor lad, unaccustomed to the water, quickly lost all presence of mind, and was striking out wildly and clutching at the air. Ernest saw the danger there would be in approaching him, and therefore, instead of swimming directly for him, took a circuit and then darted rapidly at him from behind. Grasping him by the collar, by a strong turn of his arm he threw him on his back, and then he held him while he himself trod water, and assisted himself to float with his left hand.

"Don't be alarmed, now, Arden, my dear fellow; keep your arms quiet and you will float easily," he exclaimed. "There, just look up at the sky; now you find that your face is perfectly out of the water; never mind if your head sinks a little; steady, so, all right, old fellow."

With words to give confidence and encouragement, Ernest tried to calm poor Arden's fears; yet he himself turned many an anxious glance towards the yacht.

The instant Ellis had heard Arden's cry and saw Ernest in the water, he leaped up and hauled the punt, towing astern, up alongside.

"Wait, sir, wait till we are about," said Hobbs; "you'll be nearer to them then, and on the same side they are."

Ellis saw this, and as the cutter came round he jumped into the punt and shoved off. Ernest saw his friend coming. He began to feel more anxious than before. The punt was small, and he was afraid, should Arden struggle, she also might be capsized. He therefore urged Arden to remain perfectly quiet, while Ellis hauled him in. The moment Ellis reached them he threw in his oars, and wisely leaning over the bows, caught hold of Arden's collar and lifted him partly out of the water, while Ernest swam round to the stern and climbed in over it. He now was able to come to Ellis's assistance, and together they hauled in poor Arden, more frightened than hurt, over the bows. They soon made him safe in the little cabin of the cutter, with his clothes stripped off, and he himself wrapped up in a blanket. The clothes quickly dried in the warm sun and air, and he was able to be the first to describe his accident to his parents, and to speak of Ernest's gallant conduct in saving him.

"My dear Arden," replied Ernest, when the former was overwhelming him with thanks, "I learned to swim, and know how to retain my presence of mind. Had you been able, you would have done the same for me; so say no more about it."

Young Arden did not say much more about it, nor did Mr Arden to Ernest himself; but he had powerful friends in India, and when, after some months Bracebridge arrived there, he found himself cordially welcomed, and placed in a position where he had full scope for the exercise of his talents.

For some time Ernest Bracebridge had not heard from any of his old schoolfellows. War was raging. His regiment, with others, was appointed to attack a stronghold of the enemy. He led on his men with a gallantry for which he had been ever conspicuous, but they met with a terrific opposition. Almost in vain they struggled on. Again and again they were beaten back, and as often encouraged by their brave leader, they charged the foe. At length he fell. His men rallied round him to carry him off, when there was a loud cheer—a fresh regiment was coming to their support. Ernest looked up. They were Queen's troops. He saw the face of the officer who led them, as, waving his sword, he dashed by. Ernest shouted, "Ellis—Ellis!" The enemy could not stand the shock of the British bayonets. They fled in confusion. Ernest heard the cry, "They run—they run." Then he sunk, exhausted from loss of blood.

At length the blood was stanched, a cordial was poured down his throat, and looking up, he saw the countenance of his old friend Edward Ellis bending anxiously over him. Ellis bore him to his tent, and nursed him with the care of a brother. Together in many a hard-fought fight they served their country, and often talked of their old schoolfellows, of the kind Doctor, and of the happy days they spent at Grafton Hall.